No sooner had Teldin disappeared than the shrike ship slowed to a hover over the *Trumpeter*'s deck. Three immense creatures landed nimbly on the swan ship's deck, creatures identical to the one hidden in the landing behind Vallus.

Everywhere on deck the elves froze. All had heard stories of battles the bionoids had fought and won for the elves in the first Unhuman War. No one had the faintest idea how to fight *against* such creatures.

The bionoids, standing shoulder to shoulder and armed with huge swords or pikes, were daunting even to the battle-hardened elves. Vallus shot a glance over his shoulder, half expecting to see a halberd swinging at his neck, but Hectate, in his bionoid form, still stood guard.

One of the creatures stepped forward and spoke into the silence. "We have come for the human. If you turn Teldin Moore over to us, we will leave peaceably."

In response, Vallus swept an implacable, narrowed glare across the immobile elven crew. "Attack," he said simply.

THE CLOAKMASTER CYCLE

● ● ●

BOOKS

The Radiant Dragon

Elaine Cunningham

THE RADIANT DRAGON

First Printing: November 1992
Printed in the United States of America
Library of Congress Catalog Card Number: 91-66488

9 8 7 6 5 4 3 2 1

ISBN: 1-56076-346-9

TSR, Inc.
P.O. Box 756
Lake Geneva, WI 53147
U.S.A.

TSR, Ltd.
120 Church End, Cherry Hinton
Cambridge CB1 3LB
United Kingdom

To Sean, my avid swordsman
and elfling extraordinaire,
despite whom this book was written.

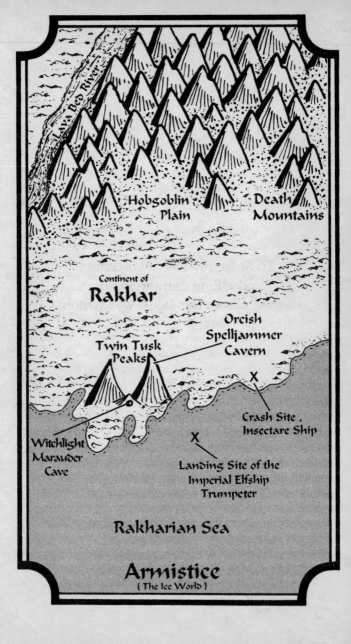

Prologue

•••

For untold centuries, many had sought the truth behind the legend of the *Spelljammer*, but few had returned to tell of their quest. Now, in a distant corner of Realmspace and in the shadow of the great ship itself, the crewmen of a reigar vessel wondered if they soon would join the thousands whose stories had ended in silence.

The awestruck crew members could not judge the *Spelljammer*'s size; at times they perceived it only as an immense blackness that curtained the stars behind it. Their navigator informed them that they had orbited the vessel twice, a feat that had taken many hours. In truth, it was a ship a third of a mile long and half a mile across, shaped like an enormous manta ray with a shining city atop its back. It was the largest ship in all of known space, and persistent rumors said it was both a ship and a living entity.

The other ship, a reigar esthetic, was a rather unorthodox vessel for such a voyage of exploration. The race known as the reigar was famous for its unusual ships, but the flamboyant artiste who captained this vessel had taken reigar individuality to new extremes. The ship's base was a conventional wooden hull with a deep keel, but upon the deck was a small forest and a stretch of green meadow. On the stern of the ship a tree-shaded mountain rose abruptly. A stream cascaded down the mountain, ending in a pond filled with bright fish and surrounded by flowers.

The beautiful sylvan scene was all the more remarkable for its origin: the reigar had magically grown everything—including the singing birds, fish, and other woodland creatures—from multicolored crystal. Each plant was so realistic as to appear alive, even to swaying in the magical breezes, but the whole had a color and sheen more intense than any found on even the most magic-laden elven world. A small, sunlike globe orbited the outer edge of the ship's atmosphere, casting an illusion of day and night even in the midst of wildspace. At the bow of the ship was a small, retractable platform on which the sun-globe could come to rest when the ship's helm went down, and the bridge was aft, located at the top of the mountain. There the ship's captain, a reigar woman known as Cholana, sat cross-legged in the shade of a giant crystalline oak.

Around the reigar huddled a semicircle of arcane, the blue-skinned humanoid giants who served as the ship's crew. To one side of Cholana paced her lakshu bodyguard, a muscled amazon warrior, and on the other side sat the ship's wizard in a unique helm that was carved directly into the crystal rock of the mountain. Cholana was lost in magical revery, and tension and foreboding encircled the small assembly just as surely as the glory—a glowing, glittering halo of twinkling motes—surrounded the entranced reigar.

"By the Departed Elders!" swore one of the arcane in a harsh whisper. His six-fingered blue hand trembled as he pointed to the reigar captain. "Look at Cholana's glory. It's fading!"

For a time even the great ship was forgotten. The arcane muttered among themselves, debating in hushed tones what the omen might portend for their revered captain. Viper, the lakshu, stopped her fierce pacing and studied Cholana with narrowed eyes. In sharp contrast to the arcane's concern, the lakshu's scrutiny of Cholana's glory held no hint of distress.

Yes, the bright mist that surrounded the reigar had faded.

How interesting, Viper noted with cynical detachment. Of course, she found it interesting that the reigar was there at all.

Viper had been on board the esthetic during Cholana's last, spectacularly unsuccessful experiment. The reigar had taken a small longboat out into the flow, where she had attempted to magically channel the rainbow-hued phlogiston into a wildspace mural in her own honor. After the explosion's aftershocks had finally died away, the crew's search had yielded no trace of Cholana or her small boat. The reigar had been presumed dead, and, despite the evidence seated before her, Viper saw no reason to believe otherwise.

Many years before, on the very day she had reached her full fighting weight, the lakshu had pledged her strength and her life in the service of Cholana. As was the custom, Viper had been named for the reigar's *shakti*, a magical animal totem of great power. The lakshu had been given a matching *shakti*, the stylized jeweled snake that curled around her wrist and matched the one entwining Cholana's forearm. These *shakti* were powerful weapons, powerful enough to protect the physically fragile reigar and to secure the allegiance of the wild and warlike lakshu. A single word of command would change the ornament into an enormous, deadly snake, big enough to ride upon. A second command word could transmute the *shakti* into a suit of scaled armor that gave its wearer the ability to strike with viperlike speed and to spit blasts of deadly venom at even distant attackers. Each *shakti* was different, but each was a fearsome weapon. Viper wore hers with pride, as befitted a reigar-pledged lakshu warrior.

Since the explosive mishap in the phlogiston, however, Viper's *shakti* had been nothing more than a pleasant ornament, as dead as the lakshu believed her master to be. The return of the reigar Cholana had not restored the *shakti*'s power.

With a patience uncharacteristic of the wildspace ama-
zons, Viper kept her weapons sheathed and her tongue still
as she studied the entranced reigar. The lakshu did not know
who or what presumed to sit in her master's place, but she
would wait and she would learn. And then she would kill.

Still deep in trance, "Cholana" made a small, restless
motion, and her hand grasped the sapphire pendant that
hung around her neck. Her narrow fingers curved around
the huge gemstone, which shone with a deep, magical blue
light. The reigar's fidgeting brightened the motes surrounding her and sent them into dizzying motion.

She did not hear the arcane's collective sigh of relief, nor
did she notice the lakshu's suspicious glare. Lost in her
magical inquiry, she was barely aware of the body that had been
so amusing to assume. Reigar! she mused silently. Pretentious
little creatures, really, but they did have a certain flair.

This one had been a female with short, red-gold ringlets,
a body as slim as a snake's, and flamboyant facial makeup
consisting of tiny, iridescent scales that transformed her
triangular face into an exotic parody of the *shakti* on her arm.
Except for the ancient, sapphire-studded pendant, the reigar's
clothing showed the usual creative flair. She wore tight green
leggings of some pebbly, shining fabric and a matching silky
shirt that bared her midriff. An elaborate tattoo wound up
one thin arm, and jewelry in abstract forms glittered at her
ears and fingers. Even the nails on Cholana's hands and bare
feet showed typical reigar élan; they had been gilded, dusted
with crushed precious stones, and then ensorcelled to show
elaborate designs that changed colors in random patterns. As
guises went, it was amusing enough.

Amusing, but not entirely effective. She had assumed the
reigar's form in an attempt to avoid detection by the great
ship, yet even in her frail and flashy new body she sensed
that the ship had detected her. She was, however, a creature
of great power and will.

For some time now she had resisted the questing, demanding voice of the ship, intending to learn all she could about it before landing on it. Celestial Nightpearl had not lived all these centuries by being imprudent. Since the day the magical pendant had come into her possession, she'd spent an elf's lifetime exploring its powers and promise. She had defeated enemies who had wanted the pendant for themselves, and she had overcome Others—beings who had held similar magical objects. Now that she'd found the *Spelljammer*, the first part of her quest was complete. She had yet to determine what would come next.

And so she sent out her seeking thoughts upon the magical stream flowing from the pendant. She searched for the minds of Others, creatures who either aspired to take or formerly had become the great ship's helmsman.

Without warning, her thoughts hit a magical wall. The creature's glittering reigar hand gripped the sapphire tightly, and she poured all her own considerable magic through the stone in an attempt to breach the barrier. Before the power of her will and her magic the wall wavered, became insubstantial, and finally dissipated. The great ship yielded its secrets.

To her surprise, there were three Others on board. Three! she raged silently. Was she supposed to share power with three?

Her fierce concentration slipped and the wall slammed down again. Once again, by sheer force of will and magic— and, she suspected briefly, the intrinsic power of her ultimate helm—she again forced aside the magic barrier.

Three Others were there, yes, but what had they become? Stripped of power, locked in a dark tower, and condemned to a life of imprisonment and isolation? Perhaps they had seen the ship's wonders and had learned its powers, but what good had their knowledge done them? They were pitiful, helpless.

Rage rose in the creature like a dark tide, washing away her desire to delve into the minds of the Others. The information she had sought for centuries seemed insignificant beside the living death she had glimpsed. This fate could not befall one of her kind. Celestial Nightpearl vowed to find another way.

The "reigar's" trance broke, dispelling the glory that surrounded her and sending the tiny glittering motes flying outward with the force of an explosion. Roaring her dismay, the creature leaped to her feet.

The assembled arcane tumbled back, stunned by the explosion, but Viper had the presence of mind to fling herself out of range the moment "Cholana" cried out. The lakshu rolled away and came up in a fighting crouch.

What she saw did not surprise her. The being that had taken the form of the reigar Cholana was now changing, growing into a creature of almost unimaginable size and power.

As a good warrior, Viper knew when to attack and when to retreat. She lunged for the arcane wizard. Grabbing his long blue hand, she yanked him out of the helm. With a vicious push, she sent the stunned arcane tumbling down the mountain, then she followed him in a barely controlled roll. They hit the ship's deck hard, but Viper was on her feet instantly. With one hand she grabbed the wizard by the scruff of the neck, and she sprinted toward the esthetic's longboat, easily dragging the dazed twelve-foot giant behind her. She tossed him into the small craft and dove in after him, keeping her head low as her nimble fingers loosened the ropes of her escape craft.

When the longboat was free, Viper peered cautiously over the edge. The creature's transformation was almost complete, and the wooden frame of the esthetic groaned under the weight of a body some five hundred feet long. A rapidly growing tail snaked around the mountain, twitching and stretching as it reached its full length. Every movement of the tail sent crystal shards splintering off into wildspace, and the creature's roars seemed to vibrate deep in Viper's bones. Scales the color of wildspace covered the immense beast, catching the starlight with an opalescent shimmer. Finally, the creature unfolded its wings and beat them like a newly hatched butterfly would as it lay drying in the sun. Anger blazed in its intelligent golden eyes, and a huge sapphire gleamed from the enormous pendant that hung around its neck.

With a final, mighty roar, a full-grown radiant dragon burst away from the reigar ship and sped off into the blackness of wildspace. In its rage, it did not notice that a switch of its tail had shattered the reigar ship, sending debris and the broken bodies of Cholana's faithful crew into the void.

Chapter One

•••

Teldin Moore edged his way through the crowded marketplace, ignoring the exotic wares and the hawking cries of the merchants whose stalls crowded both sides of the narrow streets. For all its enticements, the market was a scene Teldin had seen many times before and on a dozen different worlds. Here, on the cluster of entwined asteroids known as Garden, he wished only to supply his ship and snatch a few hours of peace before resuming his quest.

A year earlier, Teldin had been a solitary farmer scratching out a living on faraway Krynn, unaware of the worlds beyond his own. Then a spelljamming ship had crashed on his farm and its dying reigar captain had bequeathed Teldin the cloak he now wore. Since that night he had searched for answers to the cloak's mysteries, always with deadly rivals in close pursuit. He had learned that the cloak was an artifact that would enable him to command the legendary *Spelljammer*, and he had vowed to find the great ship. Recently a brilliant wildspace sage, an enormous slug known as a fal, had advised Teldin to seek the *Spelljammer*'s birthplace: a broken crystal sphere. Teldin knew nothing of such a place, but after a disastrous experience with the elven Imperial Fleet he was not willing to depend on legend and hearsay for answers. He had purchased his own ship using money given to him by the fal One Six Nine, and he had stopped on Garden to stock up for a long voyage of exploration.

Because of Garden's peculiar shape, sunset came with the speed and drama of an eclipse. Before Teldin's eyes could adjust to the sudden darkness, a passing centaur jostled him, sending him stumbling into one of the gray lizard men engaged in lighting the gas lamps along the street.

The creature turned and hissed at Teldin. Its reptilian eyes narrowed in challenge and its clawed hand curled around the hilt of a dagger. Teldin was not afraid of the lizard man, but neither did he wish to draw attention to himself with a street fight. He held up both hands in a temporizing gesture and murmured a few words of apology. Even as he spoke, he realized his mistake. To such a creature an apology was a sign of weakness, a virtual invitation to attack.

Far from attacking, the lizard man fell back a step as if in surprise. After a moment of silence it burst into hissing laughter. Its scaly shoulders shook as it nudged its partner and repeated something in a sibilant language. The other lizard man wheezed out a chuckle and bobbed an appreciative nod in Teldin's direction.

It took the nonplussed human a moment to realize what had transpired; somehow the magic of his cloak had translated his ill-advised apology into a gem of reptile humor. As Teldin walked away, he could hear his mysterious *bon mot* making the rounds of the lizard men, and the amused hissing behind him brought to mind the sputter of a gnomish steam engine. With a quiet chuckle of his own, Teldin slipped gratefully into the obscurity of the crowd.

As usual, Teldin was careful not to bring attention to himself, but even in the colorful bustle of the marketplace he drew enough glances to make him feel uncomfortable. The cloak again, he thought with a touch of resignation. He recently had learned that its extraordinary magical aura acted as a lure, even to those who were unaware of the cloak's significance. Indeed, some of the beings who cast glances Teldin's way did so with a distinctly puzzled air, as if the magic they sensed could not be reconciled with its rather commonplace incarnation.

In Teldin Moore an ordinary observer would see only a tall young man wearing a black shirt and trousers and a laced tunic of suede leather. His passably handsome face no longer bore the mustache he'd once worn, but now was clean-shaven, and his light brown hair was brushed back from a decided widow's peak. His shoulders were broad and draped by a long, dark cloak.

A more perceptive eye would note that the man's lean muscles were the sort earned by a life of unrelenting labor. He wore his short sword with assurance, but his stance and walk were not those of a trained fighter. His square jaw and craggy features gave him the type of face that in later years would be said to "have character;" on a young man that face suggested blunt honesty and a stubborn nature.

In startling contrast were his eyes, bright cornflower blue eyes that lent him an almost boyish mien. The network of fine lines at their corners suggested a sense of humor; the dark hollows beneath spoke of recent struggle and loss. Finally, there was something unusual about the man's cloak. It was an elusive hue, a deep, intense purple that was almost black. The cloak seemed to adjust its color and length almost imperceptibly as its wearer edged his way through the crowded streets.

A little unnerved by the curious glances, Teldin drew the cloak closer as he walked. It had brought him great danger, but it also offered a measure of protection. By now, Teldin had learned many of the cloak's powers through a painful process of trial and error and by its own response to danger. Several times its magic had taken over during a critical situation, giving him a preternatural clarity of mind and seemingly slowing down the action around him so that he could think and react. Teldin could also use the cloak to change his own appearance into whatever form he chose.

Although he did so with reluctance, he had employed this magic often; there were many who sought a tall, blue-eyed man with fair hair and a flowing cloak. His disguises did not seem to hamper some of his pursuers, but Teldin hoped that they at least deterred others who wished to join the race for the cloak. The cloak also translated unknown languages, enabled Teldin to shoot magical missiles and—most importantly—functioned as a helm powerful enough to propel a spelljamming ship at tremendous speed. It often occurred to Teldin that he still had much to learn about the cloak. He tried not to dwell on that thought any more than he had to, though; it was too much like waiting for the other boot to drop.

Teldin's stomach rumbled sharply, reminding him that it had been many hours since his last meal. He rounded a corner and looked for a likely place to eat. At the end of the street was a tavern, of the sort that he could have encountered in any small village back on his homeworld.

The tavern looked cozy, safe, and welcoming. It was long and narrow, with low eaves, a domed, thatched roof, and thick, ancient beams separating expanses of fieldstone and mortar. Teldin quickly made his way to the offered haven and pushed through the broad wooden door. An involuntary sigh of satisfaction escaped him as he took in the scene sprawled before him.

The patrons were a mixed group; merchants and travelers of many races drank alongside local fisherfolk and yeomen. To the left side of the tavern was a huge stone fireplace big enough to roast a whole boar with room to spare. A red-cheeked cook basted the sizzling roast with a fruit-scented sauce while two halflings struggled to turn the immense spit. Fat, fragrant loaves of bread baked in open ovens on either side of the fireplace. Scattered about the room were small, round tables draped with brightly colored cloths, and a long, well-stocked bar stretched almost the entire length of the back wall. A barrel-shaped dwarven barkeeper was passing out tankards of something that foamed and smelled suspiciously like Krynnish ale. Teldin inhaled deeply and followed his nose to a table near the bar.

He ordered dinner and asked for a mug of ale and a goblet of sagecoarse, the smoky liquor that Aelfred Silverhorn had favored. Teldin did not care for hard liquor, but it seemed appropriate to lift a glass in honor of his friend.

Teldin was still stunned by Aelfred's and Sylvie's deaths, even more so than by his male friend's unexpected and unwilling treachery. Teldin did not hold Aelfred responsible for his actions—Aelfred had acted under the spell of an undead neogi wizard—but his loss had shaken Teldin deeply. Betrayal was something Teldin almost had come to expect; the death of his friends was another matter altogether.

Nothing could inure him to the pain and guilt he felt over bringing danger to those around him. So many had fallen that Teldin, by nature a solitary man, had begun to distance himself still more in fear that caring for others could only result in their deaths. His hippolike friend, Gomja, was gone as well, having left to seek employment and a new life elsewhere.

As if by reflex, his hand drifted to the small bag that hung from his belt. Through the soft, worn leather he fingered the medallion that had been given to him by Gaye, the beautiful, exuberant kender whom he hadn't dared to love. Like most kender, Gaye had a talent for "finding" things, yet she'd gone against kender nature and given up the magical trinket, thinking that Teldin could use it on his quest. Indeed, the fal had told Teldin that the medallion could be used to track the *Spelljammer*, and Teldin had tried several times to follow the sage's instructions. Every attempt had failed; whatever magic the ancient disk once possessed apparently had faded. He kept Gaye's gift, however, wearing the bag on his belt exactly where her delicate fingers had knotted it. Leaving

Gaye hurt more than he cared to admit.

A polite chirp interrupted his ruminations. Teldin glanced down as small, feathered hands placed a dinner platter before him. He nodded his thanks to the serving wench, a penguinlike creature known as a dohwar, then he attacked his meal without giving the servant a second thought. A year earlier Teldin would have gaped at the dohwar like a farm lad at a two-headed calf, but he'd grown accustomed to encountering peculiar creatures on his travels. He was therefore startled by the involuntary shiver that ran down his spine when his gaze happened to settle on one of the tavern's other patrons.

The robed figure of a tall humanoid male paused just inside the front door. His face was deeply shadowed by the cowl of his brown cloak, but Teldin noted that the face was thin and angular and dominated by a pair of slanted, distinctively elven eyes. One side of the cowl had been pushed back slightly to display a pointed ear. To all appearances, the newcomer was an elf, but it struck Teldin that something was not quite right. The robed figure began to make his way slowly back toward the bar. He moved with elven grace, but there was something foreign and somehow *brittle* about his movements. It occurred to Teldin that the creature was not quite what he seemed to be: he was elf*like* but not elven.

There was a certainty to this notion that startled Teldin. He had the oddest sensation that he'd caught a glimpse behind appearances to the elven creature's true nature. Where had that perception come from? he wondered briefly. Was it yet another power of the cloak?

At that moment a very drunken human challenged the newcomer to a knife-throwing contest. Weaving unsteadily, the man thrust his face into the deep folds of the cowl, a show of belligerence apparently calculated to either intimidate his opponent or overcome him with fumes. As Teldin watched, the drunk recoiled in horror. Pale and shaken, he backed away, sputtering apologies. Whatever the creature was, it was dangerous, Teldin concluded. In his opinion, elves were bad enough. Any variation on the species created possibilities he did not care to contemplate.

A hard-muscled female adventurer at the table next to Teldin's let out an oath, one colorful enough to distract him momentarily from the mysterious elven creature. He followed the line of her gaze, and his jaw dropped. Hovering in the doorway like an obscenely large eyeball was one of the most feared monsters in all of wildspace: a beholder.

Teldin had heard a score of horror stories about beholders, and he'd seen one stuffed and mounted as a trophy. From time to time, he had wondered whether he might have to face such a creature in battle, but he'd never dreamed he might bump into one in such a cozy, innocuous setting. So intent was he on this new threat that he barely noticed the elven creature leave by the side door.

The beholder, levitating about four feet above the floor, floated into the tavern, leaving a spreading wake of silence behind it. As the monster glided the length of the room, firelight glistened on the brainlike folds and crevices of its circular body, and its ten eyestalks turned this way and that as it took in the local color. It made its way to a corner table and came to a stop, hovering in the air over one of the chairs.

Speaking flawless Common, it issued instructions to the suddenly servile tavern keeper. Within moments a terrified serving girl appeared, bearing a bowl of raw meat, which she tossed piece by piece into the beholder's fanged maw. As it chewed, the beast occasionally blinked the one large eye that was located on its spherical body.

"Bless me, Trivit, I believe that's a beholder. By the Dark Spider, he is a homely fellow," piped an ingenuous voice. The remark carried to the corners of the tavern, and, although the beholder did not appear to take offense, every other patron in the room began to eye the exits.

Teldin's hand strayed to the clasp of his cloak, a habit he'd developed in moments of impending crisis. Out of the corner of his eye he cast a glance at the imprudent speaker. Surprise made him turn his head and stare openly.

Two green dracons stood at the mug-littered bar, observing the beholder with open-mouthed fascination. The reptilian equivalent of a centaur, each dracon boasted a dragon's neck and head, an upright torso with heavily muscled arms ending in clawed hands, and the thick four-legged body and powerful tail of a brontosaur. One of these two beasts had the pale green hide of a tree lizard, and its torso was covered by a shirt of fine chain mail. The other's skin was a mottled moss green, and its armor was fashioned of leather elaborately painted with a swirling pattern of lavenders and deep rose. A chunk of rose quartz hung on a chain around his neck, and an ornamental silver axe was displayed in a shoulder strap. Their open, innocent curiosity indicated that they knew nothing of a beholder's fearsome reputation, and they just as obviously were too ale-soaked to recognize the tension that filled the taproom. Dracons were big, and they were tough, and these two were heavily armed, but they still were no match for a beholder. Someone ought to tell them that, Teldin mused as he took a quick sip of ale. Someone *else*.

"I'm reminded of a jest, of the sort that makes the rounds of the washroom after a kickball tournament," chirped the pale green dracon. He giggled briefly. "For that matter, I'm reminded of the *kickball*."

"A ribald jest! Oh, splendid." The darker dracon—who somehow reminded Teldin of an effete, adolescent human—clasped his mottled green hands in anticipation. "I'm fond of such. Say on, do."

The pale green dracon cleared his throat with much ceremony before reciting, "How does a beholder, er, shall we say, reproduce?"

His friend cast a smirk at the hideous, still-dining monster and shifted his huge shoulders in a delicate shrug. "With all eleven eyes shut, I'd warrant."

The would-be jester's visage twisted in disappointment. "You heard it already," he accused.

"I most certainly did not," huffed his friend, one clawed hand clutching at his pink jewel in exaggerated, fussy outrage.

"But you must have."

"Upon my word, no."

"You did."

"Did not."

"Did."

"Did *not*."

The dracons began to shove at each other like two boys in a schoolyard fight. Giving a longing glance at his half-full mug of ale, Teldin tossed back the rest of his sagecoarse and rose to leave the tavern. In his opinion, things could get only worse.

As Teldin edged toward the side door, a troop of aperusa burst into the inn, flowing around him in a whirl of sound and color. Laughing and chattering with boisterous humor, the wildspace gypsies immediately took over the taproom. To Teldin's surprise, not one of the aperusa spared the beholder so much as a glance. Obviously the gypsies were hardier souls than he'd been led to believe.

The tavern's patrons seemed relieved by the distraction, and they welcomed the gypsy invasion with what Teldin considered an unwarranted degree of enthusiasm. What he had seen of aperusa so far, he hadn't particularly liked.

One of the gypsy women brushed past Teldin, deliberately too close. She cast a sidelong, provocative look at him through lowered lashes, then stopped abruptly. Her feigned interest turned into wide-eyed speculation, and she reached up to trace Teldin's jawline with a slender, bronzed hand, crooning an aperusa phrase that the cloak didn't bother to translate. Her tone made the effort unnecessary, and to his chagrin Teldin felt his cheeks flaming. He was accustomed to feminine attention—his rugged good looks had attracted the glances of farmers' daughters since he was a lad—but the boldly appraising look in the aperusa woman's black eyes made him feel uncomfortably like a mackerel in a fish market.

Teldin murmured something that he hoped would grant him a polite escape, and he began to back away. The woman pouted and claimed his arm with a surprisingly strong grip.

"Why you go, *nyeskataska?*" she purred in a brown-velvet contralto. Although there was no reason why he should, Teldin knew the aperusa's endearment roughly meant "one whose eyes are fine blue topaz." He had yet to figure out a pattern to his cloak's capricious translations.

With her free hand, the aperusa made a sweeping gesture that started with herself and encompassed the taproom. "Look, *nyeskataska*, here there is much to enjoy." Her liquid black eyes challenged him as she drew him firmly into the room.

Extricating himself without a scene would not be easy. Fighting down a wave of frustration, Teldin allowed the woman to lead him deeper into the tavern. From what he'd heard of the aperusa's fickle nature, he supposed this one would lose interest in him as soon as she saw a man who appeared wealthier. That, Teldin noted wryly, shouldn't take long. And what would it hurt to spend a few minutes in the company of a beautiful woman?

Beautiful she certainly was, as ripe and full of promise as an autumn morning. Her tight-laced dress was the color of pumpkins, and the sachet pendant that nestled in her cleavage gave off an earthy, spicy aroma. Even her dark, braided hair had an auburn sheen that reminded Teldin of harvest trees viewed by moonlight. Well, he thought, what harm could come of a few more minutes?

As the gypsy woman elbowed a path for them through the tavern, Teldin marveled at the instant carnival atmosphere the aperusa troop had created. Some of the gypsies played wildly infectious music; others shoved tables aside and enticed the inn's patrons to join in the dance. Teldin counted four card games, three fortune-tellers, and several boisterous games of skill. His lovely captor edged past three human mercenaries and an aperusa man embroiled in a dart contest, pulling Teldin toward a small table near the bar.

Presiding at the table was a stunning woman with an untamed mop of glossy black hair and a dress of vivid purple silk. Her customer was a gray-bearded, gray-clad dwarf who perched stiffly on the edge of his chair and firmly anchored his sack of coins beneath his boots. A small knot of people had gathered around the table, awed by the dexterity of the gypsy woman's flashing hands as she flicked the cards into an intricate pattern on the table.

The game was not one Teldin recognized; he'd never been one for gambling. Still, he found the gypsy's skill and the whimsically painted cards intriguing. Teldin became so absorbed in the card game that it was several minutes before he realized he was alone. He glanced around the crowded taproom, and a flash of orange caught his eye. "His" gypsy was on the other side of the tavern, luring a clearly besotted sailor toward one of the fortune-tellers. A small, self-deprecating smile twitched Teldin's lips. So that was her game.

A discordant note in the happy cacophony drew Teldin's attention back to the card table. The card-playing dwarf punctuated his stream of innovative curses by throwing his losing hand down on the table.

"I say you cheat," he growled through his beard. He thumped the table with both hands for emphasis. "And, by Reorx, I'll prove it."

One stubby-fingered hand shot forward. With surprising speed and delicacy, the dwarf picked a card from the front of the gypsy woman's purple blouse. He held it aloft. "See? Always a paladin, whenever she needs one," he said triumphantly. The crowd around the table began an ominous mutter.

Not put out in the slightest, the gypsy smiled and playfully touched a fingertip to the dwarf's bulbous nose. "Card game is over," she admitted with a little shrug. She reclaimed the Red Paladin card from the indignant dwarf and openly tucked it back into her blouse, then she leaned suggestively closer to the rugged, little man. "But much, much more I have where you found that one, hmmm?"

The dwarf responded to her purred invitation with a snort and a ready axe. "You could be packing a whole deck in your drawers, woman, for all I'd care," he said as he rose to his feet. Shaking his axe, he roared, "Now give me back my coins!"

At the mention of money, blades flashed as several aperusa men formed a semicircle behind the seductress.

"Nine Hells!"

The exclamation came from the other side of the tavern. Teldin looked over to see a large, red-bearded human wearing an outraged expression as he frantically patted himself down. "Damned if someone didn't pick me clean!"

"Me, too!"

"Hey, where's my bag?"

As the indignant chorus rose, several aperusa women melted into the night as silently as brightly colored shadows. Seeing this, Teldin understood. The women had taken the opportunity handed them by the dwarf's outburst to quietly work the room. His hand dropped to his own belt. Reassured that his coin bag was still full and that the medallion's bag was in place, Teldin eased away from the gypsy's card table. The gods knew, he drew more than enough attention by

virtue of his cloak without putting himself in the center of a
senseless tavern battle.

The storm definitely was brewing. Insults and accusations
flew like hailstones, quickly followed by thrown fists. Within
the span of two score heartbeats the fight engulfed the
tavern.

As he carefully edged toward the back door, Teldin
noticed the beholder now floating high above its chair. One
of its eyestalks slowly rose, somehow giving Teldin the
impression of a crossbow being notched and aimed.

Teldin flashed a look over his shoulder. Sure enough, the
impertinent dracons stood directly behind him, watching the
battle with stupid, tipsy smiles curving their reptilian mouths.
Two things simultaneously occurred to Teldin: the beholder
probably did not have much of a sense of humor, and he
himself was standing in the line of fire.

An enormous aperusa man near Teldin apparently came
to the same conclusion. With a shriek, the gypsy launched
himself into the air and away from danger. His precipitous
lunge caught Teldin and sent him sprawling under a nearby
table. Slightly dazed, Teldin shook his head and started to
crawl out from under the tablecloth.

"No! Not to go yet," hissed a bass whisper. Teldin started.
Somehow the huge aperusa also had taken refuge under the
table and was crouched on all fours behind him. After
motioning for Teldin to stay put, the gypsy thrust two fingers
under his black mustache and blew. A shrill whistle cut
through the clamor of the fight.

At the signal, the purple-clad woman jumped onto the
card table and began a sinuous, suggestive dance. Some of
those fighters nearest the table stopped in midbrawl, oblivious to their own upraised fists or drawn daggers as they
gaped at the sensuous display. As she whirled and stamped
and beckoned, several of the tavern patrons forgot their
grievances and drifted closer to her makeshift stage, opening

a path between Teldin's hiding place and the rear door of the tavern.

The gypsy woman seemed to notice the same thing. Smiling seductively, she caught up her swirling skirts and ripped them from hem to sash, revealing a small arsenal of knives strapped to shapely legs. She began to snatch up knives and throw them with chilling accuracy.

"Now," intoned the aperusa man. He slid out from under the table and bounded to his feet. "We go now."

Teldin crawled out and cast a look toward the beleaguered gypsy woman. Her knife collection almost depleted, she now lashed out with bare feet at anyone who ventured within range. "But—"

"Please to hurry," pleaded the aperusa, pushing Teldin toward the back of the tavern. "Must go out back door, and quickly. Amber can hold them only for so long."

"And then?" Teldin asked pointedly, brushing the man's hand off his shoulder. The aperusa's black brows knitted in befuddlement, so Teldin tried again. "What will happen to her then?"

"Ah." Understanding lit the gypsy's eyes, but he shrugged as if the answer were of little consequence. "A short stay in prison. Amber will charm the jailor and leave when she chooses."

A bolt of blue light shot past Teldin's head with a sharp, sizzling hiss. He stared in stunned amazement at the stars glimmering through the smoking, black-edged hole in the tavern wall. The charred remains of what used to be bar patrons lay on the floor, as crumpled and dried as fallen leaves. They might as well have been leaves, for all the identity that was left to them.

"Eye of disintegration," moaned the gypsy, again shoving Teldin toward the exit. "Angry beholder, very dangerous. We go *now*."

A thunderous rumble nudged Teldin out of his shock and

indecision. He looked up to see the pair of dracons, panic etched on their dragonlike faces, stampeding toward him. Teldin leaped for the door, but not soon enough. The dracons, the human, and the aperusa crashed through the doorway and into the alley.

As he pulled himself free of the bruising tangle of tails, limbs, and splintered wood, Teldin thought that it would be a cold day in Reorx's Forge before either of the dracons told another beholder joke.

Chapter Two

● ● ●

The grand admiral sat at the very center of the secret command base called Lionheart, her tiny form almost lost in the deep blue leather of her chair. Despite her diminutive size, the ancient ruler of the Imperial Fleet was an imposing elf who wore her years like hard-earned battle trophies. Her bearing was still erect and proud, her close-cropped silver curls were thick and lustrous, and her face was a triangular network of lines framing eyes of tempered steel. The power that came with the office of grand admiral shaped and defined those who wielded it, and the passing of centuries had left little to the elven leader that spoke of personality, name, or even gender. Yet her office was furnished throughout in deep blue, a color that uniquely complemented her silvery appearance. There was enough personal vanity left in the elven woman's soul for that.

Her office was in a tower, and from any of the circular room's windows she could see the ring of armadas, enormous butterfly ships planted wing-to-wing on a remote asteroid of Garden. She stared idly at one of these titanic butterflies as she pondered the strange message an elven wizard had just delivered to her.

The grand admiral turned slowly to face her adviser and studied the wizard with shrewd, pale eyes. Vallus Leafbower stood stiffly as he awaited her response. The gossamer chain mail of his uniform glittered in the dim lamplight, and his blue tabard was embroidered with a wizard's insignia as well as elven runes naming his house and rank. He had been with the Imperial Fleet only a short time, yet Vallus Leafbower was highly regarded by the command of Lionheart. He was a powerful wizard of impeccable lineage, and he'd brought information deemed vital to the elven war effort. Had the report he'd just given come from any other adviser, the grand admiral likely would have dismissed it as hysteria.

"Ghost ships are not uncommon. Perhaps you should tell me why this particular one was brought to my attention," she suggested.

Vallus hesitated, and the admiral did not miss the foreboding in the wizard's eyes. "The abandoned ship was an armada. It was adrift in Winterspace," he said.

The ancient admiral's face turned gray at this news, but her disciplined features showed no other sign of her distress. "I see." She nodded curtly. "Very well, you may bring the patrol ship captain to me now."

Vallus Leafbower bowed and left the small chamber. Alone, the grand admiral slumped low in her chair and passed one hand wearily over her eyes. The power and authority of her position fell from her, and for a moment she was no longer the grand admiral, the representative and embodiment of all elves; she was only a frail and heartsick elven woman, exhausted by the weight of centuries and the responsibility of directing an escalating war.

She dragged herself from her chair and began to pace, relying on the motion of her legs to nudge her numbed mind into action. There was time to collect her thoughts, for it could be a good while before Vallus returned with the rescued captain.

Lionheart was a vast place. The base under her command was actually a fleet of ships connected by magically animated walkways and enveloped by a single atmosphere. In addition to the armada battleships, Lionheart included patrol ships, supply barges, docking bays, warships, and, of course, the enormous, coin-shaped vessel that housed the magnificent blue-and-silver Elven Council, a chamber large enough to seat representatives from every known elven world. Soon, the admiral feared, she might have to call a general council of the elven peoples. Such a thing had not been done in living memory, but the war was going badly.

In the first Unhuman War, the goblinkin had been unorganized and undisciplined. Unfortunately, her people's disdain for all goblin races had left them ill prepared for the scro. Descendants of orcs, the highly evolved, fiercely militaristic scro were a force to fear both in wildspace and on world-to-world combat. Already the scro had overcome and destroyed whole elven worlds. Now, as if the elves hadn't problems enough, it seemed that the mighty armadas were somehow vulnerable.

A small knock on her office door interrupted the admiral's troubled thoughts. Vallus Leafbower had returned, and with him was a young male elf clearly long past exhaustion.

"Captain Sirian Windharp reporting, Admiral," Vallus said gently, unobtrusively supporting the haggard elf.

The admiral motioned the captain to a chair. "Please have a seat, Captain Windharp," she said kindly. "We will try to keep this interview as brief as possible, so that you may be free to rest and recover from your ordeal."

Sirian Windharp sank gratefully into the offered chair, and the admiral took the seat behind her desk and folded her hands on the polished expanse of blue marble. "I understand that you have something important to tell us. Please start at the beginning."

The elf nodded. "I am captain of the *Starfoam*, a dolphin patrol vessel recently assigned to duty in Winterspace. As we approached our post, we came across an abandoned armada—"

"Where, precisely?"

The captain blinked, startled by the interruption. The elven custom of long, uninterrupted narrative was deeply entrenched, even in situations of greatest import. "It was adrift in Winterspace, about two days' travel from the planet Radole. I'm afraid the exact coordinates were lost with our navigator."

"The armada was old? Derelict?" she demanded.

"No. It was of recent metamorphosis."

Silver eyebrows flew upward. "You're quite sure of that?"

"Oh, yes," Sirian said with quiet certainty. "The armada's wings were patterned in purple and yellow, marking it as a newly developed strain. I believe that only one or two generations of this particular ship have been grown."

The admiral nodded slowly. "That is so. Go on."

"There was no sign of life on board, and the armada's air was fouled. The *Starfoam* could not land on the ship, but we sent down a boarding party." A haunted look filled the elven captain's eyes. "Not one member returned."

"It is a great loss," the admiral said gently. "We will speak of it again when you are well. For now, please describe the damage done to the armada."

The elf's gaze turned inward as he tried to recall the details. "The ship was virtually unscathed," he said slowly. "The only mark on it was a few broken boards on the top hull, as if the armada had been bombarded. The damage wasn't severe enough to explain why the armada was deserted, though."

"Did you attempt to destroy the ship?" She had to ask; policy decreed that any adrift elven vessel was to be reclaimed or annihilated, at all costs. Always important, in time of war this policy was now vital. Allowing the scro to obtain an armada—particularly in Winterspace—could result in disaster.

"Yes, we tried." The elven captain was silent for a long moment. The loss of his crew showed in his eyes like a physical pain. "I sent down two more parties, with the same result. The ship seemed to swallow them whole. In order to report back, I kept only the barest minimum crew needed for the return trip."

"But you left the armada in a spaceworthy condition," the admiral stated, in the manner of one who must be absolutely sure.

"What else could I have done?" Sirian Windharp cried with a sudden burst of emotion. "I could hardly tow an armada back to Lionheart behind the *Starfoam*!" As soon as the words were out, the captain blenched, horrified by his own grievous breach of protocol. The grand admiral, however, appeared not to notice.

"It seems incredible that an enemy capable of overcoming the armada would resist claiming it," she mused aloud. A long silence filled the chamber. Dread hung in the air as the three elves contemplated an unknown force that could render the most powerful vessel in the elven fleet a lifeless hull.

Finally the admiral looked over at the captain. "Thank you for your report, Sirian Windharp. You did well in returning to Lionheart with this news. Be assured that we will do all we can to find and reclaim the armada."

The elven captain rose, but, despite the obvious dismissal, he hesitated. "With your permission, I would like to be among the searchers."

"If you remember your history lessons, you realize that this matter is of grave importance," she said. "The fleet must leave at once. Can you be ready?"

"Yes," he said simply.

The grand admiral held his gaze with eyes that saw and measured. Finally she gave a crisp nod and clapped her hands twice. A uniformed aide appeared at her door. "Take Captain Windharp to the supply master," she directed. "His ship, the *Starfoam*, is to be prepared for flight, provisioned, and crewed. Give the captain whatever he requests." She turned to Sirian Windharp, and a rare smile brightened her face. "Go, then, Captain, and may you find sweet water and light laughter."

The traditional elven farewell, seemingly incongruous in such grim circumstances, was an affirmation of the unquenchable elven spirit and a personal tribute to Sirian Windharp. The elven captain bowed deeply, then followed the aide from the chamber.

The admiral's smile faded abruptly, and her eyes drifted shut. After a moment she shook off her dark introspection and turned to Vallus Leafbower. "We need the ultimate helm," she stated. As legend had it, an ultimate helm was the only device that could be used to control the mighty ship *Spelljammer*. Such helms were said to be ordinary artifacts imbued with special powers by the great ship itself, and they were exceedingly rare.

"An attempt was made to recover the Cloak of the First Pilot, as Captain Kilian reported," Vallus reminded, referring to elven admiral Cirathorn's effort to take Teldin Moore's cloak. "It was not an honorable attempt."

"What, then, do you recommend? The war is taking a great toll, with a high loss of lives and ships. Kilian's own ship is the sole survivor of the fleet we had stationed at the Rock of Bral. Now we learn that our newest and most powerful armada is vulnerable to some mysterious enemy. As highly as we value life, even a life as fleeting as a human's, can we risk the survival of the elven nation on this principle?" she asked. From her dispassionate tone, they might have been discussing the menu for eveningfeast. "No, I think we must recover the cloak, and soon."

She paused, and the gaze from her sharp, ancient eyes met and held Vallus's. "*You* will recover the cloak. I tell you this because you must be the next to wear it."

The wizard's fine-boned face paled almost to transparency. "Why me?" he asked with unelven bluntness.

A faint, sad smile thinned the admiral's lips. "Because, dear Vallus, you do not *wish* to wear the cloak. We have seen that such power can be dangerous in the hands of those who covet it too dearly. The Imperial Fleet must ensure that the cloak, and the *Spelljammer*, will be brought to bear on the side of the elves. You would use it as you were bid."

Vallus's silence affirmed the older elf's insight, but his face remained troubled. "There may be another way," he suggested cautiously. "I believe that Teldin Moore could be persuaded to join our cause."

"Do you?" She sniffed. "May I remind you that this conflict is widely called 'The Second *Unhuman* War'? Humans, with the exception of the scro's riffraff mercenaries, consider it none of their concern. As long as the war doesn't inconvenience them, they're more than happy to ignore it."

"But—"

"Another issue," she continued, pointedly overriding Vallus's interruption. "Many of our people have made finding the *Spelljammer* their lifework, without success. Have you any reason to think that Teldin Moore can succeed where we have failed? Or that he could command the ship if he should find it?"

The admiral paused and shook her silver head adamantly. "My dear wizard, your plan is—at best!—taking a long shot with a short bow."

"You may be right," Vallus allowed. "However, while serving aboard the hammership *Probe*, I had ample time to observe Teldin Moore. It is true that he is limited by his youth and inexperience, but many times he showed signs of *ryniesta*," he argued, using an Elvish term roughly meaning "the seeds of heroism."

The admiral frowned, startled by Vallus's word choice and what it implied. He had deliberately used a term that conferred great honor, and that was reserved for things elven.

Vallus pressed his point. "The cloak obviously has accepted Teldin Moore. From what we know of the *Spelljammer*, there is no reason to assume that the great ship will not do likewise. The human has shown the strength to endure and to persevere. I believe he possesses the potential to command. We could do worse than to have such a human on our side."

The elven woman considered him carefully, weighing his obvious conviction against his self-interest. "Hmmm. And you think the human could be persuaded to join us? Even after the attack on him by our Admiral Cirathorn?"

"I do." Vallus paused, choosing his words carefully. "You've brought up another important issue. If we were to take the cloak from Teldin Moore by force, or even by attrition, in what way would we be better than the other races that pursue him?"

Silence, as palpable as an autumn mist, hung in the admiral's chamber.

"If you truly believe that Teldin Moore would be an asset, I give you leave to try to enlist his assistance," the admiral said evenly. However—" she broke off and leveled a steely gaze at the elven wizard "—you have one hundred days to convince the human, no more. We can ill afford even that much. When that time is spent, we will use whatever means are necessary to obtain the cloak."

"But how can we—"

The admiral abruptly raised her hand, cutting off the wizard's heated objections. Her hand faltered, then dropped heavily to her lap. For a fleeting moment the grand admiral's powerful visage crumbled, leaving only the troubled face of an ancient elven woman. "My dear Vallus," she whispered, "how can we *not*?"

* * * * *

In the alley behind the tavern, Teldin rose and gingerly tested his aching joints. With a loud grunt, the aperusa heaved himself out from under the dark green dracon and began to brush off his multicolored finery. The dracons lumbered to their feet and shook their heads as if trying to clear them.

The gypsy stooped to pick up a jeweled dagger, then he cast an uneasy look toward the splintered remnants of the tavern door. He adjusted the bright green sash that girded his immense waist, then tucked the dagger back into place with the air of one ready to travel. "Come, my friend," he urged Teldin. "The aperusa have earned much trouble this night. We must leave quickly, for I am their leader."

Teldin stopped taking inventory of his injuries. "You'd desert your own people?" he demanded.

"What you mean, desert?" the gypsy asked with genuine amazement.

"Abandon, forsake, leave behind, run out on, turn one's back upon," the pale green dracon said helpfully.

"Hmmph." The aperusa cast a scathing glance toward the dracon and turned back to Teldin. "The Astralusian Clan has much trouble. I am their leader, so I have *more* trouble," the aperusa explained patiently. He stared at Teldin, obviously waiting for the man to see reason.

Teldin huffed in disbelief. Before he could tell the gypsy what he thought of such self-serving "logic," the darker dracon clasped his clawed hands to his cheeks and shrieked like a just-pinched farm maiden. Teldin twisted to see what had frightened the creature.

Bright light spilled out of the tavern and shone on the wooden wall of the alley. Against the wall was a spherical shadow bristling with eyestalks and growing ominously larger. The beholder was following them into the alley.

"Come on!" yelled Teldin, breaking into a run. His oversized companions fell in behind him without argument, showing surprising talent for speed and self-preservation.

As they dashed through a twisted maze of streets, Teldin found himself wondering whether the dracons had been the beholder's real target. After all, the shot had gone past *his* head. Beholders were not known for having bad aim. For that matter, beholders were not known for self-restraint. As Teldin thought about it, it seemed unlikely that the monster would sit calmly by as a joke was told at its expense. It must have had some reason for holding its peace, something compelling enough to stay its natural urge to commit instant and gratifying mayhem. Dread rose in Teldin like a dark tide. So far, the beholders had stayed out of the race for the cloak, but they could prove to be his deadliest antagonists so far.

On and on Teldin ran, the aches of his body forgotten. Fear, his troubled thoughts, and a disinclination to be trampled by the panicked dracons behind him pushed him along. The alleys widened into streets, and soon the dock area was in sight. Teldin raced across the village green toward the relative safety of the dock, where he'd have a clear view of an approaching beholder.

Teldin stopped when he reached the boardwalk. He bent over to grip his knees as he struggled to regain his breath. A hand on his shoulder startled him, and he jerked upright. With a stab of relief he recognized Hectate Kir, his half-elven navigator.

"Steady, sir," Hectate said in his quiet voice. He studied Teldin's companions, and, as he did so, he reflexively flattened the cowlick at the crown of his auburn head. After each pass of his hand, the cowlick popped obdurately up, lending the half-elf a puckish air completely at odds with his gravely puzzled expression. "Are you in any trouble, sir?" he finally asked.

Teldin held up a finger, indicating that he could not yet speak. As he gasped for air, he noted that the dracons also were winded, and their deep, ragged breaths set up a scratchy din reminiscent of a gale blowing through winter trees. The aperusa, on the other hand, did not seem the least bit inconvenienced by their precipitous escape. He merely smoothed a bejeweled hand over his bald pate and straightened the amethyst-silk tabard that covered his quilted yellow coat.

"Ready to sail?" Teldin asked as soon as he could draw enough breath.

"I don't know, sir. I just got back myself." Hectate glanced at a tall, robust woman, clad in only a short tunic and soft leather boots, striding across the dock. He raised his voice to hail her. "Dagmar! Were all the supplies delivered?"

"Aye," she replied, coming close enough to tower over both Teldin and Hectate. "Delivered and stowed. Ready to set sail."

Still breathing hard, Teldin merely nodded up at the first mate. Dagmar was a striking woman with blue-gray eyes and thick braids of ash-blond hair so fair that the gray streaks woven in it were almost indiscernible. Her superb physique belied the years etched into her face; Teldin assumed she had seen at least a dozen more summers than his thirty-three. She was also at least two hands taller than any man on board, and she probably could best any two of them in unarmed combat. Noting Teldin's condition, Dagmar placed a firm hand under his arm and began to help him toward the ship.

"Wait!"

The sonorous bass plea stopped Teldin. He extricated himself from Dagmar's grasp and turned to face the aperusa man. The gypsy stepped forward, sweeping into an elaborate bow. "I have yet to thank you for saving my poor life," he said dramatically and inaccurately. "Before you stands Rozloom, King of the Astralusian Clan."

"We're honored," Teldin said dryly, not bothering to offer his own name. Experience had taught him to protect his identity even in innocuous circumstances.

"A king! What a shame, Your Majesty, that you lost your crown defending your clan," put in the dark green dracon in a snide tone. His sarcasm would have done credit to a Krynnish fishwife, and Teldin flashed the creature an amused look as he turned to leave.

"No! Not to go yet." Rozloom dropped to his knees. "Please, Captain, you see before you a man in great danger."

Suspicion came easily to Teldin. "Captain?" he echoed.

Rozloom's eyes flicked over Hectate Kir, taking in the slight navigator's almond-shaped eyes and slightly pointed ears. "This one calls you 'sir.' An elf shows you respect?" The gypsy slapped a hand over his heart in pantomimed shock. "If you are not great captain, you must be small god."

The gypsy's apt sarcasm so closely paralleled his own opinion of elves that Teldin couldn't resist a smile. To his surprise, the wry smile on Hectate's face echoed his own response.

Encouraged, the gypsy sprang nimbly to his feet. "No trouble will I be," he said in a wheedling tone. "My people were born to wildspace. We need but little air."

Teldin's eyes dropped to the sash of emerald silk that girded the gypsy's immense waist. If the ship should ever lose one of its smaller sails, there was enough fabric in that sash to make a passable jib. "Maybe you don't require much air. What about provisions?" he said, as tactfully as he knew how.

"Provisions?" The gypsy roared with laughter and swatted Teldin's shoulder companionably. "Today much luck has come your way, Captain. Rozloom will be galley master, and never will you feast as well."

"You can cook?" Hectate asked, hope glowing in his voice.

At the half-elf's reaction, the guilt that was never far from the surface of Teldin's mind welled up once again. Of his skeleton crew, not one person could claim basic culinary skills. So far, not one meal had been more than edible, and few had achieved even that status.

"Cook, certainly. *And* run fine shipboard tavern," the aperusa said smugly.

Teldin bit his lip and pondered. Considering the danger he asked his crew to face, providing them with decent food was little enough. He'd learned from Aelfred the importance of crew morale. But taking on an aperusa? He looked Rozloom over carefully.

The gypsy was several inches taller than Teldin, and almost broad enough to carry off his immense girth. Despite his size, Rozloom moved with a nimble, fluid grace. Everything about the man was flamboyant and theatrical: his voice, his gestures, his clothes. The bronzed skin of the gypsy's bald pate gleamed in the dock's lamplight as if it had been oiled, and his long black mustache flowed dramatically into a curly beard. Thick black brows shadowed Rozloom's small, unreadable black eyes, but his broad smile suggested both open friendship and supreme self-satisfaction. Teldin doubted that the gypsy would be much of a fighter; aperusa seldom were. The jeweled daggers tucked into Rozloom's sash and boots obviously were ornaments, not weapons.

Still, the gypsy said he could cook. Teldin turned to Dagmar. "What do you think?"

The mate shrugged. "Aperusa are wildspace camels. He's right about that much. He won't use up much air or provisions. On the other hand, if this one breeds true, you can trust him to run from a fight, drink like a duck, and pester the women."

Rozloom's eyes brightened as he took in the woman's substantial charms, and he rubbed his meaty hands together with anticipation. "And who is this beauty?" he asked in liquid tones.

"Dagmar, the *Valkyrie's* first mate," Teldin said. The gypsy's bug-eyed disbelief at this revelation was almost

comical. Since aperusa men regarded women as inferior—
necessary only to the fine art of seduction—they were not
accustomed to finding women in positions of power. Teldin
considered this attitude to be one of the aperusa's less
attractive traits, and he couldn't resist pushing the knife a
little deeper. "As galley master, you'd be under Dagmar," he
warned.

The gypsy gave Teldin's comment a moment's lewd
consideration, then he flashed a leer at the first mate. "That
will be a pleasure," he said, and looked her over with a
lingering gaze.

"It's your call," Teldin told Dagmar with dry humor.

She seemed neither interested nor insulted by the aperusa.
"We could use a cook. You, gypsy, belay the prattle and stow
your gear. Serve eveningfeast at two bells, night watch." She
turned and strode toward the ship, shouting orders to the
hands as she went.

The first mate's mention of gear surprised Teldin; Rozloom
had fled with nothing but the clothes on his back. Then the
gypsy turned to ogle the departing Dagmar, and, for the first
time, Teldin noted the large, lightweight silk sack strapped
to Rozloom's back. His eyes narrowed.

"All business, that one," Rozloom mused, unaware of
Teldin's scrutiny. He chewed pensively at his mustache, then
shrugged. "Ah, well, probably she was too old, anyway."

"Sir," importuned the pale green dracon, his hands
clasped together and his reptilian face earnest. "If you
please, I am Siripsotrivitus, and this is my brood-brother
Chirpsian. Since life is short, most prefer to call us Trivit and
Chirp. I beseech you to grant us safe passage to our ship."

Not understanding, Teldin shot a glance over the rows of
ships bobbing at dock. "Which one of these is yours?"

"Surely you jest!" piped Chirp, the darker dracon. "Our
clan flies a ship too large to land at this port."

Taking in the creatures' size, Teldin could believe that.

They easily were five feet tall at the shoulder, plus about two feet of neck and head. He couldn't imagine a ship that could hold a clan of dracons. "Then how—"

"Chirp and I were dispatched by shuttle to acquire certain supplies." Trivit paused, shamefaced. "We were derelict in our duty, and our *kaba*—our high leader—will be most displeased. The quality of the tavern's ale was such that we lingered too long. Our shuttle doubtlessly took off at its appointed time, and it will not return until the same hour tomorrow." The dracon leaned in confidentially. "I fear we might have offended that, er, that round gentleman in the tavern. Staying until tomorrow could prove to be injudicious in the extreme."

"True enough," Teldin said, struggling to keep a straight face. He found himself warming to the earnest, comical creature.

"Our clan awaits us just outside Garden's atmosphere. I can give the coordinates to your navigator," offered Trivit quickly.

Teldin glanced at the *Valkyrie*, a slender drakkar, or longship, built on Dagmar's icy homeworld, then skeptically considered the dracons. Each beast had to weigh at least a quarter ton. "I'm not sure we can carry you, even for a relatively short distance."

"Dagmar would know for sure," Hecate put in.

Teldin nodded. He'd acquired Dagmar along with the drakkar, and the first mate knew the *Valkyrie* down to its last plank and barnacle. Teldin led the way to the ship, then sprinted up the boarding plank and caught Dagmar's arm as she rushed past.

"These dracons want passage. Their ship is orbiting Garden. Can we handle the extra weight for a couple of days?"

The first mate studied the huge creatures, taking in their fine armor and weapons. As they awaited her decision,

Chirp shifted his weight from one massive foot to another and Trivit nibbled nervously at his claws. Finally Dagmar nodded crisply. "The *Valkyrie* could use a couple of fighters. They come." Her tone was without expression, and she strode off without a backward look at her new crewmen. Teldin and Hectate exchanged a glance and a shrug. Teldin was beginning to suspect that the brusk first mate had a soft spot for strays.

It took three extra planks and a tense half hour to maneuver the overjoyed dracons onto the *Valkyrie*, and during that time Teldin saw no sign of pursuit by the beholder. With a sigh of relief, he gave the order to sail.

At Teldin's signal, Om, the ship's taciturn gnome technician, fired up the machine that drove a mysterious tangle of pipes and gears attached to the oars. The machine started with a smoky belch and a long, grinding whine of protest. Om crouched beside the contraption, her small brown face wrinkled in concentration and her tiny hands flying as she wielded one gnome-sized tool after another. From time to time she stood and augmented her efforts with a well-placed kick.

Teldin watched, amused. At first he had been put off by the idea of a gnome-powered ship, but since the machine took the place of twenty oarsmen per watch, it kept the crew to a minimum. To Teldin's way of thinking, the fewer people he endangered, the better. The contraption worked quite well, thanks to the gnome who apparently devoted her life to keeping it running. Om was a rarity among tinker gnomes. For one thing, her inventions worked; for another, she never said two words when one would do the job and spoke not at all when a grunt would suffice.

Soon the oars began to move rhythmically. As the ship backed away from the dock, the dracons raised their high, fluting voices in one of the bawdiest chanteys Teldin had ever heard. He was pleased to note that the dracons were excellent sailors. Under Dagmar's instruction, they hoisted the sails with disciplined exuberance. Rozloom had retired to the galley, somewhat crestfallen from the discovery that the only women on board were Dagmar and Om.

Leaving his strange crew to their tasks, Teldin headed for the ship's stern, to the small raised room that housed the bridge. Hectate Kir was already there, bent intently over a star chart. Teldin took his place on the helm, and his cloak began to glow with the pale sunrise pink that signaled the start of its spelljamming magic.

Until just recently, Teldin was only able to use his cloak as a helm when there was no other working helm on board. With his limited crew, however, he could hardly break a helm every time he needed to move. He'd practiced until he could wield the cloak in the presence of a functional helm. He made a point of sitting in the helm at such times—no sense in advertising the fact that the spelljamming magic came, not from him, but from his cloak—yet he could do nothing to dim the cloak's magical pink glow. Teldin slid a sidelong glance toward the navigator. The half-elf took note of the cloak's latest color shift and shrugged.

Not for the first time, Teldin felt a surge of relief over Hectate's utter lack of curiosity in matters not directly relating to star charts. Hectate Kir seemed to be the only being in wildspace who had no interest in the cloak. He was a simple soul, content to do his job and mind his own business. For a moment Teldin envied the half-elf. His own average, ordinary life on Krynn seemed so distant that it well could have been a story he'd heard about another man. That life had been taken away, leaving him with a dangerous legacy and a quest that he had yet to fully comprehend. With a sigh, Teldin turned his concentration to the task at hand.

As the cloak's magic waxed, Teldin's senses expanded to encompass the ship and its surroundings. He *was* the ship, and at the same time he had the odd sensation that he was floating high above it, looking down over it and the dock. Teldin knew the moment the cloak helm was fully operational, for the sounds and scents of the river port were cut off abruptly as the ship became encased in its own envelope of air. It was uncanny the way all sounds of life on the asteroid—the cries of the gulls, the congenial insults exchanged by the fisherfolk on nearby boats, the faint distant bustle of market life—could be extinguished as abruptly as one might blow out a candle's flame. The sound of water lapping at the drakkar's hull was their only sensory tie to the port. At Teldin's silent command, the *Valkyrie* rose straight out of the river. Water rushed off the hull with a thunderous roar, and the drakkar rose into the night sky.

The archaic design of the bridge limited Teldin's natural vision, but with his expanded senses he could see the river port fall quickly away. Within moments the trade asteroid below them was an oddly shaped lump of rock, then just one of many that clung to the roots of the celestial plant known as Yggdrasil's Child. It was a bizarre construction, but Teldin did not doubt that the image in his mind mirrored the reality beneath the ship. Despite his recent travels on a dozen worlds and through the wonders of wildspace, Teldin's imagination was not capable of conjuring such a place. Garden was just the roots of the "plant," and it looked like a tangle of odd-shaped beads that some giant child had strung and, tired of them, flung aside. Or, perhaps, a young potato plant torn from the soil, complete with small, clinging tubers.

"I wonder where the rest of the plant is," Teldin said idly.

"Well, it's not on the star charts, sir," replied Hectate Kir with his usual flair for understatement.

The navigator's unintentional humor brought a quick smile to Teldin's face. Having heard some of the legends concerning Yggdrasil's Child, he could see why it'd be hard to chart. It was said to be a celestial plant so large that it

encompassed, not only worlds, but other planes of existence. Such a thing was so far beyond Teldin's ken that
merely thinking about it made his mind spin.

The ship shuddered faintly as it passed through the edge
of Garden's atmosphere. As always, Teldin was amazed at
the intense blackness of wildspace. Back on Krynn he'd
thought of night skies as black, but since then he'd seen that
a thousand shades lay between the blackness of wildspace
and the midnight blue skies he'd witnessed with his feet on
his homeworld.

At two bells, Teldin turned the helm over to Klemner, a
minor cleric of Ptah. He made his way below to the small
mess, curious to know whether Rozloom's boasts had been
founded in reality. He was amazed by the festive atmosphere
that the aperusa had created. The galley tables had been
pushed into a companionable cluster. Conversations were
muted and fragmented as the crew members tucked away
fresh fish and vegetables, bread still warm from the oven,
and a sticky confection made of flaky pastry, dried fruit, and
honey. Rozloom made the rounds of the room like a genial
host at a well-run party. Teldin quickly filled a tray and
seated himself.

"Join you, sir?"

Teldin looked up into Hectate's thin, serious face. He
nodded, and the navigator set his well-laden plate down on
the table and took the chair across from Teldin. "I see you
approve of our new cook," Teldin said dryly.

Taking in Teldin's rueful expression, the half-elf asked,
"Having second thoughts, sir?"

"Always," Teldin acknowledged with a touch of sadness.
He could ill afford to trust even those who seemed trustworthy, and the gypsy "king" hardly qualified as that.

"Rumor has it that Rozloom has started a batch of ale
brewing," Hectate said, dangling Teldin's favorite indul-
gence before him. "He couldn't be all bad, sir."

Teldin winced—imperceptibly, he hoped—and returned the half-elf's smile with a fleeting one of his own. Teldin's attitude toward elves had been soured by a series of bad experiences, and for some reason Hectate's features took on a decidedly elven tinge whenever he smiled. Thank the gods that he didn't do it very often, Teldin thought wryly.

"Rozloom seems likable enough," Teldin said cautiously, surprised to find that he could in fact like a man who was so blatantly self-serving.

"But . . . ?"

Teldin shrugged, struggling to form his reservations into words. "The man seems to have no convictions," he began. "Most people, for good or bad, have some set of principles that guide their actions. From what I've seen so far, I'd have to say that Rozloom runs on pure self-interest. How can you sail with someone who'll follow the prevailing wind, no matter what?"

The half-elf's smile disappeared, and his eyes dropped. For a long moment he sat in silence, his meal forgotten.

"What is it, Hectate?" Teldin asked at length.

"Sometimes, sir, staying a chosen course despite the winds can be dangerous. There's such a thing as holding too strongly to convictions," the navigator said softly. Without explanation, he rose to his feet and walked out of the galley, leaving Teldin staring blankly after him.

Chapter Three

● ● ●

Tekura leaned farther into the dome of the port window, drawn by the austere beauty of the world below her, set in wildspace like a vast opal against a black velvet cloth. The swirling pattern of white streaks on the orb's surface charmed her even though it probably indicated that a numbing blizzard awaited them. Intending to share the beauty, the elflike woman glanced back at the three ship's officers.

Zeddop, their lamentable wizard, was slumped in the thronelike helm, his eyes glazed as he poured magical power into the ship, and his short silvery hair sticking up in random spikes around his pointed ears. Behind him stood the captain and the navigator, huddling together over a stolen star chart and completely absorbed with the challenge of charting their course. Sadness touched Tekura as she studied her adopted kin: Wynlar, a quiet scholar forced into a role of war leader, and his niece Soona, who possessed an exotic, flame-haired beauty reminiscent of elven royalty, as well as a reluctant talent for seduction. Soona had employed both gifts to learn of the secret gateway into the ice planet's atmosphere.

As part of a centuries-old pact, a magical network enveloped the planet and alerted elven patrol ships when-ever a craft entered or left the planet's atmosphere. A long-ago elven admiral had created a randomly shifting gate to allow elven spy ships to slip through the net. Eventually the admiral's overzealous activities were detected by the Imperial Fleet. The elves had supposedly reprimanded him, but they kept the gate open and secret. Tekura would bet her left hand that they weren't above using it either.

"Merciful Ptah!" the captain swore in a dull whisper. His gaze was fixed on the starboard window, and the star chart he had been studying a moment before dropped unheeded to the floor.

Soona and Tekura stared into the velvet blackness, squinting as they tried to make out the danger their sharp-eyed captain perceived. "Over there, near Vesta," Wynlar directed them, pointing toward the domed windows that were set like eyes on either side of the forecastle. Each window yielded a view of Vesta, one of the three large moons of the ice planet Armistice.

A shadow touched the edge of the pale violet disk. The small group watched with horrified fascination as the shadow grew, slowly metamorphosing into the silhouette of a huge, twisted butterfly.

"Man-o-war," murmured the captain, stating what they all knew. An elven man-o-war was one of the most powerful and feared ships of wildspace. Their shrike ship was a sleek, birdlike vessel that could dart and maneuver like a spacebound sparrow, but in battle it would present little challenge to the elven ship. If the stolen cloaking device did not hide the shrike ship from the elves, their illegal cargo would not reach Armistice and their dream of revenge would die with them.

"It's coming straight at us," Soona reported in a voice tight with fear.

And coming fast, Tekura noted silently. The man-o-war had changed its course and was growing larger with frightening speed. Within moments they could see plainly both the ship and the dark purple shadow it cast back upon the moon.

"Tell me, Tekura, is your plan worth tackling *that?*" demanded Zeddop, nodding toward the approaching ship.

A small, hard smile twitched the young woman's lips, but her gaze never left the man-o-war. "If the cloaking device works, Zeddop, we won't have to fight," she replied, absently tucking a strand of silvery hair behind one pointed ear.

It *has* to work, Tekura thought fiercely, as if the force of her will could strengthen the magic cloaking device. The price she'd paid to obtain it was simply too high for her to accept the possibility of failure. The cloaking device already had cost years of her life, years spent pretending to be everything she abhorred. Passing as an elf, she had worked as a technician on one spelljamming vessel after another until her reputation earned her a post with the Imperial Fleet. Finally, her mission had required her to kill. The ironic justice of this did not escape her—after all, the elves had designed her kind as living weapons—but the necessary act had bruised and sullied her spirit. Whenever the burden grew too heavy, Tekura remembered the look on those elves' faces when she had gone into the Change: first shock, then terror incongruously mixed with disgust. They had disdained her even as she had cut them down.

The man-o-war came on, pushing aside Tekura's memories. Soon they would have to either run or fight. Tekura shot a glance at the captain. As she expected, Wynlar's angular face was contorted by powerfully conflicting emotions. Although their mission depended on getting past the elven patrol ship, every instinct urged the captain toward battle. It was a compulsion Tekura knew too well, a compulsion she read upon every face in the room. To their race, running from a fight was not only unthinkable, but almost impossible. They were, after all, living weapons.

Tekura gritted her teeth, fighting the gathering battle-lust that threatened to overwhelm her every thought and sinew.

Her hands yearned for the feel of a weapon, and she rubbed her palms against her thighs as if the pebbly fabric of her uniform could quiet the itching, insistent desire to fight. She forced herself to ignore the weapons that the officers kept close at hand—the enormous swords and the two-pointed halberds that they could barely lift until battle brought the Change upon them. Tekura knew that, throughout the shrike ship, every member of the crew had similar weapons at hand. Perhaps some already had succumbed to the Change.

The man-o-war moved steadily closer, and throughout the shrike ship there was not a word, barely a breath. The sensitive bodies of the space-bred race could feel the first persuasive tugs of the large ship's approaching gravity field. If the shrike ship continued on its carefully charted course, the man-o-war's atmosphere would engulf it even if the stolen cloaking device *did* work.

After a long moment of silent struggle, the captain's features settled into taut resolve. "Evasive action, Zeddop, at full speed," he said in a soft tone as he briefly touched the helmsman's thin shoulder.

The wizard nodded, looking faintly relieved. His hands clenched around the arms of the helm as he transformed magic into motion. The shrike ship turned in a tight arc and sped away, quickly putting distance between them and the man-o-war. Suddenly the elven ship banked sharply, leaving the pale violet moon behind and soaring with silent majesty into the darkness.

The small group expelled a collective sigh. The shrike ship had not been seen after all.

"Congratulations, Tekura." Wynlar laid a hand on her shoulder. "Your vision and sacrifice have saved our plans."

Now that the immediate danger had past, Tekura felt a little giddy. "I steal only the best," she quipped, then she joined the others in a burst of tension-breaking laughter. Predictably, Zeddop remained immune to humor. The wizard clutched the arms of the helm with white-knuckled hands, and his thin, elflike face predicted disaster. Theirs was a contemplative race, but Zeddop habitually took this trait too seriously and too far.

"Now we face the simple task of dealing with orcs and ogres," Zeddop noted. His words brought an involuntary grimace to every face. Fueled by this reaction, the wizard continued. "Odds are, the savage beasts will tear us to shreds, then kill each other fighting over our cargo," he intoned with the grim satisfaction of those who expect the worst and are seldom disappointed.

"Thank you, Zeddop. That was truly uplifting," snapped Soona. She tossed a handful of red curls over her shoulder and glared at the wizard. "Instead of blinding us with your sunny disposition, why don't you concentrate on the shrike ship? We're off course."

"I know my job," Zeddop said stiffly.

"Then do it, both of you," Wynlar told them, fixing a stern gaze on the pair. The captain's tone indicated that further bickering would be imprudent, and the navigator and helmsman returned their full attention to their tasks. Within moments the birdlike vessel slipped through the invisible gap in the elven warning net, apparently without incident, and began the spiraling descent toward Armistice.

Tekura resumed her place at the forecastle window, dimly aware that Wynlar had left the bridge to address the crewmen gathered on the main deck just outside the forecastle.

"There is danger ahead, but we've laid our plans with care. The orc tribe under Ubiznik Redeye is one of the strongest groups on all of Armistice. It rules the land of Rakhar virtually unopposed. But remember, we must Change before meeting with the orcs. They would be, shall we say, *put off* by our elven forms." A polite chuckle greeted the captain's wry understatement.

Wynlar continued to speak, but Tekura's growing excitement crowded out his words. Her dreams were edging closer to reality with each downward spiral of the shrike ship. The end of the elven domination of space had never seemed so close at hand. Beneath her feet, packed away in the ship's hold, was a cargo that would steal the overwhelming advantage now held by the Imperial Fleet.

The cargo was not terribly impressive: a few battered ship fragments, two small, dead helms. It was but the first shipment of many. Over time, her expertise would help assemble the parts into a fleet, and her people would raise a new navy from among the ice world's inhabitants. With these new allies, they would change the course of the War of Revenge. It was an ambitious plot, and it held terrible risks.

For centuries, the goblin races of Armistice had been trapped on a world of icy winds and violent earthquakes. Denied wildspace travel and driven underground by the brutal climate, the goblinborn had grow more primitive and warlike with each generation. Yet they remembered that others traveled the stars and they coveted spelljamming technology above all else. In exchange for the shrike ship's cargo and skills such as Tekura's, the Rakharian orcs had agreed to release an ancient, terrifying weapon. With it, the elven forces that patrolled Armistice could be systematically destroyed, and in time a powerful new goblin navy could escape into wildspace undeterred.

And after that, Tekura prayed silently, may Ptah protect us all.

* * * * *

Rumors were the standard currency of wildspace. A good rumor could buy a round of drinks, or help to fill the tedious hours of void travel. Apart from the *Spelljammer* itself, few topics provided more speculation than the ambitions of the goblin races. Rumors abounded of vast orc fleets, ogre kings holding grim court, terrifying new war ships. But these were, after all, just rumors, stories designed to pass the time and bring a pleasant shiver or two. Few believed them to have any basis in fact.

Grimnosh, scro general and commander of the Sky Shark battalion, preferred to keep things that way for as long as possible. Even his ship, a newly built version of the ogre mammoth called a dinotherium, was the stuff of legend. Entirely built of metal and weighing almost a hundred tons, it was a grim and efficient war machine fitted with two long ramming tusks, six heavy ballistae, and four catapults. With good reason, the dinotherium had been named *Elfsbane*. Most elves did not expect to find such a monster lurking in the phlogiston rivers, and so far none who did had survived to spread the tale. It was the *Elfsbane*'s mission to meet and destroy elven ships on their way to the Winterspace crystal sphere, and thus weaken the elves' formidable presence in that sphere. Grimnosh was doing his job well—far better, in fact, than his superiors suspected.

Not that his assignment was so difficult, Grimnosh mused with scorn. The elves were disorganized; they lacked vision, discipline, and leadership. It was ironic, really, that the very failings that had brought down the goblin races in the first Unhuman War now characterized their elven conquerors. But what had destroyed the goblins would just as surely destroy the elves. Soon the elves would prove the old bromide that those who disregard history are condemned to repeat it.

Actually, the elves made Grimnosh's job pitifully easy. Communications between the elven ships and their elusive command base were notoriously bad; a ship could disappear almost without notice. Elves abounded who had been drummed out of the Imperial Fleet or who preferred a larger measure of autonomy than the elven command permitted. By restricting their attacks to lone ships or isolated elven worlds, the scro had inflicted significant damage over a period of time without drawing the notice of the elven high command.

The scattered and disorganized elves finally were awakening to the scro threat, however, and, once it bestirred itself, the Imperial Fleet could put up a credible fight. Of late scro losses had been heavy. When full-scale war finally erupted, Grimnosh intended to be ready. The scro general had glorious victories planned for the Sky Sharks, ambitions that vaunted far beyond his assigned mission.

Of course, such gains were not without risk. The plan required regrettable alliances—scro as a rule disdained lesser races—but finding others who hated the elves and enlisting their aid had not been difficult. More challenging was keeping the fools in step with the plan: Grimnosh had learned that the damndest difficulties could arise when dealing with the lower goblin races and elf-spawned freaks such as the one seated before him, swathed in that ridiculous cowled robe.

"My dear K'tide, I'm afraid this ancient weapon of yours is proving far too costly," Grimnosh observed mildly.

The speaker's calm demeanor did not fool K'tide. As head of intelligence for the scro general, he collected information. Everything he knew about Grimnosh confirmed his own belief that the scro was a deadly foe and a dangerous ally.

"It is true that a few orcs were killed when the weapon was released," the spy master said, deliberately choosing his words to minimize the loss. Although mere centuries of evolution separated the scro from their orc ancestors, the scro considered all other goblin races to be inferior and barbaric.

"As a rule, the death of a few orcs would not be a matter for concern," Grimnosh conceded, folding his well-manicured hands on the polished wood of his desk, "but few orcs have the ability to control this weapon. Seven orc priests and three hobgoblin witch doctors are therefore a significant loss. Is it possible that the depleted ranks will prove insufficient to keep the situation, shall we say, under control?"

"Our allies on Armistice assure me that this is not the case," K'tide said firmly.

"I should hope not, for all our sakes." The statement was calm, offered in the deep, rounded tones that often made listeners pause and puzzle to identify an accent.

K'tide nodded briefly, acknowledging the implied threat. A wise person never took any scro threat lightly, and K'tide was a highly trained observer who was not fooled by Grimnosh's cultured manner or elegant surroundings.

The office in which they met was a civilized marvel of polished wood and deep leather chairs, tastefully decorated with *objets d'art* from a dozen worlds. Books from many cultures lined the walls, as well as exquisite framed maps and star charts. It was, without doubt, a gentleman's study.

The gentleman in question, however, still was a scro. Over seven feet tall and powerfully muscled, the general was the single discordant note in his elegant study. Grimnosh was a rare albino, with a white hide and almost colorless eyes. He wore the regulation black leather armor studded with small sharp spikes, but, while many scro painted the studs in bright patterns or even substituted cut gems, his studs were fashioned from a dull, expensive silver-toned metal. The scro version of understated elegance, K'tide noted.

Although Grimnosh's garments suggested a certain refinement, his ornaments revealed his true nature. His large canine teeth had been sharpened and decorated with mini-totems, and his pointed, wolflike ears were festooned with tatoos. About his neck hung a *toregkh*, a necklace made of

teeth taken from opponents who had met their deaths upon
the general's fangs. By scro custom, no other tokens of battle
prowess were worn, though the scro carried many weapons
and were expert with each. It was taken for granted that a
scro warrior had many kills to his credit. The *toregkh* was
therefore a nose-thumb gesture, a way of saying that scro
could kill quite handily with no weapons other than those
granted by nature. Perhaps Grimnosh had taken the recent
evolution toward culture farther than most scro—indeed,
farther than most members of any race—but he was no less
deadly for it.

Other scro tended to overlook Grimnosh's pretensions, as
snide comments tended to lead to dismemberment. In fact,
the general's assistant, a sullen olive-green scro who skulked
in a nearby corner, was missing one ear and the small fingers
of both hands. Rumor had it that Nimick had offered some
small insult to Grimnosh during their training. Grimnosh
kept the green scro around as his adjutant, knowing that the
maimed soldier's presence was a powerful object lesson to
others.

"Perhaps it is time to rethink our strategy," Grimnosh
suggested. "This weapon might not be worth the risks."

K'tide inclined his head, acknowledging the scro's remark
while respectfully disagreeing. "Its first use was highly
successful. The creature was catapulted aboard an elven
armada, and it destroyed the entire crew. More than one
hundred elves," he concluded, weighing each word with
quiet emphasis.

The scro seemed somewhat mollified. "Most impressive,"
he murmured, fingering his *toregkh* reflectively. "What of the
armada?"

"It is virtually unharmed."

"This *is* good news," Grimnosh said, at last visibly
pleased. "Has the ship been secured?"

"Not yet." K'tide paused, choosing his words carefully. "It

will be some time before the weapon runs its natural course. We needn't fear losing the armada. Since it is much closer to Radole than to Armistice, it will escape discovery by the elven patrols that protect the ice planet. If anyone should find the ship and attempt to board, the creature will simply destroy them."

"How long before we can claim the armada?" Grimnosh demanded.

The spy considered. "Once the supply of elven flesh is depleted, the creature and its inevitable offspring will turn on each other. The whole process will take only a few score days. The creatures do not live long without a food supply."

"Excellent." The scro general nodded crisply. "Our first concern, however, must be getting the new troops spacebound. To do so we need spelljamming battle wizards and priests. At this point we cannot afford to risk more goblinkin mages to this weapon."

"Perhaps we cannot afford *not* to," the spy said.

Dark, cold wrath welled through the scro's cultured veneer. The expression on Grimnosh's face would have sent most battle-hardened scro warriors into flight. "I should hope you have a good reason for contradicting me," he said in clipped tones. "It is not an experience I enjoy."

K'tide held his ground. "Indeed I do. We are preparing a second target, one even more attractive than a mighty elven armada."

Grimnosh raised one bone-white brow. "You have my attention."

"Lionheart."

A long silence followed K'tide's triumphant announcement. "Lionheart," repeated the scro commander, his colorless eyes lighting with interest. "An intriguing notion."

"In your estimation, destroying the elven high command would be worth a risk?"

"If such a thing can be accomplished, certainly," Grimnosh

agreed pleasantly, "though I'm not certain that your smug tone is worth the risk that accompanies it." The scro smiled, baring gleaming tusks. "Now, your progress report."

"The Armistice goblinkin soon will be flight ready," the spy master assured him. "We are building a small fleet of ships and training the orc priests in the basics of spelljamming." K'tide's fleeting sneer spoke of utter contempt for the orcs. "Progress in that matter, you understand, is painfully slow."

"Indeed," returned Grimnosh dryly as he leaned back in his chair. "As depleted as scro ranks have become, I sometimes question the wisdom of seeking orc allies on Armistice. Centuries of living underground has hardly improved the strain. That Ubiznik fellow of yours looks like some unholy cross between a dwarf and a goblin. Appalling chap."

"The orc chief is a strong ally. All the Armistice orcs have great physical strength," pointed out K'tide. "The gravity on the ice planet is three times that of most worlds. Once the goblin races are spacebound or fighting world-to-world, their strength will give them a distinct advantage in close combat. I'm assuming that you intend to use them as, shall we say—"

"Cannon fodder," supplied Grimnosh with uncharacteristic bluntness. He glanced down at his hands, grimaced, and held up a thumbnail for closer inspection. "Oh, Nimick," he said, looking over toward his adjutant, "be a good fellow and put an edge on this claw, won't you? While you're at it, you might touch up the engravings as well."

The greenish scro shot his general a look of pure hatred, but he rose with instant obedience and retrieved a small set of tools from a nearby desk drawer. He dragged a stool over to Grimnosh's side, and, taking up a tiny chisel, Nimick began to work on the huge white paw, tracing the tiny, elaborate scenes carved onto each of the general's claws. The murderous expression on the adjutant's face left no doubt that he was contemplating other, more satisfying uses for the tool. Grimnosh took this in with a bland, urbane smile and turned back to K'tide.

"Your argument has merit. As first-strike troops, the Armistice reinforcements are ideal: strong, motivated, and expendable. Now," the scro said briskly, "why don't you tell me a little more about your plans for the good elves of Lionheart?"

Chapter Four

●●●

"We do so appreciate passage, Captain Teldin Moore," Trivit said for what Teldin guessed was the twentieth time. "Our *kaba* certainly is most concerned about our welfare, and once she learns of our rescue I'm sure she will wish to reward you handsomely."

"That's not necessary," Teldin said absently, again.

"Oh, but we insist," said Trivit. "At the very least, perhaps we can share information."

Suddenly the dracons had Teldin's full attention. Seeing this, Chirp's face brightened and he draped a convivial green arm around Teldin's shoulders.

"Our clan travels to the secret homeworld of the dracon people," Chirp confided. "We will cross uncharted crystal spheres and travel seldom-used phlogiston rivers."

"Our *kaba* is wise," Trivit added, his soprano tones rounded with hero worship. "Her knowledge surely can aid you in your own quest."

"What do you know of it?" Teldin demanded. Reflexively he ducked out from under the dracon's chummy embrace. Chirp and Trivit seemed harmless enough, but he didn't want a clan of lizard-centaurs joining those who hunted for the cloak.

"You're bound for the Broken Sphere, are you not?" Chirp asked, clearly surprised by Teldin's suspicious tone. "If that is supposed to be a secret, it has been badly kept. Your destination is common knowledge around the *Valkyrie*."

"You must meet our *kaba*," the pale green dracon repeated. "She has been traveling the far corners of the void for nearly three centuries. Surely her knowledge will serve you well."

Teldin regarded the twin dracons carefully, his eyes darting from one to the other. Their green faces were earnest and open, and Teldin doubted it was in their nature to dissemble. At one time Teldin had considered himself a fairly good judge of character, finding that when he trusted his instinct he seldom went wrong. But since the cloak had come into his hands, life had changed. Telling friend from foe had become difficult, and he had made some near-fatal mistakes. Teldin wasn't sure he could trust his instincts anymore.

Chirp interrupted Teldin's thoughts with an excited squeal. Hugging himself in his excitement, the dracon began a heavy-footed little dance of glee. "There! Look over there!" he burbled, pointing toward a distant light. "That's the *Nightstalker*, or I'm the Dark Spider's next dinner."

Teldin squinted out into the darkness of wildspace. There was a light, all right, but something about it was wrong. From this distance, most ships had a faint, whitish glow and looked a bit like faint stars. This one was like no star he'd ever seen. It glowed with a dim but intense purple light. The strange sight drew the other crew members to the railing, and a worried muttering spread across the drakkar. Teldin reached for the brass tube that hung from his belt and raised it to one eye. Seen through the glass, the dracon ship appeared to be a giant, deep purple wasp. It looked very much like an elven battleship.

"Man-o-war," said Dagmar, confirming Teldin's suspicions. The first mate had sprinted to the railing during Chirp's impromptu dance, drawn by fear for her beloved ship. After curbing the dracon's board-breaking glee, Dagmar stood at the rail by Teldin's side, gazing out into the void. Worry deepened the lines around her eyes. "*That's* the dracons' ship?" she asked.

"So they say," Teldin replied, studying the ship with growing concern. He'd never heard of any race other than elves flying a man-o-war. Was this some sort of trap, or did dracons legitimately use such ships? Teldin lowered the glass and turned his attention to Chirp and Trivit. Their delight in the coming reunion with their clan was so genuine and childlike that Teldin's suspicions ebbed. And if their far-traveling clan leader had answers to the riddle of the Broken Sphere, he'd be foolish not to take the opportunity to listen.

Teldin turned to the first mate. "Prepare the longboat and get the dracons on board. I'll be going with them, but we'll need another helmsman. Get Klemner," he directed, naming the minor priest who did double duty as Rozloom's galley helper. Teldin could easily power the small boat himself, but he did not want to use the cloak's spelljamming magic in front of the dracon clan.

"Aye, Captain," Dagmar said reflexively, but her eyes slid involuntarily to Teldin's cloak. When he'd purchased the drakkar, Teldin had told Dagmar a little about the cloak and the various foes who sought it. Every member of his small crew knew that the voyage held great potential for danger, but Teldin felt he owed his first officer a little more.

While the woman got the dracons aboard the longboat, Teldin shrunk the cloak until it was no more than a silver necklace. Again, he didn't intend to take unnecessary chances with the cloak.

With Klemner at the helm and the dracons wielding the oars, Teldin was free to sit in the longboat's bow and observe the man-o-war. He had heard that these ships were grown by the elves, carefully pruned and twisted into their final shape. He had to admit that the result was beautiful. As they drew near, Teldin noticed that the enormous wings—he guessed a wingspan of at least three hundred feet—were of some glittering, translucent substance that resembled crystal. The wings were webbed with ribs, as if they were giant purple leaves.

As soon as the longboat entered the man-o-war's atmosphere, Chirp took a small silver pipe from the pocket of his leather armor and began to blow busily on the thing. Teldin did not hear a sound, however, and seeing the human's puzzled expression, Trivit leaned forward on his oars to explain.

"It's a signal pipe. One can't be too careful, you know, even when the approaching ship is as small as this boat. Using a code of sorts, Trivit is telling them about our adventure, and he's also performing advance introductions."

"How can you tell?" Teldin wondered.

A series of emotions—confusion, abrupt understanding, and finally pity—chased each other across the dracon's mobile face. "Gracious, I've stuck my foot in it this time, haven't I? Being human and all, I don't suppose you can hear the pipe," Trivit observed with deep sympathy.

"Hard astern," Klemner prompted tersely, bringing the dracons back to the matter at hand. They maneuvered the longboat to the top deck, a narrow, semicircular strip that was suspended above the main deck and dotted with smaller vessels such as elven flitters. Once the longboat was secured to the walkway, the dracons grasped stout ropes and slid down to the main deck below, their muscled arms controlling their descent so that the four-footed impacts were not the thudding crashes Teldin anticipated. He followed them down the rope and looked around for the other dracons. Teldin blinked several times as his eyes adjusted to the strange, dim purple light.

"Captain Teldin Moore, may I present to you our *kaba*, Netarza," said Trivit in formal tones.

Teldin stared in disbelief as the *kaba*'s figure stepped out of the violet shadows. The creature before him was an illithid.

Roughly humanoid in size and stance, the mind flayer had a high, domed head and a lavender hide tinged with red. Four tentacles formed the lower part of its face, and its three-fingered hands ended in curving claws. The creature wore flowing, multilayered robes of deepest purple, which were richly embroidered with metallic threads at the cuffs and trailing hems.

Well met, Teldin Moore, Netarza said at length.

Teldin jumped, startled by the sound of the illithid's mental voice. As low-pitched and musical as a night breeze, it was rather feminine-sounding. Teldin knew that illithids did not possess gender, but he'd thought of Estriss as male and assumed that all illithids would sound pretty much the same. He decided it would be easier to consider this one female.

Summoning what remained of his wits, Teldin bowed. "Forgive me. Trivit and Chirp spoke of you as their clan leader, so I was expecting to meet a dracon."

Clan? That is a fiction to keep the lizard-centaurs happy and cooperative, Netarza said bluntly. Teldin glanced quickly at Trivit and Chirp; their green faces still held wide, expectant smiles, and Teldin realized that the illithid was directing her thoughts to his mind alone. He wondered what motive lay behind her candor.

Chirp and Trivit are the only two dracons on board, the illithid captain continued. *We hope to change that in the near future. The* Nightstalker *is a trade ship, Captain Moore, chosen to conceal our identity and our purpose. As you can see, we already have accumulated a variety of merchandise.*

Teldin followed the sweeping gesture of the creature's pale purple hand. The half dozen illithids who gathered behind Netarza were the only ones of their kind in sight, yet the ship bustled with activity. With horror Teldin realized that he had come aboard a mind flayer slave ship. Chirp and Trivit were pawns; he suspected that Netarza allowed the adolescent dracons to keep their minds and memories in the hope that they might lead the illithids to the secret dracon homeworld. Teldin remembered the neogi's claim that with the cloak they could conquer and enslave whole worlds. It seemed the neogi were not the only monsters to harbor such ambitions, and he had brought the cloak right to the illithids' doorstep. Teldin cursed himself for coming aboard.

The illithid's slaves, unmistakably marked by their dull eyes and expressionless faces, went about the business of tending the ship. Elves were the most numerous slaves, which was not surprising: Teldin assumed the illithids had somehow taken over the elven ship and enslaved its crew. There also were several other races: a few humans, a band of halflings, even a pair of ebony-skinned elves who wore glittering black cloaks.

Cloaks!

In his surprise over the dracon leader's identity, Teldin had not noticed that his own cloak had grown back to its full length. It now was a deep forest green, a color it had never before assumed. Although Teldin had little to say about the cloak's color, he could control the length at will. The cloak showed itself of its own volition only in times of great danger.

Netarza reclaimed Teldin's attention by laying a three-fingered hand on his arm. *We are delighted that you've come, Teldin Moore. We have much to learn from you, since we spend so little time talking with humans.*

Humans just don't seem to last very long around here, a black-robed mind flayer observed. There was a touch of evil humor in its mental voice, and something else as well. Its white eyes were fixed on Teldin and its facial tentacles flexed in an unmistakable gesture of anticipation. Teldin's gut twisted as he realized that *he* was the creature's first choice for a midwatch snack.

This one is not cattle, Netarza snapped, her mental words tumbling out quickly. With absolute certainty, Teldin realized that her thoughts were not intended for his mind; somehow the cloak caught and transmuted the telepathic conversation. *None of you will harm the human. Remember our orders: we must bring Teldin Moore and his cloak back to Falx unharmed, his mind untouched. The elder-brain must first harvest the Cloakmaster's thoughts. After that, the human is of little value and we can sell or sup as we choose.*

And you will make that choice, I suppose? You, a subservient minion to a dying elder-brain? relayed the other mind flayer. *We should take the human now and claim the cloak for use aboard the* Nightstalker.

Netarza turned on the other illithid, lowering her head and fixing her blank white eyes upon it. The creature recoiled. With a searing hiss, it began to tear at its own eyes in the madness of agony. In seconds it slumped, either unconscious or dead, to the deck. Teldin gaped, astounded that the illithid captain would use its lethal mind blast on one of its own crewmen.

Forgive the interruption. Ship politics, I'm afraid, Netarza said, nudging Teldin's attention away from the stricken mind flayer. *I hope you will stay for a while, as my guest.*

"Do I have a choice in the matter?" Teldin asked bluntly.

Before answering, Netarza gestured at a trio of elven slaves and issued a silent command. The elves responded immediately and dragged the fallen illithid to the railing. Without ceremony, they tossed the dead creature out to drift away. Netarza watched the object lesson in silence for several moments before turning back to Teldin. *Naturally, you have a choice. Of course, there are good choices and bad choices. . . .*

The illithid captain let her words echo in Teldin's mind for a long moment. Before he could respond, he heard beneath him the muffled sound of a scuffle. A scream of anguish came from the lower deck, and then another. Wooden steps creaked as the victor approached the main deck.

Netarza spun toward the commotion, her white eyes spitting fire. She hissed a command, and mind-controlled elven warriors drew steel and attacked with a speed and agility that made Teldin stare. In little more than a blink, a dozen elves surrounded a figure, obscuring it from view. One of the elven slaves screamed and stumbled back toward her, his hands clutching at his head and his eyes rolled back in unspeakable agony.

Netarza brutally shoved the wounded elf out of her way as she padded forward. *Now, now,* she admonished, her mental voice an evil purr. *Is this any way for a guest to behave?*

The elves parted to let her pass. Teldin fell back a step. Netarza's other "guest" was an illithid. Its eyes were without either pupils or expression, but Teldin had known one illithid well enough to perceive this one's distress. The creature clasped its three-fingered hands before it, and the four tentacles that formed the lower part of its face writhed with agitation. In the dim purple light, its flowing robe was a deep maroon, almost black. With a stab of shock, Teldin realized that he knew Netarza's guest very well.

We meet again, Teldin Moore, came a familiar mental voice, removing any doubt of the creature's identity.

"Hello, Estriss," Teldin said aloud.

Netarza's head snapped around to face Teldin. *You know each other?*

We have met, Estriss "said." The illithid's mental tone was dismissing, minimizing the importance of the relationship.

Teldin was not surprised by Estriss's coolness. At their last meeting, Teldin had suspected his one-time comrade of treachery, and he had convinced the illithid's crew to mutiny. Teldin had taken Estriss's hammership, the *Probe*, into wildspace, intending to get rid of the cloak by giving it to an arcane. There he had found the arcane slain and himself betrayed to the neogi.

Netarza studied Teldin, and one tentacle curled up to tap thoughtfully against her lavender forehead. *I know less of the cloak's powers than I would like. Estriss, as always, is full of talk of the Juna and has revealed nothing of value. Perhaps, Teldin Moore, you will tell me what you know of the cloak, and why the elder-brain wishes to possess it?*

Turning his eyes away from the mind flayer's probing gaze, Teldin deliberately kept his mind blank. Although he wasn't entirely sure Estriss had spoken the whole truth, the illithid once had claimed he could read Teldin's mind only when the human formed words in silent speech. Apparently Netarza did not get the answer she sought, for after several moments the illithid captain hissed and shot a glance over her shoulder. Immediately an elf glided forward.

It is time to earn your keep, wizard. Tell me whatever you can about this human, Netarza instructed the elf.

A hint of light returned to the wizard's eyes as Netarza allowed him to reclaim enough of his mind and memory to perform the required spell. The elf's index finger moved sluggishly through the gestures of the spell, and his voice was slurred as he muttered arcane syllables.

Teldin stiffened, enraged by the magical intrusion on his life. He had no idea what information the spell would yield, but anything would be too much.

"There is magic about his cloak," the wizard began in a dull tone.

The illithid hissed her exasperation and shoved the elf aside. She stepped forward and took the silky green fabric of the cloak between her fingers. Instinctively Teldin swatted away her hand. She released the cloak and caught his wrist in a movement almost too quick for his eyes to follow.

You don't want me to touch your cloak? I wonder why, she asked sweetly. *Perhaps there were some gems amid the rubble of Estriss's tales and theories, after all. He mentioned an artifact of the Juna, and claimed that anyone with magical ability who touched the artifact could thereafter track it. Not that I would be so foolish as to let such an artifact out of my sight,* she concluded. One of her facial tentacles arched in an approximated sneer as she cast a glance in Estriss's direction.

Despite the danger of his situation, Netarza's words struck Teldin like a blow. They confirmed something he had long suspected: from the very beginning, Estriss had known about his cloak and had tracked him down, hoping to possess it. An old sadness, one that he had thought long spent, welled up in Teldin, and he met the expressionless eyes of his false friend with an accusing gaze.

Tell Netarza nothing, urged Estriss's mental voice, throbbing with intensity. *In her own way, she and all her kind are as evil as the neogi. The* Spelljammer *in their hands is a possibility too appalling to contemplate. On this you must trust me.*

Teldin stood silently for a long moment, considering the illithid's fervent request. Once he *had* trusted Estriss. The warning given by his cloak and his own instincts told him he must do so now. Whether Estriss was friend or foe was a question for another, safer time.

Is the cloak this artifact of the Juna? Netarza asked Estriss. Whatever he said about either cloak or its potential creators was for her mind alone, and she seemed less than pleased with the answer. The illithid captain abandoned that line of inquiry and turned to her other guest. *You will tell me about this cloak of yours, Teldin Moore,* Netarza stated, her white eyes locked with his.

Teldin felt the first tendrils of control slip into his mind. He took a reflexive step backward. "Another time," he replied. "I must return to my ship now."

The illithid's shoulders shook with silent laughter. *You have a sense of humor, I see. I think I would enjoy taking your thoughts, Teldin Moore, but I must remember my pledge to the elder-brain.* She turned to her slaves. *Take our guests below and put a guard on their quarters until whatever time Teldin Moore feels like talking,* she said, broadcasting her instructions.

A sharp gasp burst from the dracons. "A guard? You mean to keep Captain Teldin Moore *prisoner*?" Chirp asked in a shrill squeak.

"But *kaba* Netarza, this is most irregular," Trivit protested. The pale green dracon had been standing quietly by, watching his clan leader with growing confusion and dismay.

"Most irregular," Chirp echoed, obviously in deep distress. "This human rescued us from a beholder, and surely he should be honored and rewarded, not—" Overcome with emotion, Chirp broke off, biting his reptilian lip to keep it from quivering.

The dracons' chagrin seemed only to amuse Netarza. She reached up and patted Chirp's dark green cheek. *Take them below,* she repeated, then she spun and walked away.

Elves surrounded Teldin and Estriss, and the two "guests" were roughly herded below deck and through a narrow hall. Teldin glanced back at the troubled dracons, wondering whether he should try to warn them about what lay in store for them. Perhaps such knowledge at this point would only endanger them; it would seem that their safety lay in their continued ignorance. Of one thing Teldin was sure: if he managed to escape the illithid ship—a distinct possibility, given the creatures' oversight in leaving him armed—he would find a way to bring Chirp and Trivit with him.

When the door to the cabin clicked shut behind them, Teldin turned to his fellow captive. "What's going on, Estriss? How did you get here? I thought you were—" He broke off abruptly.

Dead? Estriss finished coldly. He held his facial tentacles stiff and immobile, a clear sign of his emotional detachment. *Illithids require less air than humans, and I survived in the void long enough to be rescued by this group from Falx.*

There was so much to say that Teldin did not know how to start, or what to do to bridge the gap of betrayal that lay between them.

"I've heard that the mind flayers of Falx were going after the cloak—"

And you assume that I was in league with them, Estriss finished coldly. *I deserved better from you than to be judged solely on the basis of my race.*

Deeply ashamed, Teldin averted his eyes from the mind flayer's steady, white-eyed gaze. The words Estriss had just formed were not new to Teldin; they had echoed in his own mind since the mutiny, which Aelfred and Sylvie had helped him lead.

"You're here," Teldin observed lamely.

Yes, but not by my own choice, the illithid said. There was a long silence, then his shoulders rose and fell in a great sigh. *Much of what is said of my race is true, Teldin Moore, but I despise the slave trade and all those who engage in it. I find slavery morally repugnant—a view, I might add, that is virtually unique among illithids.*

Teldin nodded. From the first day he'd met Estriss, he could not consider him a monster, despite his appearance. He could not say the same thing for Netarza and her crew. Those illithids seemed to require a new word for evil. Estriss was right; in their own way they were every bit as bad as the neogi. But even if Estriss was different from most of his kind, there still was much about the past that lacked explanation.

68 ELAINE CUNNINGHAM

"The threat from the Falx illithids was only one thing of many," Teldin continued, determined to have the whole truth. "Our first meeting aboard the *Probe* could not have been a coincidence. You came after me. If not to gain the cloak for yourself, then why?"

That is a long story, one better left for another time. Estriss's mental voice was suddenly weary, and he sank down on one of a few narrow cots in the cell. *There are more immediate concerns.*

"Like keeping the *Spelljammer* out of Netarza's hands," Teldin said.

Actually, Netarza does not seek the Spelljammer, Estriss replied, *though she would hardly turn down a chance at the great ship. She does not know why the elder-brain seeks the cloak, but she harbors ambitions of her own and command of the* Spelljammer *would certainly further them. Most illithids are content to gain power through trade and information; Netarza seeks military strength as well. To what end, I am not sure. She is searching for the homeworld of the dracons, planning to raise a mindless army.*

"How can Chirp and Trivit not realize what's going on?" Teldin demanded. "Can't they see that they're surrounded by slaves?"

Estriss shifted his shoulders in a crooked shrug. *The dracons have an inborn sense of order. Each clan must have a leader and a spiritual guide. The dracons' need for this structure is so imperative that they will die if deprived of a clan setting, and perhaps this need has blinded them to the true nature of their adopted clan.*

"They've got to know," Teldin insisted. "When we escape, the dracons go with us. When the time comes, can you convince them?"

The illithid inclined his lavender head. *You have grown in confidence and daring, I see. When the time comes, as you say, I will do what I can for the dracons.*

A piercing alarm sounded throughout the ship, its insistent shriek rising and ebbing in a hideous pattern that made Teldin think of an angry, wounded eagle. Footsteps hurried down the narrow corridor outside their room, and the sounds of battle began to ring on the deck above. Teldin tried the door to Estriss's cabin and found it unlocked. He smiled at his good fortune, cracked the door open, and ventured a look. Their guard was gone, and the corridor was deserted. A woman's voice soared above the din of battle, raised in a berserker's war cry.

Dagmar!

Teldin was halfway down the corridor before he realized he had left Estriss's cabin. Fear gripped him as he sprinted up the stairs toward the main deck. His small crew had no hope of overcoming the illithids' elven warriors. He drew his own sword, glad that the contemptuous illithids hadn't bothered to take it from him.

The sight on deck stopped him cold. Somehow his crew had boarded the *Nightstalker*, and they were locked in battle with the illithids' slaves. Fighting alongside Dagmar was a ten-foot monster wielding a two-pointed halberd with incredible speed and skill.

Shock welded Teldin to the deck as he gaped at the monstrous ally. Roughly humanoid, the creature resembled a bipedal, muscular insect. A large gem was set in the center of the monster's forehead, and it cast an eerie red glow into the purple light. Two large compound eyes, like those of a giant fly, faced forward, and four more eyes darted about independently as the creature took on newcomers from all sides. Although it was surrounded, the creature did not seem to be in trouble. Weapons clanked harmlessly against its iridescent exoskeleton.

At the edge of his vision Teldin saw a black-robed illithid draw near the creature, its white eyes fixed in a wide, compelling stare. Teldin realized it was summoning a mind blast. Before he could shout a warning to the insect creature, it lunged forward with the halberd, neatly spitting the mind flayer and raising it aloft. The illithid's legs flailed beneath its black robes, but their motion rapidly diminished to a few jerky twists. With a quick, sharp shake of the halberd, the creature sent the mortally wounded illithid flying into the void.

An elven warrior crept slowly behind the monster. *The enemy of my enemy is my friend.* His grandfather's words rang in Teldin's mind. Whether the homily was true or not, Teldin saw in the enormous insect his only hope of keeping the cloak away from the illithid slavers.

"Behind you!" he bellowed, pointing with his sword toward the elf. Teldin charged toward the insect creature, not sure what he could do to help it.

He needn't have bothered. Even as his lips formed the warning, the monstrous insect kicked backward. Its heel spur sliced up and into its attacker, and the elf slumped to the deck clutching at his spilling entrails. Two more elven slaves rushed the creature from the side. A quick thrust of the halberd beheaded one, and the monster drove a spiked fist into the other elf's midsection. No, *through* his midsection, Teldin amended with horror. He skidded to a stop, just short of tripping over one of the fallen slaves.

With one movement, the monster wrenched its hand free of the dead elf's body and backhanded another attacker. A spike on the creature's forearm sliced open the elf's throat. Teldin caught a sickening glimpse of bone and gristle as the elf slumped backward into death in a pool of his own blood.

At that moment another illithid charged on to the deck, a curved knife in one three-fingered hand. It stopped dead, staring with disbelief at the seemingly invincible insect.

Bionoid!

The illithid's mental shout was broadcasted to everyone on the deck. *Aim for the crystal eye*, it commanded the slaves, then it let the knife fly.

Teldin felt the now-familiar magic of the cloak wash over him. Time altered, and the battle slowed to a grim choreography. He saw Netarza's curved knife somersault lazily toward the monster's glowing crystal eye. With unassailable clarity, Teldin knew that he must save the insect creature. He ran and leaped as high as he could, thrusting his sword into the knife's path. There was a short, ringing sound as steel met steel, and bright blue sparks flared against the purple light. Teldin landed on his feet in a crouch, and the knife fell harmlessly aside.

The illithid spun toward Teldin, tentacles flailing with rage. It drew a dagger and advanced. The dracons charged forward with astonishing speed and placed themselves between Teldin and their former clan member, blocking the attack as effectively as two avenging green golems. Chirp swung his ax, and a tentacle flew to the deck. The dracon continued to swing, and Teldin was not unhappy that Trivit's huge green body obscured the view.

An agonized shriek tore through Teldin's mind; near the head of the stairs lay a frenzied illithid, writhing and clutching at its head. Standing over it was Estriss. He sprung on his victim with the speed of a striking lizard, and his facial tentacles closed over the illithid's skull in preparation for a grizzly feast. The horror and disgust Teldin expected to feel at this act of cannibalism simply did not register. His preternatural clarity of mind kept him focused on the battle, and the only thing that seemed to matter was the female elf creeping up behind Estriss.

Suddenly Teldin's doubts and ambivalence concerning Estriss seemed as distant as a childhood memory. Without hesitation, he shouted a warning as he sped toward his friend. The elf's dagger fell in a slow, gleaming arc, and even the cloak's time-altering magic could not move Teldin across the deck in time to save the illithid. The blade bit deeply into Estriss's shoulder, releasing a flood of pale, pinkish ichor.

Estriss slumped forward over the dead illithid. A grisly, gray tidbit from his feast slid down the length of a limp tentacle and puddled on the wooden deck. With an blank smile, the enslaved elf raised her dagger again.

Teldin lunged toward Estriss, sword held low before him. A sharp clang rang out, and the dagger thrust aimed at the illithid's spine slid harmlessly aside. The force of Teldin's parry threw the elven warrior off balance, and she stumbled and fell to one knee.

The elf was back on her feet with a speed that seemed remarkable even to Teldin's altered perception. Drawing a short, curved sword, the slave attacked. Teldin stood his ground, though he had little doubt that the elven warrior was far beyond his ability. Only the cloak's magic allowed him to parry the dazzling onslaught of blows she showered upon him.

From the corner of his eye Teldin saw a long green tail arching toward his opponent. The dracons again! Teldin parried one last blow, then flung himself aside. As he rolled out of range, he heard the ringing *thwack* of impact. The force of Chirp's blow sent the elven woman tumbling across the deck. Trivit's broadsword thrust downward, neatly stopping the elf's slide by pinning her to the deck. With an uncharacteristic lack of ceremony, the dracon stomped on the fallen slave. The dracons nodded crisply to each other and moved on, working in tandem with a sort of grim efficiency. Using their whiplike tails, enormous swords, and even their teeth, they kept the illithids' slaves away from Teldin.

Feeling safe for the moment, Teldin dropped to his knees and bent over Estriss. The illithid was alive. Relief washed through Teldin, and the intense focus of battle began to slip away. His senses shifted and swam, shrinking and condensing into the focus of his normal time perception.

Dimly aware of a clicking sound coming toward him,

Teldin looked up. His eyes widened in purest horror. The insect creature loomed over him. Its armored body shimmered faintly in the dim light, and the lethal blades on its hands, arms, and head dripped blood. At close quarters, the monster was terrifying. Worse, it began to reach down toward Estriss. The creature had fought alongside the *Valkyrie*'s crew, but for all Teldin knew it might have a taste for illithid flesh.

Teldin struggled to his feet and stood over the fallen body of his friend. As he crouched in a defensive position and raised his sword, he frantically tried to summon the cloak's battle magic. The clarity and focus would not come; it was gone beyond recall.

"It's all right, sir," said the creature in a soft, familiar voice. Shock hit Teldin like a blow. His sword fell from his suddenly numb hand and clattered unheeded to the deck. "Hectate?" he whispered, not wanting to believe.

The insect monster inclined its head. To Teldin's numbed senses, the creature's acknowledgment seemed to hold a deep sadness. With a gentleness Teldin had always associated with Hectate Kir, the creature stooped and gathered Estriss in its enormous, armor-plated arms.

"Time to leave, sir," it said in Hectate's voice.

"Leave?" Teldin echoed numbly. The monster swiveled its head so that its main eyes looked out over the starboard rail. Teldin followed the gesture and recoiled in shock. Another ship, even stranger than the drakkar, had joined the battle.

A series of grappling hooks connected the dark man-o-war to an enormous, spacebound swan. Elven warriors slid down the lines from the swan ship, immediately engaging the illithid's slaves in fierce battle.

There he is! Get him. Get the cloak, demanded a dark, feminine voice. Teldin spun to see Netarza leading a group of elven warriors. An elf with skin like polished obsidian responded by throwing back his arm. One moment, purple light glinted off the steel in his hand, the next, Teldin staggered back from the force of the impact. Bright pain exploded in his left hip. He reached down and felt the hilt of the knife flush with his skin and the blade grating against bone.

Through the pain, Teldin dimly noted that the insect with Hectate's voice had deposited Estriss on the deck. It turned to meet the attack. The heavy armor that shielded its chest parted, and two plates folded back to reveal glowing red membranes that vibrated with power. A flash of bright energy burst from the creature's chest, blinding Teldin with its intensity as it hurtled like a shooting star toward the band of slaves. It hit the warriors with a burst of light and fire.

Heavy black smoke, fetid with the smell of death, roiled back toward Teldin and his strange companions. It surrounded them in a suffocating cloud, and Teldin sank to his knees beside Estriss, coughing and choking. As he struggled to hold on to his ebbing consciousness, Teldin was dimly aware that Hectate—the *real* Hectate Kir—was sprawled beside him, his elven face as pale as death. Teldin had little doubt that Hectate's fate soon would be his: the cloak's magic had drained his energy, and he was losing too much blood from the knife wound. Teldin could no longer feel the deck under his knees. He was floating, weightless, into a place of darkness and warmth. . . .

"Teldin Moore."

Strong, slender arms caught him as he fell. A familiar voice shouted orders in Elvish. Teldin summoned every vestige of his remaining strength and willed his fading senses back into focus. With a mixture of relief and dismay, he pulled himself away and looked into the face of his elven rescuer.

Even in his weakened state, Teldin could not accept the possibility that this rescue was a coincidence.

The insignia of a ship's captain adorned the elf's Imperial Fleet uniform, and his slanted green eyes were hooded, as unreadable as ever. This time, however, Teldin had no doubt about what this elf wanted.

Vallus Leafbower had returned for the cloak.

Chapter Five

●●●

"I'm not dead yet," Teldin informed the elf with as much vehemence as he could muster. Anger coursed through his veins, deadening his pain and renewing his resolve. If the elves once again hoped to take the cloak off his dead body, they were in for one more disappointment. By Paladine, Teldin vowed as he struggled to his feet, he'd live just to spite the pointy-eared bastards.

Despite the surge of energy his anger lent him, the effort was too much for Teldin, and a fresh stab of agony tore through his wounded side. Gasping through gritted teeth, he fell back to his knees, pushing away the elf's steadying hands.

Vallus Leafbower grimaced and shook his silver-haired head. "Perhaps you're not yet dead, Teldin Moore, but you soon *will* be if your wounds are not tended." The elf looked up and raised on hand in a quick, imperious gesture. Five uniformed elves hurried to his side. "Get this man aboard the swan ship and take him to the healer," Vallus directed them.

Two of the elves started to do Vallus's bidding, but something in Teldin's eyes stopped them. "I'll see you in the Abyss first," he told Vallus coldly.

"That is a distinct possibility," the elf returned with equal warmth. "The man-o-war is burning, and I will not leave you behind. If you don't let us help you, we're all dead."

"But the battle—"

"Is over," Vallus concluded firmly.

Teldin hesitated, listening. The battle sounds had dwindled to a few scattered clangs, a few faint moans. Smoke billowed up from the stairwell, and a faint, ominous crackling came from beneath the deck. "Take me to the *Valkyrie*, then," Teldin said resignedly.

"The illithid's wizard slaves hit the drakkar with a barrage of spells." Vallus's flat tone and steady gaze made it clear that Teldin's ship was gone.

"And the crew?" Teldin demanded, not able to take it all in. Vallus turned to one of the other elves and raised his silver eyebrows in inquiry.

"A small longboat got away before the drakkar exploded. We took the survivors aboard the *Trumpeter*," the elf reported.

Dread filled Teldin. "Some of my crew boarded the man-o-war. Have any survived?"

"I'm sorry," Vallus said gently.

Teldin slumped, despairing. More deaths tallied on his slate, all due to the cloak. Whatever the *Spelljammer* might be, it couldn't be worth this.

The elf rose to his feet. "Come."

He had no choice but to go with the elves, Teldin realized. He nodded dully, numb to the core. "Take Estriss first. His wounds are worse than mine."

"Estriss?" Vallus echoed in disbelief. The elf squinted through the smoke at the crumpled form beside Teldin, then with a cry of recognition he dropped to his knees beside his former captain. Gently turning the unconscious illithid over, Vallus bent to peer into the empty white eyes. "Barely alive," he murmured distractedly. He looked up at the other elves, who had formed a tight, curious circle around him. "Take these two to the swan ship, now," he commanded.

As Vallus spoke, another sharp-edged perception penetrated the pain and anger that clouded Teldin's mind:

Vallus's concern and distress were genuine. For the first time, Teldin wondered whether his harsh judgment of the elven wizard was warranted.

Two of the elven warriors exchanged glances. "Take a *mind flayer* aboard?" one of them ventured.

Vallus was on his feet in a heartbeat. "Now!" he thundered. The elves hastily lifted the wounded illithid and headed for the flitter that had landed on the *Nightstalker's* deck.

As gentle hands lifted Teldin to his feet, a faint groan came from the deck and the waxen figure of Teldin's navigator stirred. Hectate Kir was alive.

"The half-elf!" Teldin demanded weakly, clinging to what he knew about his friend. "You have to bring the half-elf."

"Why not?" one of the elves grumbled, looking on with distaste as a comrade hoisted the unconscious Hectate over his shoulder. "We might as well complete our collection of oddities."

"That's enough, Gaston," Vallus snapped. Before he could say more, the dracons thundered around the corner. Trivit, as usual, was in the lead. He drew up short when he saw Teldin, and Chirp bumped heavily into him.

"Siripsotrivitus reporting, Captain Teldin Moore, sir," Trivit announced in his fluting, formal cadences as he snapped off a salute. "The illithid slaves have been routed, though I must say we've had a beastly time telling one elf from another. Some few of the illithids and their slaves escaped in flitters, but Chirpsian and I have dispatched all those who remained on board." The dracon paused, and his lower lip trembled. "As you know, sir, the illithids deceived us. We are . . . without a clan."

Remembering what Estriss had said about the dracons' clan mentality, Teldin suspected what was coming next. Sure enough, Trivit drew his sword and raised it in a salute, then he laid it on the deck before Teldin.

"*Kaba*," Trivit said simply, but his reptilian eyes pleaded.

The dracons had adopted *him* as their clan leader! Teldin's frustration bordered on despair. Would there be no end to the responsibility he was forced to assume? He took a deep, calming breath, knowing that if he did not accept this role, the adrift dracons would die.

Teldin challenged Vallus with his eyes. "They come," he said evenly, then he turned to glare at the elf named Gaston, the one who had spoken slightingly of Hectate. The elf raised both hands in rueful surrender.

A deep boom began in the hold of the *Nightstalker*, echoing throughout the ship. The man-o-war was breaking up.

"Time to go," Vallus said abruptly. As the elves half-carried Teldin to the flitter, he found himself thinking about Netarza and wondering whether he had heard the last from the mind flayers of Falx.

* * * * *

Vallus Leafbower watched the unconscious human with deep concern. Three days had elapsed since the battle with the illithid ship, and Teldin Moore had yet to regain consciousness. The knife that had struck Teldin had been treated with poison, and after several tries the ship's healer managed to decoct a potion to counteract it. Teldin's delirium had faded within hours, and the restraints binding him to the narrow cot had been removed as soon as it was safe to do so. Vallus did not want Teldin to awaken to the perception that he was being held prisoner in some way.

Throughout the process Vallus had attended the human, praying for his recovery with a deep, desperate fervor. As if in response to his prayers, the human's eyelids fluttered, then opened. Teldin Moore's cornflower blue eyes looked dim and disoriented, but relief flooded the elven wizard. By order of the grand admiral, Vallus would have had to don the cloak if the man had died. Having seen the results with Teldin, he wasn't looking forward to the experience.

"I am glad you're back, Teldin Moore," Vallus said from the heart.

The human's eyes met his, focused, then narrowed. Vallus suppressed a sigh. Despite Cirathorn's treachery, Vallus was startled by the extent of Teldin Moore's animosity toward the elves. Perhaps, Vallus thought with dismay, his task would be more difficult than he'd anticipated.

Teldin tried to speak, but the sound caught in his dry throat and sent him into a weak spasm of coughing. He grimaced and touched his left hip. Despite the elves' best efforts, the wound was still angry and red. Vallus motioned for the healer.

Deelia Snowsong glided to the bedside. She slipped one hand behind Teldin's neck and lifted his head, holding a goblet to his lips. Teldin managed several painful swallows and nodded his thanks. As he focused on his elven attendant, his eyes widened with wonder. Deelia was pale even for an elf, with hair and skin the color of a snowdrift. The elves from her ice-covered homeworld were tiny, seldom reaching five feet, and their ethereal beauty gave pause even to other elves.

There was admiration in Teldin Moore's eyes, of course, but Vallus saw something far more important. The human's curiosity and wonder struck an answering chord in Vallus's soul, which sang with a burning, childlike need to *know*. This need had defined the wizard's life, first by his choice of profession, and then by seducing him from his homeworld and sending him into wildspace. Once again the elf saw in Teldin a flicker of the flame that burned in his own heart. Someone had implanted in Teldin Moore the need to explore, to question, and to know. Perhaps the human had suppressed this need, but it was there and Vallus would exploit it.

"Where—" Teldin broke off, painfully clearing his throat. Frustration was written clearly upon his face.

"You are aboard the *Trumpeter*, a swan ship of the elven Imperial Fleet," Vallus told him. Anticipating some of the human's questions, he continued.

"You have been gravely ill, unconscious for almost three days. The knife that wounded you was poisoned, but thanks to Deelia Snowsong, our healer, you should suffer no long-term effects. Your ship was destroyed in battle, as was most of your crew. We picked up but two survivors, a gnome woman and an aperusa."

"Figures," Teldin croaked through a small, crooked smile.

Vallus nodded, understanding. In the three days since the battle, he had noted that the gypsy Rozloom had an uncanny aptitude for self-preservation.

The human's brow knitted in sudden concern. "Estriss? Hectate?"

Vallus nodded reassuringly. "Our illithid friend is much improved. In fact, he is anxious to speak with you and has been asking for you hourly. Of the half-elf, I have less news. Since the battle he has kept to his cabin. Our healer examined him and could find no sign of injury. The effects were very similar to those following the casting of a powerful spell, and after resting for a day he recovered fully. I take it the half-elf is a mage of some power?"

Teldin hesitated, then nodded. He knew relatively little about bionoids, but they undoubtedly were magical. He vowed to himself that he would learn more as soon as he could. Vallus did not miss the troubled expression that crossed the human's face, and for the first time the elven wizard felt more than a passing interest in Hectate Kir. Whatever the half-elf's secrets were, they must not be allowed to interfere.

Vallus rose and gave Teldin another reassuring smile. "You need rest. I will leave you to it."

"No."

Teldin Moore struggled into an upright position, brushing away Deelia's restraining hands. After motioning for Vallus to stay, he accepted the healer's offer of water and took several more sips. The human's face was still pale and drawn, but it was set in grim determination as he struggled to gather his strength behind the force of his will. Vallus watched and approved.

"What do you want?" Teldin asked bluntly.

The elven wizard settled back down in his chair and began his answer at the appropriate place. "When we last met, I gave you a warning and some advice. You should have taken the cloak to the elves of Evermeet, where the Imperial Fleet maintains an embassy."

Teldin harrumphed, and Vallus held up a temporizing hand. "Yes, I know about Admiral Cirathorn. That was most unfortunate, and the Imperial Fleet has sent me to ensure that such a thing does not happen again." At this news, the human's face hardened with skepticism.

"If you had done as I'd suggested and sought out the Evermeet elves," Vallus continued, "you might have been spared that experience. The elves of Evermeet are a peaceful nation, and there you would have had the time and protection needed to seek answers. War forces individuals to make difficult choices. Even so," he allowed, "I would dare say that Admiral Cirathorn made the wrong choice."

Teldin huffed again, but this time in agreement. The elven wizard took this as a good sign and pressed his point. "The Imperial Fleet agrees. I have been dispatched to help you find the *Spelljammer.*" He paused to let Teldin digest this.

"Why?" Teldin asked.

"Frankly? We want you to find the ship, Teldin Moore."

"*Why?*" he asked again.

"We hope to persuade you to use the great ship on behalf of the elves. No, wait. Let me finish. The war is taking a terrible toll. If something is not done, the Imperial Fleet, the elven network that is the single stabilizing element in wildspace, could be no more."

"So?"

The human's response was so like the one predicted by the grand admiral that Vallus's patience wavered. Too much was depending on Teldin Moore; they must get past this newly minted bigotry of his.

"What would you have take the elves' place?" the wizard asked sharply. "The scro? Or perhaps the neogi?"

His last words hit their mark. Teldin's eyes drifted closed, and his face tightened into a mask of confusion and despair. The elf rose to leave, and his parting words were offered in a calmer tone. "I am not certain how much you have learned about the cloak since we parted, Teldin Moore, but know this: You have in your possession the ability to command the greatest ship ever known. That is power. The nature of power is that it must be used as a force for good or ill. Very soon you will have to decide exactly how to use that power."

The human's only response was a faint snore. Vallus shook his silver head, and a small, self-mocking smile curved his lips. So much for his fine speeches. The poor human had barely regained consciousness, only to be bombarded with tales of elven woes.

Teldin Moore needed time to rest and recover. Time, unfortunately, was something that the elven nation could not spare. As Vallus walked slowly from the cabin, the grand admiral's deadline pressed heavily upon him. The elven wizard paused at the door of the cabin and looked back at the sleeping human.

"I doubt this would be any consolation to you, my friend, but, in all truth, I do not envy you your decision," he said softly.

* * * * *

For Teldin, the next two days aboard the swan ship *Trumpeter* seemed to crawl by. His wound was slow to heal, and the lingering effects of the poison were so debilitating that he was not able leave his cot for more than a few minutes at a time. From what Deelia Snowsong told him about drow elves and their skill at making poisons, Teldin reckoned he was lucky to be alive at all. That knowledge, however, did little to stem his growing restlessness, or to ease his apprehension about being a virtual prisoner on an elven ship. He had no idea where the ship was or where it was bound. Several times he asked to see Vallus Leafbower, but he was always told that he was not well enough to receive visitors.

On the second day, the vigilant healer finally announced that visitors were permissible. Within moments, Estriss appeared at the door of the cabin. Teldin hauled himself upright and greeted him with an almost comic degree of enthusiasm. The illithid's lavender facial tentacles flared outward in an expression of surprise, but he came into the cabin and lowered himself into the chair at Teldin's bedside without comment.

I take it you are well enough to talk, Teldin Moore? Estriss's mental voice held a touch of wry amusement, but his three-fingered hands smoothed the deep maroon silk of his robe in quick, nervous gestures.

Teldin nodded reassuringly, wanting to put the creature at ease. "To tell you the truth, a little conversation would probably speed up the healing process. I've never been so tired of my own company," he said ruefully. "What about you? Are you fully recovered?"

Estriss shrugged. The human gesture did not translate well to illithid anatomy, and the odd, disjointed movement of his shoulders contrasted sharply with the easy grace of his weaving tentacles. Without warning, Teldin *felt* the intensity of Estriss's desire to set things straight between them. The illithid's sincerity burned in Teldin's mind, as bright and earnest as if the emotion had been his own.

The cloak again? wondered Teldin. Did these flashes of insight signal the emergence of another magic power? Teldin took a long, deep breath and held it, as if he could absorb the magic and let it sharpen his thinking for all time. He'd been wrong about Estriss once, and he realized that a second chance was a rare gift. With this in mind, Teldin exhaled slowly and began.

"We have a lot to talk about."

We do indeed, the illithid agreed avidly. He folded his hands on his silken lap and straightened decisively.

I believe I have come to understand the reason for your mutiny, Teldin Moore, Estriss began. *The news that the illithids of Falx sought your cloak, combined with the admittedly unlikely coincidence of your rescue from the pirates by my ship: these things did not supply your motivation. If you had asked me about these matters, we easily could have come to an understanding. You made no attempt to do so. I thought about this while you were ill, wondering why, after our many frank discussions, you did not see fit to bring your concerns to me. Then I remembered that the woman Rianna Wyvernsbane had placed a charm spell upon you, which meant that you were magically disposed to believe her. She probably suggested that I was not trustworthy. Was this not the case?*

"In the main, yes," Teldin admitted reluctantly, unconsciously pleating the bedclothes between his fingers. Estriss's explanation inadequately described the events during that time, and left out Aelfred's duplicity, but it was essentially correct. Rianna's influence over him had aspects that the genderless illithid could not understand, and Teldin himself did not care to dwell on the matter. Even now, the memory of Rianna's treachery made him cringe. The love he'd felt for her had faded with the effects of the charm spell, but he had to admit that he'd been an easy one to ensorcell.

From the very beginning, he had been taken with Rianna and had allowed his attraction for her to overwhelm his caution. Estriss was basically correct: to lure Teldin into the neogi's trap, Rianna had told her then lover about the Falx mind flayers and insinuated that Estriss could not be trusted. Teldin had believed her and trusted her, and his near-fatal error in judgment still haunted him.

As the victim of a spell, you were blameless in this matter, Estriss continued with what Teldin considered an excess of generosity. The illithid raised a cautioning, red-tinged finger. *You should know, however, that I have related this incident to Vallus Leafbower. As captain of the swan ship, he has a right to know about your mutiny as well as the circumstances surrounding it.*

"I suppose you're right, but I'd doubt Vallus is worried about a repeat performance." Teldin managed a crooked grin, trying to lighten the awkward conversation with a little humor. "Can you see a group of elves rising up in mutiny to aid a mere human?"

Estriss cocked his head slightly as if he were thinking the matter over. *Actually, no, but neither did I want Vallus to hear about that incident through other channels. If you and he are to join forces, it would not do to have him unfairly prejudiced against you,* he said earnestly.

Teldin nodded, appreciating the illithid's evenhandedness. This was more like the Estriss he thought he knew: a being who possessed a strong moral code and a philosophical nature. It was difficult for Teldin to reconcile this Estriss with his own lingering suspicions.

"I've often wondered why you attacked the neogi in the arcane's ship," Teldin ventured. Of all the questions he harbored, he started with the most difficult. The memory of that moment was indelibly etched in his mind: the neogi's hideous, eellike head lunging for Estriss's throat, its needle-sharp teeth glinting wickedly; the ancient Juna knife in

Estriss's hands, and the illithid's tentacles struggling to find purchase on the neogi's long neck or spiderlike body. Teldin would always remember the dull horror he'd felt when Rianna's magic missile spell broke the ship's window and sent the combatants tumbling into the void.

Estriss spread his three-fingered hands before him. *What else should I have done? I could not allow the cloak to fall into the neogi's grasp.*

"Your motivation was that simple?" Teldin wondered aloud.

Few matters can be viewed as right and wrong, black and white. The neogi are one of life's rare exceptions.

Sincerity rang in the illithid's answer, but Teldin's mind still was not at ease. "What about our first meeting?"

Your rescue from the pirates was no coincidence, Estriss admitted candidly. *You obviously have learned that the* Probe *landed on one of the moons of Zivilyn. I had arranged a meeting there with Hemar, a reigar adventurer who recently had escaped from a neogi slave ship with two magical objects, items I believed to be artifacts of the Juna. One was your cloak, of course. The other was an amulet of sorts, an ancient medallion. The second item was not in her possession.*

Teldin blinked, startled, and his eyes darted involuntarily to the chest at the side of his bed. In it was the sack containing the medallion Gaye had given him after his battle with the scro general. Could the medallion he carried be the same one Estriss sought? Teldin's impression was that it was, but the connection seemed too fantastic for belief.

Hemar would not part with the cloak, Estriss continued, *but in the course of our discussion she allowed me to handle it. After that time, I found that I could sense its presence.*

"So you came after it," Teldin confirmed sadly.

The illithid responded with another crumpled shrug, and he turned his head aside as if he were too embarrassed to meet Teldin's eyes. *That is true, but I sought the cloak for the*

*same reason I seek all other suspected artifacts of the Juna. I
realize that my theories concerning the Juna are not accepted or even respected, but it is my lifework to prove that this
race existed. As I learned more about the cloak, its connection with the* Spelljammer *seemed likely. If my theory is
correct, the Juna created the ship. If I can find the* Spelljammer, *I might find on board documents of some sort that will
enable me to validate my lifework.*

"And to control the most powerful ship known," Teldin
added with a touch of cynicism.

Estriss hissed audibly but kept his head averted. *Your
experiences have jaded you, I see. Perhaps you are no longer
able to believe this of me, but I have no interest in wielding
such power. I am a scholar, a historian. What power I seek
comes from knowledge.*

The illithid's observation reminded Teldin of one of his
grandfather's bits of homespun advice: A skunk by any name
stills stinks. "The thirst for power takes many forms," Teldin
paraphrased cautiously.

As do the uses of power, Estriss observed, fixing a white-
eyed stare upon Teldin.

The mental voice held a quiet intensity. It was obvious
that Estriss wanted to open a new line of discussion. Teldin
made a note to come back to the topic later, but he still had
questions of his own to cover. "You did not want me to give
the cloak to the arcane T'k'pek," he remembered. "Why not?"

Estriss snorted, an odd hissing sound that sent his
tentacles billowing upward in the most eloquent gesture of
scorn Teldin had ever seen. *I doubt T'k'pek would have made
good use of the cloak. The arcane are merchants. Any one of
them would love to have the* Spelljammer *as a base of
operations or, more to the point, as a source of new technology. The reigar, from whom most of the arcane technology
supposedly originated, have become so scarce as to be unre-
liable sources.*

"The reigar?" Teldin echoed, his interest piqued. He had often wondered about the beautiful creature who had given him the cloak. For once he was grateful for the philosophical illithid's tendency to be sidetracked. "The arcane inventions came from the reigar?" he repeated.

It depends on whom you ask, Estriss said, his silent voice dry with sarcasm. *Reigar creativity and inventiveness are legendary. They've been credited with such diverse creations as helots and helmsplicers.*

Neither of the terms were familiar to Teldin, but he nodded sagely in an effort to keep Estriss from defining those terms.

The reigar have no patience for repetition. The arcane, on the other hand, are eager to manufacture the more market- able reigar inventions. As we have discussed before, the arcane are highly secretive, and they habitually deny that they maintain any connection with the reigar. Those few travelers who have encountered an esthetic—a reigar spell- jamming ship—invariably report that the vessel is crewed by arcane. Of course, the arcane on these esthetics always insist that they are chance-met passengers. The illithid punctuated the anecdote with an oddly snide little wriggle of his tentacles.

Teldin acknowledged the illithid's humor with an absent smile. As he sifted through the explanation, a new thought began to form in his mind, one appallingly simple and direct. "Is it possible that the reigar woman—Hemar, was it?—was referring to her own people, the reigar, when she told me to take the cloak to the creators?"

I suppose that is possible, Estriss said slowly. One tentacle quirked as he considered the matter. *I have not heard that the reigar refer to themselves in that manner, but it would be like them. They are not known for their modesty.*

Teldin pounded his cot with a balled fist. "Why didn't you tell me all this before?" he blurted out, more exasperated with himself than with Estriss. Too much time and too many lives had been spent in his searching for the mysterious "creators" to learn now that he'd missed the most obvious path.

The possibility didn't occur to me, Estriss admitted. His mental voice echoed Teldin's consternation. *Perhaps it should have, but, as Aelfred Silverhorn often told me, my conclusions were sifted through my personal bias. Perhaps my search for the Juna blinded me to other possibilities for your quest. In all honesty, however, I don't think that this information on the reigar would have done you much good.*

"Why not?"

The illithid threw up his hands, and the movement of his tentacles reflected his exasperation. *Have you any idea how difficult it is to meet a reigar? You could search through three human lifetimes without encountering a single one, and even if you should find one, he would be unlikely to grant an audience to a human. Why?* the illithid added pointedly, noting Teldin's open mouth and anticipating his question. *The reigar are completely absorbed in their pursuit of art, and they define everything by its potential contribution to reigar art. These are beings who have little regard for the artistic ability of elves and who openly disdain the crafting skills of dwarfs. You can imagine what they think of humans. I mean no offense,* Estriss hastily added.

"None taken," Teldin murmured distractedly. "Please go on."

This determination to push the horizons of art for art's sake ultimately explains the rare occurrence of reigar. Simply put, they went a bit too far.

"A bit too—"

They blew up their homeworld, Estriss interrupted bluntly. *And that is another issue. If the reigar were to gain control of the* Spelljammer, *they would regard the ship as little more than a base for artistic experiments. Given the reigar's penchant for excess, it is an appalling prospect.*

Teldin nodded slowly, taking it all in. Everything Estriss said supported his new theory about the identity of the cloak's creators. Oddly enough, it also bolstered his decision to keep the cloak himself. The reigar may well have created the cloak, but, if Estriss was to be believed, they hardly were suited to wielding it.

So, Teldin Moore, now that this matter is settled, why don't you tell me what you have learned of the cloak since we parted.

Teldin quickly outlined what had transpired since the fight with the neogi. He'd just described the cloak's power to propel ships when he was interrupted by a timid knock at the door. At Teldin's impatient summons, two large green heads poked into the cabin.

"I must say, it's marvelous to see you yourself again. You look splendid, especially considering that you're a human," Chirp said cheerfully. The dracon's words held not a hint of sarcasm, and his huge, dragonlike mouth curved up in a smile of ingratiating innocence. Despite his irritation with the interruption, Teldin could feel himself responding to the creatures' innocent goodwill.

"It's good to see you two as well," Teldin said sincerely. "What have you been up to?"

"Vallus Leafbower has a small but splendid library. We've been making some inquiries into your family background, Captain Teldin Moore," Trivit informed him solemnly, "and I must say it's most impressive."

Teldin blinked. His father had been a farmer, his grandfather a man of inherent wisdom and lively curiosity, but still poor and obscure. Teldin supposed he had a family tree beyond that, but he'd never seen any reason to try to climb it. "Do you mind if I ask how you traced my family?" he ventured.

"Not at all," Chirp piped, squeezing his dark green body

into the cabin. "Vallus has a perfectly marvelous volume on the history of Krynn. A fascinating world, Krynn, but, of course, you'd already know that. We have traced your line back to Angor Dragonsbane, a great hero and one of the first humans on record on the continent of Ansalon."

"There are other lines of equal note," Trivit added. He edged into the room beside his brother, and the dracon pair launched into a convoluted tale, interweaving names from Krynnish history and folklore until Teldin grew dizzy trying to follow it all. So complex and detailed was the dracons' presentation that the dazed Teldin was inclined to believe it.

"We were fortunate in our choice of *kaba*," Trivit concluded in a tone ripe with self-congratulation. "As you may know, a dracon clan chief is chosen on the basis of lineage, and yours surpasses those of any ancient elvish house represented on this ship. For me to enumerate your list of titles would take—" Trivit broke off, wrinkling his rubbery face in an effort at calculation. After a moment, he shrugged. "Well, just ever so long."

"A most fortunate choice," echoed Chirp. "Our instincts were splendid, as usual," he said with blithe disregard for the illithid episode.

"Of course, we had to stop our study several generations before your birth. The elven history was not a current one," Trivit said ruefully.

The new-made nobleman smirked, suddenly understanding. His new and grandiose family tree was linked to him by no more than a great deal of wishful thinking.

"Perhaps you'd care to fill in the blanks for us?" Chirp suggested.

Teldin's smile collapsed. It was one thing to let the dracons concoct some fancy genealogy to support their choice of leader—and he got the distinct impression that his wasn't the first of such—but his innate sense of honesty would not allow him to contribute to the dracons' self-deception. Apparently sensing his consternation, Estriss took a defensive position at the foot of Teldin's bed.

At some later time, I'm sure Teldin Moore can oblige you. At the moment, however, he requires rest.

Mumbling apologies, the chastised dracons backed out of the cabin. The door gingerly creaked shut, and the hall rumbled under the dracons' version of a tiptoed retreat. Teldin gave in to a chuckle. He could have sworn that his friend's blank eyes held a hint of a twinkle, and he cocked an eyebrow at the smug illithid. "Thanks."

Not at all, Estriss demurred. *You have not been the only target of the dracons' passion for genealogy. Chirp and Trivit have passed the days tracing the connections between and debating the merits of the various elven houses, until even the most lineage-proud elf on board has lost interest in the exercise. I can assure you, however,* Estriss concluded with mock gravity, *the dracons honor the heritage they invented for you over any elven background based on fact.*

Teldin grimaced. "I suppose I should talk to them."

Don't bother. They would listen politely and then ignore anything you said. To them, you are the kaba *and that settles the matter. Now,* Estriss concluded briskly, coming to the head of the bed, *according to the ship's healer, you are ready to take a walk on deck. Are you interested?*

In response, Teldin grinned and threw back the covers. He got out of bed far too quickly, though, and the moment his feet hit the floor he got the distinct and disconcerting impression that the small cabin suddenly had been filled with turbulent gray water.

Estriss closed a steadying hand around Teldin's arm. *Perhaps the healer was a bit optimistic?*

"No," Teldin said as soon as he could hear himself through the humming in his ears. "If I don't get out of this cabin soon, I'll go mad."

Estriss helped Teldin up to the deck. After the confinement of his cabin, the vastness of wildspace held all the promise and spirit-lifting magic of a warm spring morning. Teldin's mood slid, however, at the sight of the lone figure leaning on the swan ship's starboard rail.

Chapter Six

● ● ●

Hectate Kir stood staring into wildspace, absently flattening the crown of his red-brown hair. The half-elf's cowlick popped back up after each pass. The ineffectual battle would have been almost comical if Teldin had been in the mood to be amused.

Teldin excused himself from the illithid with the promise to meet him later for a longer chat. Still feeling a bit unsteady, he made his way over to the rail. Hectate acknowledged his arrival politely, and they exchanged the usual expressions of concern before silence overtook them. For many long moments they stared into wildspace with eyes that saw only the past.

Hectate was the first to speak. "I imagine you want to know more about the battle," he stated quietly.

"Yes. I've been sorting through all that's happened, trying to make some sense of it. I couldn't help wondering how . . . That is to say, exactly what . . . " Teldin's voice trailed away, and he gestured helplessly. There simply wasn't any tactful way to word his question.

"You want to know what I am," Hectate said bluntly.

Teldin nodded, a little embarrassed by the half-elf's candor but relieved to have the issue on the table.

"You have heard of the first Unhuman War," Hectate began softly, looking fixedly off into wildspace.

Again Teldin nodded, this time with resignation. Hectate

might be a half-elf, but he obviously shared the elven fear that some small part of a story might be omitted.

"During that time, both elves and goblinkin built terrible weapons of destruction. A few elves volunteered to become such weapons. Through a magical process that has since been deliberately forgotten, these elves were transformed. In appearance they were indistinguishable from other elves, but they had the ability to change into a creature such as . . . such as the one you saw aboard the *Nightstalker*."

Hectate paused and met Teldin's eyes. The half-elf's face was sad but resigned as he awaited his captain's reaction. Teldin wasn't sure what was expected of him, but he nodded encouragingly. "Go on."

The half-elf's eyes widened with surprise. He blinked several times, then cleared his throat. "These creatures were, of course, my ancestors. The elves named us *bionoids*, the suffix implying that we were a life*like* form, not a true lifeform. The bionoid troops were a pivotal force in winning the war, but after victory was achieved, the 'living weapons' were found to have a serious flaw. We are alive. For centuries we have lived, struggling with our inherent contradictions but teaching each new generation to live in peace. Because we are living beings and not intelligent, undead weapons, the elves consider us a mistake. Elves, as a rule, prefer not to acknowledge their mistakes."

The words were softly spoken, and to Teldin's ears they held a remarkable lack of bitterness. "I'm sorry," he said, not knowing what else to say.

A sad smile crossed Hectate's face. "There is no need to be. I am reconciled to what I am, and there are a few—such as yourself—who seem to accept me as such."

Teldin reached out and briefly clasped Hectate's shoulder, a comrade's gesture that answered the unspoken question. Hectate's answering smile still held uncertainty.

"What do we do now, Teldin Moore?" he asked. "I've

heard that the Imperial Fleet has put the *Trumpeter* at your disposal."

That was news to Teldin. "Where'd you hear that?"

"In the mess. I overheard some of the elves talking."

Teldin let out a slow whistle. "I don't imagine they were happy about it," he said dryly.

"No, sir, they weren't," Hectate agreed.

Teldin's mind whirled with the implications of this news. So the elves planned to give him a ship. If this were true, he had a whole new set of problems. Feeling a sudden need for support, he turned his back on wildspace and slouched wearily against the railing. The Imperial Fleet might not have originally intended to hold him against his will, but it probably hadn't occurred to the arrogant elves that he might not accede to the wisdom of their plans, or accept their offer with suitable gratitude. Once they got over the shock of his refusal, who knew what they might do?

Hectate cleared his throat and added, "If you can arrange for the *Trumpeter* to put down as soon as possible, sir, I'll sign on with another ship. The crew would not be happy to have a bionoid aboard."

"Who says they have to know?" Teldin asked bluntly.

Hectate's mouth dropped open, then closed with an audible click. "But—"

"And for that matter," Teldin continued with more resolve, "who says I have to take them up on their offer? I plan to continue my search for the Broken Sphere, but I'd prefer to do it on another ship, my own ship. When I do, I'd like you to be on that ship." He paused, searching for the right words. "I need people with me whom I can trust. When you're, well, *yourself,* you're a fine navigator, and as a bionoid you're among the best fighters I've seen."

"I'm always a bionoid," Hectate corrected softly. "My outer form may alter, but the dual nature is always within."

An image of a ten-foot, invincible insect flashed into

Teldin's mind, bringing with it echoes of the terror he'd felt when the creature first approached him. He was surprised that the memory was as reassuring as it was unnerving. "I need you with me," he repeated. When Hecate hesitated, Teldin asked, "Are you saying you would prefer not to sail with me?"

The half-elf shrugged. "Considering what I've just told you about myself, I would not blame you if you didn't want me to."

"That's not the issue," Teldin said with a touch of impatience. "What is it, Hecate? Do you have other plans? Or maybe you think the search for the Broken Sphere is a waste of time?"

Hecate gave the matter such a lengthy consideration that Teldin began to think his hastily spoken words touched on truth. "For me, no," Hecate finally said. "You might remember that I jumped at the chance to sign on with a long voyage of exploration."

"But for me?" Teldin pressed.

"I don't know," the bionoid replied honestly. "You have told me only that you seek answers to a personal quest, and that you are pursued by dangerous foes. Knowing so little, I could hardly advise you one way or the other."

Teldin had to acknowledge the truth in Hecate's reasoning. He had spoken of his trust in Hecate, but he had extended little. If he wanted Hecate to continue with him—and he was surprised to realize how much he wanted this—he would have to trust the half-elf.

"I have a story of my own," Teldin began, fingering the edge of his cloak. "About a year ago—that is, as time is reckoned on my homeworld—I lived on Krynn, making my living as a farmer. A spelljammer crashed on my farm, and the dying reigar captain handed me this cloak, insisting I keep it from the neogi and take it to the creators. I've been trying to do just that ever since."

Hectate observed Teldin carefully as he spoke. "And you hope to find at the Broken Sphere the answers to these creators?"

"That was once my goal, yes," Teldin admitted. "Finding the cloak's rightful owner and getting the burden off my own shoulders was all I could think of. As time went on, though, it began to look as though I might well *be* the rightful owner. Everyone who wants the cloak—and that includes pirates, illithids, arcane, scro, neogi, even the elves—has shown less than perfect motives."

"Why do they want this cloak?" the bionoid asked, eyeing the black garment with mild interest.

"It's the key to the *Spelljammer*," Teldin said tersely. "The cloak I'm wearing is an artifact, thought to be the Cloak of the First Pilot. According to the best information I've been able to get, whoever wears the cloak can control the *Spelljammer*—provided, of course, that they can find it," he added dryly.

"Then the old stories are true," Hectate said, and wonder shone in his voice and his eyes. "When I was a child, I heard tales about a ship as big as a small world, which escaped its crystal shell like a chick coming from an egg. Do the two stories fit together? Could this be the Broken Sphere we seek?"

Teldin warmed to the bionoid's "we," and he met Hectate's gaze squarely. "It's possible. The only thing that the fal—the giant slug sage, but that's another story—told me, was that I could find answers to the *Spelljammer* at the Broken Sphere, and since that's the best lead I've had so far, I've got to take it. Before someone beats me to it, I have to find the ship and take command."

The bionoid thought this over for several long moments, then he nodded in grave agreement. "Yes, I think you should. But, if I might ask, to what purpose?"

Teldin blinked, stunned into silence by Hectate's words.

He dimly remembered that Vallus had said something like that, but Hectate's calm, reasonable question brought the reality of his situation home. He finally had accepted his destiny as Cloakmaster, but now he saw that acceptance was not nearly enough. His destiny was his to shape, and Hectate had a valid point: To what purpose?

"The elves want me to join their war effort," Teldin admitted carefully, steeling himself for Hectate's reaction.

Hectate merely nodded as if he had anticipated this answer. "Many of my people fight alongside the elves," the bionoid said.

That seemed incredible, given what Hectate had told him about the elven attitudes toward Hectate's race. "And *against* the elves?" Teldin asked, looking his friend in the eye.

"Some, yes." Hectate's gaze was steady, giving away nothing.

Teldin raked a hand through his hair. "How do *you* stand?" he asked outright. "Look, I'm sorry if I offend you, but this is a time for plain speaking."

Again the half-elf turned his sad smile toward wildspace. "If the truth must be told, I had hoped to avoid taking a stand either way." He glanced up at Teldin. "You were too ill to notice, but I kept to myself for the first days after the battle. It is traditional after the Change for a bionoid to spend a period of time mourning the lives he has taken. We don plain silver robes, meditate, and cleanse our souls from the stain of blood. We are a gentle people who kill efficiently but with great regret." Hectate's face took on a faraway look. "I had hoped to put away my silver robes."

Teldin absorbed this, understanding the half-elf's feelings but still saddened by them. "And that won't happen if you stay with me," he concluded.

"Probably not," Hectate agreed. The eyes he turned back to Teldin held resignation and the sadness of a dream deferred. "But you soon will get your own ship, and you will need a navigator to help you on your quest. And once you succeed?" He shrugged as if trying to make light of the matter. "Even the *Spelljammer* needs to be told where to go, I imagine."

"But if I decide to stand with the elves?" Teldin pressed.

"Then I will stand with you, Teldin Moore." The half-elf extended his hand, offering a pact. "You trusted me. To one of my race, that is a rare gift. In return, I'll trust your decision."

Startled but deeply moved, Teldin took the offered hand in a firm grip, and the first genuine smile in many days brightened his face. Wanting to put the conversation on a lighter, happier footing, he switched to a topic dear to Hectate's heart: food. "Now that the future's settled, maybe you'd care to join me for eveningfeast?" he asked. "I hear Rozloom is galley master tonight."

Hectate answered him with one of his rare, elfin grins. "Just when I'd concluded that this ship had nothing to offer."

* * * * *

Wrapped in a magical cloak of secrecy, the invisible shrike ship darted after the star-traveling swan. The disgruntled crew mates listened sullenly to the captain's explanation of their new mission.

"Our liaison, Lord K'tide, has requested that we follow the human," Wynlar began. "The human may have changed ships, but that does not alter our orders. Drakkar or swan ship, it matters not. K'tide is depending on us to report the human's movements, as the informant's messages have not proven sufficient."

"What does baby-sitting an elven ship have to do with the Armistice mission?" demanded Tekura. The silver-haired technician flipped an exasperated gesture toward the white, tufted tail of the swan ship. "We should be outfitting the orcs, not trailing some human. The swan ship is heading toward Toril, and each wasted day takes us farther from our goal."

"And what have we to show for this little detour?" the wizard Zeddop whined. "Obscure messages about a broken sphere and a cloak that changes color. Bah!"

The captain's angular, elflike face betrayed his discomfort. "I do not know all that K'tide has in mind. He said only that the cloak is important, not to our current alliance with the orcs, but to some later strike against the elves. K'tide promised to say more when the time is right."

"And you accepted that?" Zeddop sniffed, and his thin lips twisted with scorn. "You always were a bit too credulous, little brother."

Wynlar turned to glare at the wizard. "What would you have me do? K'tide is a necessary intermediary. Would you rather deal directly with the scro?"

His challenge was met with silence, and after a moment he sighed deeply. "I know that this new development is difficult, but we have given pledge loyalty to K'tide, and we are honor-bound to carry out his plans."

"Whatever *they* may be," Zeddop murmured in the manner of one who must get in the last word.

Tekura came to stand at Wynlar's side. She gave her foster-father's arm a reassuring squeeze. "We know that K'tide desires the destruction of the elves. As long as we are working to that end, we can do whatever is required."

Chapter Seven

●●●

The mess was crowded when Teldin and Hectate arrived. Rozloom strode in from the galley, bearing an enormous platter heaped with shiny, cone-shaped loaves of bread, which he set down on the serving table with a flourish.

Hectate's eyes lit up at the sight of the confection, and he hastened to pile several of the small loaves onto his tray. Given the half-elf's appetite, that did not strike Teldin as unusual until he noted the usually spartan elves flocking to the table to do likewise. He himself did not particularly care for sweets, but he took one on the chance that he might otherwise be missing something.

The elven crew seemed unusually expansive that evening, and, as Teldin followed Hectate to a corner table, he fielded a number of questions and accepted numerous good wishes on his recovery. By the time Teldin and Hectate had settled down with their dinner trays, Teldin had made two unsettling observations: the elves treated him with considerable respect, but they virtually ignored the half-elf. Teldin was acquainted with the Imperial Fleet's high-handed ways, but nothing prepared him for this utter dismissal of Hectate Kir.

The half-elf did not seem to notice anything amiss. He broke one of the loaves apart and inhaled the fragrant steam with deep satisfaction. "*Quinpah,*" he breathed in a reverent tone. "I haven't seen any in years. It's a traditional elven bread, but it varies from one world to another. This one is very like what I remember from my childhood."

"Really. I wonder how Rozloom got the recipe for something like that," Teldin said absently. He broke off a piece and popped it into his mouth, and his eyes widened in surprise. The outside of the bread was crisp and sticky with a honey glaze, but the middle was a soft, airy delight that dissolved in his mouth into a foaming mist.

"How do the aperusa acquire *anything?*" Hectate observed without malice.

Teldin grinned. During the few days Rozloom had been aboard the *Valkyrie*, a number of "lost" items had been discovered in his possession. The gypsy's explanations were always so entertaining that none of his victims could hold their ire for long. Only Rozloom's offbeat charm—and remarkable culinary prowess—kept the exasperated crew from loading him into the drakkar's catapult and letting fly.

After several days of eating nothing but broth and thin porridge, Teldin was ravenous. He devoured the *quinpah* and thought he might like another, but aside from Hectate's private hoard, the sweet bread already had disappeared. As he ate the rest of his dinner, Teldin pondered the elves' strange coldness to Hectate Kir. The only reasonable conclusion Teldin could come up with was that somehow the crew must have found out about Hectate's bionoid persona. When Teldin suggested this possibility, Hectate's well-laden spoon froze halfway up to his mouth.

"What makes you think so?" Hectate asked, cautiously lowering the spoon back to his bowl.

As tactfully as he could, Teldin commented on the elves' decided lack of friendliness. To his surprise, Hectate burst out laughing, drawing brief, chilly stares from the other diners. "What's so funny?" Teldin groused.

Still chuckling, the half-elf shook his head. "I'm sorry, sir, but I'd forgotten that some people really don't care what I am." He seemed on the verge of saying more, then his eyes fell on the last loaf of *quinpah* on his tray. In a gesture more eloquent than words, the half-elf picked up the treat and broke it in two, handing the larger piece to Teldin.

Teldin didn't need his newly acquired perceptivity to recognize the offering as much more than elven bread. He accepted the gift and nodded his thanks, and human and half-elf munched in companionable silence.

They were licking the last sticky drops from their fingers when the chiming of bells signaled the beginning of the third watch. "If you'll excuse me, sir, I've got duties," Hectate said as he rose from the table.

"Good," Teldin said. He gathered up his tray and prepared to follow the half-elf. "Do you think anyone would mind if I came to the bridge with you? I'd like to see some star charts and get a fix on where we are."

The half-elf hesitated. "My duties aboard this ship don't include navigation, sir."

"Oh?"

"Hectate, come!" boomed a familiar bass voice from the galley. "Always there is a price to pay for pleasure, is that not so?"

Hectate noted the gathering storm in Teldin's narrowed eyes. "It's all right, sir. Work is work. I don't mind, really." He gave Teldin a reassuring smile and disappeared into the galley.

Teldin tossed his tray back onto the table, ignoring the clatter of scattering dishes as he stalked after the half-elf. Enough was enough. He wanted some answers about Hectate's treatment, and if he had to file the points off a few elven ears before he got those answers, all the better. He threw open the door of the galley and surveyed the busy scene with angry eyes.

The galley was larger and better equipped than any kitchen Teldin had ever seen. The shelves that lined the walls held more steel implements than a battlefield, and the

pots and vials and jars and vats suggested a diversity of
ingredients that would rival a wizard's laboratory. Elven
crew members glided efficiently about the galley, some
putting away the remnants of the evening meal and others
chopping and mixing in preparation for dawnfry. On one
side of the room crouched Om, the gnome technician who
had been rescued from Teldin's ship. She was busily
engaged in "improving" the vast cookstove, muttering gnomish imprecations as she worked. In the center of the room
was a long table used for food preparation. Rozloom sat at
the head of the table, his broad posterior distributed over
two high-backed stools and his polished boots propped up
on another. One meaty bronze hand held a large silver
tankard, and a bottle of elven spirits sat on the table beside
him. There was no sign of Hectate, but several doors led out
of the main galley.

Rozloom caught sight of Teldin and bounded to his feet.
"Captain!" he boomed, waving the tankard at Teldin with
ebullient good cheer. The gypsy's resonant bass voice rattled
the crockery. "My very dear friend! Come in! Sit! Drink!"

Some of Teldin's anger melted under the warmth of
Rozloom's extravagant greeting. He remembered that the
aperusa, despite his self-absorption, had shown himself to
have fairly decent powers of observation. Rozloom might be
able to shed some light on the elves' treatment of Hectate.

So thinking, Teldin greeted Rozloom and settled himself
on the offered stool. He paled when the gypsy set a half pint
of pale amber liquid before him. The elves—who, despite
their delicate appearance, had an astounding capacity for
potent spirits—traditionally served the stuff in tiny, fluted
glasses. In his still-weakened state, Teldin figured that two
sips would put him eye-level with the diminutive Om. "You
seem to be adjusting to life aboard ship, Rozloom," he
observed, unobtrusively pushing his drink aside.

The aperusa resumed his seats and nodded avidly. "And

why not?" He took a long pull at his tankard and smacked his lips with gusto. "Fine drink this ship has, good food, and many women." A gleeful leer lit Rozloom's face as he jerked his head toward a lithesome elven woman measuring spices into a huge bowl of batter. He elbowed Teldin companionably. "Look and learn, Captain. Your last crew, it had no such women. Without them wildspace is a cold place, yes?" The gypsy punctuated his foray into philosophy with a chuckle and another solid nudge to Teldin's ribs.

An agitated clatter forestalled Teldin's reply. Om picked up the tool she'd dropped and leveled a brown-eyed glare at Rozloom. "No women, eh? And what would you call me?"

Black brows flew upward in genuine surprise. "A gnome?" guessed the gypsy.

Om huffed indignantly and squared her tiny shoulders. Teldin watched, fascinated, as she drew herself up to a regal four feet. He'd never seen Om show interest in anything other than machinery, yet there she was, the very picture of female pique. "Among gnomes, I'm considered very attractive," the tiny woman informed Rozloom with dignity.

The aperusa looked pointedly at the stove parts scattered around the floor. "Among gnomes, you're considered a *technician*."

Teldin winced and braced himself for the gnome's rejoinder. To his surprise, Om's small brown face relaxed into a coquettish smile. Being a gnome, she'd taken Rozloom's insult as the highest possible praise. She acknowledged the "compliment" with a satisfied nod and returned to her tinkering. Teldin shook his head in silent amazement. The shipboard gossip that had trickled down to Teldin's sickroom had included Rozloom's vow to charm every woman on board. Teldin had considered this to be so much amusing bluster, but subsequent gossip suggested that the aperusa was succeeding more often than not.

Oblivious to his effect on the smitten gnome, Rozloom

drained his tankard and wiped his mustache with the back of his hand. "Ah, that is good. You will have more?" When Teldin shook his head, Rozloom shrugged and emptied most of the bottle into his own mug. "So, Captain, to what shall we drink?"

Teldin edged his tankard even farther away from him, hoping to signal his lack of interest in toast-making. "Actually, there's something about Hectate Kir."

Rozloom nodded agreeably. "If you say so, Captain." He raised his mug in salute. "His health!"

Teldin caught the gypsy's wrist while the tankard was still south of the enormous mustache. "No, I have a *question* about Hectate."

"Ahh." Rozloom set the mug down carefully and folded his arms over his vast belly. His bronze features arranged themselves into a parody of a sage adviser. "What would you know, Captain?"

"Well, to start with, why is he working here in the galley when he's so skilled in navigation? Why do the elves act as if he's not worthy of their notice?"

Rozloom twisted one bushy eyebrow into a sardonic quirk. "That is unusual for an elf?"

Teldin conceded the point, but added, "They are far more cordial to you and me than to Hectate. I can't figure that out."

"It is not so very difficult. These elves of yours, Captain, they do not believe that half an elf is better than none."

"Pardon?"

"Hectate Kir is a half-breed," the aperusa said bluntly. "The elves, they are an ancient people with old ways. They do not like change. A half-elf is a step toward becoming what they are not. They do not see what might be gained, only what is lost." Rozloom held up a finger and waggled it, indicating that an idea had occurred to him. He picked up the almost empty bottle of elven spirits and splashed a little of the amber liquid into another tankard, then he called for a pitcher of water and filled the huge mug to the brim. He presented the resulting pale yellow fluid to Teldin with a theatrical flourish. "Care to drink, Captain?"

Teldin waved away the disgusting stuff. "You've made your point."

"Good," Rozloom murmured distractedly, no longer interested in the lesson. His small black eyes followed an elven woman who was carrying a stack of nested bowls toward what appeared to be a larder. She shot an arch, inviting glance over her shoulder before she disappeared. The aperusa was on his feet instantly, preening his massive beard with an air of anticipation.

"Ah, but hypocrisy is a wonderful thing in an elven woman!" he noted with deep satisfaction. "My apologies, Captain, but you understand?"

Rozloom was gone before Teldin could reply. With amazing speed for one of his bulk, the gypsy made his way across the galley and shut the larder door firmly behind him and his latest conquest.

The strange conversation left Teldin puzzled and suddenly exhausted. He made his way back to his cabin, and was just tugging off his boots when a crisp knock sounded at the door. "Come in," he called wearily.

Vallus Leafbower stepped into the room, resplendent in his blue-and-silver uniform. "You look much different from when we last spoke. I trust you're feeling better?"

"Well, I'm a little tired," he hinted.

"I'll leave you to your rest momentarily. You should know that we make landfall tomorrow, three bells into the first watch."

Suddenly alert, Teldin motioned the elf into the room. "Where are we going?"

"Toril."

Teldin's blue eyes narrowed. "Why Toril? And don't bother to tell me you were on your way there when you just happened to bump into my ship."

Vallus took the chair at the side of Teldin's cot and faced down the angry human. "We are going to do what I advised you to do months ago: We are going to seek answers to your cloak and your quest from the sages of Evermeet," he said with quiet finality.

"Really. And do I have any choice in the matter?"

"Have you another destination in mind?" the elf asked mildly. "My orders are to help you find the *Spelljammer*. If you can suggest a better way to go about it, I'd be happy to listen."

That stopped Teldin. As he thought it over, he realized that Vallus's choice fit his own plans rather well. If he wanted to continue his search without relying on the elves for transportation, he would have to purchase a new ship. That problem had been pressing on his mind for days, and perhaps Evermeet presented a solution. There was enough gold left in his bag for a modest down payment, but Teldin knew that as an unknown, inexperienced captain making a voyage of exploration into deep space, he was not exactly a good risk. He doubted anyone would be willing to extend him credit. The elves, perhaps, might prove an exception. They regretted the treacherous behavior of one of their own, Admiral Cirathorn. Although Teldin didn't like the idea, he figured he would have to find out how far the elves would go to make amends.

"Evermeet's fine," he muttered grudgingly. "Hectate and I will be looking for another ship."

Vallus shook his head. "I'm afraid that's out of the question."

So it was true, Teldin thought. He was a prisoner of the elves. "You're saying I can't leave the swan ship?"

The elf's surprise seemed genuine. "Not at all. You may come and go as you will, but Hectate Kir cannot set foot on Evermeet."

Teldin's resentment over his friend's treatment returned in full measure. "Why? Because he's half-elven?"

"Yes."

Teldin shot both hands through his hair, astounded that the elven wizard didn't even bother to hide his bigotry. "That's ridiculous," he sputtered.

"I agree," Vallus said evenly, "but the decision is not mine to make. I personally have no objection to Hectate Kir."

"Is that so? Then why is the crew treating him like a pariah? Why is a skilled navigator—the best I've seen!—washing dishes instead of taking shifts on the bridge?"

The elf's green eyes remained steady. "I am the captain of the *Trumpeter*, and therefore my dictates are followed. I cannot, however, transfer my beliefs and values to the crew. Elves tend to be an insular people, and many of my crewmen distrust the half-elf. Putting your friend on the bridge would create more tension that the exercise merits."

Teldin shook his head adamantly. "No. I can't agree that you should abandon a principle merely because upholding it might create a little discomfort," he said with scathing sarcasm. To his surprise, his wrathful answer brought a smile to Vallus's face.

"You do not disappoint me, Teldin Moore."

He threw up his hands in exasperation. "I live to please. Now, I'm sorry if this ruffles a few elven feathers, but I need to bring Hectate with me. If I'm to purchase a new ship, I need the advice of someone I can trust, someone from my own crew."

"Surely you know that the swan ship is at your disposal," Vallus told him. "After we visit Evermeet, you may choose whatever course you wish. You do not need another ship."

"Sorry, but I don't care for the strings attached to your offer," Teldin said bluntly.

The elf received this information with a long silence. "Very well. I ask only that you keep an open mind and not make your final decision until after we speak with the elves of Evermeet."

The human shrugged. "If you like, but Hectate comes with me," he insisted.

"That is not possible," Vallus repeated. "No half-elves are allowed on Evermeet. It is not permitted for me as an ambassador of the Imperial Fleet to violate a rule of the groundling elves. If you wish, you may bring other, more acceptable crew members."

"Like Rozloom?" Teldin asked with heavy irony.

Vallus had the grace to smile. "That choice might not further diplomatic relations. Actually, I had the dracons in mind."

"Chirp and Trivit?" echoed Teldin in disbelief.

"Why not? They are fine sailors, born and raised in the void. Since they now are part of your family, so to speak, they have a very personal stake in choosing your next ship."

Teldin's eyes narrowed. He suspect that Vallus was teasing him, but he could detect no sign on humor on the elf's angular, aristocratic face. Neither could he see any real reason for leaving the dracons behind, so he gave in with a gut-deep sigh. "All right. They can come."

"Then only one minor matter remains." Vallus excused himself and left the cabin. He returned almost immediately with a large, paper-wrapped bundle, which he handed to Teldin. "Since your possessions were either lost or damaged in the last battle, we took the liberty of replacing some of them."

With a feeling of apprehension, Teldin untied the string. He had a mental picture of himself gadding about in the shining silver favored by the Imperial Fleet. He didn't particularly like the idea of appearing before elven royalty in his only set of battered clothing, but wearing an elven uniform would be making a statement of allegiance that he could not support.

To his surprise, the bundle contained several dark garments. He shook out the first, a shirt of fine black silk. Black trousers, a dark jacket, and several other garments completed the package. The cut of the clothing was almost identical to his old wardrobe, except that the quality of fabric and workmanship far surpassed anything he'd ever owned. At the bottom of the package were finely tooled leather items: boots, a belt and scabbard, even a new money sack.

"We had these made while you were ill, using your old things as a measure. I trust they are satisfactory?"

"Very," Teldin murmured, still stunned by the thoughtfulness of the gift.

"Then we shall meet after we make landfall. Sleep well." Vallus was gone before Teldin realized he'd forgotten to thank him.

Chapter Eight

• • •

Chirp and Trivit responded to the news of their furlough with such glee that Teldin was glad he'd agreed to Vallus's suggestion. However, Teldin made a point of talking to Hectate and explaining the position of the Evermeet elves. The half-elf seemed quietly pleased by Teldin's concern, but he shrugged off the rebuff as if it were of no consequence. Teldin got the distinct impression that the whole thing mattered more to him than it did to Hectate.

Everyone whose duty schedule permitted gathered at the swan ship's railings to watch the descent to Evermeet. Rozloom was there, uncharacteristically surly over not being allowed ashore. Following him like a tiny brown shadow was Om, who remained more or less invisible to the aperusa. Despite his professed lack of interest, Hectate joined Teldin at the railing, as did Vallus Leafbower. Chirp and Trivit kept up a running dialogue, speculating about the wonders that awaited them ashore, until Teldin began to give serious consideration to throttling them.

Vallus acknowledged the exasperated expression on Teldin's face with a faint, sympathetic smile. "Try to appreciate the dracons' curiosity," the elf suggested. "So few maintain it past youth that your clan's enthusiasm is actually refreshing."

Kaba or not, Teldin was about to take issue with the elf's casual reference to clan, but he saw that he no longer had

Vallus's attention. The elf was absorbed in the scene spread out before them, and his angular face was rapt with wonder. The elf's expression was a perfect replication of what Teldin always felt upon making landfall. For the first time Teldin felt a touch of sympathy—even kinship—with the elven wizard. He turned his own attention back to the rapidly approaching world.

Teldin watched, fascinated, as the jewellike island of Evermeet came up to meet them. "So many shades of green," he murmured. "I didn't know so many different greens existed."

"Evermeet is heavily wooded," Vallus explained. "There are ancient forests on the island, but much of the foliage has been cultivated to produce shades of green, blue, gold, and silver. In different lights and at different times of year, certain colors predominate. From this height all meld into the unusual green you see before you."

The swan ship spread its wings and began its descent, finally splashing down about a league off the coast. The small group clung to the railing for balance as the ship rocked, and Teldin heard the deep, creaking groan of turning gears.

"They're lowering the paddles now," Hectate informed him.

"Paddles?" broke in Om, her small brown eyes lighting with interest. Gnomes, Teldin recalled, had a perverse fondness for paddle-driven ships and were always on the alert for new variations on the theme. "What do these paddles look like?" she demanded.

"Like any swan's feet, only very large," Rozloom supplied absently, his tone morose.

The gnome harrumphed. "Inefficient," she muttered. "Give me a day or two, and I could improve the design."

Rozloom rolled his black eyes. "If only they knew, many swans would rejoice this night." His insult earned him a playful swat from the tiny gnome woman.

Once the rolling motion subsided, the ship began to move forward. Almost immediately the swan ship was surrounded by a host of elves, strange fey creatures with webbed hands and skin beautifully patterned in hues of mottled blue and green. They formed two lines, one on each side of the ship, and began to swim toward the shore.

Teldin leaned far out over the railing to watch, awed by the elves' exotic beauty. Their eyes were large and lacked the characteristic almond shape of other elves. Their hair was like nothing he had seen: masses of wet, silvery curls that caught the early morning sunlight and reflected it back as if through a prism. The elves sang as they swam, communicating in a lyrical language that mixed windsong voices with a haunting counterpoint of clicks and whistles.

"What are they doing?" Teldin asked in a hushed whisper.

"They are guiding the ship safely along a channel of deep water," Vallus explained. "The waters around Evermeet are extremely treacherous. The island is guarded by lethal rock and coral formations, underwater currents strong enough to rip apart unwary ships, powerful magical wards, and even a guardian monster or two."

The elves guided the ship through the channel to the docks, then disappeared into the deep. As he stared out into the waves, Teldin found himself wondering what world within a world existed under the surface of the water.

The elven port soon claimed his full attention. The elves that greeted them at the dock were more familiar to Teldin. Slim and supple as aspen trees, the golden elves were very like those with whom he had sailed many months earlier on his native Krynn. These harbor workers set about securing the swan ship, and another contingent of elves met them with great ceremony and escorted them to a floating, odd-shaped litter. Teldin stared dubiously at the thing, but he clambered aboard. Since the dracons were far too large to ride the elven conveyance, they ambled along beside, drawing stares as they went. Teldin noted many curious glances cast in his direction as well.

Vallus leaned close to Teldin. "As you may have guessed, your presence here is an unusual occurrence. In elven memory—which is long—the humans allowed on Evermeet can be counted on the fingers of one hand."

"I'm honored beyond speech," Teldin said with grave formality.

Vallus's silver eyebrows rose slightly, acknowledging the human's sarcasm. He refrained from commenting, but his expression tightened. "I have arranged an audience with the queen. With her will be some of Evermeet's most renowned sages." He paused to let the import of his words sink in. "Am I safe in assuming that you are unaccustomed to the ways of royalty and scholars?"

"For one who knows as much about me as you do, that seems like a safe assumption," Teldin returned. He did not care for the elf's patronizing tone.

Vallus sighed deeply and passed a hand over his forehead. "You may not believe this, Teldin Moore, but I'm trying to help you. With all my heart I want you to find the *Spelljammer*." Teldin made no attempt to hide his skepticism, and the elf sighed again. "You still don't believe me."

"I'm not completely convinced," Teldin admitted. "The elves don't need me to get the *Spelljammer*. There are other ways to achieve that goal. Forgive me for being so blunt, but what's in this for you?"

"Freedom." The elf's eyes took on a distant look, and he scanned the colorful market scene outside their litter. "Freedom," he repeated softly.

Teldin's brow furrowed, but Vallus did not seem inclined to elaborate. The elf dropped the subject and began to describe the sights along their route. Teldin only half listened, so absorbed was he in the sights of the elven city.

Evermeet was a place beautiful beyond Teldin's dreams.

The harbor led through a market, where elven merchants offered exotic produce, musical instruments, jewelry, gossamer silks. They passed a bakery redolent with the subtle spices of *quinpah* and surrounded by a flock of elven children. The elflings licked honey off their slender fingers and darted about in games common to children of all races. Some of them, agape or giggling, pointed at the dracons. Teldin had never seen an elven settlement before, and he was fascinated by the vital, joyful atmosphere. Aloof with other beings, elves apparently could be high-spirited, even fun-loving, in the company of their own kind. As the litter floated slowly through the city, Teldin began to perceive something of the fabric of the elven society. Tradition and magic wove through elven life, giving it a beauty and resonance Teldin had never before imagined.

As he pondered this insight, the market gave way to a residential area. Enormous trees were everywhere, meeting over the broad streets to make uninterrupted canopies of blue and green. The streets were lined with elven residences, each with its own gardens. These houses were neither uniform nor built upon the angular, four-square designs that humans favored. Some structures resembled wood or crystal and seemed to be organic, grown as were elven spelljamming ships. Other homes were in the trees themselves, and a complex system of suspended walkways connected the homes in a gossamer network.

Teldin knew little of magic, but it occurred to him that elven magic was subtly different from that wielded by a human wizard. It was somehow more harmonious, using life-forms and working with nature. That was an engaging thought until he remembered Hectate Kir and what that sort of magic could yield. Teldin hastily pushed the thought aside. It seemed almost irreverent to contemplate the elves' dark side in this land of bright magic and green light.

After a time the litter came to a large square surrounded

with official buildings. The palace, a marvel of gem-en-crusted white marble, glistened faintly blue in the distance. It was surrounded by gardens, and to one side stretched a vast green forest. Magic hung in the air like mist.

"I should tell you a little about the royal family," Vallus said, breaking into Teldin's thoughts. "Evermeet is ruled by Queen Amlauril, who heads the moon elf royal family."

"What are moon elves?" Teldin asked.

"They are but one of several elven peoples on Toril," Vallus began. "They are uncommon on other worlds, so it is not unusual that you have not encountered one before this."

Vallus gestured to the pale, black-haired elven woman who walked alongside the litter, exchanging pleasantries with Trivit.

"That is a moon elf," Vallus said. "A slight blue tinge to the skin is common, but apart from that, they are more like mankind than are other elves."

The elf's discourse was interrupted by the creak of gates. They had reached the palace grounds, and several guards fell in with the procession to escort them up to the palace. As they neared the palace gardens, Teldin noted with interest that the lawns were a deep, vibrant blue, as were the tall bushes that formed the garden maze. He shook his head in silent amazement. Hearing about blue foliage did not prepare him for the strangeness of the sight.

Teldin turned his gaze to the palace walls. Instantly he recoiled. There were no doors into the palace; the vast wall looked as if it had been carved from a single precious stone.

"How do we get in?" Teldin asked bluntly.

Vallus pointed upward. "The gate is there."

As Teldin craned his neck to see, the litter began to float straight up. The door was far above them, but the distance was closing rapidly. Teldin cast a look downward. The dracons were pacing about uncertainly, and he noted the guards pointing them toward the gardens. The dracons looked delighted at this turn of events and took off with an odd, four-footed skip. Teldin smiled, relieved that he could concentrate on the elven sages without the dracons' endless questions and prattle to distract from important matters.

Vallus also had noted the dracons' detour. "This is just as well. If Chirp and Trivit were involved in this conference, they would feel compelled to trace the royal family's lineage back beyond Myth Drannor, to the forging of the first moonblade."

Teldin caught the touch of wry humor and responded with a delighted, if confused, grin. "I'm afraid you lost me."

"I'm sorry?"

"Take a left turn at Myth Drannor," Teldin suggested helpfully.

Vallus looked startled, then he laughed outright. Teldin's jaw dropped in astonishment. Somehow, he'd never thought of the elven wizard as possessing much of a sense of humor. Since their arrival in Evermeet, however, Vallus seemed to have shed much of the aloof, distant manner that Teldin associated with him.

"Would that I could," the elf said, with a chuckle. "That particular center of elven culture fell many centuries before my birth. By all telling, it would have been a sight worth seeing."

"You know a great deal about Toril's elves," Teldin commented.

"Learning is my passion," the elven wizard said avidly. His pale green eyes settled on Teldin's dark cloak, and an involuntary, almost imperceptible shudder rippled through his slender frame.

Teldin blinked, startled by the sudden intensity of the elf's emotion. He had never before been able to "read" Vallus's expressions, but he couldn't miss the apprehensiveness with which the elf regarded the cloak. Reflexively, Teldin drew the somber black garment a little closer and glanced out the window.

The ground was far below now, and the litter had reached a height even with the oddly shaped door. The gate disappeared suddenly, slipping with a smooth swish into a hollow in the palace wall. They floated forward, and Teldin noted that the litter's unusual shape matched the door as precisely as a key might fit its lock. The litter glided into a hall, and the passengers stepped out onto a green carpet that led down a winding incline to a council chamber. Through the arched doorway Teldin caught a glimpse of a dais shaped like a crescent moon and dotted with thrones.

At the door the elven guard announced them as ambassadors of the Imperial Fleet. Vallus preceded Teldin, giving a ritual phrase in a dialect of Elvish that Teldin had never heard, but nonetheless understood.

"We welcome you, Vallus Leafbower, for your own sake and also as a representative of the Imperial Fleet."

The formal words were spoken in a clear contralto voice that held all the music and promise of the sea. The speaker was a female elf as beautiful as any Teldin had ever seen or imagined. Her age was impossible to guess, for her smooth white skin was flawless and touched with blue where a human woman's face would flush rosy. Vallus's mention of blue skin had brought to mind the dusty, unappealing complexion of the arcane, but the elven woman possessed a beauty as cool and elusive as moonlight on a pond. Her face was angular, delicate, and dominated by large, almond-shaped eyes as blue as Teldin's own, though flecked with gold. The elven queen's hair was elaborately arranged in a cascade of waves and ringlets, and the color was a startlingly deep, bright blue that looked as if it had been spun from fine sapphires.

Around her throne were thirteen chairs. One chair, Teldin noted, was pointedly empty. Seated in the others were six princes and six princesses, all bearing a strong resemblance to Amlauril. Some of them had her wondrous blue hair, others black. All were dressed in court robes of palest spring green, all had the moon-kissed skin and golden blue eyes, and all regarded him with friendly curiosity.

Vallus again bowed to the queen, holding his hands palm up as he did. "*Quex etrielle*, may I present Teldin Moore, Cloakmaster," he said, giving Teldin a significant glare.

Teldin stepped forward and performed a passable imitation of Vallus's bow. "Thank you for seeing me, Queen Amlauril."

The elven monarch leaned forward, slender hands folded in her silken lap. "We are honored, Teldin Moore. Your quest is of greatest interest to us all, but to me you bring an answer I have sought for many centuries." The queen paused and glanced around the room, and a touch of uncertainty softened her regal face. "You see, I have seen the great ship *Spelljammer* myself."

"Why have you not spoken of this before, my queen?" The demand was made in a voice that crackled with age and astonishment.

Teldin followed the direction of the speaker's voice, and for the first time he noticed another group of elves seated to one side of the moon-shaped dais, all of them robed in pale gray. These, he supposed, were the elven sages of whom Vallus had spoken.

A wistful expression crossed Queen Amlauril's face as she answered the sage. "If I had told such a tale when it occurred, who would have believed me? Wildspace travel was not a well-known thing in Evermeet some eight hundred years past. Even after I heard tales of the great ship, I could not be certain that was what I saw. The earliest memories of a child are so dreamlike that dream and reality are virtually indistinguishable." Her smile held great charm and self-mocking humor. "Until we received your message, Vallus Leafbower, I am not certain I believed myself."

"What did you see?" Teldin demanded, taking a step

closer. In the corner of his eye he noted the warning look Vallus shot him and surmised that he had violated some protocol code. In his eagerness to learn of the *Spelljammer* from someone who had seen it with her own eyes, he didn't particularly care.

"Before we begin, perhaps you would take a seat?" the queen said graciously, gesturing toward the table placed directly in front of the throne. Teldin and Vallus took their places, and Amlauril began her tale.

"My family's ancestral lands lie on the northernmost shore of the island," she began, taking a leisurely elven pace. "As a child, I spent much time on the coast, sometimes walking the shore, sometimes sailing in the protected coves with my sisters. One night, when the moon was full, I slipped away alone, compelled by some childish impulse to catch sight of the merfolk. My nursemaid had recently told me tales, you see, of the marvelous dances the merfolk held on the water's surface on each full of the moon, and I was eager to see this wonder.

"I saw instead a giant ship, shaped like a manta ray, flying slowing through the sky and all but blocking out the moon. At that time, of course, I did not know of other worlds, nor did I dream that ships could sail among the stars. I remember looking from the ship above to the sea below. Seeing its reflection on the still waters of the cove seemed a complete reversal of all I had ever known or imagined. I was terrified and fascinated all at once."

A fleeting smile touched her lips. "Of course, I fled like a frightened ground squirrel, back to the safety of my own bed. At daybreak, I was not sure whether I had seen the ship or only dreamed it. Even in later years, I heard so many conflicting stories about the *Spelljammer* that it was not possible to know what I had seen.

"And now, Teldin Moore," she concluded, "it is time for your tale. Permit me first to present your audience."

One by one, the queen introduced the members of her court. Teldin bowed his head to each prince or princess in turn, trying to commit the unfamiliar elven names to memory.

When the introductions were completed, the queen asked Teldin to tell his story. He nodded and did as he was bid. Keeping in mind elven patience and the elves' delight in long and fantastic tales, he left out little of what had befallen him since the day he first had donned the cloak. Throughout his telling, the elves' rapt attention never wavered. As he spoke, Teldin noted with surprise that he was beginning to understand elven reactions and emotions. By and large, they were more subtle than those of humankind, as different as the slow, stylized dances he'd seen on the world of Chimni were from the boisterous frolic of a harvest dance on his homeworld. Less heavy-footed, he noted, pleased with his own analogy.

Their faces betrayed guarded outrage as Teldin told the story of the elven admiral Cirathorn and his attempt to seize the cloak for his own purposes. Finally, he described the battle with the illithids and his rescue by Vallus Leafbower.

"Vallus has offered to aid me in my search, with the understanding that once we find the *Spelljammer*, the ship will join the elven side in the war."

"War? What war?" asked an elderly sage in a querulous tone, his face puckered with dismay. It seemed to Teldin that the elf was distressed not so much by the prospect of war, but that such a thing could happen outside of his knowledge.

The perceptive Vallus stepped in to soothe the elven sage. "The war of which Teldin Moore speaks is a matter for other worlds. It rages far from your shores, Master Tseth."

The elven queen leaned back in her throne, her expression suddenly unreadable. Her gold-flecked gaze settled upon Teldin. "Where does your search take you next?"

"The Broken Sphere."

His answer apparently surprised them, for over a dozen pairs of elven eyebrows leaped upward in perfectly choreographed unison. The elven sages exchanged arch glances. "Might we ask why?" asked the elderly Tseth in a supercilious tone.

"A fal, a giant space sage known for its long life and great wisdom, told me I might find the answers at the Broken Sphere."

His response sent the elves into a chorus of laughter. The sound made Teldin think of fairy bells and delighted babies. "I take it you don't agree?" Teldin asked as soon as he thought he could be heard. He was as bewildered by their reaction as he was charmed by the music of their laughter.

"Along with wisdom and longevity, the fal are known for their cryptic responses," remarked the sage who had spoken before. The elf's smile struck Teldin as unbearably patronizing, and his patience slipped. He had come here for answers, not oblique ridicule.

"Perhaps that's a trait common to sages of all races, Master Tseth," Teldin shot back, meeting the ancient elf's eyes steadily. His response sent the elves into a renewed bout of merriment, an intimate, shared laugh that made Teldin feel as if he inadvertently had stumbled upon a favorite family joke. Far from insulted, the ancient sage actually seemed pleased.

"Well said!" congratulated a black-haired elven prince, wiping his streaming eyes. He beamed at Teldin and added, "You've met Master Tseth before, I take it?"

"That's enough, Asturian," Amlauril murmured in the manner of any mother curbing an adolescent son, but, when she turned to Teldin, her eyes still danced with laughter. "We do not disagree with your sage slug, Teldin Moore. The answers to the mystery that is the *Spelljammer* may well be found at the Broken Sphere."

"And the answers to every other question as well," added Prince Asturian, still grinning.

"I'm afraid I don't understand," faltered Teldin.

"Permit me?" asked Tseth. Amlauril nodded, and the aged elf began. "In simple terms, elven philosophy holds that the Broken Sphere is the primordial sphere, the mother of the universe, if you will. All other spheres, all life, for that matter, erupted from this single source in an explosion of unimaginable power. In time, new spheres formed and began their path outward upon the phlogiston. According to records gleaned from the Elders—an ancient people long since vanished—and from our own observations, it would appear that the spheres still move away from the source."

"Then couldn't you trace these paths back to the source, and locate the Broken Sphere that way?" Teldin asked, excited by the notion.

The sage shook his head. "Such a path cannot be traced. The movement is so minute as to be almost indiscernible, and the time involved is beyond fathoming." He paused, a look of deep contemplation etched into the lines of his face. "The universe is of unimaginable age. One ponders the ephemeral nature of elven life compared to such vastness." The distant look vanished when he met Teldin's eyes, to be replaced by chagrin.

Teldin bowed his head to acknowledge the elf's comment and to show that he had taken no offense. "Go on, please." He smiled ruefully. "As you say, life is short."

The elves' delighted smiles showed appreciation for Teldin's self-deprecating humor, and once again he was struck by the charm and impelling charisma of the moon elves. He could see why this family ruled.

Another sage spoke up, this one an elven woman of middle years. "Despite such evidence as we have gathered, we cannot know the nature of the Broken Sphere. It may be an actual place, but it may not. It is but one theory, albeit a favored one, of the origin of life. If this theory is correct, it would follow that all answers could be traced back to the Broken Sphere. In essence, your fal was correct in saying this."

Teldin listened with growing dismay. Frustration as palpable as a fever flowed through him. If Cirathorn had known all this, why had the elf sent him to the fal?

Teldin slumped in his chair, defeated. "Then I'm back to where I started."

"Not necessarily," said Tseth softly. "You carry an object of great power. In some way that I do not understand, it is linked to your quest."

Hadn't the sage heard a word he'd said? wondered Teldin with exasperation. "The cloak and the ship are linked, yes," he responded as evenly as he could.

Tseth shook his head. He rose and came over to the table where Teldin sat. "No, I wasn't speaking of your cloak. You carry another magical object. The power comes and goes, but at the moment I feel it waxing."

The sage could be referring to only one thing. Teldin reached into the bag at his belt and drew out the medallion Gaye had given him. Immediately he was hit with a wall of emotion as overwhelming as a tidal wave. He gripped his forehead with the fingers of his free hand, struggling to ride out the mental storm. Occasionally a random thought or feeling became separate from the cacophony in his mind, and somehow he realized that he was being buffeted by the emotions of every person in the room. When he felt as if he could bear no more, Teldin became aware of a new sound, a voice of incredible power that drove back the mental assault. Slowly the storm receded. Teldin lowered his hands and tentatively opened his eyes. Tseth stood over him; the saving spell had come from the ancient elf.

The sage extended a wizened hand. "May I see the artifact?" he asked, and his voice once again held the reedy quaver of age.

Teldin nodded and handed the amulet to the sage.

Holding it in one palm, Tseth wove an intricate pattern in the air above it with the fingers of his other hand. Finally he shook his head and handed it back.

"Nothing," he said with a touch of surprise. "Whatever magic it once possessed has almost faded. Can you describe what happened to you just now?"

Teldin did the best he could to explain the sudden assault of emotion. On impulse, he also described the sudden flashes of insight that had started coming to him since he'd acquired the medallion, and the sage's face lit up.

"An instrument of true seeing," Tseth murmured. He looked at Teldin. "It seems to me that the two objects are related. Perhaps the magic of the cloak can augment the medallion's failing power."

Following Tseth's instructions, Teldin focused on the amulet, concentrating on the sigils engraved on its face and slowly moving into them, through them.

As if from a great distance, he heard gasps of surprise from the elves and he noticed that his cloak had taken on the glowing, red-gold hue of molten bronze. The elven council chamber blurred and faded before the bright light, and Teldin had the notion that reality itself was melting before the cloak's bright magic.

Then he was beyond the cloak, far from his own body, far from the elven kingdom. He saw the blackness of wildspace, sprinkled with unfamiliar groupings of stars. The sense of immediacy was incredible, as if he actually were seeing it through eyes that not only saw, but felt and measured.

Accepting the strange perception as reality, Teldin began to focus intently on the scene before him. The vast, majestic emptiness of wildspace was familiar, but it held dimensions that he had never been able to see before. In the silence was song, and the blackness had depth and texture.

Suddenly the dreamlike quality of his vision exploded into a frenzy of anger and flight. A dragon burst into sight, but such a dragon as Teldin had never imagined. Teldin's vision registered the dragon's opalescent black scales and enormous wings, and his more subtle, magically enhanced senses staggered under the impact of the creature's rage. The serpentlike dragon wheeled and flew away at tremendous speed. Lacking points of reference, Teldin had no idea how big the creature was. Its emotions struck him in a bright burst of power, leaving Teldin with the impression that he had spent a moment in the dragon's mind. The feeling stretched his own mind to the point of explosion. If a small world was sentient, if a star could feel rage, then that might approach the vast intelligence that flickered briefly in Teldin's expanded vision.

So this is how a dragon thinks, he thought dazedly. He might as well have said, So this is what it feels like to be struck by lightning.

The enormity of it shattered Teldin's vision and threw him back into the elven council chamber.

With only his own human senses to gather information, Teldin felt suddenly blinded and silenced. The elves plied him with questions, cautiously at first and then with growing excitement. He put the medallion down on the table and told them in as much detail as he could remember what he had seen and felt.

Vallus spoke with great wonder. "I have heard tales of this medallion, but I was not certain of its existence and had no idea it was in your possession. Its magic enables you to see what the *Spelljammer* has seen."

Teldin had no idea of what benefit that might be, and he let his expression say so.

"Don't you understand?" Vallus persisted. "If you can see what the ship sees, you can figure out where it is. The creature you described is a radiant dragon, a very rare being indeed. Perhaps there have been other, recent sightings of this creature. That would give us a general idea of the ship's location. Can you remember anything else that might be used as landmarks? Star formations? Planets? Anything?"

The elf's excitement was contagious. Teldin's hollowed eyes brightened. Determined to try again, he reached for the medallion. Tseth's withered hand captured Teldin's wrist before his fingers could close on the ancient disk.

"No. The use of magic takes a great deal of strength. You are not ready to try again. At any rate, the effort would be to little purpose," the sage admitted with obvious reluctance. "The elves of Evermeet have little knowledge of other spheres. We could not tell you what you saw."

"It seems to me that our best course would be to proceed to Lionheart," Vallus said thoughtfully. Understanding the risk he was taking in revealing such information, he turned to Teldin and explained, "Lionheart is the secret base of the Imperial Fleet. Elves from many worlds are stationed there. Surely with their combined resources we can find the answers you need."

Teldin instinctively recoiled from the plan. He was not ready to commit to the elven cause, and he feared that walking into their command center would take this choice out of his hands. With a surge of relief he remembered Hectate and the uncanny knowledge the half-elf had of star charts and navigation. He was sure Hectate could provide the needed answers, but he wasn't about to announce his decision to a room full of elves.

After a long, typically elven discussion, it was decided that nothing more could be accomplished. Queen Amlauril suggested that they break so that Teldin Moore could rest until time for the evening meal. The exhausted Teldin followed an elven aide out of the chamber, feeling as though he were wading through swamp water.

The elf showed Teldin to a guest chamber. His peripheral vision suggested that the room was sumptuously appointed, but his fading attention was focused solely on the bed. Preparing to flop into exhausted slumber, he pulled back the bright silk coverlet and recoiled in surprise. The bed, which had looked solid enough when draped, was a thin mattress that floated roughly three feet from the floor. A childhood image from his grandfather's stories popped unbidden into his mind, a tale of a magic mat that would bear the rider to magical destinations. For all he knew, he could wake up from his nap to find himself in Vallus's Myth Drannor.

He was still debating whether or not to chance sleep when a knock sounded on his door. At his summons Vallus came into the room. "Am I interrupting your rest?"

Teldin cast a rueful glance toward the bed. "I doubt I could sleep on that thing."

The wizard laughed. "They bear some getting used to. If you're not going to sleep, perhaps we could take a walk before eveningfeast? The palace gardens are lovely."

Despite his fatigue, Teldin agreed. He and the elf made their way through a bizarre garden maze fashioned of tall blue hedges. Vallus watched him with amused understanding as Teldin plucked a tiny leaf from the hedge, crushed it between his fingers, and sniffed. The plant yielded a spicy fragrance not unlike the pines of Krynn.

The garden into which they emerged was just as unusual. Tiny bell-like flowers actually tinkled, playing intricate music that responded with the shifting afternoon breezes. Teldin assumed it was springtime in Evermeet, because several small ponds were ringed with flowering trees. The flowers were being pushed aside by the newly budded blue leaves, and fallen petals foamed at the shores of the ponds. At the far side of the garden, happily snacking on the rare foliage, were Chirp and Trivit. Teldin wondered idly what blue leaves tasted like, and what color they might turn in autumn.

Vallus stopped under the azure shade of a tree and pointed to a small knothole. "Look in there and tell me what you see."

Puzzled, Teldin stepped up and squinted into the hole. A

tiny blue frog stared back at him with bulging yellow eyes.

"That's a zenthian tree frog," the elf explained. "Its life span comprises a single day. A minute to you, the time in which you might pull on your boots or kiss your lady, marks the frog's lifespan from hatchling to adult. How well can you understand this frog, or it you?"

Teldin thought this over silently. Sifting an experience through centuries of life would give elves a very different perspective. Once Vallus had said something like . . .

Vallus.

A thought that had been struggling to gain form all day finally came together with jarring clarity.

"What is it, Teldin Moore?" the elf asked softly.

"You're a wizard and a scholar. Is the elven philosophy about the Broken Sphere so obscure that you've never heard of it?" he demanded.

Vallus met his gaze squarely. "No. It is widely known."

Teldin pressed his lips firmly together to keep from screaming with frustration. "If you knew the elves of Evermeet couldn't help me, why did you bring me here?"

Instead of responding immediately, the wizard locked his arm with Teldin's and drew the human through a gate. The garden beyond was steeply terraced, providing a view of the elven city, the dock area, and the sea beyond. Several levels down Teldin saw a cluster of elven children at play. Their bright clothes fluttered as they ran, and their happy laughter drifted upward. Some of Teldin's anger ebbed, and he thought of his own childhood and wondered what effect it would have on a person to have that magic era extended for years, perhaps decades.

Vallus allowed him several quiet moments. "Evermeet is a thriving, vital elven society. I wanted you to see elves as we see ourselves. Perhaps I was being naive, but I hoped this would seduce you to the elven side." The wizard cast a wry, almost wistful smile at Teldin.

Teldin was touched by the elf's admission, but his answering smile was a little uncertain. "I haven't decided yet."

"There is still time before you must make your decision," Vallus said. "At the moment, though, we should return to the palace. The evening meal is traditionally served at birdsong—the time of day just before twilight, when the birds begin their evening songs."

So I still have time? echoed Teldin silently. There was a strange undertone in Vallus's voice that suggested that this time might have its limits. He tucked that question away with the rest of his doubts.

Oblivious to Teldin's speculation, Vallus said almost gaily, "Come on. Whatever else you may think about elves, after tonight you'll know beyond doubt that we can throw a party."

Chapter Nine

• • •

In the unlikely guise of a hummingbird, Celestial Nightpearl darted around the palace garden like a nervous, multicolored gemstone. The Other was close at hand; she could sense his presence and every now and then she could feel the storm of confusion that was his mind. She was beginning to despair, however, of ever focusing in on any one creature on this island cluttered with elves and disconcerting blue plants.

A duet of high, piping giggles drew her attention, and she whizzed around a stand of flowering bushes to investigate. Her tiny black eyes settled on a pair of dracons, two males just entering adolescence. Finally, she thought with a surge of relief, some creatures she could understand!

"Try this one next," offered the pale green dracon, handing his fellow a branch lush with blue leaves and pale orange flowers. "It's a bit odd, but on the whole extremely palatable."

The other dracon, a mottled green one with overly dainty mannerisms, accepted the plant and took a discriminating nibble. The first dracon absently stuffed his mouth with the rare foliage, looking around the garden for his next course. Suddenly his reptilian eyes bulged with excitement, and his long neck craned in the direction of the garden maze. "See those two people? Isn't that Captain Teldin Moore?" he asked through a mouthful of blue leaves.

"Trivit! How could you not know such a thing! Of course it is," huffed the dark green dracon. He popped a flower into his mouth and chewed, a meditative expression on his green face. "At least, I'm almost certain *one* of them is," he qualified.

"Oh? And which one would that be, my dear Chirp?" Trivit asked in a snide tone.

Chirp leaned forward and squinted hard enough to distort his entire face. Finally he gave up and rolled his eyes with exasperation. "Well, all right, I'll admit it. I can't tell them apart at this distance. Why these two-legged beings set such store by the tiniest differences is beyond my grasp."

"Oh, I suppose the differences are there to see, if one looks closely enough," Trivit said thoughtfully. "For example, upon close study, one can separate males from females."

"You can tell?" Chirp marveled, pantomiming goggle-eyed shock. "I never could. It always seemed to me that the sex of a human was discernable—or of interest—only to another human."

The dracons shared a companionable giggle, then sudden mortification overtook the paler creature. "Chirp, we forget ourselves. It is unseemly to make our *kaba* the subject of so coarse a jest."

High leader, eh? mused the hummingbird. A human named Teldin Moore was a dracon clan leader? She absently took a sip from a red trumpet flower as she weighed the possibilities. An Other certainly would be in a position of leadership. The hummingbird swooped in closer, hoping to hear more, and one of the distracted dracons batted her away as if she were a pesky fly. Celestial Nightpearl, venerable radiant dragon, barely dodged an offhanded swipe that would have reduced her to pulp and feathers had she been a real hummingbird.

"Wait! I know! Captain Teldin Moore is the taller one, the

one with the cloak," Chirp said triumphantly.

To test this theory, the disguised dragon sent her thoughts out through the seeking magic of the pendant, which was now little more than a speck of gold and blue against the tiny ruby feathers of her throat. Yes, the human male was the Other she sought, and the dark cloak that surrounded him with magic was the twin to her own pendant.

"Do you think the *kaba* will join forces with the Imperial Fleet?" Chirp asked. Suddenly alert, the hummingbird listened intently for the other dracon's response. She had sensed uppermost in the human's mind his deep preoccupation with the elves. It would appear that she might have a rival.

"I should think not," Trivit returned thoughtfully. "He has his own affairs to consider, after all. Fighting a war, no matter how entertaining that might be, certainly would not further his search for the Broken Sphere."

"Ah, yes." The dark dracon sighed lustily. "Just think of it! A grand quest! A true adventure!"

So the human had not yet found the great ship. If he truly was looking for the Broken Sphere, he was farther off track that she'd dared to hope. Celestial Nightpearl smirked, a satisfying response even if it did not register on her hummingbird anatomy. Let the elves trot out their best threats and blandishments. She had a bargaining chip that the human Other could not resist.

Still, it never hurt to fight a battle on two fronts, she mused as she pondered her next step.

"You know, there is one thing about our *kaba* that concerns me," Trivit said thoughtfully. "He apparently is without a consort, and he's unlikely to find one on a journey into deep space. If the line of clan succession is to be assured, we must remedy this situation as soon as possible. And taking the short view of the matter, his solitary state is not healthy or natural, even for a human."

Chirp's face drooped into an expression of glum agreement. "I know whereof you speak. For that matter, it would do our own constitutions a world of good to meet some lusty green wenches."

The dracons shared a manly soprano chuckle and a few knowing nudges. Their posturing, absurd though it might be, gave Celestial Nightpearl an amusing idea. A burst of silent, sardonic laughter shook her tiny frame, sending her crashing into a flower-covered trellis. She staggered out of a large blossom, dazed and dusted with pollen. As she flew off unsteadily toward the privacy of a nearby grape arbor, she admonished herself to be more careful. Flight in wildspace was one thing: serene, majestic, powerful, and faster than lesser creatures could begin to comprehend. The obstacle course provided by this cluttered little world made flight another matter altogether.

Perching on a blade of blue grass, the hummingbird beat her tiny wings for balance as she brought to mind the name, face, and form she wished to assume. Her new identity would be perfect, as well as vastly entertaining.

The transformation came easily. She had seen the creature depicted in an ancient, illuminated manuscript of dragon legend. From the perspective of a radiant dragon, there was not that much difference, after all, between a hummingbird and an elf. Her shapechanging was accomplished in moments, and Celestial Nightpearl stood upright on two booted feet.

She examined her new hands, pale and slender and without ornament, the nails blunt and the palms hard with calluses. An assortment of well-used weapons hung about her person, and thick braids of ebony hair brushed the back of her knees. Granted, the adventurer's drab leathers were a far cry from the jeweled feathers of a hummingbird, but she'd learn to adapt. At least, she mused with a half-smile, her new name continued the avian theme.

As Raven Stormwalker, the radiant dragon strode through the palace gardens toward the dracons. The Little Ones, for all their clannishness and odd, militaristic ways, could prove to be valuable allies. They would help her on the strength of her new identity alone, but "Raven" thought she might clue them in on her real identity as well. Dracons had a proper and most satisfying reverence for dragons. A little adulation would be a pleasant side benefit, and with all she'd gone through recently, she certainly deserved a treat.

The look of awe on the dracons' faces brought a gratified smile to her true dragon's visage. At last, things were starting to work out as they should.

* * * * *

The silver sea around Evermeet was stained with sunrise pink by the time Vallus Leafbower brought his charge back to the *Trumpeter*. On the whole, the elf thought, the trip had gone well. The moon elves had been gracious and welcoming, the festive dinner and the starlit dance that followed an unrestrained and joyful celebration of elven life, such as humans seldom saw. Although Teldin Moore had been enthralled by it all, he doubtlessly was feeling a bit overwhelmed. He had spoken but little since the diplomatic litter had left the palace.

Perhaps Teldin's silence was a good sign, Vallus thought. At least the man was no longer taking refuge behind sarcasm. Vallus was fairly confident that, in time, Teldin would come around to the elven side. The man had not seemed upset when informed that the dracons had preceded them back to the *Trumpeter*, and he made no further mention of his plan to take "his" crew members out looking for a new ship.

As they strode across the dock to the swan ship, Vallus decided to test the strength of his perceptions. "Shore leave ends at daybreak. We'll take off as soon as the last of the crew boards, if that's acceptable," he said in a deferential tone.

His manner took the distracted human by surprise. "You're asking me?"

"But of course."

Vallus removed an odd-shaped silver insignia from his tabard and held it out to Teldin. The elf knew that Teldin's cloak could translate spoken communications, and he was counting on its ability to transmute the meaning of the elven rune. Judging by the way the human's blue eyes widened as he stared at the captain's insignia, the cloak had done its job.

"This is yours," Vallus said simply. "As I have said, the swan ship is at your disposal. Matters would be simpler all around if you were the actual as well as the de facto captain."

Since Teldin continued to eye the emblem with suspicion, Vallus added, "In case you're worried, wearing the insignia will in no way be construed as a commitment to the elven navy. The insignia merely identifies you as captain, and it is specific to this particular ship."

After a moment of hesitation, Teldin Moore's face firmed with resolve and he took up the insignia. He pushed back the cloak and pinned the captain's emblem onto the left shoulder of his jacket. He met Vallus's gaze squarely. "Let's get this ship underway, then."

"Aye, Captain," Vallus agreed mildly. As the elf followed the new captain up the plank to the main deck, he had to call upon the discipline earned through centuries of rigorous training to keep from shouting out loud with elation.

The red rim of the sun was just breaking above the surface of the water as Teldin and Vallus walked onto the deck, and the swan ship was alive with a bustle of activity as the elves prepared for departure.

"As soon as you give the order, we can take flight. The crew has been instructed to set course directly for Lionheart," Vallus explained helpfully. Teldin stopped abruptly, and the elf raised his hands in a mildly defensive gesture. "I thought the matter had been decided," Vallus said.

"Not as far as I'm concerned," Teldin replied. His sudden ire melted under the elf's mild, earnest gaze, and he raked a hand through his hair and swallowed his frustration. Vallus Leafbower obviously was doing all he could to help, and from the elven wizard's perspective Lionheart was the best way to go. The elf didn't have a clue why that idea might bother Teldin.

"Look, Vallus, I trust you about as much as I do anyone, but I'm not sure that walking into the elven stronghold would be a wise move. Too many people want this cloak too badly. If some group of elves in Lionheart decided to take it, there isn't much I could do to stop them."

"I see," Vallus said slowly. Teldin noticed that the elf did not bother to contradict him. "I take it you have an alternate plan?"

"Well, almost," Teldin said with a wry smile. Out of the corner of his eye he saw Gaston Willowmere, the ship's first mate. He quickly flipped aside his cloak so that the captain's insignia was prominently displayed, then he caught the first mate's arm as he rushed past.

Gaston did a double take at the sight of the emblem on a human's chest, but he quickly pulled himself up and snapped off a salute. "Aye, Captain?"

"Take off as scheduled and follow the course you were given until you hear from me otherwise," Teldin said crisply. "Oh, and one more thing," he added as the elf started to turn away. "Find Hectate Kir and send him to the bridge immediately."

The first mate saluted again and hurried off to tend to his orders. A high, piping signal floated out over the deck, and everywhere the crew members braced for takeoff. The swan ship lifted smoothly out of the Evermeet harbor and rose into the morning sky.

Vallus arched a silver eyebrow. In response to the silent inquiry, Teldin said sternly, "If I'm to be the captain of this ship, there's one thing you're going to have to do."

"Oh?" the elf replied. His angular face showed a touch of apprehension.

Teldin's scowl collapsed into a teasing grin. "You're going to have to show me where the bridge *is*," he said.

* * * * *

Working quickly, K'tide's informant slipped his latest message into one of the tiny, specially designed boxes he'd been given. Since coming aboard the swan ship, he'd had second thoughts about his assignment and he'd been less than faithful about sending them regularly, but this one he sent the moment the swan ship broke free of Toril's atmosphere. He spoke the words that activated the magical tracking device, then tossed the box into a refuse barrel.

His lowly work assignment brought him hours of tedium, but it also gave him access to the ship's cargo doors. He jettisoned the barrel and two others and watched them tumble out into wildspace. Reaching into a pocket, he took out a small, specialized looking glass and squinted out at the barrels. Sure enough, one of them gave off a pulsing, greenish light that would easily be detected by the crew of the shrike ship that shadowed Teldin Moore. The thought of those proud beings sorting through the elves' garbage for their message brought a tight smile to the informant's lips. Not taking any particular precaution—no one who saw him perform this "duty" would spare him a second glance—he turned and made his way to his quarters.

Some time later, the barrel was picked up by the shrike ship. The message brought excitement to them all, even the usually peevish wizard. Immediately he took out his scrying crystal to send messages to K'tide and to the Clan Kir members stationed on Garden. The moment they had so long awaited was at hand.

The swan ship was headed for Lionheart!

* * * * *

A barrage of firepower—a final gift from the retreating elven forces—shook the massive frame of the ogre dinotherium. The ship-to-ship battle was over, but the crew of the *Elfsbane* had taken a severe beating. In the hold of the ship, a makeshift infirmary had been set up to tend the scores of wounded. The scro warriors endured their injuries with stoic pride, but the less disciplined goblins filled the air with a cacophony of groans and inarticulate oaths. Worse still were the kobolds; a pack of the tiny goblinoid creatures huddled together in whining, yapping misery.

At a safe distance, K'tide followed Grimnosh on his rounds of the troops. The scro general was livid over the loss of so many of his best fighters, and his veneer of culture could be stretched only so thin. K'tide doubted that Grimnosh would actually lose his temper, but the scro had a way of calmly issuing the most appalling orders when riled. Adding to the spy master's discomfort was the chill; the hold was deliberately kept cold to slow the flow of the goblinkin blood. K'tide's insectlike exoskeleton provided him little protection from the cold, and he drew his brown cloak closer as he moved stiffly after the scro general.

The sound of chanting wove through the cries of the wounded. One of the scro war priests was tending to a badly wounded half-orc, a female whose heavy leather armor—and a good deal of her brownish hide—had been split from gut to gizzard by an elven sword. Grimnosh stalked over to the priest and dropped a huge white paw on his shoulder. The priest stopped in midchant.

"Perhaps you might direct your efforts more judiciously,

good father," the scro suggested, voicing the title with heavy irony. Grimnosh gestured pointedly to the two scro lying on nearby pallets. "Heal one of those."

"But which?" stammered the unnerved priest.

Grimnosh's brows rose, and his expression plainly inquired why it was necessary for him to tend to such matters himself. Nevertheless he crossed the distance to the wounded scro and stooped over their pallets. He took up and examined their *toregkhs* in turn, then rose to his feet. "This one," he said casually, pointing to one of the scro.

The general took K'tide's arm and drew him to the side of the room. "They'll be back," he said grimly. "We must have new troops. Do whatever you must, but I want the Armistice fleet."

"Surely the scro rulers could reassign a few squadrons to your command on a temporary basis," K'tide prevaricated. His people had been making regular shipments, and, in truth, the goblinkin were almost battle-ready, but K'tide had no intention of releasing the new troops. The alliance with Grimnosh was a convenient ploy, no more. In his opinion, this second Unhuman War was a marvelous thing. With the elves and goblinoids decimated, there would be more room in wildspace for his own kind.

"Just order up a few squadrons, eh?" Grimnosh glared at the spy master. "If the scro had troops to spare, do you think I'd take the risks involved with the Armistice plan?" the general asked with a touch of exasperation.

"But with a fresh supply of troops so near at hand, surely the scro command could make an exception for you," K'tide pointed out.

Grimnosh's tiny pause was telling.

"Your superiors do not know about the Armistice project," K'tide stated as objectively as he could. To reveal a trace of the elation he felt over this news would be courting certain death. Still, he could not resist adding, "I take it they would not approve?"

"The scro command approves of success," the general said. He spun and walked away, absently resuming his rounds of the infirmary. "Once I get the Armistice troops, I'll have the strength needed to launch an attack on the elven communities of Radole. Once we control this crystal sphere, we will go on to Realmspace. I must have those troops," he reiterated.

"But we must destroy Lionheart first," K'tide said firmly as he hurried to keep up with the scro.

"Must we? Perhaps you'd be so kind as to explain why," Grimnosh said with dangerous calm. He stopped to examine a black-hided scro warrior who, despite a number of grievous wounds, had propped himself against a wall in a ramrod straight pose. Even so, the scro's eyes were glazed and his breathing shallow. It was apparent to K'tide that the warrior would die if not tended soon. Grimnosh reached for the scro's *toregkh*. There were but five trophy teeth, and all but one were human or dwarven. The general dropped the trophy with a derisive sniff, then scanned the room.

"Oh, Nimick," he called out, spotting his gray-green adjutant in the doorway. "Be a good fellow and put this soldier down."

Nimick hurried to his general's side and carried out the order by running a single claw across the wounded scro's throat. He watched with detached pleasure as the black scro gurgled and fell heavily to the floor, then he turned to his general and saluted. "Will there be anything else, sir?" he asked, raising his voice over the yapping, howling anguish of the nearby kobolds.

"Actually, yes," Grimnosh said dryly. "You might jettison the kobolds. They're becoming rather tiresome."

Lacking Grimnosh's macabre sense of humor, the green scro took the comment at face value and gave a sneer of agreement. "Load them into the catapult, sir? The last of the elven ships might still be within range. Might as well get some use out of the miserable ankle-biters."

Grimnosh looked pleasantly surprised. "What a clever notion. You do that." His assistant saluted again and began to herd the unfortunate creatures above deck. K'tide watched this with a mixture of apprehension and relief. Having vented his ire, perhaps Grimnosh now would be receptive to K'tide's plans. Perhaps.

"You were about to explain your last impertinent comment, I believe," Grimnosh prompted.

K'tide did not consider the scro's choice of words to be a good sign. "The goblin navy needs additional time for training—battle training," he stressed. "Small raids, minor battles. If you send green troops against current elven strength, the goblins will be decimated and *all* the risks of the Armistice project will be for nothing."

Grimnosh did not miss the implied reference to scro command, and his colorless eyes narrowed dangerously.

"And think of this: What success would be more highly esteemed than the destruction of Lionheart?" K'tide hastily added.

The scro general regarded K'tide with cold, calculating eyes. "Let's say we do attack Lionheart. How do you propose to find the base, much less penetrate it?"

"We will send the weapon in aboard an elven vessel, an oddly appropriate one. The captain is a direct descendant of Aldyn Leafbower, the elf whose vile bargain condemned the Armistice goblins to an icy hell."

The albino chuckled, a harsh canine growl of genuine amusement. "Why, K'tide, you have the soul of a poet. Quite a valuable thing in a spy master, I must say. You must tell me how you plan to accomplish this miracle of poetic justice."

"We have placed an informant on board the ship."

"An elf? Is that so?" The scro's amusement deepened, but his eyes also betrayed his fascination with the concept.

K'tide shifted his shoulders, not committing either way. "The swan ship is being followed by some of my allies. The informant passes information on to them, who, in turn, relay it to me. According to my latest report, the ship is bound for Lionheart. They will put down on Garden for supplies, and we will load the weapon on board at that time. It has already been dispatched and is being held for the swan ship's arrival. Our informant is placed highly enough to get the weapon smuggled aboard and then see it released once the swan ship reaches Lionheart."

Grimnosh was silent for a long moment. "A risky proposal, I would think. The weapon could destroy the swan ship long before it reaches the elven base."

"Believe me, we have taken precautions. The ship will be amply protected."

Something in the spy master's fervent response caught Grimnosh's attention. "What is so special about this ship?"

Teldin Moore, K'tide answered silently. He hesitated, weighing the benefits of telling Grimnosh against the risks. "There is a human aboard who possesses an artifact of great power."

Like many warriors, the scro general held magic in low esteem. "If you wish me to die of suspense, you'll have to do better than this," Grimnosh said with dry sarcasm.

"The human's name is Teldin Moore, and he possesses the Cloak of the First Pilot. Whoever wears the cloak can control the great ship *Spelljammer*," K'tide said bluntly.

The spy master's response shocked Grimnosh into silence. Then his lupine face twisted into an expression of savage rage. "Why haven't you told me this before?"

"I just recently learned of it," K'tide lied smoothly.

With visible effort, Grimnosh pulled control over his face as if it were a mask. "You have no designs on this cloak yourself, I suppose," he asked in an arch tone.

"Hardly." K'tide punctuated his denial with a dry, brittle chuckle. "My people survive by weighing odds and choosing battles carefully—"

"Your people survive by getting others to fight their battles," Grimnosh pointed out.

"Be that as it may, the fact is that whoever takes the cloak faces a wide variety of powerful enemies. That is not our way."

"Indeed," Grimnosh agreed. "Who might these foes be?"

"The neogi, the mind flayers of Falx, the arcane, a band of pirates sponsored, I believe, by the reigar, and especially the elves. The Imperial Fleet is attempting to recruit the human to the elven side. Any attempt on the cloak at this point would draw too much attention to you and your other activities."

"I see your point," Grimnosh acknowledged thoughtfully. "If I were to acquire the cloak from this Teldin Moore now, I also would inherit all his enemies."

"Precisely. The elves must be dealt with first. As for the cloak, our informant is prepared to rescue Teldin Moore from Lionheart and bring him here. Once the Imperial Fleet is in disarray and the cloak is in your hands, you will have both the means and the opportunity to establish a true base of power."

Grimnosh thought over all the spy master had said. He had heard scuttlebutt about this cloak and about General Vorr and Fleet Admiral Halker's incompetent attempts to retrieve it. Grimnosh had the scro contempt for failure, though he expected little more from Vorr, an orc-ogre mongrel. He could do better himself, of that he had no doubt.

The legendary *Spelljammer*, under his command, trailed by the Armistice goblin fleet. Grimnosh permitted himself a smile. There would be no trouble with the scro command. As captain of the *Spelljammer* and the scro responsible for the destruction of Lionheart, he would *be* the scro command. The plan had a rightness that he could not deny. Grimnosh nodded slowly.

"Very well, K'tide," he said. "It will be as you say."

Chapter Ten

• • •

Toril was a blue-and-white spot in wildspace by the time Teldin and Vallus had finished filling Hectate in on the details of the elven meeting, including the newly discovered power of the medallion. "Vallus thinks we should take the amulet to Lionheart," Teldin concluded, "on the theory that once the elven experts there tell me what I'm seeing, we'll know where to find the *Spelljammer*."

A strange expression crossed Hectate's face, and one hand absently drifted up to the red-brown tuft at the crown of his head. "I suppose you'll be wanting me to leave the ship then, sir," he said quietly as he reflexively flattened his cowlick.

Teldin blinked. "No. Why would you even ask?"

"The location of Lionheart is a closely guarded secret," Vallus explained. "Those of other races are not admitted. In your case, obviously, the Imperial Fleet will make an exception, but I'm afraid the other *n'tel quess* would have to leave the ship."

"*N'tel quess?*" Teldin echoed with a touch of anger. His cloak did not translate the elven phrase for him, but he didn't care for the sound of it.

"Anyone who is not elven," Hectate supplied hastily. Teldin did not miss the warning glance the half-elf shot at Vallus, and he made a mental note to pursue the matter with Hectate at some later time. Teldin took the medallion from his bag and laid it down on the navigation table.

"We're not going to Lionheart, Hectate. I'm going to use this again, and I want *you* to tell me what I'm seeing."

Understanding, then the excitement of a professional challenge, dawned in the half-elven navigator's eyes. Teldin sat down in the captain's chair and took the medallion in his hands, and Hectate took a place nearby at a table spread with star charts.

Vallus stepped back, leaned against the wall, and watched as Teldin dropped into deep concentration, much more quickly this time that he had in the moon elf palace. Before Vallus could draw three breaths, the cloak began to glow with the eery molten bronze hue that signaled its connection to the magic medallion. The human's expression became remote as his vision focused on a place far from the ship's bridge.

Although the elven wizard had witnessed the process just the day before, he was shaken by Teldin Moore's transformation. Vallus had seen that degree of focus and concentration many times, but only on the faces of highly skilled wizards or priest. What the untrained human had achieved amazed him, and it steadied his faith in the stand he had taken against the grand admiral.

"What do you see?" Vallus asked softly.

For a long moment Teldin did not answer, then the molten bronze glow faded from his cloak, and his face settled into a mask of pure frustration. "A purple cloud, a river of rainbow colors. I've never seen the phlogiston in quite that way."

"The *Spelljammer*'s in the phlogiston? It could be anywhere," Vallus said in dismay.

Hectate took a step forward, "Can you describe what you saw the first time?"

Under Hectate's detailed prompting, Teldin recalled some of the details of his first vision. Hectate identified them as constellations around Toril.

"So the *Spelljammer* was in Realmspace." Teldin felt both excited and frustrated by this news. "It must move incredibly fast to have already left the crystal sphere."

"So where do we go now, sir?"

Teldin shrugged. "Set the shortest possible course for the edge of Realmspace's crystal sphere. Maybe once we're out in the phlogiston, I can get a better idea where the ship is bound."

"Are we going to stop on Garden first?" Hectate asked.

"That won't be necessary," Vallus broke in. "We obtained all the supplies we'll need from the Evermeet elves."

Hectate nodded and turned to the navigator's table. Picking up a triangular tool, the half-elf bent over a star chart and quickly became lost in the task he loved. Teldin left the bridge behind to acquaint himself with his new command.

The first two days passed quickly. On the whole Teldin was satisfied with the way things aboard the swan ship were progressing, though he still noted a marked coolness in the bridge. The first mate, in particular, made little effort to hide his displeasure over Hectate's promotion. The half-elven navigator handled the slights with more grace than Teldin thought he himself could manage under similar circumstances.

On the third day of travel, Teldin and Hectate ended a watch together and headed toward the mess for eveningfeast. They nearly bumped into the exiting dracons. Chirp and Trivit exchanged guilty, furtive glances and looked at the dinner tray in Chirp's mottled green hands.

"Er, lovely night, wouldn't you say, sir?" fluted Trivit nervously. He stepped forward, deliberately blocking Chirp from view. Chirp looked frantically around for a place to put his tray. Seeing none, he reached around and placed it on his own broad green back.

"Lovely night," Teldin agreed, struggling to keep a straight face. "Carry on with whatever you're doing."

Trivit snapped off a salute and scuttled off down the corridor. Chirp fell in behind, in his haste forgetting about the dinner tray balanced on his back. Both creatures took on a nonchalant, four-footed swagger as they headed for their cabin.

"What do you suppose they're up to?" wondered Teldin.

Hectate shrugged. "Maybe we could look into it after we've eaten," he hinted delicately.

Teldin suppressed a smile. After they got their meal, he noticed that Om was sitting alone, and they went over to her table. Her dinner sat untouched and she was absently toying with a gnome-sized wrench. "May we join you?" Teldin asked.

"Why not?" she responded glumly.

"Problems?" Hectate asked sympathetically as he dropped into a chair.

The gnome's only response was a morose grunt. A quick glance at the neighboring table revealed what was bothering the tiny technician. Rozloom was sprawled on a couple of chairs, regaling three elven women with a wild tale of adventure that, though obviously fabricated, nonetheless was entertaining. Teldin noticed that the aperusa had preened himself to an almost blinding degree. His blue satin pantaloons were embroidered with stars and tucked into boots that had been polished to a mirrorlike finish. He wore a shirt of flowing red silk with voluminous sleeves and a leather vest upon which was tooled several complicated abstract designs. Intrigued, Teldin squinted at one of the designs. The picture was a clever illusion that under his scrutiny focused into a scene of campfire revelry. The explicit gypsy "art" brought sudden heat to Teldin's face. As he hastily averted his eyes, he caught a whiff of the faint, spicy odor that wafted from the small silk sachet suspended around the aperusa's neck. The scent reminded Teldin of the similar pendant worn by the gypsy seductress in the tavern back on Garden, and he asked about it.

"Love potion," Om grunted.

"What gnomes are to machinery, aperusa are to herb lore," Hectate elaborated. "They have potions for everything. This is the first time I've seen Rozloom resort to a potion, though."

"For whose benefit, I wonder?" Teldin mused.

Om's brown eyes narrowed dangerously. "I don't know . . . yet," she intoned. As she spoke, she smacked her palm with the wrench in an unconscious, ominous rhythm.

Teldin and Hectate exchanged a quick glance of guilty amusement. Although the gnome obviously was disconsolate over Rozloom, it was difficult to take her infatuation seriously. Back on Krynn, Teldin once had owned a bantam rooster that became attached to the plow horse, following it around and even roosting on the horse's back. To his mind, anything between the tiny, serious Om and the flamboyant gypsy was almost as improbable. When several attempts to engage the taciturn gnome in conversation failed, Teldin and Hectate finished their meal as quickly as decently possible and left Om to enjoy her misery alone.

That night Teldin's sleep was restless and broken, haunted by a recurring dream. When he finally rose, he retained only fragmented images and an impression of the dream. He remembered a questing voice, powerful but wounded, and he sensed a web of magic being cast, seeking all those who might answer. A few phrases, too, stuck in his mind: "Winged captain resistant . . . followed her, lost her. Another captain on the ribbon, might be ready . . . Must find!"

Deeply troubled, Teldin went in search of Hectate. The half-elf was already on the bridge, and he listened intently to Teldin's story. He eagerly agreed when Teldin suggested they try the medallion again. As Teldin dropped into concentration, Vallus came quietly into the bridge, drawn by the powerful magic and the bronze glow.

"Wildspace," Teldin murmured, and his voice seemed to come to them through time and distance. "Stars, but no constellations that I know."

"Can you describe what you see?" Hectate spoke softly, so as not to disturb the Cloakmaster's concentration. "Any clusters? Formations? Worlds?"

Teldin nodded to acknowledge the question, and he tilted his head back slightly as if going deeper into himself. "There's a distant cluster, very small, that looks a little like an hourglass," he said finally.

Hectate looked up abruptly, and apprehension was keenly etched on his face. "Are the stars all white, or do any of them show color?"

Teldin squinted at something only he could see. "Umm, yes. Near the top, one of the stars has a faint yellow tinge."

"Look at the center star, right where the top and bottom of the hourglass join," Hectate directed. "Any pink?"

"A little," Teldin agreed. His brow furrowed suddenly. "The formation's gone now. The ship must be turning, because the backdrop of stars is moving. It's moving incredibly fast," he repeated in an awed whisper.

"If I'm right, you should be able to see a sphere soon," Hectate said. "It'll be very faint, so look carefully."

"What are you looking for?" Vallus asked quietly. Hectate just shook his head and held up a hand for silence.

"I think I do see a world," Teldin said in that odd, detached voice. "It looks like a strange-colored smudge, though."

"Reddish gray?" prompted Hectate. His shoulders were hunched and his wiry frame knotted with visible tension. Feeling a little unnerved by the half-elf's reaction, Vallus drifted closer.

Teldin nodded. "Yes. That's right."

"What *is* it?" Vallus hissed in Hectate's ear.

"Radole," Hectate said quietly, though his tension did not noticeably abate. "The world he sees is called Radole.

Merciful Ptah," he swore in a harsh whisper. "That means that the *Spelljammer* is in Winterspace."

"Winterspace," Vallus echoed dully. With dread he remembered the armada ghost ship. Was it possible that the *Spelljammer* somehow had destroyed the crew of the elven battleship? If so, what kind of being controlled the ship? If somehow the scro had gotten control of the most powerful ship in the void, it could mean the end of the elven nation. "Are you sure it's Winterspace?"

"I'm afraid so," Hectate replied. The horror on his face echoed Vallus's feelings with uncanny precision. Suddenly the intensity of the half-elf's reaction worried the elven mage.

"You know elven history, I see," Vallus said softly.

Hectate averted his eyes. "My ancestors had a part in it," he replied.

Vallus nodded. It was possible that Hectate's elven forebears had fought in the first goblin wars. Still, the half-elf's response was a little too immediate and too extreme to be based on family history. Before Vallus could explore the matter, the cloak's glow faded and Teldin shook himself as if to dispel the effects of the magic.

"Where is this Winterspace? How long to get there?" Teldin asked, his blue eyes alight with excitement.

The half-elf considered. "There are rivers in the phlogiston between Realmspace and Radole's crystal sphere, small rivers that are unusually fast but very hard to find. If you can catch them, a swan ship should be able to make landfall in about forty-five days," Hectate calculated. He turned to Vallus and shrugged apologetically. "Of course, that's just an educated guess. Not knowing whether you've made any changes to the ship's basic design, I can't say for sure what the *Trumpeter* could do."

"That's going to change right now," Teldin decreed. "Hectate, you've just been promoted to chief navigator. I want you to set a direct course for Radole. Vallus will see that you get whatever information you need about the swan ship."

Teldin Moore turned to the elven wizard, and a cocky smile lit his weary face, making it look almost boyish. "Well, Vallus, I hope you don't mind taking back your insignia soon. It looks as though I'm going to be getting my own ship after all."

* * * * *

The *Trumpeter* had traveled the phlogiston rivers for several days before Teldin discovered the dracons' secret. He was rounding a corner in the lower deck when he bumped into a solid female frame. Instinctively he caught the woman's elbows to steady her and began to murmur an apology—

And stopped dead.

The woman was taller than any other female on board, slender but hard with muscle. Her hair was a sea of wavy black satin, and her pale, blue-tinted skin reminded him of cream and summer skies. Most arresting were her eyes, one of which was a typically elven shade of silver, the other an unusual shade of amber so pale it was almost gold. Her leather garments were of a quaint cut Teldin had never seen, and ancient weapons were tucked into her belt, boots, and shoulder strap.

Teldin stared at the moon elven woman for a long, startled moment. He'd never seen her on board, so he assumed she had boarded at Evermeet. Why hadn't Vallus mentioned a passenger?

His mind had barely formed the thought when his vision shifted and swam. Suddenly he saw superimposed over her lovely face a reptilian visage that looked like a nightmare rendition of Trivit's. As suddenly as it had come, the moment was gone and a moon elf stood before him, regarding him with a quizzical smile. When he did not speak, she lifted her shoulders in a delicate shrug and pulled away, gliding down the hall toward the dracons' cabin.

"A beauty, eh, Captain?" rumbled a voice next to Teldin's ear.

He whirled to face Rozloom, feeling a little sheepish about being surprised. He'd forgotten how silently the aperusa could move. "Do you know her?" he asked, taking note of the gypsy's avid interest.

"Not yet," Rozloom said, and his tone was both a vow and an innuendo.

"Who is she, and why haven't I seen her around the ship?" he wondered aloud.

"The woman is called Raven Stormwalker. Beautiful she is, but not friendly. And what good is beauty locked away?" Rozloom asked rhetorically, nodding toward the converted storeroom that served as the dracons' cabin.

"So you do know a little about her," Teldin prompted.

"Only what I could make the dracons say in exchange for her food," the aperusa said. "She is a warrior—a sell-sword, as you say—who wishes passage to Radole. How long before we are there, Captain?" Rozloom asked with an abrupt change of mood.

"What? Oh. About forty days."

"Hmmm." Rozloom fingered the sachet-potion as if considering his chances. "Is maybe too little time," he mused.

So that was the way the wind blew, Teldin thought. "I take it the lady is immune to your charm?" he asked.

The gypsy turned serious black eyes toward Teldin. "Who would have thought it possible?" he marveled.

"Well, let's go meet our new passenger," Teldin decreed, turning away before he insulted the gypsy by smirking in his woebegone face. Together they approached the dracons' door and the mysterious moon elf. Teldin's knock was answered by a long, heavy silence. He pounded again, and finally Trivit asked who was there.

"Your *kaba*," Teldin said firmly. Rozloom rolled his eyes at the title but for once did not comment. Behind the door they could hear a nervous, whispered consultation. When Trivit finally opened the door a crack, Teldin pushed through and came into the cabin.

The dracons hung back, Trivit nibbling his claws and Chirp wringing his hands in a picture of prissy distress. The elven woman stepped forward to greet Teldin, however, and her odd eyes held his in a steady, compelling gaze.

"Well met, Captain Moore. I understand that I have you to thank for my passage," she said. Teldin's surprise must have shown, for she fell back a step and gestured toward the distraught dracons. "Is that not so, Captain? Chirp and Trivit assured me that they spoke for you when they invited me aboard."

Teldin leveled a glare at Trivit. The dracon bit his lip, and his eyes darted between the captain and the moon elf. "Well?" Teldin prompted. Raven smiled sweetly at the dracons.

"Yes!" blurted Trivit. "Yes, indeed, that's the utter and absolute truth. It certainly is." His words burst out with the force of a small explosion.

The captain bit the inside of his cheek to keep from laughing aloud at the dracon's fervent fib. "Perhaps you believed you could speak for me on this matter, Trivit, but you should have checked first before bringing on a passenger," he chided gently. "Apart from such issues as adequate air and provisions, the elves have a right to know who's on their ship." The miserable dracon nodded and hung his head.

"What do you plan to do with me, Captain?"

Raven's voice was low, smoky, and slightly husky, and it brought vividly to Teldin's mind both the flavor and the wallop of sagecoarse liquor. Rozloom seemed to have been similarly affected, for his sudden leer assigned her innocent question any number of salacious responses.

"You're not to blame for the dracon's misunderstanding," Teldin said, not too sure that it was an accurate assessment of the situation.

"That's right!" Trivit shrieked in nervous agreement.

"All the same, I would like to know more about you. Please report to the bridge at three bells," he said to the elf, naming a time about an hour away. "You will meet with the ship's officers, and a decision will be made then. If you are to stay aboard the *Trumpeter*, duties will be assigned to you."

"As you wish," she agreed.

"We'll be there promptly, sir," Trivit vowed. "Indeed we shall."

"Three bells it is," put in Chirp.

Raven caught Teldin's eye, and his sudden quandary brought a glint of humor to her gold and silver eyes. She turned to the dracons and placed a hand on the shoulder of each. "Thank you for your kind offer, Little Ones, but I've created enough trouble for you. I will talk to the officers alone."

"As you wish, Celestial One," the dracons murmured in unison. They bowed deeply to the elven woman, and Teldin's brow furrowed in sudden concern. He had become accustomed to the dracon's formality and their obsession with rank and title, but there was something different in their treatment of Raven Stormwalker, something that disturbed him.

Reverence. That's what it is, he realized suddenly. Chirp and Trivit treated the elf as if she were a demigod. Deeply puzzled, he nodded a farewell and turned to go. Rozloom elected to stay, and for the first time Teldin noticed the bottle of pilfered elven spirits tucked under the aperusa's arm. Somehow, Teldin doubted the offering would do Rozloom much good. The thought gave him a quick stab of satisfaction that he didn't want to examine too closely.

Compelling and beautiful though she might be, the unexpected passenger was deeply disturbing. Why had she virtually hidden away since they had left Evermeet? What about her had the dracons in thrall? And what about the other face he had seen superimposed over her beautiful elven features; what could such a thing mean? Rozloom had said she'd requested passage to Radole, but . . .

Radole.

The thought took form suddenly, exploding in his brain and immediately settling in his gut in a hard knot. As Teldin hurried down the corridor, he damned himself for a fool for not picking up on that sooner. Certainly the moon elf had boarded before the new destination was chosen, which meant that she probably had expected to be taken to Lionheart. It looked as if Raven Stormwalker was some sort of spy. Vallus would have to know.

Teldin hurriedly made his way to the bridge in search of Vallus. The elf was there, writing in the log required by the Imperial Fleet. All other duties pertaining to the ship's captain had been relegated to Teldin, but Vallus faithfully kept the log and no one else was permitted access to it. When he wasn't writing in it, the elf kept the log in a locked cabinet in his own cabin.

Vallus looked up when the agitated human burst into the bridge, and his pale green eyes widened. "Is there a problem?" he asked, immediately laying down his quill and rising from his chair.

Teldin raked a hand through his hair. "Maybe. Do you know anything about someone called Raven Stormwalker?"

"Yes, of course," Vallus replied with a puzzled smile.

Relief flooded Teldin. If Vallus knew her, she wasn't likely to be a spy. "Then I suppose you know she's on board?"

The elf stared at him blankly. "That's impossible."

"No, I just spoke with her."

"Describe her," Vallus demanded. As Teldin did so, horror and denial fought for space on the elf's countenance. He sank back down into his chair. "Where is she now?" he asked in a dull whisper.

"On her way to the bridge," Teldin said, deeply puzzled by the elf's reaction. His surprise deepened when Vallus abruptly rose jerking to his feet like a puppet on a tangled string. In the doorway stood Raven Stormwalker, looking somehow mythic with her ancient weapons and quaint garments. The elven wizard backpedaled, rapidly putting as much distance between him and the moon elf as possible.

Teldin had never seen the sedate elven wizard so nonplussed, and for some perverse reason he found it vastly amusing. He covered his mouth with one hand and coughed delicately to keep from laughing aloud at the expression of horrified recognition on Vallus's face. Whatever dealings Vallus had had in the past with Raven Stormwalker had not ended well, apparently. Since Teldin couldn't see Vallus skipping out on a debt, he imagined that the moon elf was a former lover.

"She's already here, Vallus, so you might as well stay," Teldin observed dryly.

The elf continued to back away until he had reached the far side of the bridge. "You say your name is Raven Stormwalker," Vallus said tersely, his words dispelling Teldin's entertaining notion.

"And with good reason," Raven replied with a smile.

"When did you come aboard?"

"On Evermeet," she asserted as she came to stand at Teldin's side, "at the invitation of your dracons."

"Why?"

She looked long and deeply into Vallus's eyes before replying. "I have lived for centuries on one world. It occurred to me that I would like to see something of other worlds, to know a little about many places."

"Sounds a lot like your philosophy, Vallus," Teldin observed.

The elven wizard turned strangely pale. "You have never traveled the stars, then?"

"Did I imply that?" Raven asked innocently. "I did not intend to."

"I've been told you requested passage to Radole," Teldin interrupted, coming back to the question that most disturbed him. "Is that true?"

"Not especially," she said. "I wanted an adventure, and I didn't particularly care about the destination. I was happy enough to learn that the swan ship was bound for Radole. There's an elven settlement there that might have use for a hired sword." She patted the strap of the shoulder harness that held her broadsword.

"Radole is a peaceful place," Vallus said coldly. "Do you have any reason to believe it might soon be otherwise?"

The moon elf shrugged. "Even the most sedate world has an occasional tavern battle."

"But you are accustomed to much larger conflicts," Vallus said softly.

Again Raven held the elven wizard's gaze for a long moment, then she cast a roguish glance around the bridge. "I'm accustomed to larger *everything*," she rejoined gaily. "No offense, but this ship is not as roomy as some."

"Then you *have* traveled the stars."

"Oh, we're singing that tune again, are we?" the moon elf said with acerbic sweetness. She cast Teldin a sidelong glance through half-lidded eyes. "Persistent fellow, isn't he?" she asked out of one side of her mouth.

Teldin grinned, and felt himself warming to the elven woman despite his lingering reservations. "You might say that," he said, folding his arms and preparing to enjoy the sparring match.

"I would appreciate an answer," Vallus said.

"I'm sure you would," she said in the manner of one humoring a small and unreasonable child. "Very well then, I have traveled the stars before."

The elven wizard looked away, deeply shaken. After a moment's silence he rose abruptly. "I have duties elsewhere. If you'll excuse me, Captain?" He fled from the bridge without waiting for Teldin's response.

"Hmm. Persistent *and* jittery," Raven observed wryly. "Tell me, is he always like this?"

"Well, no . . . " Teldin paused, feeling he ought to apologize for the elven wizard.

"Never mind," Raven said as if she discerned Teldin's intent. She took his arm and flashed him a comrade's grin. "Is there a spot anywhere on this ship where I can get a mug of ale?"

Suddenly Teldin felt a little dry himself. "The mess, I think. I'm sure you could charm Rozloom out of a couple of mugs."

A flicker of distaste crossed the elf's beautiful face. "Charm the aperusa?" She dropped Teldin's arm and shuddered delicately. "I'd need more than a couple of mugs before I'd consider that."

Her sardonic tone sent Teldin into a burst of surprised laughter. The elf's beauty was so delicate that her sharp-edged wit came as all the more unexpected. What appealed most to him was her straightforward manner. In that she reminded him very much of Aelfred Silverhorn.

"Come on," he said suddenly. "I've requisitioned a bottle of sagecoarse, if you'd like to come by my cabin for a drink. It's an acquired taste, I'm afraid," he added somewhat lamely, faltering a little under Raven's steady, amused gaze.

"Sagecoarse! I've already acquired *that* taste." A mischievous glint lit the elf's unusual eyes, and she reclaimed Teldin's arm. "Lead on, Captain."

Chapter Eleven

● ● ●

At first the pounding seemed to be part of the dream. Teldin was back on Krynn, a mule skinner in the War of the Lance, trudging toward yet another battle and choking on the dust kicked up by the league of soldiers in front of him. He awoke slowly, painfully, and his first waking observation was that his mouth felt as dry as that Krynnish road. Dimly he recalled a possible explanation for his condition. He groped for the bottle of sagecoarse—which had been full the night before—and upended it. A single, smoky drop fell to the floor. Strange. He didn't remember drinking that much. Raven had matched his every drink with at least two.

The pounding continued, more insistent. Before Teldin could respond, the door of his cabin flew open so hard it slammed against the cabin wall. Teldin winced and clutched at his temples, glaring weakly at Vallus Leafbower.

"Raven Stormwalker must leave the swan ship immediately," Vallus said without preamble.

Teldin blinked stupidly, trying to make some sense out of the elf's pronouncement. As he did, he hefted the bottle in his hand, giving brief but serious consideration to flinging it at the invader. "All right, I'll play," he said wearily. "Why does she have to leave the ship?"

Clearly agitated, Vallus raked both hands through his silvery hair. "This is not a matter for jests. You have no idea what she is. She's dangerous, and if she remains on board, she could destroy us all."

A memory flickered through Teldin's numbed brain, an image of the scaly, night-black head he had seen reflected in the elven woman's face. "What is she?" he asked cautiously.

Being an elf, Vallus did not answer the question directly. He began to pace distractedly, and the expression on his face made it clear that he was weighing his next words carefully. Watching the wizard made Teldin dizzy, so he closed his eyes and sank back on his cot. With a sigh of resignation he waited for the latest elven saga to unfold.

"There is a legend from Toril, from a time when humankind was still young, its cities and civilizations still centuries in the future. A certain magical land, a group of living islands, was besieged by an alliance of evil dragons. These creatures attacked not only the elven, fairy, and animal populations, but the good dragons as well. Soon only a handful of the magical fairy dragons still drew breath, and even the powerful silver dragons seemed destined to follow them into extinction.

"Then an elven warrior, an adventurer named Raven Stormwalker, gathered an army from the far-flung elven kingdoms. She was a fierce fighter, a master of the bow and broadsword, and she had an uncanny ability to rally her troops. Under her banner came a score of races, including good and even neutral dragons. The evil dragons were driven from the island, but Raven Stormwalker was grievously wounded in the final battle. She was carried away by a gold dragon whom she had befriended, and from thence she passed into folklore. She was not seen again, and although there were rumors and legends, no one learned what her true end was."

Teldin massaged his aching temples. "A point," he pleaded.

"Raven Stormwalker was a moon elf of exceptional beauty," Vallus continued, as if he had not heard the man. "She wore her night-black hair in plaits that fell to her knees.

Her most striking feature, however, was her mismatched eyes. One was gold, the other silver. The good dragons considered this a favorable omen, I believe." Vallus paused to let the import of this sink in. "It goes against elven culture to name someone after a hero or a historic figure. I have every reason to believe there is only one Raven Stormwalker."

Teldin opened his eyes cautiously. "Wait a minute. You think your Raven Stormwalker and mine are one and the same?"

"Yours, is she?" Vallus asked sharply.

Teldin flapped one hand in a vague, helpless gesture. "A figure of speech, that's all."

"I hope so," Vallus mused, looking deeply disturbed. He gazed at Teldin with somber eyes. "There is more to my tale, and it gets more disturbing. Have you noticed that the dracons all but genuflect before her, and the dogged perseverance with which the aperusa pursues her? You should have seen her holding court in the mess at dawnfry. Almost without exception the crew is quite taken with her."

"So? Maybe they share your fascination with elven history," Teldin said with heavy sarcasm.

"No." Vallus shook his head emphatically. "The legend of Raven Stormwalker is well known to all dragon races—including dracons—but, except for Toril's elves, few who are not scholars or historians know it."

"Enough about this thrice-damned legend," Teldin snapped, getting unsteadily to his feet. "How can you tell a tale like this with a straight face? How old would she have to be? One thousand years? Two?"

"Four," the elf said softly.

Teldin's eyebrow flew up. "Do elves live that long?"

"Not normally, no."

"Then how—"

"*She's not an elf!*"

The wizard's shout shocked Teldin into silence. Vallus

composed himself quickly and continued in a softer tone. "Even four thousand years ago, some ships traveled the stars. I believe that Raven Stormwalker took to the stars and met some mishap. She became a *survivor*. Do you know that term?" When Teldin shook his head, Vallus continued. "A being who is set adrift in the phlogiston does not necessarily die. Some remain in a suspended state for centuries, floating in the rainbow rivers until rescued by some well-meaning fool."

"I've no idea how you came up with this," Teldin observed with honest astonishment.

"How, then, do you explain her appearance? Her antique weapons? Even her name?" Vallus asked sharply.

Teldin gave a helpless shrug. "Look, I'll admit that there's more to Raven Stormwalker than meets the eye, but this theory of yours is beyond belief. Even if—and that's a very big if—you're right about this, what's the harm of it?"

"A survivor changes," Vallus said quietly. "It becomes an altered demihuman driven by insatiable hungers. To make up for centuries of sensory deprivations, she will take over the minds of every member of the crew, draining us of thought and emotion and intellect like a vampire drains his victims of blood. Not to think, not to know," he concluded softly. "It would be the worst kind of living death."

Teldin laughed outright, earning a shocked look from the wizard. "I'm sorry, Vallus, but I just can't believe any of this."

"Oh no? It's happening already. Remember yesterday in the bridge? When we asked her why she took to the stars, she gave *my* answer. She took it from my mind."

"Actually, Vallus, it just might mean you two have something in common," Teldin suggested with false gravity. "Are you in the market for a Mistress Leafbower?"

The elf chose to ignore his gibe. "The aperusa's obsession with her is not normal, and the dracons haven't been themselves since she came on board. Those three have had the most contact with her. I fear for you, Teldin Moore," he said earnestly, "and I fear what would happen to the cloak if she were to hold you in thrall. Next to the power of a survivor, the effect of Rianna Wyvernsbane's charm spell would be nothing."

Teldin sucked in a sharp, surprised gasp. For a long moment he felt as if someone had gut-punched him. No matter how upset Vallus Leafbower might be, the reference to Rianna was unforgivably tactless. Teldin nodded pointedly toward the cabin door.

"I'll give your words all the consideration they deserve," he said coldly.

"Not enough," Vallus insisted. "Any delay could be disastrous. She must leave the ship at once."

Teldin cast a glance at the cabin porthole. The rainbow hues of the phlogiston tumbled by in lazy, random patterns. Out there was vast space and unimaginably brilliant color, but nothing else. "How do you proposed to accomplish that?" he asked. "We're several days from any port, and we haven't a small craft to spare."

"Jettison her," Vallus said firmly. "It's that or lose everything we are."

Teldin stared at the elven wizard, utterly horrified. He shook his head in disbelief, then, without a word, he yanked on his boots and strode from the cabin.

Left alone, Vallus sank wearily onto the cabin's only chair. If the human was coming under the sway of a survivor, Vallus would have to take the cloak after all. The elven wizard dropped his head in his hands, and for several long moments he mourned for Teldin Moore and for the loss of his own freedom.

*　*　*　*　*

Teldin came on deck just in time to see the damselfly touch down. A small crowd was gathering around the spindly, insectlike craft, and the elves had their weapons handy. The ever-curious dracons were there, of course. Teldin also spotted Estriss in the crowd and hurried over to him. He had not seen the illithid for several days; Estriss had kept to his cabin and had declined visitors.

"What's going on here?" he asked the illithid.

The damselfly appeared, suddenly, just outside of the swan ship's air envelope, Estriss informed him. Teldin noted that the illithid's mental voice seemed somehow edgy, agitated. *They raised the flag for ship in distress and then landed. It all happened so suddenly that there was no time to summon you or Vallus.*

Before Teldin could speak, the door of the craft swung open and a lone arcane, bent almost double to keep his blue domed head clear of the door, ducked through the too-small opening. The creature awkwardly descended the rope ladder to the deck. He unfolded himself to his full twelve-foot height, then spread his six-fingered blue hands to show he was without weapons. "I am called Npamta. We mean you no harm. We come seeking trade," the arcane said in the oddly expressionless voice Teldin had come to associate with the race.

A second figure exploded from the craft, disdaining the ladder and landing on deck beside the arcane with a clank of armor. Immediately elven steel flashed as the crew circled the newcomer, an exotically beautiful female warrior dressed in plate armor and intricate body paint. The woman glared defiantly at the elven warriors. "Where's the dragon?" she demanded.

A lakshu. Estriss's words formed in Teldin's mind, holding a touch of wonder and excitement. *You might meet a reigar after all. The snake bracelet on her forearm is a* shakti, *a sign that she is pledged in service to a reigar.*

The arcane edged away from the lakshu and shifted uncomfortably. "What my, er, associate means to say is that we're seeking an artifact of great power. The creature who wields it is not necessarily a dragon. It can take whatever form it wills," the arcane explained hastily. "Whatever the case, I will pay dearly for the artifact."

Teldin tensed, his hand going to the clasp of his cloak. He'd received such offers from the arcane before, but never one that began like this. The magical garment gave him the ability to change his face and form, and although he'd never tried so drastic a change as a dragon, he supposed it was possible. Perhaps one of its previous owners had done so. "The cloak is not for sale," he said firmly.

"Cloak? What cloak?" The arcane blinked, then stunned realization dawned on its blue face. "You are Teldin Moore, I take it? This is an unexpected turn of events. I have heard of your cloak."

Then the cloak is not the artifact you seek? Estriss asked sharply.

"Stick to the point," snapped the female warrior, not hearing the illithid's mental question. She strode forward through the circle of elven blades, batting them aside as easily as another woman might tear through a cobweb. Teldin motioned for the elves to hold peace. She came toe-to-toe with Teldin and glared down at him. "You in charge here?"

"I am," he said.

"Good. I want the dragon. That's all. All you have to do is point her out to me, and I'll do the rest," she said.

For some reason, Teldin remembered his first encounter with Raven Stormwalker and the fleeting image of a dragon he had seen on her face. Now that he thought about it, the perception had all the earmarks of the flashes the medallion brought him. Was it possible that Raven once had owned the cloak? Had she met the lakshu while in a dragon form? Perhaps before losing the cloak she had taken the form of Raven Stormwalker, and had somehow became stuck with it. It was an odd theory, but it was certainly easier to swallow than Vallus's explanation. Out of the corner of his eye he saw Trivit slip away from the crowd and hurry below deck, undoubtedly to warn Raven of the fearsome newcomer.

"Well?" snapped the warrior, impatient with the man's delay.

"I'm sorry," Teldin said, flashing the woman his best smile, "but dragons seem to be in short supply on this ship."

"It could have taken any form," added the arcane. "You will know the creature by the pendant it wears, an antique gold piece set with a dark sapphire. Have you seen such a piece?"

"I'm sorry, no," Teldin said firmly.

"But the artifact is on this ship, of that I'm sure," protested the arcane, its blue face wrinkling in an expression of petulance.

How do you know this? Estriss broke in, broadcasting his words this time so that all could hear them.

The lakshu sniffed. "When the dragon was a reigar, this obsequious blue bastard couldn't kiss her pendant often enough."

The meaning of the warrior's cryptic statement hit Teldin like an icy fist. The fal had spoken of other artifacts, objects with powers similar to those of his cloak. The arcane was a wizard—he'd have to be to propel the damselfly—so he could track such an object. Teldin cast a quick glance at Estriss, wondering whether the illithid had come to the same conclusion. Estriss's expressionless eyes gave no indication of his thoughts.

Teldin took control of the situation. "You raised the distress flag to gain access to the swan ship. Is this how you usually do business?"

"Our apologies," the arcane said, his voice utterly without regret. "A necessary deception. The ship is perfectly functional."

"Couldn't hurt to check her over, though," put in Om. The tiny gnome woman had edged her way through the growing crowd to Teldin's side, and she eyed the damselfly with a disturbing degree of fascination. Her ubiquitous wrench glinted in her brown hand.

Teldin placed a restraining hand on the gnome's shoulder, and turned to address the arcane. "I have no knowledge of the object you seek."

"Forget the pendant," growled the lakshu. She leaned in closer, her eyes glinting. "I want the dragon."

"You've made that quite clear," Teldin said coolly. "Now I'll be equally frank. You have boarded this ship under false pretenses, and by your battle garb and demeanor you threaten my crew. I want you off the swan ship immediately."

The lakshu glared, then shrugged. "Your funeral. Maybe you'd sing a different song if you knew that the last crew who sailed with the dragon is floating through Realmspace in bits and pieces."

"Viper!" protested the arcane. The lakshu shot him an unrepentant glare, then folded her muscled arms and defied Teldin with her eyes.

"Realmspace?" Teldin asked. Viper gave one curt nod. "It seems we may have a something to talk about after all," he said slowly. "I will gather the ship officers and meet you on the bridge in an hour. Since there are no dragons to slay on this ship, perhaps you would consider removing your battle armor before the meeting?" He gestured to the wary, armed elves. "It puts the crew off."

Viper considered the offer. She whipped off her helmet, to reveal rows of tightly braided, vibrantly green hair. The end of each tiny braid was decorated with colored beads, and the flamboyant style complemented the warrior's un-usual beauty. Her face was broad, defined by high, sharp cheekbones, fierce black eyes, and green brows that slanted sharply up at the corners.

"Armor or no, if I find the dragon, she's dead," Viper growled. Despite her harsh words, the lakshu's tone offered a concession.

"That sounds perfectly reasonable," Teldin agreed with a touch of sarcasm. Deal made, he pointed to the first mate. "Gaston, post a guard to protect our guests from passing dragons. The rest of you, return to your stations."

Teldin left the strange duo in the care of the elven warriors and went in search of Vallus Leafbower. As soon as most of the crew members had drifted away, Estriss glided silently up to the damselfly. Projecting his thoughts to the arcane and the lakshu, he said, *If you will trust me, I believe I can help you both obtain what you desire.*

*   *   *   *   *

The anger Teldin felt over Vallus's callous attitude toward Raven had not faded, but Teldin felt that the wizard should hear about the new developments immediately. If Teldin's suspicions were right, the quest for the *Spelljammer* could be more difficult than either of them had dreamed. Not only would Teldin have to battle and evade the many who would take the cloak from him, but he might also have to overcome other potential captains. If Raven Stormwalker was one of these, if she did have the pendant the arcane sought, why else would she be on board but to destroy him?

To Teldin's surprise, Vallus was quite willing to discard his own theory in favor of Teldin's. In fact, the elf seemed relieved to discard the notion that Raven might be a "survivor." He agreed, however, that the moon elf would have to be watched carefully.

"Our more immediate concern is the lakshu," Vallus observed. "If Raven does indeed possess another ultimate helm, I'm assuming she used it to take the form of Viper's reigar master. If that is true, the lakshu is looking for vengeance and will not willingly leave the ship until she is satisfied. Even one lakshu can do a great deal of damage, I'm afraid."

"I don't plan to hand Raven—or whoever she is—over to the lakshu," Teldin said firmly. "I know what it is to be hounded for the cloak."

The sound of a muffled explosion interrupted their conversation, and Teldin and Vallus quickly made their way to the main deck. The damselfly was gone, and where the ship had stood lay the bodies of the three guards Gaston Willowmere had posted. They had died quickly and silently, their throats cut before any of them could draw a weapon.

"The lakshu," Vallus explained to Teldin. Assuming that the revenge-bent warrior would stay aboard the swan ship until she found what she sought, the elven wizard sent teams of heavily armed elves out to search the ship for her.

They found Viper—or what was left of her—in the cargo hold. A blast of enormous power had gone through her armor and body, leaving little more than shattered ribs and a few shards of steel and flesh. In stark contrast to her ravaged body, her beautiful, sharp-boned face was untouched. Her eyes were wide, but the fierce glare had faded with death. Beyond the hollow shell of the lakshu was a black-edged hole in the wall of the ship. Clearly visible through it were swirls of green and purple phlogiston that curled around the far side of the swan ship's air envelope.

Teldin's gut twisted at the sight, but Vallus knelt to examine the body and the damaged wall with dispassionate interest. "A spell of unusual power," he mused. "This is beyond our wizards. None could summon a spell in time to stave off a lakshu's attack. Who could have done such a thing?"

Hectate Kir could, Teldin thought with horror. He recalled the ball of force that Hectate in his bionoid form had thrown at the band of attacking elves. It would have taken something that powerful to do the type of damage they saw before them. As logical as the conclusion was, Teldin found he could not believe it. "The arcane?" he suggested weakly.

Vallus shook his head. "Not likely. The damselfly took off before the attack on the lakshu, I believe. Once the arcane realized he was unlikely to acquire either artifact, he probably saw no need to stay. I'm guessing the lakshu insisted on staying behind to seek out her revenge. She has not been long dead."

The elf rose slowly to his feet and ordered a second search. He and Teldin first questioned Raven Stormwalker, but Chirp and Trivit fervently swore that she had never left their shared cabin. Frustrated but unable to refute the dracons' claim, they carefully questioned the rest of the crew. Om noted that Estriss had gone up to speak to the arcane, so they sought out the illithid to see what light he might shed on the matter. Estriss, however, was nowhere to be found.

After much discussion, Vallus concluded that the illithid, who possessed magical abilities far beyond those of most of his kind, had killed the lakshu and gone off with the arcane. No one could fathom why. The illithid had been strangely elusive since the trip to Evermeet.

Deeply shaken by Estriss's desertion, Teldin returned to his cabin to think the matter over. He entered and stopped short; someone had been in the cabin and had left the lid of his sea chest open. Curious, he stepped closer and peered down. In the chest, next to a book he'd borrowed from Vallus several days earlier, was a small figurine.

The piece obviously was very old, and it depicted a creature fashioned on tripartite lines, holding in each of its three hands a familiar three-petaled flower. Teldin flipped over a corner of his cape and looked closely at the elusive pattern woven into the silk lining. The flowers were identical. Was this statue, obviously a souvenir of Estriss's endless hunt for the Juna, some sort of parting gift?

Teldin could not bring himself to touch the strange figurine. Feeling oddly betrayed, he swallowed hard and raked both hands through his hair. Just when he had laid to rest his doubts over Estriss's strange behavior, the illithid had left without a word.

Teldin retrieved a bottle of sagecoarse from the sea chest, then he quietly closed the lid. Filled with a sense of despairing recklessness, he went in search of his new drinking companion.

As Teldin made his way down to Raven Stormwalker's quarters, he noted that he still had no idea who or what she might be, or what she wanted from him. At the moment, that hardly mattered. In Teldin's current frame of mind, those doubts put her on an equal footing with any of his most trusted friends.

Chapter Twelve

•••

"How could such a thing happen?" thundered the scro general.

"There is a certain, unavoidable delay in getting information from the elven swan ship. Since our last dispatch, it seems that the human, Teldin Moore, changed the ship's destination from Lionheart to Radole," K'tide said. "It was most unexpected."

Grimnosh stopped his pacing to level an icy glare at the spy master. "I pay you to make sure I know what to expect. So far, your efforts have created little benefit and much potential for disaster."

"But our informant is still in place. In time, the elven ship will return to Lionheart—"

"We don't *have* time, you imbecilic insect," Grimnosh growled, thrusting a menacing forefinger into the spy master's chest. "Understand this: Lionheart is no longer the issue." He punctuated each word with a sharp stab, his claw banging painfully against K'tide's exoskeleton.

"But destroying the elven high command—"

"Was a pleasant fantasy," Grimnosh concluded firmly. He shook himself down as if to dispel both his rage and the notion of destroying Lionheart, and he strode purposefully over to his desk and lowered himself into his seat. "Now then. Under the circumstances, the Armistice project has become a problem. Given the elves' interest in Teldin Moore, as well as the fact that half the races of known space seem to be chasing the human's cloak, Winterspace soon will be infested with more ships than a bugbear has fleas." He paused to let K'tide absorb his words. "Now, where are the bionoid ships?"

K'tide blinked, startled. "Nearby. Why do you ask?"

"Summon them. Have them all land on the *Elfsbane* immediately."

"But that is impossible," the spy master stammered. "The bionoids work with me only with great reluctance. They will never take direct orders from you."

"Oh, come now, K'tide," Grimnosh chided. He folded his beautifully manicured hands on his desk. "Don't you think it's time we dispense with this ridiculous pretense?"

"But—"

"Call them!" thundered the scro.

Seeing that he had little choice, K'tide removed a small scrying globe from a pocket of his robe and sank deep into concentration. The telepathic argument was every bit as fierce as he'd anticipated, but finally he called upon the bionoids' pledge loyalty and demanded that they land on the dinotherium. Finally, feeling drained and depleted, he looked up at the glowering scro.

"It is done," he said.

"Excellent." Grimnosh turned to his ever-attentive adjutant. "Nimick, I want you to go to the landing deck. Wait for the shrike ships, then bring the officers to me at once."

"Sir?"

"The officers?" Grimnosh prodded, seeing that Nimick's astonishment had rendered him immobile. "I would like to see them? Here?"

The adjutant saluted and turned to carry out the order. "Oh, Nimick," Grimnosh drawled as if a new thought had just occurred to him. "You might stop by the barracks on your way. Select a dozen or so of my personal guard to help you escort our allies to my office. If some of our scro become overly conscientious in their duty, I should hate to have to break in a new adjutant."

Nimick disappeared through the doorway. "What is all this about?" K'tide demanded, rising from his chair and moving forward with several jerky strides.

"Sit."

The scro's suggestion was offered through a snarl of pure menace. K'tide took the chair Grimnosh pointedly indicated and waited for the bionoid officers.

Their approach was heralded long before their arrival; the presence of the guard did not prevent scro from shouting highly articulate, alliterative insults at their unlikely allies. The commotion grew progressively louder until Nimick's knock signaled their arrival.

"Enter," Grimnosh called sharply. He looked first to his adjutant. "Nimick, take the guard and inform the troops that this unseemly display is to stop immediately. The rest of you, please do come in."

"Leave you alone with them, sir?" the gray-green scro asked in disbelief.

"I'm touched by your solicitude, Nimick," Grimnosh said with dangerous calm. The adjutant saluted and shut the door behind him.

The scro general turned his attention to his allies, hiding his disdain for their elflike appearance only with great effort. He got the impression that the bionoids were struggling to maintain similar facades. There was little love lost between the scro and the bionoids at the best of times, but since times were not good for either race, they had decided to make a mutual exception.

"I have an assignment for you," he said, rising to his full seven feet so that he towered over the deceptively fragile creatures. Their leader, a male named Wynlar, cast a quick glance toward K'tide. "Since time is of the essence, perhaps we should discard the pretense of an intermediary," Grim-nosh said.

"As you wish," Wynlar replied in an even voice, meeting the scro's gaze squarely.

The general nodded slightly, pleased by the bionoid leader's control. Less disciplined were the other officers: a red-haired female's eyes flashed fire, another wench kept smoothing back her silver hair in an unconscious gesture of agitation, and their wizard looked as if he were ready to weep. It was hard to equate these wretched, elflike creatures with the magnificent fighting machines they could become at will, but, since one could not be had without the other, Grimnosh was prepared to make allowances.

"Some of your people have been following the elven vessel called *Trumpeter*, so you know that this ship soon will be entering Winterspace, bound for the planet Radole. On that ship is a human who is attracting an unseemly amount of interest. Rather than risk drawing attention to our work on Armistice, I want the human out of the picture. You will find his ship, board it, and retrieve him. I want him. Dead or alive makes no difference. His name is Teldin Moore, and he is distinguished by the long, dark cloak he wears."

"An easy task," Wynlar said, a question in his quiet voice.

"Make it look difficult," Grimnosh said flatly. "Take every ship you have. Make a display of force, as if the elves themselves are your primary target."

"And the elves?" asked Wynlar.

Grimnosh smiled, thinking that he understood the bionoid leader's concerns. The combined bionoid forces numbered more than a score, and the fierce creatures would hardly be content with a surgical strike. Under similar circumstances, he would be hard pressed to hold back scro warriors from seeking trophies, and he was prepared to be generous with his allies.

"Kill as many elves as amuses you. I want only the human.

Find him and bring him to me, Captain," Grimnosh said with quiet emphasis. "I want this group to see to the task personally. The rest of your people need not know the true target of this attack." There was a warning in the gentle suggestion that the shrewd bionoid could not miss, and Wynlar nodded.

The scro spread his hands in dismissal. "That's all. See to it."

Without a word, the bionoids turned and filed from the room. Four officers, twenty-odd bionoids altogether, Grimnosh mused. That might seem a small band to send against an elven swan ship, but conventional military odds favored one bionoid against ten fully armed scro. The scrawny bunch that had just left his office probably could have the elven crew for dawnfry without breaking a sweat.

"I thought that went rather well, didn't you, K'tide?" Grimnosh taunted.

"As you predicted," the spy master acceded in a tight voice. He rose. "If you have no further need of me?"

"No, K'tide," Grimnosh said meaningfully. "I have no further need of you."

K'tide bowed deeply and left the room. He moved as quickly as his brittle body allowed, taking a shortcut in order to beat the bionoid team back to their craft. His mission—not to mention his life—depended on his getting out of sight before Grimnosh decided who would have the honor of doing away with him.

The insectare made his way to the landing deck. He ran a pale green hand over the sleek surface of his own ship, a vessel shaped like a grasshopper's head with two long, trailing antennae. It had been too long since he had been aboard a klicklikak, the ship of his own people. Perhaps the alliance with the scro had broken down, but he still had influence over the bionoid band. It would have to be enough.

The group rounded the corner and pulled up short to see K'tide waiting for them. "There has been a slight change of plan," K'tide announced.

"The scro general sent you?" Wynlar asked, suspicion in his voice.

For a moment K'tide debated whether to present his own agenda as his or Grimnosh's. The bionoids had always been unhappy about the alliance with the scro; they were bound to be unnerved by their meeting with the fearsome general. Perhaps he should play into those feelings.

"The scro has betrayed you," K'tide answered firmly. "He plans to do away with you four as soon as you retrieve the human."

The bionoids exchanged worried glances, and K'tide saw that he had struck a nerve. "And the other members of Clan Kir?" asked Wynlar.

"He needs them still, and he will until the Armistice goblins are released. As long as your people remain ignorant of the scro's treachery, they will remain safe—at least for the time. You four are highly skilled and battle proven. That is why Grimnosh has chosen you to achieve his purpose. A short-sighted decision, but one to be expected from such as he."

"Why does the scro want this human?" demanded Wynlar.

"The human has a cloak, an artifact of great power. As do all scro, Grimnosh wants this power for himself."

"Would it help him destroy the elves?" asked Tekura fiercely. K'tide suppressed a smile. Of all the bionoids, the silver-haired female had been his most stalwart ally.

"Oh, yes, as well as every other race in wildspace," K'tide said dryly. "Believe me, you would not want this cloak falling into scro hands." The spy master came several steps closer. "There is more. In his lust for personal power, Grimnosh is abandoning the attack on Lionheart. I take it your first concern is to end the elven domination of the spaceways?"

"Our first concern is the freedom of our own people," Wynlar corrected him.

"These are one and the same, are they not?" asked K'tide smoothly. "If we do not take matters into our own hands now, our goals will be lost. Once the Armistice goblins are released, they have no further need of our services and we have no bargaining chips to use for their weapons. We must act now."

"What do you think we should do?" Wynlar asked quietly.

The insectare took a step forward. "Attack the elven swan ship, as Grimnosh directed. Get the human's cloak, but leave the ship and its crew intact."

"Why do we want this cloak?"

"To be quite honest, at this point we don't," K'tide said firmly. "But the elves do. If their captain, Vallus Leafbower, should lose the cloak, he will be obliged to return to Lionheart and report his failure. We have an informant on board, though he has not proven as reliable as I would have hoped. A bionoid ship, armed with the stolen elven cloaking device, will follow the swan ship to Lionheart and release the secondary marauder."

"A risky plan," Wynlar said cautiously.

"Our only chance," Tekura stressed, rounding on the captain. "K'tide is right. If we don't move now, we'll never have another chance at getting a Witchlight Marauder, and we'll never have another chance to get one into Lionheart."

The bionoid captain bowed his head in resignation. "All right. We will tell Clan Kir only what Grimnosh asked of us: that we attack the elven vessel."

"We will travel together," K'tide said. "I will follow aboard the klicklikak. Assign two of your ranks to serve as my crew."

"Bionoids, traveling on an insectare ship?" the bionoid wizard demanded. "Only an insectare can run the helm. You can't power the klicklikak alone—"

"There is an auxiliary helm," K'tide broke in, "a lifejammer."

K'tide did not miss the bionoids' shudders and the shocked glances they exchanged. "You will not use my people to power your ship," Wynlar said, clearly appalled at the notion.

The spy master suppressed a smile. It amused him that such fierce killers could have so soft a core. Of course, they had not had the benefit of Grimnosh's tutelage, as he had. And he, K'tide, was a fast study.

"I assure you, Wynlar, that won't be necessary. I've had some kobolds packed in the hold. They should suffice as fuel."

Chapter Thirteen

● ● ●

Raven Stormwalker was the first to see the approaching ship. On her insistence, she'd been assigned duty on the forward watch. Although Vallus was a little leery of having her on the bridge, he had thought it wise to treat her as if she were what she claimed to be: a moon elf adventurer. The elven wizard watched Raven carefully, though always, Teldin noticed, from a considerable distance. It took Vallus several days before he could completely discard his theory of Raven as a "survivor," and to shake his overwhelming horror of the type of living death such a being could deal. Teldin puzzled over the elven wizard's strange reaction, but he had to admit that his own, private response to Raven Stormwalker was equally disturbing. She was, by appearances, an elf, and quite possibly the possessor of another ultimate helm, but Teldin was undeniably drawn to her.

Almost daily Teldin found himself on the swan ship's bridge during Raven's watch, and more than once they'd spent the entire watch together, sometimes talking, sometimes gazing into wildspace in equally companionable silence. Not since Aelfred's death had Teldin felt so at ease with another being. Perhaps Raven was a competitor for the *Spelljammer*, but who was not? If she was a competitor, she was also a comrade, and a palpable sense of kinship drew them together.

Teldin could not, however, dispel the image of the

monstrous face he'd seen superimposed on Raven's features. What *was* she? Obviously, she was not the Raven Stormwalker of elven legend. If she could transform herself into an elf and—if the lakshu had been right—into a dragon, what was her true form? As Teldin puzzled this, it occurred to him that he'd reached a sad state of affairs: he found the prospect of a dragon less threatening than a woman.

Whatever she was, Raven turned out to be a great favorite around the ship. She'd traveled widely and told her experiences in a wry, understated style that the story-loving elves found engaging. Her practical experience was also in demand; she even advised Hectate of a gate into the crystal sphere of Winterspace, a new one that the half-elven navigator hadn't known existed. "Let's just say I was there when it opened," she had observed cryptically. She was good company: intelligent and amusing as well as easy to look at. And so Teldin's days had slipped by, busy but uneventful . . . until now.

Teldin and Vallus were on the upper deck when Raven gave the first alert. "Captain!" she bellowed from her perch in the swan's head. She leaned far over the railing that separated the bridge deck from the long drop to the main body of the swan ship, and her long midnight braids swayed as she gestured wildly for Teldin.

He sprinted up the stairs leading up the swan's neck to the bridge. "What is it?" he demanded.

"Well, it's something you don't see every day," Raven replied. Despite the flippant remark, her voice held a new, serious note. "Look there," she directed Teldin, pointing off into wildspace.

Teldin took up the brass tube that hung from his belt and peered through it at a distant, peculiar ship. The vessel was almost round, and two long streamers trailed behind as it approached the *Trumpeter* at a businesslike pace.

What now? Teldin thought with a touch of resignation. He

passed the glass to Vallus Leafbower, who had come up behind him.

Vallus squinted at the approaching vessel, and his angular face tightened. "What do you make of that?" Teldin asked.

"It's an insectare ship," Vallus said in a worried tone. "A klicklikak."

Teldin grimaced, not liking the mental picture that the buglike name conjured. "What are insectare?"

"A mysterious race," the elven wizard said absently, still peering through the glass at the odd ship. "At first glance, they appear to be elves. Pointed ears, angular features, and so on. They usually wear heavy robes with cowls, though, to hide their true nature."

"Which is?" Teldin asked, eyeing the distant ship with a growing sense of foreboding.

"Imagine an intelligent insect, about the size and shape of an elf," Raven suggested. "If you get a good look at their eyes, you'll see that they're multifaceted. They have long antennae sprouting from behind their ears, and the way they move is a little different, too, since their bodies are covered with hard plating." She shrugged. "Apart from that, they're pretty much like elves. Oh, except that their skin is light green, about the same color as Trivit's, maybe a little brighter."

"With such minor differences," Teldin said, "no wonder they're mistaken for elves."

Raven acknowledged his sarcasm with a fleeting half-smile. "Not many get close enough to get a good look at one. I have."

Suddenly Teldin recalled the mysterious, elflike creature he had seen in the tavern back on Garden, and the terrified reaction of the drunken man who'd peered directly into the creature's face.

"I may have run into one myself," he said. He answered Vallus's questions with a quick version of the story of the tavern battle and the strange, elflike creature shrouded in brown robes. "At the time, I had a strong perception that it was no elf," Teldin concluded.

"True seeing," Raven mused, sliding a sidelong glance at the cloaked human. "The medallion at work?"

Her seemingly innocent question startled Teldin. He hadn't mentioned the medallion or its powers to her; how had she learned of it? He noted the peculiar expression on her face—a smug, almost feline satisfaction—and a second shock overpowered the first. She knows, he thought dazedly. She knows that I suspect she's carrying an ultimate helm and wearing a face that is not her own. As he stared into Raven's gold and silver eyes, Teldin knew precisely how a mouse must feel when a cat toyed with it. He broke eye contact and drew in a long, calming breath.

"I wonder if there's any connection between the creature you encountered on Garden and our new visitors," Vallus said, oblivious to the exchange that had taken place.

"The cloak," Teldin said wearily. "That always seems to be the connection."

"Especially in this case," Vallus agreed. "The insectare are a secretive and devious race. It's safe to assume they crave the cloak's power."

Teldin sighed and reclaimed his looking tube from the elven wizard. The klicklikak was still a good distance away, but coming directly for them. "I suppose it's also safe to assume they'll fight?" he asked with resignation. Vallus nodded.

"I'll alert the crew," Raven volunteered. Reflexively Teldin caught Raven's arm as she brushed by.

"I want you to stay out of the fight, Raven," he said quietly. "Sound the alarm, then go directly to your quarters. Whatever happens, stay below."

"I can handle myself," she assured him. She patted the shoulder strap of her broadsword's scabbard and smiled, but to Teldin's hypersensitive eyes her smile seemed to hold secret, ironic amusement.

"Oblige me," Teldin insisted. "I don't want to have to order you below, but I will."

A baffled expression crossed the moon elf's face. Teldin wondered briefly if she might be picking up his own feelings. That certainly would account for her confusion, he thought wryly.

Despite the mysterious power Raven had just flaunted, despite whatever game she might be playing with him, Teldin was afraid for her. Just because she looked like a legendary elven warrior, it didn't necessarily follow that she knew how to use the sword she carried. On those occasions when Teldin had used the cloak's power to alter his own appearance, he'd kept his own voice and his own abilities.

"Now," he repeated quietly.

"If you say so, Captain," she replied, still looking puzzled.

As she spoke, Teldin's vision wavered. Raven's mismatched eyes became yellow, hooded orbs slashed by vertical pupils. In the instant before he blinked away the vision, he caught a flickering glimpse of a reptilian face. He released Raven's arm as quickly as he would have dropped a live coal.

As soon as Raven had left the bridge, Vallus turned to Teldin. "That was well done," the elf said somberly. "Until we know for sure who and what she is, it's wise to keep her out of battle."

The image of a metamorphosing dragon flashed into Teldin's mind, and he silently agreed with Vallus. Since he didn't care to reveal—or even examine!—his other motives for sending her away, Teldin acknowledged the elf's praise with a curt nod and returned to their immediate problem. "How many insectare can we expect, and how do they fight?"

"Ten to twenty. They use long swords and antennae."

"Antennae? But how—"

"Whips," Vallus broke in grimly. "Eight-foot whips that

can break an opponent's neck in a single strike. Even if you can get close enough to lay a sword on one, its body armor is virtually impenetrable. Ten or twenty insectare could give us serious problems."

"*If* they manage to board," Teldin replied. "Let's make sure they don't."

He hooked the brass tube back onto his belt and strode out of the bridge. As he sped down the steps to the upper deck, it occurred to him that he had never before directed a battle. The prospect was not as daunting as he would have expected. Thanks to the cloak, he'd had plenty of battle experience.

Teldin quickly shrank his cloak down to its smallest size so it would not hamper him in battle or mark him as an immediate target. He loosened his sword in its scabbard, and as he circulated among the elven troops he was surprised at how little fear he felt at the impending battle. The swan ship had a crew of some thirty elves, each a crack sailor and fighter, and Teldin felt an unexpected twinge of excitement over the prospect of directing such a force.

Raven had spread the alarm, and the upper deck was humming with tension and activity as elves took their battle stations at the railing. Loaded crossbows lay in piles, as well as pikes to repel boarding attempts, and a small band of wizards gathered under Vallus's direction. The tufted tail at the stern had been folded down to reveal a deadly catapult. A team of four elves busily cranked the mechanism into place and loaded the weapon. Teldin could hear whining of gears from the cargo deck below as the ballista was readied for firing. He positioned himself on the upper deck at the head of the stairs. There he had full view of the approaching foe, and his shouted commands would carry to the two lower decks as well as up to the bridge.

The wooden stairs behind him creaked in protest as the dracons lumbered up onto the deck. Both were in full battle finery: Trivit wore his practical chain mail and wielded the enormous broadsword, and Chirp sported the purple-hued leather armor and carried his ornate two-headed axe as if it were a fashion accessory. Having seen the pair in battle, Teldin was not fooled by Chirp's frivolous appearance. The dracon brothers had proven themselves excellent fighters, but suddenly Teldin thought of a better use for their talents.

"I want you two to go below and guard Raven Stormwalker's quarters. Whatever happens, don't let anyone or anything get near her." Can't have her goaded into changing form during the battle, he added silently.

The dracons exchanged worried glances. "But she sent us up to guard *you*," Trivit blurted out.

Chirp hissed and rolled his eyes in exasperation. "Oh, marvelous. 'Act natural,' she said. 'Be discreet,' she said. Aren't you the very soul of discretion?" he said nastily.

"Well, I'm a bit unnerved by the dilemma in which we find ourselves. Moral dilemmas do strange things to one," Trivit replied thoughtfully. "I've always wanted to experience just such a thing—for the intellectual exercise, mind you—but now I've thoroughly repented of my wish. Moral dilemmas are damnable nuisances."

"Below," Teldin ordered firmly.

The dracons responded instantly to his tone, saluting and clumping down the protesting stairs toward the moon elf's quarters. Teldin glanced toward the starboard railing, where Vallus had gathered the ship's battle wizards. Once Teldin had thought that six wizards was a frivolous use of crew space, but at the moment he was glad to have them.

The klicklikak had drawn close enough that details were clearly visible, and it had slowed almost to a hover. It was a relatively large ship, about one hundred feet long, and had an odd, oblong shape. Two windows shaped like bulging eyes dominated the front of the vessel, and the long streamers that had trailed along behind while the ship was in rapid motion now stuck straight up before it. The ship was covered with intersecting plate armor, and two pairs of short metal rods protruded from the bottom. Landing gear, Teldin supposed, though something about them suggested the feelers that hung down on either side of a locust's mouth.

That's it, he realized with a sharp feeling of distaste. The klicklikak was shaped to look like the head of an enormous grasshopper. The disembodied head seemed to possess an eery sentience, and Teldin had the uncanny sensation that the buglike eyes were watching and taunting. The insectare ship halted just out of ballista range, as if it discerned the elves' intent.

A strange, scraping sound distracted Teldin, and he cast a sideways glance toward the source. He immediately turned and gave Hectate Kir his full attention. The half-elf labored up the stairs to the deck, half carrying and half dragging an enormous, two-headed halberd. Like the halberd Hectate had lost in the battle with the mind flayers, the weapon had blades easily two feet across and a staff fashioned from an eight-foot length of stout oak. This weapon, however, boasted a bewildering overlay of bolts and levers that marked it as a gnomish design. Om's work again, Teldin supposed. The gods only know what "improvements" the gnome had made. Whatever the case, Teldin could have no doubt about Hectate's intent.

"Don't you think you should sit this battle out?" Teldin asked him pointedly. The racket of Hectate's approach had drawn the attention of the elves on deck, and all were eyeing the half-elf and his enormous weapon with astonishment and suspicion. It was not an auspicious moment to debut as a bionoid.

"If possible, sir, I will," the half-elf replied, "but I've fought insectare before. My experience may prove useful."

"You have?" Vallus asked, coming over to stand by Teldin.

"A swarm of the creatures destroyed my home and family

when I was little more than a boy," Hectate said quietly. "I know how they fight, and how they attack. I'll do whatever I can to help."

Teldin gripped the half-elf's shoulder, accepting his offer with a mixture of gratitude and foreboding. If Hectate was willing to reveal his bionoid nature before a swan ship full of elves, the risk presented by the insectare must be serious indeed. "What do you think they are up to?" he asked the half-elf.

Hectate squinted at the monstrous insect head. "That's not a battleship. The ballistae ports that should be around the base have been closed up. It looks as though it's been stripped down, either for crew or cargo."

"So?" Vallus prompted.

"I'd say the ship's a diversion," Hectate said. "A klicklikak is rare enough to get attention and keep it. Insectare only fight if they have to. What they're likely to do is to—"

His last words were lost in a piercing whistle. Teldin ducked reflexively, then shot a glance in the direction of the approaching sound and saw . . .

Nothing.

Their invisible adversary whistled in with a rising shriek. With horror Teldin recalled the banshees of his grandfather's tales—ghostly creatures with a keening cry. He'd seen strange things in wildspace, but so far all of them had been alive. As Teldin formed the thought, a current of air swept over them and he grabbed for the stair railing to keep his balance. Suddenly the banshee had passed, and its voice abruptly dropped in pitch to a thrumming roar. It approached and shrieked past again, and then a third time. Each cycle came in closer and lower. Just as Teldin thought he might scream aloud, a small, birdlike ship appeared from nothing but sound and air.

"A cloaking device," Vallus said tersely. "One of ours, on a shrike ship!"

Hectate tensed as the shrike ship approached again, his brown eyes narrowing as he stared fixedly at the ship. Suddenly he grabbed Teldin's arm and, with surprising strength, shoved him toward the steps. "Get below, sir," he shouted.

Teldin didn't answer, staring upward in disbelief as the small craft veered sharply from its path, making a suicidal lunge directly for the swan ship's long, curved neck. Twin bolts of light, magic balls of incredible power, burst from the shrike ship's forecastle and hurtled forward. The balls of force hit the bridge tower with an explosion of magical power and splintered wood. Teldin watched helplessly as the severed top half of the tower plummeted toward the deck, shattering boards and pinning several members of the elven crew. The shrike ship dove straight through the opening it had made and continued on its frenzied, circling path.

"They got the bridge," Vallus said in disbelief.

"And the helm," Teldin noted grimly. The ship was essentially what it appeared to be: a beheaded swan. The crew would be every bit as dead if he didn't act quickly. Teldin doubted there would be time to get up the secondary helm before the battle began.

In response to the crisis, his cloak began to glow, its pale sunrise pink signaling its spelljamming magic. Teldin felt his awareness growing, spreading to every part of the wounded ship. He could see the elves hurrying to rescue their fellows, Deelia Snowsong bending over a wounded elf as her tiny, pale hands forced a dislocated shoulder back into place. He saw Rozloom taking refuge under a stout table in the galley. Suddenly he could feel the ship itself, as if wood and iron were no more than a continuation of his own bone and sinew. Soon he would *be* the ship, and his untended body would be exposed and vulnerable on the deck, despite the bionoid protector that now loomed over him.

"Vallus, you've got to take command. I'm going to take the helm," Teldin said in a faint, faraway voice, and he gathered up a handful of the luminous, pale fabric. "*This* helm."

The elf shot a glance at Teldin, and his eyes widened at the sight of the glowing cloak. A mixture of comprehension and wonder suffused the wizard's face, and he gave Teldin a quick nod. As Teldin turned to leave, he couldn't resist adding, "Watch yourself, Vallus. Stay close to Hectate, and you'll be safe."

The elf's eyebrows rose, and he turned quizzical eyes toward Hectate Kir. He recoiled in shock and horror. In the shadow of the stairwell where the half-elf had just stood was a ten-foot, muscular insect holding the halberd in a guard position as it watched the shrike ship slowly circle in for another pass. The Change had overtaken Hectate silently and instantaneously.

Teldin slapped Vallus's shoulder. "There's something you should know about Hectate," he said casually, then he turned and left the wizard alone with the bionoid fighter. While he was still able, he pushed open the door that led to his cabin.

No sooner had Teldin disappeared than the shrike ship slowed to a hover directly over the *Trumpeter*'s deck. Three enormous creatures leaped from it to land nimbly on the swan ship's deck, creatures identical to the one hidden in the landing behind Vallus.

Everywhere on deck the elves froze. All had heard stories of battles the bionoids had fought and won for the elves in the first Unhuman War. No one had the faintest idea how to fight *against* such creatures.

The bionoids, standing shoulder to shoulder and armed with huge swords or pikes, were a daunting sight even to the battle-hardened elves. Vallus shot a glance over his shoulder, half expecting to see a treacherous halberd swinging at his neck, but Hectate, in his bionoid form, still stood guard.

One of the creatures stepped forward and spoke into the

silence. "We have come for the human. If you turn Teldin Moore over to us, we will leave peaceably."

In response, Vallus swept an implacable, narrowed glare across the immobile elven crew. "Attack," he said simply.

The battle that followed was ghastly. The elven crew fought with bravery and skill, but they fell so rapidly that the dead and wounded piled around the bionoid band. Two other bionoid ships closed in, and each ship discharged two more of the fearsome creatures. The light emanating from their crystal eyes bathed the deck with a reddish glow. Some of the bionoids battled the elves; others seemed to be searching the swan ship.

In his cabin, now fully taken up in the spelljamming magic of his cloak, Teldin's expanded senses took in the battle with a growing sense of horror. If Hectate alone had destroyed dozens of the mind flayers' slaves when in his bionoid form, how could the *Trumpeter*'s crew stand against the bionoid invaders? If there was a way the creatures could be overcome, perhaps Hectate would know it.

Like a hawk circling a meadow, Teldin's magically enhanced vision searched the ship for his friend. The bionoids, however, were eerily identical, and Teldin was not sure he could recognize Hectate when he found him.

One of the bionoids fought at the head of the stairs, barring the way to the lower decks and to the captain's quarters, and its flashing halberd held off two of the invaders. Teldin's instincts told him with unerring certainty that Hectate lived within the creature.

As Teldin watched, one of the invaders leaped, a spiked foot kicking out with lightning speed. The Hectate bionoid apparently anticipated the move, for he nimbly sidestepped and circled upward with the staff of his halberd, catching the attacker behind the knee. A quick twist threw the creature off balance. It landed heavily, and Hectate was upon it instantly. He planted one enormous foot on the creature's back, pinning it to the deck, then he hooked the curved blade of his halberd under a plate of insectlike armor and wrenched his weapon back toward him as if it were a giant lever.

A horrible cracking sound rent the air as the bionoid's armor gave way, followed by a woman's scream of unbearable anguish. Hectate's enormous body shuddered, but he quickly plunged the blade of his halberd deep into the opening. Ichor puddled on the deck, and the red light faded from the fallen bionoid's crystal eye. With a creaking groan the creature's body began to compact, for in death it reverted to its elven form.

As if from a great distance, Teldin noted that the fallen bionoid had become a tiny, red-haired elven woman with a huge, gaping wound under her left shoulder blade. Teldin saw his monstrous friend slump, and he felt Hectate's grief and despair as if the emotions were his own. He knew with certainty that Hectate had known the bionoid he had just slain, and known her well.

The second bionoid advanced, its enormous sword held out before it, and Hectate halfheartedly raised his dripping halberd into a defensive position. The creature came closer, but it did not attack. Its insectlike head tilted to one side, giving it an oddly quizzical air.

"Hectate? Hectate Kir, can that really be you?"

The creature spoke in a woman's voice, a voice that was soft, intimate, and full of longing. It sheathed its sword and stepped forward, massive hands reaching out and up as if to cradle Hectate's bionoid face. Hectate's weapon lowered reflexively.

At the last moment, the creature's fist smashed into Hectate's vulnerable crystal eye. Teldin's bionoid friend slumped as if lifeless to the deck.

"No!" Teldin screamed. A second keening cry escaped him, only to be lost in an explosion that shook the swan ship to its keel. With effort he forced aside his grief to attend the ship. Again he slid his expanded vision over the elven vessel.

The *Trumpeter's* stern had been damaged almost past recognition. One of the bionoids had loosed a spell, taking out the swan ship's rear catapult and sending the heavy machinery crashing to the lower level. The blasted bodies of elven crew lay amid shattered boards and smoking debris.

To Teldin's surprise, the invaders abandoned the fight as abruptly as it had begun. One after another, the shrike ships dove in, hovered, and threw down boarding ropes. Within moments the bionoids were gone. *All* of the bionoids; try as he might, Teldin could not locate Hectate anywhere on the ship. The klicklikak faded from sight, and the shrike ships darted off into wildspace after it.

Teldin took inventory of the ship's wounds. The bridge was gone, and with it the lookout tower and the primary helm. Their heavy weaponry had been destroyed. The *Trumpeter* was without eyes, power, or defenses. They had to put down for repairs, but they still were many days from Radole.

He sought outward for a solution. Below them was a world, a tiny gray sphere streaked with white. From this distance, it looked very much like his last glimpse of his native Krynn. With sudden resolve, Teldin sent the swan ship into a rapid descent.

Vallus Leafbower burst into Teldin's cabin. His silver hair was disheveled and the shoulder of his uniform had been slashed open. His once-proud tabard was stained with blood and ichor. "What in the gods' names are you doing?" he demanded.

"Landing," Teldin murmured. "We're landing."

"No!"

"The ship is damaged. The helm is gone. We've got to put down."

"But that's Armistice. We can't land there."

"Why not? Doesn't it have large bodies of water?" Teldin

asked in sudden concern. The swan ship wasn't designed to put down on land, and an attempt would doubtlessly reduce the battered ship to kindling.

"Vast oceans, but elves must not land on that planet."

"Spare me your elven scruples," Teldin said wearily. "We haven't got much choice."

"We do. The secondary helm is operational. I've got someone on it now, but we can't override the magic of your cloak."

"Damn right," Teldin muttered.

"Let go, Teldin Moore," Vallus insisted, taking a step closer. "We cannot land on Armistice. It's heavily patrolled by the Imperial Fleet, and for good reason. There are huge nations of orcs and hobgoblins there, landlocked monsters who would do anything to obtain spelljamming capability. If the swan ship lands, we present them with not only a ship and a helm, but also your cloak."

"Vallus, let's fly that hawk when its feathers are grown," Teldin said. "The swan ship needs repairs now, or we're in serious trouble. We might not make it as far as Radole."

"I know," Vallus said quietly, "but it would be better to lose the swan ship and everyone on board than to put the cloak in goblin hands."

"Haven't enough people died for this damnable cloak?" Teldin snapped. "I won't put the crew at risk."

"Really? And what do you think would happen to these elves in the hands of the Armistice orcs?" Vallus demanded. When Teldin hesitated, the elven wizard repeated, "Do not land the ship."

Teldin's resolved firmed. "I'm sorry, Vallus."

"So am I," the elven wizard said softly. He began to cast a spell, his long fingers gesturing as he murmured arcane syllables.

Teldin tensed, not sure what to expect. The cloak's magic had protected him from physical attacks many times before, but he had no idea whether it would turn aside a spell, especially one from a wizard as powerful as Vallus Leafbower.

A second voice joined the chanting, then suddenly there was only one. Vallus's fingers and lips moved, but no sound came from him. Chagrin flickered across his face, then fury. He spun to face the second spellcaster. In the doorway stood Raven Stormwalker, arms crossed as she leaned casually against the doorjamb, a catlike smile on her face.

"About time someone put him in a sphere of silence," she observed. She leaned her head back to look over her shoulder. "Oh, Chirp! Take the so-called wizard to his quarters, won't you? Keep him there until the captain orders otherwise."

The dracon poked his mottled green head into the cabin. He hesitated, though, his reptilian face uncertain as his gaze flicked from Teldin to Vallus to Raven. His green shoulders slowly slumped under the weight of such a mind-boggling question of hierarchy. Seeing Chirp's dilemma, Raven shoved Vallus out into the hall.

"This elf attacked your *kaba*," she said briskly. She pointed across the hall that separated Teldin's quarters from those of the elven wizard. "Throw him in there and see that he doesn't get out. I'll stay here and protect the captain."

Chirp's rubbery face embodied outrage. "On your command, Celestial One," he said. He prodded the silent Vallus across the hall with a series of shoves, haranguing him as they went. The dracon's voice faded in and out as he entered and exited the sphere of silence surrounding the wizard.

Raven came into the cabin and seated herself on the cot beside Teldin. "Go ahead and put the ship down, Captain."

Suddenly Teldin wasn't so sure that Vallus was wrong. "There are orcs down there. I've fought scro—space orcs— before, and if those orcs are anything like them . . ." His voice trailed away uncertainly.

"Look at me," she demanded.

The elf's voice thrummed with power. Startled, Teldin glanced up into her mismatched eyes. His vision swam, and it seemed to him that Raven's eyes glowed with a compelling, golden light. He felt himself drawn into that light, into a swirling, sleepy haze. As if from a great distance, he heard her voice again.

"You don't look well, Captain. I think you could use some help." Still holding Teldin's gaze, she reached into the front of her leather jerkin and pulled out an antique pendant set with a blue stone. Even through the golden haze that held Teldin in thrall, he felt a stab of dread and dismay. It was as he'd feared. Raven had an ultimate helm of her own, the one described by the slain lakshu.

Raven's fingers tightened around the sapphire pendant. In response, the rich blue color faded from the gem, and a faint pink glow dawned in the heart of the sapphire. "Rest," she suggested. "I'll take over."

Despite his weariness, Teldin regarded the pendant-helm warily as he remembered his first attempt at using his cloak as a helm. "You've done this before?"

"Spelljamming? Since the day I was hatched," she quipped lightly. "Not with this magic bauble, of course, but how hard could *that* be?"

A twinge of panic twisted Teldin's gut, and suddenly he feared he'd handed a death sentence to the ship's crew. Raven's vanity and utter self-confidence could easily blind her to the real difficulties ahead. He felt he had lost Aelfred's hammership, as well as some good people, the first time he'd tried landing a ship. Even if Raven succeeded . . .

"Maybe we shouldn't land there." Teldin fingered the edge of his glowing cloak. "The scro want this. I think you know why."

"Sure do," she said in a jaunty tone, "but don't worry about the scro. I've met worse creatures on my travels, and you've come this far wearing most of your skin. Between the two of us, we can handle a few overgrown goblins."

"But—"

"Oh, stop fussing," Raven chided him with a touch of impatience. She leaned closer, and it seemed to Teldin that the golden light of her eyes intensified. An image filled his mind, the memory of a long-ago trip to market, with his grandfather driving the wagon and himself as a lad curled up in the back.

All would be well, Teldin thought with drowsy contentment. He could sleep and be safe. With a sense of relief he began to release his hold on the cloak's spelljamming magic. As his cloak faded, the light in Raven's sapphire correspondingly increased. The transfer from one helm to the other was as smooth and effortless as if they'd rehearsed it a dozen times.

Suddenly it occurred to Teldin that he'd just turned the ship over to his most serious rival for the *Spelljammer*. He struggled to free himself from the lure of slumber.

Raven hissed with exasperation. "By the gods, you're being difficult! Let *go*, would you? After all the time I've spent looking for you, Teldin Moore, I'm not about to let anything happen to you now."

Her words puzzled Teldin, but he was too weary to examine them. As he drifted into a half-conscious sleep, his last thought was that Raven had sounded a little surprised by her own cryptic admission.

When Teldin Moore finally was snoring, Raven shook her head in disbelief. "Must be losing my touch," she muttered to herself. "That damn human was harder to charm than a dwarf's in-laws." Despite her disgruntled tone, she regarded the ensorcelled, sleeping human with a measure of respect. Maybe, just maybe, Teldin Moore would be a credible partner—even for a radiant dragon.

Less than an hour later, the wounded swan ship splashed safely down in the frigid oceans of Armistice.

Chapter Fourteen

●●●

When Hectate awoke, his first observation was that he'd regained his half-elven form. His head hurt and his vision was still blurry, but he could see well enough to know he was aboard an unfamiliar spelljamming ship. Beside his hammock was a chair, and in it sat a slender feminine form.

His eyes focused on the familiar face, elven and delicate, and his heart ached with sadness. The beautiful woman beside him was utterly unlike the monster who had attacked him aboard the *Trumpeter*, yet there was more similarity between her two aspects than Hectate could bear. She was wearing a uniform of sorts, and Hectate took that to be a bad sign. After experiencing the Change, bionoids traditionally wore loose, silver robes for a period of meditation and purification. Tekura wore no robes; she did not mourn the lives she had taken.

"How are you feeling?" Her voice was soft, and her green eyes were as warm as if Hectate had never left the Clan—had never left *her*.

"Puzzled," he answered frankly, not knowing what else to say. "Why have you brought me here?"

"You belong here, now more than ever. We're nearing a great prize, a great victory." Tekura leaned forward, reaching out to take one of Hectate's hands between both of hers.

Hectate's fears crystalized into a dull, aching certainty. Clan Kir had entered the race for Teldin Moore's cloak.

"Ah, our guest is finally awake," said a voice behind them.

The scratchy whisper startled both bionoids. At the door stood a tall, robed figure with an elflike face. He came into the room and lowered the cowl of his robe. The dim lamplight revealed a narrow, pale green face, above which prehensile antennae slowly unwound to rise high over elflike ears. Hectate recoiled from the insectare with a surge of horror.

A second shock came with the insectare's shadow. Behind the creature stood three bionoids, all from Clan Kir, all of them known to Hectate since late childhood. Wynlar, the scholar, and his two brothers: the wizard Zeddop, and a wiry, flame-haired farmer named Enester. Their faces brought a flood of memories. The extended clan had taken him in when he was a confused, wounded lad grieving the death of his parents. Clan Kir had been a warm, closely knit community made up of several related families and a number of adopted bionoids such as himself and Tekura, and it had been his entire world. Yet he'd left over ten years ago when he realized that Clan Kir had been formed to be a battle clan. Seldom in bionoid history had such a clan been gathered, and the results had been so appalling that both elves and bionoids shrouded those episodes in secrecy. Refusing to be a party to another such disaster, Hectate had left Clan Kir and gone his own way. Even so, he was gladdened by the sight of his family after so many years.

Wynlar had greatly aged in the intervening years, and Zeddop's perpetually worried expression had chiseled deep, parallel lines into his forehead. The red tabard that signified the death of a beloved was draped over Enester's uniform as the farmer-turned-warrior mourned his daughter's death. The sight brought a despairing chill over Hectate, and his vision swam, to be momentarily replaced by the sight of a red-haired girl lying dead on the deck of the swan ship.

Hectate turned his eyes back toward the insectare. The

evil monster at his bedside was easier to contemplate than the death of merry little Soona—his childhood playmate—at his own hands.

Tekura had risen immediately upon seeing the insectare, and as she stepped forward to greet the creature, her deferential attitude brought new, raw pain to Hectate's heart.

"You keep strange company, Tekura," he said softly.

She shot him a look of unmistakable warning, then turned back to the newcomer. "Lord K'tide, this is—"

"I know." The insectare's voice reminded Hectate of the snapping of dry twigs. The creature walked to Hectate's bedside and lowered himself into the chair Tekura had just vacated. Hectate heard a faint chittering sound beneath the robes, and he shuddered. He knew that the insectare's body was covered with hard, interlocking plates, with only the exposed face and hands covered by humanoid skin. As he regarded the elflike creature, Hectate had the strange sensation of being confronted with the dark side of his own dual nature. He often had feared becoming trapped forever in his own monstrous form. What manner of creature would he become? The answer was one he did not care to face in his darkest dreams, yet here it was, sitting at his bedside.

"Your clan speaks highly of you, Hectate Kir," said the insectare in his dry, brittle voice. "When we were forced to abandon the elven ship without the human, acquiring a fighter of your caliber made the attack not entirely without gain. Your skills, not to mention your connection to Teldin Moore, make you an invaluable ally."

"I'll not fight with you," Hectate stated. His voice was quiet but inflexible.

"Let me tell you an ancient tale, Hectate Kir," K'tide said as if the half-elven bionoid had not spoken at all. "Many centuries past, orc priests developed a mighty weapon of destruction. Like them, it was crude and difficult to manage, but effective. Oh, yes, undoubtedly so."

Hectate swallowed a wave of revulsion as he realized the nature of the weapon. "The Witchlight Marauder," he whispered as soon as he could speak.

One of K'tide's antennae quirked, the equivalent of an arched brow. "You know history," the insectare said approvingly. He leaned forward, his multifaceted eyes compelling. "The question is, are you ready to *make* history?"

Tekura stepped forward. "One of the secondary Witchlight Marauders has been tested in battle, with great success." She paused significantly, giving him time to absorb her revelation. "We soon will release another!"

"Where?" Hectate whispered.

"Lionheart." Tekura's voice rang with triumph, and her eyes held cold fire. "The first marauder ate its way through an elven armada. Let us hope its twin is equally hungry."

Hectate had to turn away from the sight of her. "What manner of creature have you become, Tekura?" he asked softly. His gaze shifted to the insectare, and the implication was unmistakable. Tekura flushed, but she lifted her chin in defiance.

"An outcast," she said flatly, "like all bionoids. Our only hope of improving our lot is to break the power of the elves."

"But what happens once the elven high command is destroyed?" Hectate argued. "How will that aid the bionoids? The goblin races, particularly the scro, will simply fill the void. They hate all things elven or elflike. Do you think *they* will regard us with tolerance and respect?"

"So far, they've—" Tekura broke off abruptly, biting her lip in chagrin. She looked quickly at the insectare, who merely regarded her with his strange, expressionless eyes.

"No, Tekura. You can't be working with the scro," Hectate said, aghast. Despite everything he'd seen, he could not bring himself to believe *that* of Clan Kir.

"We are *using* the scro," K'tide corrected. "The alliance is regrettable, but necessary. Only orc priests know the rituals that hold the primary Witchlight Marauder in thrall."

Hectate shook his head in disbelief. The primary Witchlight Marauder was an enormous slug whose mouths consumed everything in its path—metal and minerals as well as living things—and produced poisonous gas and more marauders. A well-fed primary marauder periodically would spawn secondaries, which were gray monsters twenty feet tall with six-taloned hands and insatiable appetites for elven flesh. They, in turn, ejected tertiary marauders, miniature versions of themselves that had two metallic swords for each hand. The tertiaries were incomparable berserker warriors who finished off any living thing the larger monsters might have missed. Once the creatures ran out of food, they turned upon and destroyed each other; not, however, before their entire environment had been laid waste.

"The orcs were willing to revive the primary marauder and feed it until it released secondaries?" Hectate asked in disbelief. "The risks are incredible!"

"Indeed they are," the insectare agreed. "A number of orc priests were killed during the process. But the goblinkin are so eager to wash their hands in elven blood that they are willing to endure such losses."

Hectate felt numbed by the appalling revelation. "And you share that emotion, Tekura?"

"Why not?" The silver-haired bionoid stepped closer, and Hectate saw the unmistakable flame of fanaticism in her eyes. "The primary Witchlight Marauder, the source of our secondary weapons, was hidden on Armistice, frozen under a time-stop spell." She paused, and her smile was grim. "I don't think the goblins had much to do with that decision."

"What are you saying?"

"Think, Hectate. Do you think the Witchlight Marauder exists on Armistice due to elven *oversight*?" she demanded. "I'd wager my life that the elves not only know about it, but that they deliberately trapped the goblins on Armistice with that monster. It gives them a convenient way to destroy the goblinkin if the urge arises."

"I can't believe that," Hectate said flatly. "Assuming the elves would sanction the destruction of an entire world, they would never deliberately allow a marauder to live."

"Believe it," she said flatly.

Hectate was silent for many moments, then he looked up into the grave face of Wynlar, the clan leader. "What does a bionoid clan have to do with this?"

"Bionoids," Tekura echoed bitterly before Wynlar could respond. "The name we were given says it all. *Bionoid*, a simulated life form, not quite alive. Don't you see, Hectate?" she concluded passionately. "As far as the elves are concerned, we are monsters that they once created and now regret, not true and living beings. They have no concern for us; do not waste yours on them."

Hectate's eyes drifted shut. He had no arguments for her. He had left Clan Kir because he could not agree with their increasingly militant goals, yet he had no illusions about the elven opinions concerning his race. For years he had traveled alone, gaining a measure of acceptance because of his skills. More than anything, Hectate wished to be known and valued for his ability as a navigator, not be defined as a bionoid or even a half-elf. Despite Teldin Moore's persistent efforts on his behalf, life aboard the swan ship *Trumpeter* had been a painful reminder that this dream was unlikely to come true, at least not as long as the elves ruled wildspace.

"What do you want from me?" Hectate asked finally.

"You travel with Vallus Leafbower," K'tide observed. "Since he is wizard to the grand admiral of the Imperial Fleet, he certainly will know the current location of the command base."

"Vallus Leafbower is not in the habit of confiding in me," Hectate said dryly.

"Nevertheless, he will take you to Lionheart, and you will lead us there."

"But how?" the bionoid hedged.

Again the antennae quirked, this time into a skeptical angle. "Surely the swan ship has logs, records of some sort. You could find them and relay the information to us."

Hectate considered. "But if your plan succeeds, the scro will have an almost endless supply of new troops."

The insectare permitted himself an evil smile. "Not at all," he assured Hectate. "I assure you, the thousands of orcs, hobgoblins, bugbears, goblins, and kobolds that now live on Armistice will die on Armistice. Once the destruction of Lionheart is accomplished, one of our training crews will kill the priests and witch doctors whose spells keep the primary Witchlight Marauder in time-stop hibernation. Let the monster forage for a year or two, and there will be no life left on Armistice."

"You see?" broke in Tekura, her pale eyes bright with fierce excitement. "With one hand we behead the Imperial Fleet. With the other we destroy a goblin world!"

"The swan ship *Trumpeter* was badly damaged in battle, and far too many of its crew members were killed." K'tide leveled a glance at Wynlar. "Some of our troops were too caught up in the joy of battle to follow orders, it would seem. Since Lionheart is our primary goal and the swan ship merely our means of finding the elven base, I called off the attack before the elven vessel was destroyed. It landed on Armistice."

A small sigh of relief escaped Hectate. "Then Teldin Moore is unharmed?"

"For the present," the insectare said meaningfully, "but, as you can imagine, the Armistice orcs are unpredictable allies." K'tide shrugged. "The temptation of an elven ship may prove too great for them to resist."

"Unless . . ." Hectate prompted.

"If you will agree to return to the swan ship as a spy, we will send down a bionoid team to stall the orcs until we get the necessary information from you. Although the goblinkin are not known for being farsighted, perhaps we can persuade them to allow the swan ship time for repairs so that it might lead us to Lionheart."

"If it's Lionheart you're after, you have to keep the swan ship safe," Hectate countered.

K'tide inclined his head in a gesture of congratulations. "That's an astute observation, but not entirely correct. We easily could persuade our orc friends to lay waste the elven ship and bring us any information they find on board."

"But what makes you think you could get near Lionheart, even if you discover its location?"

"Aboard the swan ship, of course," K'tide said smoothly. "Whether the *Trumpeter* is manned by elves or bionoids in elven form, it will be admitted to the elven base and it will carry with it a secondary marauder."

Hectate was silent for a long moment. "I owe Teldin Moore pledge loyalty," he said slowly, counting on the insectare's knowledge of the bionoid battle code.

"I understand your dilemma." K'tide's thin lips stretched into a magnanimous smile. "All the more reason for you to return to the swan ship, for then you can see that Teldin Moore is safely removed from Lionheart once the marauder is released."

"That is reasonable," Tekura urged Hectate.

Hectate looked at Tekura and then at the expectant faces of the other Clan Kir bionoids, all known to him, all dear, yet all were strangers.

"And if I don't help?" he asked.

"You die, and every member of Clan Kir with you," K'tide said flatly.

The bionoids responded with an quick intake of breath. Tekura's eyes widened, but she did not look unduly surprised. Even if the rest of Clan Kir did not, Hectate thought sadly, Tekura knew insectares well enough to expect such treachery. She'd come to the clan as a young girl, under circumstances identical to his own.

Wynlar stepped forward. "I would like to believe that you are bluffing, K'tide, but I can't make that assumption when the safety of my clan is concerned. On what basis do you make such a threat?"

A strange gleam lit the insectare's multifaceted eyes. "When I called off the attack on the swan ship, I instructed the other members of Clan Kir to return to the scro ship. Very soon they all will be aboard the *Elfsbane*, under the albino paw of our good friend General Grimnosh."

"But they were to reconnoiter on Vesta!" cried Wynlar.

"I took the liberty of changing that order," K'tide said. He raised one green hand in a placating gesture. "Oh, I wouldn't be overly concerned about your clan, Captain Wynlar. At the present, they are useful to Grimnosh. I imagine, however, that their value would tarnish considerably if the scro general knew they were plotting to destroy the goblins of Armistice."

"But they are not," protested the bionoid leader. "We in this room did not learn that aspect of your plan until this very hour."

K'tide laughed, a dry, grating sound. "Do you think that will matter to Grimnosh, when his plans lie in ruins around him?"

Wynlar's face crumpled into a mask of despair. "My people are doomed."

"Not at all," K'tide said pleasantly. "If all goes well, I should be able to get a message through to the bionoids aboard the *Elfsbane* before we release the primary Witchlight Marauder on Armistice. They can be safely away before Grimnosh learns of his ultimate failure." The insectare's eyes fixed meaningfully on Hectate. "If all goes well," he repeated with quiet emphasis.

For a long moment, Hectate weighed his options: On one hand, the destruction of a planet of goblins and the haughty elves' high command; on the other, the lives of his adopted family and his first love.

"Hectate . . ." Tekura whispered, her voice a barely audible plea.

Finally he bowed his head. "It would seem that I have only one choice," he murmured.

"Splendid," the insectare said with quiet triumph. "Now, suppose we plan how we'll get you back into the good graces of Vallus Leafbower and Teldin Moore."

* * * * *

Aboard the elven man-o-war *Windwalker*, a battle wizard sat in deep trance despite the eery, low-pitched hum that pulsed from the magical alarm. An ancient disk hung from the ceiling of the bridge on a thick chain, and each pulse of sound that came from it pushed the fears of the assembled crew to new heights.

The battle wizard was oblivious to the other elves in the room. Waves of golden hair fell around her, curtaining her abstracted face and the narrow hands that cupped a scrying globe. On the wall before the entranced elf was a large, mirrorlike panel, a thin, shimmering oval sliced from the heart of a giant crystal. The captain and officers of the patrol ship *Windwalker* stood behind the wizard, and their eyes were fixed on the crystal panel in tense anticipation.

For centuries the elven ships that patrolled Armistice had been alert for the magical alarm, but this was the first time one had ever been activated. Its ancient voice warned them that a ship had breached the Armistice net. Slowly the battle wizard's magic reached out through the scrying globe, seeking the intruder. As a picture formed in her mind, the panel before her began to glow as magical energy transferred her mental image to the ensorcelled crystal panel, so that all could see what she saw. It was an impressive feat of magic, one for which she had trained since childhood, but it was not a unique skill; every patrol ship carried at least two wizards with this ability. As the picture on the panel firmed into detail, the humming alarm faded away.

"One of ours," the elven captain marveled as he stared at the image before them. Framing the downed ship were two distant mountains, the distinctive fang-shaped peaks that marked the domain of the Rakharian goblinkin. The ship's standard plainly identified it as a vessel of the Imperial Fleet. Closer scrutiny identified it as a swan ship, though, with the swan-head tower gone and the tail section shattered, it was difficult to classify. The battered swan ship tossed in the restless seas of Armistice, obviously seaworthy. It clearly had not crashed, so it presumably had a working helm and was therefore spaceworthy as well. The only possible conclusion was that it had landed deliberately.

Rage coursed through the captain like a cold tide. What elf would land on Armistice, so close to the land of Rakhar, and risk putting a spelljamming vessel in the hands of the powerful orc tribe there? To choose this over death was more than an act of cowardice; it was an act of treason!

The captain's jaw tightened. Whomever the swan ship's captain might be, he or she would answer to the grand admiral. And he, as the *Windwalker*'s captain, would find intense pleasure in escorting the rogue back to Lionheart in chains.

"Stay with it," he murmured to the battle wizard, speaking softly so as not to disrupt her concentration. "When you are tired, Circe will take your place, but we must keep that ship under observation. She can fly, have no doubt about that, and sooner or later she'll escape into wildspace. And whether her crew at that time be elven or orcish, we'll be there to meet it."

* * * * *

The first night on Armistice was spectacularly beautiful.
Few stars were visible through the ribbonlike wisps of clouds
that whirled and spun in the strong wind, yet the night was
not dark. Three huge moons lit the skies; a pale lavender
moon, one a rich amber reminiscent of winter ale, and the
third—the closest and largest moon—white faintly tinged
with green. The multicolored moonlight was reflected in
vivid, ever-changing patterns by the restive sea that surrounded the battered *Trumpeter*, as well as on the snow-
covered mountains on the distant shore.

The surviving crew of the swan ship began work on the
repairs as soon as the ship splashed down, with nearly every
crew member pitching in. Rozloom, naturally, took advantage of the excessive moonlight to press his suit with Raven
Stormwalker. When word reached Teldin of the aperusa's
rather spectacular failure, he smirked, sighed, then headed
down to the infirmary to check on the gypsy's injuries. As the
ship's captain, he had a certain duty to the well-being of his
crew.

Teldin found Rozloom seated on a cot, flirting outra-
geously with Deelia Snowsong. The elven healer's tiny
fingers flashed as she stitched a small gash on Rozloom's
forehead, pausing periodically to bat aside a straying, bronze
hand. Teldin noticed that the elven woman did not seem
offended by the gypsy's playful advances, and he wondered
why Rozloom persisted in his pursuit of Raven when there
were more receptive targets aboard ship—not to mention
less dangerous ones. In addition to the cut, Rozloom had
collected some colorful bruises. One eye already had swol-
len shut.

"Why?" Teldin asked simply.

His question startled both the aperusa and the elf.
Rozloom's hand froze, cupping air several inches from the

elven woman's derriere. Deelia's face flushed with embarrassment, and she edged away from the gypsy and hurried out of the room, murmuring something about needing herbs for a poultice.

"Why Raven?" Teldin repeated, this time with a hint of amusement.

Rozloom considered Teldin's question for a long time, a faintly quizzical expression on his battered face. Finally he shrugged his great shoulders and shook himself as if to dispel the uncharacteristic moment of introspection. A wicked gleam lit his one good eye, and he gave Teldin a gold-toothed grin.

"Believe me, Captain, there is much to be said for a woman with fire," he said, his jaunty air restored.

The image of a dragon flashed through Teldin's mind, and he laughed aloud. If you want fire, Rozloom, you're closer than you know, he thought with a surge of black humor. The aperusa's one good eye narrowed as he drew his own conclusions about Teldin's outburst.

"You also know this to be true?" Rozloom asked with an effort at nonchalance. Teldin's amusement died abruptly. He had heard the odd rumor linking him and Raven, and he immediately got the gist of Rozloom's inquiry. As Paladine's my witness, Teldin thought, what do I do with a question like that?

As if in response, Rozloom's huge hand drifted to the hilt of the jeweled dagger in his sash. Teldin's eyes widened, then he realized that Rozloom's gesture was no more than a reflex; knife fights over women were so common among aperusa that reaching for a dagger was a response as natural as sneezing over spilled pepper. To Teldin, the idea of Raven as a prize to be won was utterly ludicrous. He was tempted to tell Rozloom so, but such a notion lay too far outside an aperusa's way of thinking.

Teldin was spared the necessity of making any response

by the return of Deelia Snowsong. Rozloom's jovial leer returned and his hand drifted away from the dagger's hilt to preen his curling black beard. Murmuring captainlike platitudes that no one heard, Teldin backed out of the infirmary.

As he mounted the stairs to the upper deck, Teldin debated what he should do about the fight. He'd often thought it was just a matter of time before one of the ship's female crew had more than enough of Rozloom. Even in light of the gypsy's unflagging and often irritating pursuit, Raven's response was a little extreme. Protocol probably demanded that he talk to her, but even he if was inclined to discipline her, he'd no idea how he could make it stick. As he did a dozen times a day, the captain wished he had the wisdom of a sage. Never a fal around when you need one, Teldin thought wryly.

A new thought hit him with the force of a fireball. Raven had a volatile temper, and she'd shown considerable magical ability in silencing Vallus's spell. Had *she*, not Estriss, cast the magic missile that had killed the lakshu warrior?

If she had, Teldin didn't blame her. He knew all too well that wearing an ultimate helm meant fighting to stay alive. His concerns were practical; magic missiles were powerful weapons, and if Raven could command them, that was one more thing he could add to the arsenal of skills possessed by the surviving crew members. They had lost far too many in the battle, including Hectate Kir. Teldin's bionoid friend had simply disappeared, which had prompted a lot of speculation by the surviving elves. Gaston, in particular, seemed annoyingly gratified that his suspicions about the half-elf had been justified.

When he reached the deck, Teldin noted that the repairs were progressing much too slowly. The elves' thin silver uniforms offered little protection from the bitter winds, and the intense gravity force of Armistice slowed their movements to a sluggish, exhausting struggle. Walking was

difficult enough, but with the gravity force making everything feel three times its normal weight, lifting was nearly
impossible and climbing became hazardous. A wiry elven
sailor attempting to climb the ship's rigging tore through the
sturdy net and earned himself a painful fall. The final blow
was a literal one: while perched on what was left of the
tower, Om "accidentally" dropped her gnome-sized wrench
on the latest recipient of the irrepressible Rozloom's flirting,
sending the unfortunate elven woman sprawling, senseless,
to the deck.

Teldin immediately sent one of the wizards to the secondary helm, guessing that conditions would be more tolerable
if the swan ship maintained its own air envelope and gravity
field. The results were immediate, and the elves worked
much more effectively. Teldin also reasoned that it wouldn't
hurt to have the helm up in case Vallus's goblins materialized
in force.

Three watches came and went before dawn broke over
the distant mountains. Vallus, who apparently was somewhat of an authority on the ice world, informed Teldin that
days on Armistice were about sixty hours in length. The
presence of three moons made the tides unusually strong,
and as the sun rose the morning tides receded in a turbulent,
compelling surge. The swan ship strained against its anchors
and several times was nearly swept out to sea. Teldin
suggested that they bring the swan ship closer to land,
hoping that they might find a sheltered cove, but Vallus
insisted that they were in less danger from the tides and
weather than from the goblins. Teldin suspected that Vallus
was being paranoid, and he agreed only with reluctance.
Since the battle with the bionoids, relations between Teldin
and the elven wizard had been strained, for Teldin's faith in
the wizard's judgment and character had been badly shaken.

Teldin had never believed that the Imperial Fleet would
give him a true choice of whether or not to use his cloak for

the elven war effort, but up to the moment when Raven had stopped Vallus's spell, Teldin had trusted the wizard personally. Now, having seen Vallus's willingness to sacrifice his crew rather than allow the goblinkin to get hold of the cloak, Teldin was not so sure this trust was warranted.

And what about Raven Stormwalker? Her use of the sapphire pendant to land the swan ship proved that she wielded another ultimate helm. Yet she had done nothing to challenge Teldin for the captaincy of the *Spelljammer*; in fact, she had been nothing but helpful. In bringing the ship down safely, she'd probably saved them all. Teldin remembered little about the landing on Armistice, other than a vague sense of unease and a dim memory of dreams filled with golden light.

As for Raven, Teldin got the impression that she considered him an ally rather than an adversary. What that meant to her, he couldn't begin to guess. Whatever her game, Teldin was getting tired of waiting for her to play out her hand.

Since the night he first had fastened the clasp of the cloak around his neck, Teldin had had little control over the events that shaped his life. He often vowed that the situation would change, but so far he'd had no inspiration on how to accomplish this. As the days on Armistice passed in ever-increasing frustration, at times Teldin could barely contain his urge to seize Raven's shoulders, shake her, and scream, "What do you want from me?" into her beautiful face.

It was almost a relief when supplies began to run low; at least it gave Teldin something tangible and immediate to address. At first he directed the crew's efforts toward the sea. The strange fish they managed to catch were ugly, spiked, eellike creatures, but under Rozloom's skilled hands the fish became palatable enough. The elves also tried harvesting some of the abundant kelp; fortunately Deelia Snowsong intervened before anyone sampled the seaweed. The ice elf

suspected anything that could grow in the frigid water, so she
tested the weeds and found them highly toxic. She guessed
that volcanic activity under the ocean bed warmed the deep
water enough to produce the kelp, but also passed poisonous gases into the seaweed. Whatever the case, Chirp and
Trivit took a dark and unexpected glee in distilling the kelp
into poison.

A more serious problem was the water supply; somehow
the storage tanks had been damaged in the landing. Soon it
was plain that—goblins or not—they would be forced to go
ashore in search of potable water.

And so, in the darkest hours of the Armistice night, a small
longboat slipped away from the swan ship and struggled
through the waves toward the forbidding shoreline of
Rakhar.

Chapter Fifteen

●●●

Teldin was on the upper deck when the returning longboat was sighted. The search party brought water and tales of a hot spring inhabited by a monster similar to a remorhaz and guarded by yetilike creatures. The elves guessed that the yeti probably were bugbears—one of the more abundant goblinoid races—who had uniquely adapted to the climate of Armistice. These creatures had put up a token fight but had not given chase.

Vallus was puzzled by this uncharacteristic behavior. According to his theory, the Armistice goblins would do anything to obtain spelljamming materials. In addition to this, bugbears were notorious and vicious carnivores, highly unlikely to let such tempting game as an elven search party escape their stew pots. After a typically long-winded elven discussion, Vallus conceded that they should further investigate the situation on shore.

Teldin volunteered to lead the search party, a notion that Vallus quickly shot down. The elven wizard argued, convincingly, that taking the cloak into goblinoid territory was a foolhardy risk. Raven stepped in to fill the breach, and, with a uncharacteristic burst of bravado, Rozloom quickly signed on with her. Om followed the aperusa like a small brown shadow, and they rounded out the party with a couple of elves, both of them skilled rangers and fighters.

With a deep sense of unease, Teldin watched the longboat

pull away a second time. It was difficult for him to send others into danger; he would have preferred to go himself.

Raven, on the other hand, felt grateful for a change of scenery. The swan ship was becoming much too confining, and her gold and silver eyes gleamed at the prospect of adventure. Her sojourn aboard the *Trumpeter* was tedious but necessary. She needed time to observe Teldin Moore, to make sure he really was the one she sought.

Think of it, she mused dreamily as she struggled with her oar. Her name, Celestial Nightpearl, forever a part of the *Spelljammer* legends. In every known sphere songs would be sung about her, and races not yet discovered would know her name and stand in awe of her glory. By Bahamut, it was wonderful! she mused, in praise of the god of good dragons.

She had learned something about the *Spelljammer* that few others had imagined: it was a living being of vast and mysterious intelligence. Centuries of study had brought her to the grudging conclusion that the ship-creature was even more powerful and brilliant than a radiant dragon, and she'd decided early on that the venerable Celestial Nightpearl would never play second zither to an overgrown boat.

Yet the pull of the great ship was difficult to resist, and several times the dragon had nearly succumbed to the seeking, compelling voice of the *Spelljammer.* In Teldin Moore she saw a possible solution: a captain to take her place. The way she saw it, the only other way to be free of the *Spelljammer* was to die, and she had no intention of doing that anytime in the next millennium or two.

The question remained: Was Teldin Moore an appropriate choice? After observing the human for many days, she'd become quite impressed with him. People tended to like and trust him, which was a mark in his favor. He had an honest, decent core to him, and she had little doubt that he'd stick with whatever bargain they struck. She'd had a hard time dragon-charming the man, which, though annoying, was another huge mark in his favor. The dragon was very close to offering him a deal, but something held her back. To her way of thinking, an aspirant to the captain's chair of the *Spelljammer* should have a deep, true love of adventure and a bold spirit. Teldin Moore did not lack strength, nor was he timid, but he didn't seem inclined to take charge. To her eye, he was drifting in the stream of events. She suspected that unless things changed, he would never survive the challenges that awaited a potential captain aboard the great ship. She knew a little of these things, enough to make her fear for the man she had chosen to be her surrogate. Guilt was out of the question, of course. Such trivial emotions were utterly foreign to a radiant dragon.

The scraping of rocks against the bottom of the longboat brought Raven's attention back to the mission. She wasn't exactly thrilled with her crew. Gaston Willowmere, the first mate, had an unreasonable grudge against moon elves. The other elf, a gorgeous female warrior of sorts who was named after some plant or other, had a nasty habit of upstaging her. Om was a gnome—enough said—though remarkably taciturn for the species, Bahamut be praised. Fear and cold had reduced the voluble Rozloom to silence, which was just fine with Raven. The aperusa had crossed the line between adulation and familiarity once too often.

The odd search party came ashore without incident and skirted the hot springs, not wanting to alert the bugbears to its presence. The night was uncommonly clear, and the winds were calm. After wading through the snow for an hour or so, the party members found two sets of bearlike tracks and followed them to the base of one of the two large mountains. Beneath a rocky overhang was a tunnel into the frozen ground. The search party exchanged uncertain glances.

"I say we go in," Raven voted, stooping down to peer into the opening. "That boring wizard of yours says the goblin people live underground."

"Agreed," Rozloom said firmly. He struck a heroic pose, one meaty fist clasped over his heart. "I will stand guard here."

With an amused smile, Raven nodded to the aperusa. A coward he undoubtedly was, but even if he were as brave as a dracon, he'd have to stay behind. Rozloom stood several inches above six feet and was prodigiously broad; she doubted he'd fit the tunnel ahead.

Rozloom forgotten, Raven turned her attention back to the tunnel. It sloped downhill at an alarming angle and rounded a sharp corner after a few feet. It was wide enough, but none too tall. Either the orcs on this world were a petite variety, or they'd stumbled upon the servant's entrance, noted the disguised dragon.

She slipped into the tunnel, followed by the elves and gnome. Fortunately her elven body came equipped with night vision, so she was able to discern patterns of heat in the rock. There was little heat to be had anywhere on Armistice, but a faint red glow gradually increased as they made their way along the winding path.

Finally they came out on a walkway that overlooked a vast, natural cavern. Raven grabbed Gaston's arm and pulled him down behind the cover of a large boulder, then she motioned for the others to do the same. Thus hidden, she turned her attention to the bizarre scene that sprawled out before them.

A large hot spring bubbled and gushed in the center of the chamber—that would account for the heat, Raven supposed, not counting the scattering of dung-fueled fires. Phosphorescent fungi grew along the base of the walls and lent a sickly green glow to the cavern. This light was augmented by a few oil lamps made from large mollusk shells. The lamps emitted more rancid smoke than light, but after the darkness of the tunnel the chamber seemed as bright as highsun.

Although the scenery was as dismal as any Raven had

seen, more disturbing was the chamber's occupants. The place was littered with goblinkin of every description. There were the squat, deeply furred bugbears the first elven party had mistaken for yeti, packs of tiny, pale gray kobolds, and slightly larger goblins. The orcs were the most grotesque mutation. Although they still had the tusks, wolflike ears, and upturned snouts common to orcs, centuries of living underground had compacted more orc into less space. They appeared to be no taller than five feet, and their barrellike chests and large arms brought to mind dwarven warriors. They had no fur, but their hides appeared to have thickened to an unnatural degree. All of the creatures ranged in color from pale gray to dirty white, and almost without exception they were unclothed. Most of the weapons Raven saw were crude mallets: carved stone lashed to a long bone with a length of dried sinew. A few orcs carried deeply pitted blades or axes—family heirlooms or war trophies, Raven supposed. Armistice was metal-poor and lacked fur-bearing animals, so the goblin races didn't have much to work with. The "culture" that had evolved was squalid, brutal, and apparently chaotic.

But someone had brought order to it. After she watched for a while, Raven could make out certain patterns. Amid the chaos, the creatures went about tending their motley vessels in an inefficient but purposeful manner.

"Ships?" she asked in a whisper. "If this is their fishing fleet, I'll put good odds on the fish."

Om shook her tiny brown head. "Spelljammers. *Working* spelljammers."

The first mate rounded on the gnome. "Impossible," Gaston hissed.

In the longest speech any of the others had ever heard from her, the gnome insisted that the ships, despite their appearance, were spaceworthy and ready for flight. Om concluded her argument by pointing up. The others looked. Far overhead was an opening big enough to reveal all three moons. The cone-shaped cavern apparently was the interior of a long-dead volcano. Raven guessed that any ship in the motley fleet easily could make it through.

"I've seen enough," Gaston announced. The others nodded, and they made their way out as quickly as possible, fighting both the steep incline and the punishing gravity force.

Rozloom was where they had left him, half-frozen and edgy. He claimed he'd seen nothing, which struck Raven as odd. She would have expected him to invent a battle with fearsome creatures, a story that cast him in the hero's role. Dismissing the aperusa, she headed back toward the shore. She would have liked to stick around for a better look, but Gaston Willowmere was nearly turning himself inside out in his anxiety to return to the swan ship to report.

By the time they reached the longboat, Rozloom had regained his usual ebullient nature. As he rowed, he sang an obscene aperusa ditty in his deep bass voice, punctuating it with an occasional wink or leer. By the time they reached the swan ship, Raven was ready to throttle him.

Vallus received their news with alarm and insisted that they must send word of this development to elven high command as quickly as possible. The elves redoubled their efforts to repair the swan ship, but not for this reason alone.

The three moons of Armistice were almost in alignment.

* * * * *

"Well, where is it?" snapped Grimnosh.

The bionoids of Clan Kir, now back in their elven forms, exchanged uncertain glances. They barely had docked their shrike ships aboard the *Elfsbane* when the scro general came striding into their midst, followed by his surly, gray-green adjutant. Wynlar, who usually dealt with the insectare and scro, had not yet arrived.

"Sir?" one of the bionoids ventured.

"The cloak!" thundered Grimnosh. He grabbed the bionoid who had spoken by the front of his shirt. "Where is Teldin Moore's cloak?"

Another bionoid, a female warrior with the crooked nose and fierce amber eyes of a hawk, stepped forward and met the scro's glare squarely. "I am Ronia, a lieutenant under Captain Wynlar. In his absence I will speak for the battle clan. We do not have the human or his cloak."

Grimnosh's lip curled into a disdaining sneer. He tossed aside the first bionoid and faced down the female warrior. "Teldin Moore was lost with the swan ship? That was careless, even for elf-spawned insects."

Ronia's amber eyes narrowed to slits at the deadly insult. "In a manner of speaking, he was lost, but carelessness had nothing to do with it."

"Enough of these elven subtleties," Grimnosh snarled. "Give your report, Lieutenant."

The bionoid warrior was soldier enough to respond to a direct order, and she drew herself up to attention. "When we withdrew from the elven vessel, it was damaged but not destroyed. I do not know what course the swan ship took, but almost certainly the human was still aboard."

"Withdrew? Against orders, you *retreated*?" Grimnosh echoed, his voice rising in a roar of rage and disbelief. In perfect Elvish he began to berate the group for their ineptitude and cowardice. By using the language of a race the bionoids both resembled and despised, he amplified his already scathing insults threefold.

At length Ronia could take no more. The Change came over her as she closed the distance between her and the general. In her insectoid form she loomed a good three feet over the ranting scro. One armored, spike-studded hand shot out toward the general's throat, circling his massive neck and effectively cutting off his tirade. She easily hoisted the seven-foot scro so that his snout was inches away from her multifaceted eyes. The glowing crystal eye in the center of her forehead cast an angry red light on the scro's pale hide, turning it a ghastly purplish blue as he struggled for air.

Two other bionoids quickly transformed into their monster forms and moved to hold back the general's adjutant. The gray-green scro put up a token struggle, but he watched his superior's distress with a manic gleam in his yellow eyes.

"You name us cowards, orc pig," Ronia told Grimnosh coldly, "when even a kobold knows that a bionoid warrior never withdraws from a fight of his own accord. If any showed cowardice, it was your minion, K'tide. *He* called off the attack."

Contemptuously, the monstrous insect tossed the scro to the ground, then folded her massive, armor-plated arms in a gesture of defiance.

For several moments Grimnosh dragged in long, ragged breaths, one white paw gingerly massaging his throat. When he rose to his feet, he had collected himself and his unnerving, urbane facade was firmly back in place. "You state your case forcibly, Lieutenant," he managed to croak out. "Where is our green friend?"

"I don't know. Several of the clan are missing as well."

"What is that damnable insect up to?" Grimnosh muttered to himself. He turned to regard the bionoid who had attacked him, giving the audacious monster a lengthy appraisal. She would suffer for her actions later, but at the moment he had a use for her. "Tell me, *Captain* Ronia, how much longer before the orcs of Armistice are flight ready?"

"They're ready now," the bionoid responded warily. Her voice revealed her suspicion with both the question and the promotion. "They have been ready for some time."

Grimnosh's colorless eyes narrowed. "I beg your pardon?"

"Some twenty ships are ready, complete with functioning helms. Many more are near completion."

The scro nodded slowly. "Yes, of course. Do you know the gate into the Armistice atmosphere? You do. Very well, Captain, you will take one shrike ship to the ice world and prepare the orc recruits for an immediate mission. The rest of you, prepare yourselves for battle. All of you, meet in my study at four bells to receive further assignments and tactics. Go now."

The scro spun and stalked out of the bionoids' quarters, silently berating himself as he went. He should have known better than to let K'tide out of his sight even for a moment. He should have squashed the insectare like the bug he was.

Grimnosh had no doubt about K'tide's goal; the insectare was obsessed with the destruction of Lionheart. It had not escaped the scro's attention that the klicklikak—the insectare's hideous ship—was no longer aboard the dinotherium. K'tide apparently had taken a crack crew of bionoids with him, and where else would they go but Armistice? The klicklikak had been stripped for cargo, and K'tide and his crew easily could load a secondary marauder and its attendant priest in the hold. K'tide would then chase down the swan ship, use the bionoid warriors to overtake the elven crew, and use the swan ship and the elflike bionoids to smuggle the marauder into the elven base. Not a bad plan, Grimnosh admitted grudgingly, *providing* one was willing to go one step further.

So far Teldin Moore had escaped every attempt to relieve him of his cloak. The human and his elven allies could not stand against the force that he, Grimnosh, would bring against them. In battle the *Elfsbane* alone was more than a match for a swan ship. K'tide might have culled the bionoid force somewhat, but a dozen of the monsters still remained under Grimnosh's banner as well as three shrike ships, and soon a fleet of orcs would complete his personal navy. To ensure victory, Grimnosh would direct the battle himself.

Once the Cloak of the First Pilot was in his possession, his first act would be to take revenge on the presumptuous

K'tide. Grimnosh personally would peel the insectare's exoskeleton away plate by plate, then have the creature slowly flayed to death with its own antennae. The scro's fierce scowl relaxed under the soothing prospect of pleasures to come.

Once he had dealt with K'tide, he would borrow the traitor's scheme to use the bionoids, the captured swan ship, and the Witchlight Marauder to bring down Lionheart. Grimnosh was a practical scro, and he saw no reason why the insectare's plan should die when the spy master did.·

Chapter Sixteen

● ● ●

When the first morning rays of sunlight touched the swan ship, they fell upon a frenzy of activity. Only two days remained until the three moons of Armistice would come fully into alignment. According to Vallus, this event occurred every twenty-eight local days, and at such times the planet was racked with earthquakes, volcanic activity, and violent high tides. Getting off Armistice as soon as possible absorbed every member of the crew.

To Teldin's way of thinking, things couldn't get much worse. Turbulent seas already were buffeting the swan ship, and rumblings could be heard not only from the shore, but deep in the seabed beneath them. Blizzards were almost a daily occurrence, many of them punctuated with bone-shaking thunder and lightning.

During one such storm, a random flash of lightning caught Teldin's attention. As he watched, a long, insistent streak blazed above the snow-covered ground, touching down between the shoreline and the mountains. Teldin stood at the upper deck's railing for a long time, squinting in the direction of the vanished light.

Something about the flash stirred his memory. As he thought it over, Teldin recognized the true nature of the light. When last he'd seen the night sky lit by such a streak, a spelljamming vessel had crashed on his farm and had begun the nightmare he now lived. Time slipped away, and for a moment Teldin was a bewildered farmer again, helplessly cradling a dying reigar woman in his arms.

Not again, Teldin vowed silently. It was not likely that he could do anything for the crew of the vessel, but he had to at least try. With a surge of resolve, Teldin strode off in search of his improbable ally: Raven Stormwalker.

He found the moon elf down on the main deck, in what remained of the storage area. She directed Chirp and Trivit's efforts to patch the gaping hole in the roof where the ballista had crashed through. A group of elves disassembled the ballista according to Om's terse instructions, preparing to take the weapon above to the upper deck to be remounted.

Although Teldin was gratified to see the work progressing so well, the bustle was not conducive to his mission. Teldin walked up to the moon elf and quietly spoke a few words to her. She nodded, and he slipped away to the cargo hold. Within moments Raven joined him, wearing the warmest clothes she could find aboard ship.

"What's on your mind, Captain?"

Fleetingly, Teldin wondered at her use of the title. Raven always called him that, with subtle but deliberate emphasis. Was she baiting him, or perhaps mocking his pretensions toward commanding the *Spelljammer*? He added it to the bottom of the list of questions he planned to ask her—if and when they got back from Rakhar.

"Can you shapechange?" he asked bluntly. When Raven quirked an inquiring eyebrow, he hastened to explain the ability his cloak gave him to change his appearance at will. Raven listened, a strange smile curving her lips and speculation glinting in her gold and silver eyes.

"That presents some interesting possibilities," she said at last, more to herself than to Teldin. "Why do you ask?"

Teldin quickly told her about the fallen ship and his decision to investigate and, if possible, help survivors. "If we took the form of one of the native races, we'd be less likely to run into trouble," he concluded.

"Unless someone speaks to you in Orcish," she pointed out.

Teldin shrugged away her objection and gathered up a handful of his cloak. "It translates."

"Hmmm. Handy garment to have, Captain." She pulled the sapphire pendant from its hiding place beneath her jerkin. "This trinket has a different set of tricks, but shapechanging happens to be one of my hobbies," she said in a wry tone. "As for changing into goblin form, that might best be done a safe distance from the swan ship. If it's all the same to you, I'm in no mood to be fireballed by a bunch of elven wizards."

Teldin conceded her point with an uncertain smile, and they worked together to drag a spare longboat from the cargo hold. A ballista was mounted at the bow of the lower level, and they lowered the longboat through the opening the weapon port provided. The longboat was painted a silvery white, making it deliberately conspicuous in wildspace but providing effective camouflage in the icy water. The boat was almost invisible in the churning waters, which tossed the small craft about as effortlessly as if it were a fisherman's float.

For more than an hour, the pair struggled with the oars. Merely staying afloat was an accomplishment, but at the end of the hour they still were no more than an arrow's shot from the swan ship.

"Time to change," Teldin gasped out.

Raven nodded, brushing a frozen lock of hair out of her face and securing her oar in the gunwale. "I've seen the creatures. I'll go first."

She closed her eyes. Immediately her outline blurred and her elven form was replaced by a nebulous gray haze. As Teldin watched, fascinated, the gray mist shifted and expanded. Like a boat comes into focus as it emerges from a fog bank, so the details of her new features began to sharpen. The transformation was over in a matter of seconds, and Teldin recoiled instinctively from what Raven had become.

Beside him was a huge, vaguely humanoid creature covered with a dingy, whitish fur. Seated, the creature towered over Teldin, and its massive torso and thick arms gave mute testimony to its strength. Its shoulders were as wide as a broadsword, and its short, squat legs ended in the clawed feet of a bear. Indeed, much about the creature was bearlike. Its prominent snout had the distinctive pug shape of a bear, and its mouth was full of sharp, curved fangs. Its eyes were a pale, sickly green with blood-red pupils, and the tips of short, wedge-shaped ears protruded from the thatch of white hair that crowned its sloped forehead.

"Should I be glad I don't have a mirror?" the creature asked in Raven's wry voice. Teldin nodded dumbly, and her tusks glinted as she smiled at the dumbfounded man. "Your turn, and hurry. I'm heavier than you now, and the boat's listing my way something awful. I don't fancy trying to swim in this fur coat."

Teldin stared intently at Raven, taking in the details of her new face and form. He closed his eyes and conjured a mental image of himself, replacing it in his mind with a replica of the creature beside him. He knew the transformation was complete when he heard long, ripping sounds, followed by a woman's laugh. Belatedly he remembered his clothing. He cracked one eye open and looked down. His fine, elf-crafted garments were not equal to the transformation and they hung about his massive new body in ribbons.

Raven shook her shaggy white head. "Don't think ahead much, do you?" she said with a chuckle. "Might as well toss those rags, Captain, though you'll raise some eyebrows when you change back to human form."

Silently agreeing, Teldin ripped off the remains of his clothing and dropped them into the sea. The thick fur insulated him from the cold better than his own clothing had, and he didn't miss it. His only garment was the cloak, which, as always, adjusted its size to accommodate his form.

"You might do something about that cloak," Raven suggested, pointing to the regal purple that flowed over his furred shoulders. "You'll be the best dressed yeti-bugbear on Armistice. People will talk."

Teldin grinned through his tusks and shrank the cloak down to its necklace size. The silver chain easily hid in his thick fur, and he caught a glimpse of the gold and blue pendant buried in Raven's fur. Their transformation completed, the pair resumed their rowing. Having the strength of the Armistice-bred creatures sped their progress, and soon they pulled the craft up on a pebble-strewn beach.

They followed a barely discernible wisp of smoke and tromped up the first of several small foothills. As they walked, the winds picked up and yet another blizzard began. Even in his yeti form, Teldin found the climate punishing, and, to conserve their energy, he and Raven trudged on without speaking. As they crested the fifth hill, the wreck came into sight. Teldin fought back the memory of that first crashed spelljammer, and he led the way as they half-ran, half-slid down the snowy hill toward the downed ship as fast as their stubby legs allowed.

The ship, or what was left of it, had been cracked wide open by the force of impact and now was little more than a smoking hull. Four thin, twisted protrusions rose from the wreckage, and to Teldin's eye the ship looked like a dead thing, lying on its back with it legs sticking up. Something about the ship seemed oddly familiar . . .

"The klicklikak," Teldin breathed. His words formed a cloud, instantly condensing into icy droplets that clung to his facial fur. Raven squinted at the ship, then nodded confirmation. A quick investigation showed that no bodies remained in the ship; all apparently had been thrown out when the ship had split in two. Snow-covered mounds were scattered around the hull, however. Not sure what compelled him, Teldin insisted on checking each one. Together he and Raven dug out four dead elves, their bodies mangled and already stiffening from the cold.

"No insectare. That's odd," Raven mused. "Only an insectare can use that helm." She pointed to the smoking, hooded throne that was fitted with two curling, long pipes. "No antennae, no power. It won't do the orcs much good. That's one comfort."

Teldin rubbed his forehead with a half-frozen paw. Suddenly he wondered why he'd come here, what he'd ever thought he could accomplish. He didn't see how anything could have survived the crash, and he said so. Raven wasn't as sure.

"Ever see an insectare without his robe and cowl?"

"No. Am I missing something?" Teldin said wearily.

His humor was unintentional, but Raven's appreciative smirk registered even through her yeti form. "They're tough, hard to kill."

Too cold and exhausted to talk, Teldin just shrugged and gestured back toward the shore. Raven nodded, and they plodded back in the direction from which they'd come. The snowfall had dwindled to a few swirling flakes, but the driving wind already had obliterated their footsteps. A few yards from the klicklikak they slogged past yet another mound. Teldin saw no reason to investigate. He'd seen enough dead elves for one day. He averted his eyes from the snowy grave, but not before he'd caught a glimpse of something that chilled him to the soul.

Frozen and stubborn, the tip of a familiar reddish brown cowlick protruded from the snow. Teldin was on his knees in a heartbeat, pawing aside the snow.

"Why?" Raven asked. Her question chased a puff of steam.

"I know this one," he mumbled.

Raven cast her bugbear eyes toward the moons in a gesture of exasperation. "Captain, these frozen elves of yours give new definition to the word *stiff.* You can't help this one."

As she spoke, Teldin uncovered the pallid form of Hectate Kir. Maybe not, Teldin acknowledged silently, but I'm not going to leave him here either.

Raven moved in for a better look. The half-elf was almost as white as his snowy blanket, but no injuries were visible. She knelt beside Teldin and lay her furred ear directly on Hectate's chest. After a moment she sat back on her heels. "What do you know. He must have changed to his bionoid form before impact. Bounced once or twice, I'd guess, but that's about it."

"He's *alive?*" Teldin demanded.

"Didn't I just say that?"

Teldin didn't bother to answer. He hoisted the half-elf over his fur-covered shoulders, and the two yeti-bugbears hurried back to the waiting longboat.

* * * * *

Moving with painful slowness, the insectare hauled himself into the small craft. Despite the loss of the klicklikak and his bionoid crew, K'tide was more determined than ever to go through with his plan. He'd get to Lionheart if he had to ride there on the back of a void scavver.

Battered by the crash and stiff from the cold, the insectare crawled deep into the hull of the longboat and looked for something with which to conceal himself. There were a couple of flotation devices—rings of extremely lightweight wood—and a torn piece of sheeting. With numb fingers K'tide shook out the canvas and covered himself with it, curling up as small as possible. Even if he were discovered, he figured his chances of survival were better with the swan ship's elves than with the goblins of Armistice. The bionoids always changed into their monster forms before facing the Rakharian orcs, but he had no such ability and his elflike face probably would earn him a slow and brutal death at the hands of the Armistice orcs.

If he could just get aboard the swan ship! His informant there was not among his most reliable employees, but with even a little help he'd find a way to ferret out the information he needed. Then he could send a message to the surviving bionoids of Clan Kir, have them rescue him, and take over the swan ship. The destruction of Lionheart could proceed as planned, and then he would don the Cloak of the First Pilot.

* * * * *

Aboard the patrol ship *Windwalker*, elven warriors stood ready for battle. The man-o-war's captain left preparations to his first mate, preferring to spend his time on the bridge in fascinated observation of the rogue swan ship.

The swan-head tower that once had housed the bridge had been replaced by a raised deck covered by a hastily constructed shed. The stern had been patched and heavily reinforced. Mounted there was a massive tail catapult that obviously was of gnomish design. By all appearances, the ship was spaceworthy. They had to take to flight soon, the captain mused, or risk destruction during the coming lunar alignment.

They *had* to take flight soon, he repeated silently. The *Windwalker's* battle wizards were near exhaustion from the effort of keeping the rogue ship in view, day after day. Even as the captain acknowledged that problem, the battle wizard on duty swayed in her chair, and her hands began to slide unheeded down the sides of the scrying globe. The captain squeezed her shoulder, pulling her back into her fading trance.

"Stay with it," he admonished softly. "The swan ship will take off soon. We must get it as soon as it clears the atmosphere shield."

Before the elven woman could respond, a second alarm sounded. Her eyes snapped open, and the image of the swan ship vanished from the magical panel. Not having much choice, the captain directed her to investigate the new threat.

Now fully alert, she bent to the task. In response to her magical inquiry, the panel darkened to the star-sprinkled blackness of wildspace. To one side Vesta glowed like a pale amethyst, its purple orb framed by the larger green light of the primary moon behind it.

The alignment, thought the captain, noting the thin rim of amber light visible to the left of Vesta. The three moons would align this night, and, by all reports, Armistice would resemble a frozen version of the Plane of Chaos. For a moment he almost pitied the orcs and goblins that lived there.

A moving pinprick of light caught his eye, ending his charitable thought abruptly. There was a second light, then a third. Before the horrified gaze of the officers, the lights multiplied, and soon a small fleet of spelljammers—patchwork vessels that defied classification—flew crazily into view. A dozen or more of the vessels sped through the atmospheric boundary and into the freedom of wildspace.

"The orcs are escaping," the battle wizard said in a dazed, distant voice. "How could this happen?"

"It hasn't happened yet." The captain spun to face the helmsman. "New course. We pursue those vessels."

After a hurried consultation with the navigator to determine the location of the goblin ships, the captain set a course toward them. Fortunately, the ragtag fleet was not far from the much faster *Windwalker*, and soon the scene outside the bridge window mirrored that on the crystal panel.

The man-o-war closed rapidly. Following the captain's orders, the weapons crew fired a catapult at the nearest ship. The shot scored a direct hit, and the fragile ship exploded into flame and scattering fragments.

In their jubilation, the elves did not notice the approach of the second fleet. Or perhaps the fleet was not there to see, for with the suddenness of magic three shrike ships appeared, circling directly above the man-o-war.

One of the elven wizards got off a fireball spell, and it hurtled toward the lead shrike ship in a stream of blue flame. An answering flash of magic burst from their birdlike attacker, and the two spells collided over the man-o-war with an explosion that shook the ship and sent its crew tumbling to the decks.

Alarms sounded throughout the man-o-war, and soon the main deck was crowded with elven warriors. The shrike ships continued to circle, and their path was so close to the *Windwalker* that the elves dared not risk using their larger weapons. With apparent chivalry, the shrike ships held off their attack until the man-o-war's battle stations were fully crewed. The lead vessel slowed, coming to hover directly over the deck of the elven vessel.

As the puzzled elves craned their necks back, waiting and watching, the cargo doors on the shrike ship's hold opened. Strange gray warriors, a dozen or so, leaped from the shrike ship and hit the deck with a metallic clatter.

Silence shrouded the elven ship as the invaders rose to their feet. Roughly four feet tall, the creatures were bipedal, and their muscular bodies were covered with hide the color of a garden slug. Their huge, fanged maws worked hungrily, and at the end of their two long arms were "hands" comprising two gleaminging swords that clanked and flashed with the dexterity of lethal fingers.

The creatures advanced in a pack, hurling themselves at the elves in a frenzy of slashing blades. Like berserker warriors, the gray horrors tore through the elven crew, feeding as they went. Their feasting did not seem to slow their attack, and the tertiary Witchlight Marauders killed and ate their way through the elven vessel with grisly efficiency.

Chapter Seventeen

•••

The return trip to the swan ship was swift and perilous. Still in their yeti forms, Teldin and Raven struggled with the oars for only a few minutes before Raven decided to shapechange into one of the giant, eellike fish that abounded in the icy waters, so that she could tow the longboat back. As soon as she made that announcement, she rose and dove into the water, disappearing into the turbulent sea. A dubious Teldin tossed a tow line overboard, and the longboat took off with a jerk that sent him tumbling to the floor. With one paw Teldin desperately clung to the side of the boat; with the other he held on to the unconscious half-elf. The longboat sliced wildly through the choppy waters, leaving behind it a small wake. Again and again the boat thudded painfully down after hitting a particularly large wave. By the time they were within sight of the *Trumpeter*, Teldin felt battered and exhausted just from the effort of staying in the boat, and he feared the effect the wild ride might have had on Hectate.

The longboat's momentum slowed abruptly, and Raven's eel head poked out of the water, along with a foot or so of scaly neck. Teldin watched, dumbfounded, as the upper part of the creature changed into the familiar head and shoulders of the elven woman. The part of Raven still submerged in the icy water retained its fish form. As she dragged herself up and into the longboat, the metamorphosis worked its way down her body. Finally she tumbled over the side and into the longboat, fully clothed and completely dry. The elf met his astonished gaze with a tolerant, one-sided smile, and Teldin realized that he was gaping like a beached carp. His fanged jaws closed with an audible click.

Fangs. There was that problem again, Teldin thought ruefully. In his current, goblinoid form he hardly could expect a kinsman's welcome from the elven crew, but if he reclaimed his human form, he'd board the *Trumpeter* clad in nothing but gooseflesh and a cloak. With a sigh of resignation, Teldin willed the cloak to grow out to its full length. He drew the dark folds over his broad, furred shoulders, hoping that the elves would discern his true identity from the magical cloak.

"Change your face back," Raven suggested. "Just your face. Keep the fur so you don't freeze, but scale the body down to something approaching your normal build."

Teldin quickly followed her advice. As he felt the goblinoid features melting away, he felt only relief. Using the cloak's power to change his appearance no longer bothered him; he'd come to regard the magic cloak as a tool and a weapon, and refusing to use it when required made no more sense than leaving his sword sheathed during battle.

As they rowed the last few yards to the swan ship, Teldin saw a light in the ballista portal. To his surprise, Rozloom was in the hold, holding a lantern aloft and peering anxiously outward. A broad grin wreathed the aperusa's face when he caught sight of the longboat, and, as soon as Raven had secured the ropes, the gypsy winched the craft up and into the hold.

"Captain!" he boomed. He grasped Teldin's furry hand and pumped it vigorously, but his eyes were only for Raven. "I am so pleased that you are not dead."

Teldin nodded his thanks and tugged his hand free. He stooped to lift the half-elf from the longboat. "Rozloom, can you take Hectate to the healer? I'll be along as soon as I change."

For the first time the aperusa's eyes focused on Teldin's furred, yetilike body. His bushy black brows shot up, but he merely nodded in agreement. "That, I see, could take time. I will care for the captain's friend, then I will come and see to the longboat. You need not trouble yourself with it." The aperusa easily took the half-elf in his large arms, and he bounded up the stairs toward the main deck.

"The elves will have questions," Raven pointed out.

"They can wait," Teldin replied firmly. "If you run into Vallus, would you let him know I'll be around to see him as soon as I can? I'll be with Hectate, and I'm not to be disturbed. If you think it's necessary, post the dracons at the infirmary door and mine to keep out intruders." He met her eyes squarely. "After Hectate's settled, you and I need to talk. It's time."

A slow smile spread across Raven's face, and she nodded in approval. "I think you're right, Captain."

* * * * *

While Deelia Snowsong checked Hectate over for injuries, Teldin paced restlessly around the infirmary until Rozloom pushed him into a chair, insisting that Teldin was giving everyone in the room "the seasickness."

Still the captain fidgeted, watching the immobile half-elf with deep concern. It still seemed incredible to him that Hectate could have survived the crash at all, much less have escaped serious injury. That was the conclusion Deelia had reached. With a shrug, she claimed she could find nothing wrong with Hectate beyond a mild case of frostbite.

The moment the elven healer left the room, Rozloom shook his bald head in vehement disagreement. "The pale one, she is beautiful but not wise," he rumbled. "To the captain's dear friend she should give better care. These elves, they have too little regard for those not their own."

For once Teldin found himself in wholehearted agreement with the gypsy. He looked appraisingly at Rozloom, remembering that Hectate himself had praised the aperusa's skill with potions. "What would you do differently?"

Rozloom shrugged. "Herbs and simples, given often with broth, to warm the body, stir the blood. With such care, your friend should soon mend. Also, one should watch over him while he sleeps."

"Would you do this?" Teldin asked, having little hope that the self-absorbed gypsy actually would agree to such a task.

"I? But of course."

"You would?" Teldin demanded, startled by the unexpected response. "Why?"

"Why, why. Always with you it is why, Captain," the aperusa said in a hurt tone. "Must a man always have a reason?"

The door cracked open and Deelia's pale, lovely face reappeared. "I'll stop in to check on the half-elf from time to time."

Teldin thanked her and shot Rozloom an arch glance. Not at all disturbed at having his romance found out, the aperusa merely smiled and preened his curly beard.

Leaving Hectate in the aperusa's care, Teldin made his way back to his cabin, noting with satisfaction that the attentive Trivit was stationed at the door. The dracon's face was unusually grave. Raven must have put the fear of the gods into the young dracons, Teldin noted with a touch of amusement.

Raven. Teldin sighed heavily. The time had come to settle matters with his strange ally, but he felt reluctant to seek the answers he needed. He was pretty confident that he wouldn't like them.

Teldin went to his sea chest and removed the book he had borrowed from Vallus days ago. Before he had it out with

Raven Stormwalker, he wanted some insight into her true nature. Maybe then he'd be somewhat prepared for whatever she had in mind. He settled down at his writing table and quickly leafed through the book, scanning descriptions of familiar races as well as creatures that stretched his imagination.

One entry caught his eye and, as he read it, bits of information he had collected about "Raven Stormwalker" fell into place: fleeting visions of golden eyes and a black, scale-covered face; Raven's natural ability to shape-shift; the dracons' reverent awe of Raven and her own delight in adulation. Then there was Raven's pendant. It matched the description given by the lakshu, whose search for the "dragon's helm" followed a path that had led from Realmspace to Teldin's ship. The wildspace dragon that he'd seen through the *Spelljammer*'s eyes—and the medallion's power—had been in Realmspace. It all came around, full circle, to an inescapable conclusion.

Teldin dropped the book on his lap and slumped back into his chair. The truth about Raven's identity had been before him all along, but it had been simply too enormous to accept. Her true form, her true nature, was that of a dragon.

And not just any dragon. The creature he knew as Raven Stormwalker was a radiant dragon: a magical creature that in maturity could reach a length of almost one thousand feet. It could travel the stars under its own power, shape-shift into any form, and breathe magical balls of force—which would explain the lakshu's violent death, Teldin concluded dazedly.

He bent over, burying his face in his hands. He briskly rubbed his face, trying to take it all in. The radiant dragon had an ultimate helm, and if the magic amulet was to be believed, she already had been within sight of the *Spelljammer*. What, then, was she doing *here?* Why hadn't she taken command of the great ship? Had she tried to do so and failed?

Teldin remembered his amulet-induced vision of a radiant dragon speeding away from the *Spelljammer* in a rage: *this* was the creature he had planned to confront. He pushed away from his writing table and stood, pacing about the small room as he tried to bring order to his whirling thoughts.

As far as Teldin was concerned, an ordinary, fire-breathing, garden-variety dragon would be trouble enough. He'd seen such a dragon back on Krynn, and even in death it had been a fearsome creature. If anyone had told him then that he would consider a pact with such a creature, he would have thought him insane. Of course, back then Teldin wouldn't have believed that any of this could happen to him, nor could he have envisioned the odd creatures he had since befriended.

As the shock wore off, Teldin tentatively began to put his strange ally in perspective. He had dealt with many creatures equally strange: Estriss, a brain-eating illithid; Chirp and Trivit, the centaurlike lizards; Gomja, a militant blue-gray humanoid hippopotamus; even the fal, a brilliant garden slug the size of a space vessel. So why not a dragon? Why the hell not?

Of course, these alliances had not been without problems. There was Estriss, for example. Teldin had tried not to think about the illithid since the day Estriss recently had left without word. Teldin's faith in his friend, and in himself, had been sorely strained by the defection.

Teldin stopped at the foot of his cot and glanced down into the open sea chest. The strange figurine that Estriss had left behind still lay there, untouched. The ancient statue seemed to beckon him, and Teldin absently reached down to pick it up.

By the time you discover my messenger, Teldin Moore, I shall be gone.

The words formed in his mind with liquid clarity. Startled, Teldin dropped the statue. It clattered to the floor, and immediately the familiar mental voice stilled. After Teldin recovered from the initial shock, it occurred to him that Estriss might have ensorcelled the statue to "speak" in his place. He'd never heard of such a thing, but he supposed it could be done. Curious now, he stooped and picked up the ancient figurine.

I regret my hasty departure, but I have compelling reasons for leaving you. The arcane Npamta has seen the Spelljammer, and from him I can learn more about the great ship than I could discover in a century of study. More importantly, he may be willing to lead me there, though I know not how.

You must follow your own path to the Spelljammer, Teldin Moore. I had hoped to accompany you on your quest, but, as the bearer of an ultimate helm, you attract many enemies. Your road may well be long and filled with danger. I am not by nature a coward, but I am no longer young. We have spoken many times of my lifework: proving the existence of the Juna. Such an opportunity as the arcane presents cannot be passed up. It may be my last.

The illithid's mental voice paused, and Teldin found himself nodding in understanding.

There is another matter. You soon will discover the slain body of the lakshu warrior. I witnessed her death. She was killed by the being who calls herself Raven Stormwalker. The attack confirmed what I have long suspected; the elven woman is not what she appears to be. She is a radiant dragon and bears an ultimate helm. What this means for you I can only guess, but tread with care. Her presence on the swan ship is another reason I must leave. There is long-standing enmity between her race and mine. I would not long be safe from her, and, in all honesty, I would destroy her if an opportunity arose. Should I attempt and fail, she could easily crush the swan ship in her rage.

This is farewell, Teldin Moore. If the gods smile upon your quest and mine, we will meet again soon aboard the great ship.

Estriss's voice faded from Teldin's mind, and the captain carefully placed the now mute statue back into the chest. He hoped that Estriss did find the *Spelljammer*, and on it the answers he sought. Teldin had no idea what trials awaited him aboard the great ship, but he cherished the thought that a friend might await him there. The prospect of being greeted by a friendly face, even one decorated with tentacles, was more than Teldin had hoped for. A deep sense of peace filled him, and for the first time he truly believed that his search could end in success.

With a new resolve, Teldin left his cabin in search of the radiant dragon.

Vallus Leafbower confronted him the moment he'd left the dracon-protected seclusion of his cabin. "You might have told someone you were leaving the ship," the elf said.

"And I suppose you would have endorsed the mission?"

The question, spoken in a woman's sarcastic voice, surprised them both. They turned to see Raven standing at the foot of the stairs, arms crossed and a supercilious smile aimed at Vallus.

Vallus cast a quick glance at the moon elf and turned his attention to Teldin. "That was a foolish, unnecessary risk."

"Actually, it was the best thing I've done in a handful of days. If you'd known what I had planned to do, you'd have tried to stop me. No, don't bother to deny it," Teldin said coldly when Vallus began to protest. "I'm tired of pretending. The truth is that from the day I was carried aboard the *Trumpeter*, I've been a prisoner. Your talk of recruiting me to the elven side is so much scavver dung. The elves intend to have the cloak, whether it's on my shoulders or someone else's. Use it or lose it. *That*'s the extent of my choice, isn't it?"

As Teldin spoke, Raven climbed the stairs. Vallus cast an apprehensive glance in her direction. "Perhaps this conversation should be held in private."

"This is her business as much as mine," Teldin said firmly. "She carries an ultimate helm, too. Do you plan to keep her prisoner as well?"

Raven looked amused at the concept, but Vallus's eyes shifted from her to Teldin with growing concern. "Another helm?" Raven responded by waggling the sapphire pendant. Vallus took in her smug expression and the way she stood at Teldin's side as if they were closing ranks against a common enemy.

"What part does she play in this?" Vallus asked Teldin.

Teldin turned and met the dragon's eyes squarely. "I haven't decided yet."

She blinked, astonished by the hard edge in his voice. "*He* hasn't decided yet," she muttered under her breath. A smile spread slowly across her elven face, and she extended a hand to Teldin.

"My true name is Celestial Nightpearl. Pearl for short. I'm your new partner."

Teldin didn't pretend to be surprised by her offer, but neither did he take her hand. "Your terms?" he asked. As he spoke, words that Aelfred Silverhorn had spoken long ago flashed through his mind: *Bargain with a dragon, and you're a fool or a corpse.* Teldin wasn't entirely sure his late friend had been wrong, but the dragon needed something from him or she wouldn't be here. He determined to keep their deal on an even footing; he had no intention of exchanging his unwilling alliance with the elves for another kind of servitude.

Pearl shrugged and withdrew her offered hand to grasp her sapphire pendant. "Your cloak has many powers. So does this bauble. Maybe you can imagine the mess we'd make if we decided to fight it out." One corner of her mouth twitched into a wry, lopsided smile. "Unfortunately, I don't have to use my imagination. I've fought other would-be captains, and to prove it I've got scars in places even

Rozloom hasn't thought about."

Teldin felt a surge of sympathetic understanding; he knew what it meant to be hunted for his ultimate helm. Yet he didn't completely believe her claim. A radiant dragon had little to fear from him, despite the powers of his cloak. Or did she? The cloak had untapped powers, of that he was sure, but was its potential such that a dragon might fear him?

"So you're proposing a truce?" he asked cautiously.

"A partnership," she stressed. "Plainly put, you want the ship, and the ship wants a captain. I'd just as soon that not be me, though I wouldn't mind if a little of the power and prestige from the job came my way. So this is the deal: I'll take you to the *Spelljammer*, you'll be the captain, and I'll go my own way. From time to time, we could join resources for mutually advantageous adventures."

"Why don't you want the *Spelljammer* yourself?"

Her answering smile was vanity personified. "Who needs it?"

Teldin nodded. What use would a radiant dragon have for a spelljamming vessel, even *the* spelljamming vessel? She probably considered a partnership between a radiant dragon and the *Spelljammer* an even exchange.

"Mutually advantageous adventures?" he asked.

"We did all right on Rakhar," she said, a comrade's gleam in her odd-colored eyes.

Teldin acknowledged that with another nod. She'd helped him when he needed her, no questions asked or strings attached. He glanced at Vallus Leafbower, who was listening to the exchange with growing dismay on his angular face. What Raven—Pearl, Teldin corrected himself—offered was more to his liking than the elves' proposal. And, he had to admit, he liked being around her. In many ways, the dragon reminded him of Aelfred: full of zest for life and always ready for a new adventure. Still, she *was* keeping something from him; Teldin was sure of that, and, despite their friendship, he'd have to keep alert for whatever that secret might be.

It was friendship that passed between him and the dragon, a healing, helpful thing that he suspected surprised the dragon even more than it did him. With the sudden, crystalline clarity he'd come to take for granted, Teldin knew the benefits of having a dragon ally would outweigh the risks. Taking a deep breath, he extended his hand to seal their pact.

Vallus seized Teldin's wrist. "Surely you don't intend to join forces with this . . . with Raven Storm—" He broke off and shook his head. "No," the elf corrected himself sharply. "She is *not* Raven Stormwalker. That elven hero died many centuries ago."

"I'm feeling remarkably well, considering," the elf-shaped dragon murmured.

"My point, Teldin Moore," Vallus continued in a determined tone, "is that you cannot trust a being who is willing to misrepresent herself so blatantly. By all the gods!" he exclaimed, throwing up his hands in exasperation, "you don't even know what sort of creature she might be."

"Actually, I do," Teldin said.

Two sets of elven eyebrows shot up. "You *do*?" said Vallus and Pearl in unison.

The dragon-turned-elf shook her head and chuckled, as if she'd made a conclusion. "Well, what do you know. Most humans would have turned tail and run. Or turned up their toes and died, just to save me the trouble. You play cards, Captain? Too bad. The way you bluff, you'd be a natural at High Paladin." She peered closely at him. "Are you sure you're not afraid of me?"

"Should I be?" Teldin retorted.

She threw back her head and laughed delightedly. "Probably, but don't bother. Being worshiped and adored is all fine and well, but I must admit, I like your salt."

Vallus stepped forward and clasped Teldin's forearms.

"You must reconsider this. Whatever she is, you have no idea where such a course of action will take you," he said earnestly.

Not sure whether Vallus was warning or threatening him, Teldin pulled free of the elf's grasp. His angry response died unspoken as his eyes caught a distant flicker of light, and his face went slack with horror.

The twin mountains of Rakhar thrust upward into the night sky, gleaming in the bright moonlight like polished tusks. Teldin blinked several times, praying that his eyes had been playing tricks. No, there was another light, and then a third, reflecting off hulls. Several ships were leaving Armistice, moving steadily upward toward the converging moons.

"Great Paladine," Teldin swore. He grabbed the elven wizard's shoulders and spun him around. "See that? The orcs are taking to the stars. We're going after them."

"Kermjin is on the helm," Vallus said in immediate agreement.

"Get him off." Teldin's voice was inexorable. "The secondary helm's too slow. Raven, we'll need yours. Use the bridge and have Kermjin stand by to take over later on, in case we need you elsewhere."

"*Pearl*," the dragon-woman reminded him pointedly, but she hurried up toward the makeshift bridge to relieve the helmsman. Teldin glanced up and caught a glimpse of pale pink light through the door of the makeshift bridge, and he turned to other matters.

"Vallus, prepare the crew for immediate flight, then get them to battle stations. Send the weapon master to the bridge."

The wizard nodded and hurried to sound the signals. The moment the high, piping tune soared through the ship, the crew members braced wherever they were. Teldin gripped the stair railing and planted his feet wide apart.

The *Trumpeter* rose straight up, so suddenly that it burst

free of the water's hold with a sound like a small explosion. The swan ship's ascent was smooth, uncannily so after the constant pitch and roll of the Armistice ocean.

As he hurried up the short flight of steps to the bridge, Teldin took stock of the ship's chances. Of the original elven crew, only eighteen had survived the bionoid attack. They were barely enough to run the swan ship, much less battle a small fleet of ships. Even with the cloak's magic, the coming battle was no sure thing. He was glad he'd had Kermjin stand by in case a better use for Raven's—Pearl's!—talents arose.

Teldin found Pearl seated cross-legged on the navigation table, star charts scattered around her. The pink glow from her spelljamming sapphire filled the small room, and her face was tense and bright with exhilaration. Whatever else she might be, Teldin noted, she was a born adventurer. He turned and squinted out the bridge window to the trio of ships ahead. Under Raven's helm the swan ship traveled unbelievably fast; in moments they were closing on the nearest goblinoid ship.

The main body of the vessel was a giant mollusk, the round, winding shell of a typical illithid ship. In front of the shell, however, was a long, shallow hull much like that of a drakkar. Huge, tusklike protrusions thrust upward from the bow, and between them was mounted what appeared to be a giant slingshot. Attached to the bottom of the hull were long, jointed legs that could have come from any number of ships: a wasp, damselfly, even a neogi spider ship. An involuntary shudder coursed through Teldin.

"What the hell *is* that thing?" he muttered.

"What *isn't* it?" Pearl retorted in the distant, detached voice Teldin had come to associate with a spelljamming wizard. "It's got more ingredients than one of Rozloom's soups."

"Slow to tactical speed," Teldin directed her, and immediately the swan ship complied. "We're almost in ballista range," Teldin guessed, turning to the weapon master. The slight elf, whose face was tattooed in whorls of green and brown, nodded grimly. "Take over, Quon," Teldin directed.

The elf stepped to the speaking pipe that led down to the cargo deck, where the fore ballista was mounted. As he did, the orc vessel ahead began to execute a clumsy circle. Teldin raised his brass looking tube, and he could just barely make out a cluster of gray orcs bustling around the ship's large weapon. He gripped Quon's shoulder. "Get them before they bring that slingshot thing to bear on us," he commanded.

The elf shouted down the order to fire, and an enormous bolt shot toward the orc vessel. It missed, soaring harmlessly over the low hull. Before the ballista crew could get off another bolt, a fireball sped toward the orc ship and its wooden hull exploded in flame. Suddenly off balance, the shell section began a dizzy, spiraling descent to the icy waters far below.

"That's one," Teldin said with satisfaction, clapping Quon's shoulder. "Keep picking them off." He left the bridge and went to the stern, where Om frantically was making last-minute adjustments on the "improved" tail catapult. Trivit and Chirp stood ready beside a pile of what appeared to be boulders and spikes. A glance over the rail showed Teldin the reason for the gnome's frenzy. A second fleet of ragtag vessels—at least a half dozen bastard dragonflies—was coming up behind them.

"Almost in range," Om muttered with a worried glance at the approaching ships. She caught sight of Teldin and rose to her feet.

"Stomp and spit, Captain," she said solemnly, naming a gnomish ritual for courting luck, then she threw herself against an oversized lever.

The catapult shot forward, and, with a sharp intake of breath, Teldin watched its strange payload unfurl. Om had rigged up a number of giant bolas: large, spiked balls connected by lengths of chain. One missile spun end over end toward an insectlike ship, and the spikes of the first ball bit deeply into the wooden hull. The second ball hurtled around the ship, held in orbit by the long, stout chain, gaining momentum and snapping off legs with each cycle. Its final impact shattered the vessel into flame and flying splinters. Another bola tore through a second dragonfly's wing, whizzing through the fragile substance. The one-winged ship tumbled out of control.

Om grinned and cranked back the catapult for a second shot, and the dracons quickly loaded a second pile of the gnome's lethal bolas into the weapon.

By the time the swan ship shuddered through the atmospheric boundary, most of the ragtag fleet had been destroyed. The "battle" was over in minutes without casualty or damage to the swan ship. Teldin should have been pleased with the ease of their victory, but he felt restless and uneasy. Something was wrong. The orc and goblin ships all appeared to be heavily armed, but not one of them had so much as fired on the *Trumpeter*.

A deep foreboding filled Teldin, and he sprinted toward the bridge.

* * * * *

For the third time in a millennium, the magical alarm on a man-o-war patrol ship sounded.

The only living occupant of the ship's bridge, a bloated tertiary Witchlight Marauder, aimed an incurious stare at the pulsing disk suspended over its head. The monster reached up toward it, and two of its swordlike fingers bracketed the thick mithril chain. With a casual, effortless snap, the creature brought the blades together and severed the chain. The disk hit the floor in a shower of spraying fragments. The tertiary marauder picked up a large splinter of crystal with dexterous foot claws and tossed the shard up and into its gaping maw.

It crunched, considered, then spat. Silently the monster directed its rapacious appetite back to its preferred food, and the bodies of the ship's captain and battle wizard quickly disappeared. Over the monster's head, the image of a ragtag goblin fleet and a battered swan ship slowly faded from the crystal panel.

Chapter Eighteen

● ● ●

Teldin burst onto the bridge. "Hard astern. Get us the hell away from here!" he shouted at Celestial Nightpearl.

Surprise registered in the dragon's elven eyes, then understanding. "Tiamat's talons!" she swore to the god of evil dragons. "Those ships are leading us, aren't they?"

The captain gave a grim nod of confirmation, then sped down to the upper deck. Gaston Willowmere rushed past with an armload of crossbow bolts, and Teldin grabbed the elf's shoulder. "Don't bother. We're breaking off the attack."

"You're letting them get away? We're *retreating?*" the first mate asked, not bothering to hide his disdain for the human captain.

Teldin faced down the elf. "When you can recognize an ambush, perhaps you'll be ready to give orders. Until then, don't question mine."

Gaston shot a glance toward the port rail, where Vallus Leafbower stood with the ship's battle wizards. Vallus confirmed the order with an almost imperceptible nod, and with a final, frustrated glance toward the fleeing goblin ships, the first mate spread the order to stand down. Vallus spoke a few words to the other wizards, then came to walk alongside Teldin.

"They did not return fire," the elf commented as they walked down the stairs to the main deck.

"You noticed," Teldin said. "I wonder what was waiting

out there for us."

"Scro, no doubt. The Armistice orcs got their ships somewhere, and who else would supply them?"

"What about those bionoids?" Teldin suggested.

Vallus stopped short. "That's impossible," he said flatly. "The bionoids obviously want to get their hands on your cloak, but why would they serve orcs? They are *elven* weapons."

Anger flashed in Teldin's eyes, but he kept his voice even. "You probably can't understand this, Vallus, but you just answered your own question." Not trusting himself to say more, he turned away and went off to check on Hectate.

Had he looked back, Teldin would have been astounded at the effect his words had on the elven wizard. Vallus Leafbower's stunned face suggested a soul who had glimpsed himself in a mirror and had been deeply disturbed by what he had seen.

Needing time alone to think over the troubling insight, the elf turned to the solitude of his cabin. Since writing usually helped him sort through his thoughts, Vallus went to the locked cabinet that held the ship's log and automatically his fingers began to rehearse the spell that released the lock. He stopped in midspell, puzzled, then leaned in for a closer look. It appeared that someone had attempted to open the lock—physically, not with magic. The signs of intrusion were subtle: the tarnished metal around the keyhole was slightly brighter where a key or picking tool had been inserted.

Vallus sped through the unlocking spell and snatched up the log. He leafed through it rapidly, checking sequence and dates to ensure that no pages were missing. To his eyes, the book did not appear to have been disturbed, and he exhaled in a slow, relieved sigh. Not that the log would have yielded much information. As was required, all of his entries were made in a unique, magical code that he himself had devised, so that the log was impossible to read without powerful spells. Of course, there was always the possibility that someone strong enough to break the magical lock could also, in time, decipher the code.

The elven wizard returned the book to the cabinet, which he locked and reinforced with additional spells and wards. That accomplished, he began to go through the motions of preparing for sleep. He strongly suspected that his dreams would be haunted, not only by Teldin Moore's accusing blue eyes, but also by the echoes of his own words, so full of blind confidence in elven right and reason.

Vallus had thought himself beyond thoughtless bigotry, and he was deeply disturbed to learn otherwise. Not long ago he'd congratulated himself for his open-minded acceptance of half-elf Hectate Kir, but the moment he'd learned that the half-elf was a bionoid, Hectate had ceased to be a person. He was simply a *bionoid*, and all the elven prejudices and reluctant guilt concerning that race had completely pushed aside any other perspective. No wonder the scro were finding ready allies against the elves. What other races, Vallus wondered, felt they had reason to rebel against the elves' arrogant dominance of wildspace?

It was ironic, Vallus thought as he crawled onto his cot, that such thoughts should come to him now, when he had good reason to suspect that Hectate Kir was a spy.

Teldin Moore, of course, would never believe this. In his current frame of mind, Vallus himself felt inclined to disregard the facts. Yet, they were there, and too numerous to ignore.

Someone with access to elven technology had stolen a cloaking device for a bionoid clan. It was likely that the bionoid shrike ships tracked the *Trumpeter* using information obtained from someone on board, and who knew the swan ship's course better than Hectate Kir, the navigator? Whoever had tampered with the locked cabinet was no thief, but someone who knew exactly what he was looking for and where to look. Other, more accessible valuables in his cabin—spell components, rare books, a few bottles of rare elven spirits—had not been touched. Finally, there was Hectate's mysterious disappearance during the bionoid attack. It could not have been coincidence that the half-elf turned up on Armistice in a crashed insectare vessel, which was almost certainly the same vessel that had taunted the swan ship during the battle. And, according to the healer, there was no reason why Hectate Kir should not have regained consciousness. What was he up to, and what did he want with the ship's log?

Vallus could not shake the feeling that Teldin Moore's cloak was not the primary issue in this mysterious plot. When the bionoids attacked, they easily could have slain every elf on board the swan ship and captured Teldin, but the creatures broke off the attack when victory seemed assured. *Why?* Vallus puzzled over this until he drifted into a restless slumber.

Much later, his troubled dreams were interrupted by a loud knocking at his cabin door. Gaston Willowmere, who, as first mate, was acting as the third watch commander, stood at attention, and his angular face was deeply troubled.

"Captain, we've spotted one of the Imperial Fleet patrol ships."

"Ahh." Vallus spoke the word on a sigh. "Well, it had to happen. I'm surprised we haven't been called into account long before this for violating the Armistice net."

"They don't want our report, sir," the first mate said. "The ship appears to be in trouble. It's adrift."

"A man-o-war, adrift?" Vallus said sharply, and Gaston nodded. A familiar, icy feeling crept through the elven wizard, the same nameless dread he'd felt on Lionheart upon hearing the tale of the armada ghost ship. A force that could overcome an armada or a man-o-war—without leaving a trace!—was a terrifying prospect. He hadn't heard the results of that investigation, but he wondered if he was about to confront the mysterious foe himself.

"Have you alerted Captain Moore?" he asked Gaston.

Vallus's question clearly took the first mate by surprise. Without waiting for a response, Vallus instructed him to get Teldin to the bridge immediately. The wizard quickly dressed and made his way to the bridge. He instructed the third-watch helmsman, Kermjin, to make a cautious approach to the man-o-war.

Teldin came to the bridge only moments later. His sandy hair was rumpled and his clothing bore wrinkled testament to several restless hours in a hammock—he'd given up his own cabin to Hectate Kir, so that the half-elf could recover in comfort and privacy. Vallus quickly explained the situation, and, when the swan ship came close enough to the drifting man-o-war, Teldin trained his looking glass at the deck. He recoiled in horror and swore an oath that would have done credit to a drunken dwarf.

The elven wizard snatched up a second looking glass and peered through it. On the deck of the man-o-war was a roiling pack of gray, hideous creatures, engaged in what appeared to be a feeding frenzy. So quickly did the monsters move that only flashes of silver and red betrayed the identity of their feast. The elf's bile rose, and he lowered the glass with shaking hands.

"If we're to save any of those elves, we'll have to move in fast," Teldin declared.

Vallus shook his head. "There is nothing to be done," he said in a dull whisper. "There is nothing left to save."

Teldin's face darkened, and Vallus wearily supposed that the human would argue the matter as usual. But the young captain took a closer look at Vallus's stricken face, and his wrath dissolved. Although his blue eyes held many questions, he merely laid a steadying hand on Vallus's shoulder.

The elven wizard nodded his thanks, and Teldin turned away and directed the helmsman to give the doomed man-o-war a wide berth. Vallus was grateful for Teldin's unexpected empathy and his good judgment. At the moment he himself felt overwhelmed with despair, incapable of speech or action.

It was almost too much to absorb. The goblins of Armistice were escaping into wildspace, a clan of bionoid warriors apparently had joined forces with the goblinkin, and the dreaded Witchlight Marauders had been released to feed. Vallus wondered if even the worst days of the first Unhuman War could compare to the threat now facing the elven people.

* * * * *

The main deck of the ogre dinotherium rang with the sounds of battle. From the walkway above, a mismatched pair of generals observed the training.

Grimnosh was, as usual, immaculate: his studded leather armor had been freshly oiled, elaborately carved totems decorated his fangs and claws, and a fine cloak of night-blue silk flowed over his broad shoulders and set off the albino scro's striking white hide. Even the trophy teeth that hung from his *toregkh* had been polished until they gleamed. Superbly muscled and over seven feet tall, Grimnosh was an imposing figure who carried both his well-used weapons and his grisly scro finery with aplomb.

His counterpart, Ubiznik Redeye, hardly could have been more different. In contrast to Grimnosh's military bearing, the orc chieftain's stance suggested the crouch of a gutter fighter. Ubiznik was a hideous creature even discounting the scars that crisscrossed his face and sealed one eyelid shut over a sunken socket. A canny intelligence blazed in the orc's good eye, however, and the beastlike yellow hue and blood-red pupil underscored Ubiznik's fierce nature. He stood less than five feet tall, but his barrel chest and great limbs spoke of incredible strength. Layers of corded muscle bulged under a gray hide thicker than the toughest leather. The orc wore no clothing but a weapon belt, and his only weapons were a bone knife and a deeply pitted axe forged by long-dead dwarves. Indeed, in many ways, Ubiznik resembled a dwarf; centuries of living underground and battling the punishing gravity force of Armistice had chiseled Ubiznik's tribe from the same sort of stone. A closer study, however, revealed the generals' common heritage; both had the upturned snouts, pointed canine ears, and lethal tusks of their ancestor orcs.

Grimnosh observed the scene below with satisfaction. The "ice orcs," as the scro soldiers had named the newcomers, were coming along nicely. Weapon training had begun immediately, to the ice orcs' grim delight. Only a few of them owned battered blades or axes, and the Armistice orcs desperately coveted such weapons. They proved embarrassingly inept with swords, so Grimnosh had quickly switched their training to battle axes. These suited the ice orcs perfectly, and they sparred so fiercely that Grimnosh wondered if they were determined to chop each other into kindling. They had an utter disregard for wounds given—or received. As advance troops, the ice orcs were incomparable: brutal, barbaric, and totally devoid of fear or wit. Grimnosh was pleased.

For the most part, the ice orcs were adjusting well to life aboard the *Elfsbane*. Although their tough hide made the regulation scro armor redundant, Grimnosh had insisted that they be properly outfitted, from the lowliest orc foot soldier to the priests who kept vigil over the terrible monster stashed in the hold of the *Elfsbane*. The scro general knew the value of ritual and outward appearance to ensuring loyalty; already he could see the difference in the bearing and attitudes of the ice orcs. They seemed eager to assimilate into the ranks of the *Elfsbane*'s crew. Only Ubiznik had resisted the encroachments of scro culture. Grimnosh was confident that the orc chieftain would come around. Despite his uncouth appearance, Ubiznik was a good officer who owned the respect and loyalty of his soldiers. Granted, his discipline did not produce the clean, precise order known to the scro, but Ubiznik kept his troops in line well enough with his grunted orders, hand gestures, and an occasion skull-shattering cuff. After Lionheart was in shambles and all the orc and hobgoblin troops had left Armistice behind, Grimnosh intended to see that Ubiznik received a real commission. The other scro commanders might not appreciate the elevation of the rough-hewn orc to general, but they could hardly argue with one *Admiral* Grimnosh. The scro's tusks gleamed as he smiled.

Ubiznik looked less happy. "No like," he grumbled. "Orcs want to kill elves, not bait snares."

The scro general nodded sympathetically, but he had no intention of changing his strategy. Why should he? The elven presence around Armistice was being systematically and efficiently destroyed. A few at a time, the goblin ships would leave the atmosphere shield and trigger the alarm. When an elven patrol ship gave chase, the cloaked bionoid shrike ships would close in and drop either bionoid warriors or the tertiary marauders to wipe out the elves.

"No like," the orc repeated. "Deal was, we fly with scro, fight many elves."

"And fight them you shall," Grimnosh agreed. "Once all of your tribe and your servant hobgoblins have escaped from Armistice, and once the elven high command is destroyed, you will be able to take elven trophies from a hundred worlds. First things first, my good fellow. As you yourself say, we have a deal."

Ubiznik grunted in reluctant agreement. The metallic click of mailed boots announced the approach of two scro soldiers. The ice orc watched warily as they snapped to attention and jammed their fists into the air, back side presented out so that their unit totem was displayed.

"Sky Sharks hail Almighty Dukagsh!" they barked out in unison.

Grimnosh absently returned the salute, but Ubiznik responded by slamming one fist into the palm of his other paw and grunting, "Gralnakh Longtooth!"

The orc's tribute to the great orc general of the Armistice Treaty was lost on the scro soldiers. Assuming that the barbarian had insulted them, one soldier snarled and let his hand settle on the grip of his short sword. Ubiznik didn't bother reaching for a weapon, and his single red eye blazed a challenge as he returned the snarl through a sharp-fanged sneer.

"At ease," Grimnosh told the scro calmly. "General Redeye's troops—and their heroic forebear—are worthy of respect. Surely we can allow for a few cultural differences?"

The scro's comment carried with it both a direct order and an unmistakable threat. With only the slightest hesitation, the soldiers crisply returned the ice orc's unorthodox salute.

"We received a message from your informant, General," one of the scro said, handing Grimnosh a slip of paper.

As Grimnosh read, a thoughtful look crossed his face. "It would appear that our friend is trying to redeem himself," he murmured. After a long moment of reflection, he turned to his orc ally. "Well, General, it looks as though you're going to fight elves sooner than we'd anticipated."

Bloodlust shone in the Ubiznik's red eye, and the ice orc bared his fangs in a fierce grin.

* * * * *

Gaston Willowmere was tired and disgruntled. Everyone aboard the *Trumpeter* was serving double watches, and he was nearing the end of two very eventful and disturbing shifts. His only remaining duty was making a final round of the ship, and he made his way down to the lower deck to begin.

The elf was not pleased with the swan ship's mission, or with many of the directions the Imperial Fleet was taking. His own homeworld was a world of deep, ancient forests and sacred tradition. To one of his upbringing the breaking of elven tradition was a serious matter. Aboard this swan ship, they had done little else. They'd harbored an illithid, suffered the constant tinkering of a gnome and the lechery of that appalling gypsy. They were forced to acknowledge a human captain and look the other way when the human made a half-elf head navigator. When the half-elf was revealed to be a bionoid, no one was supposed to mind. It was beyond belief.

Wrapped in his gloomy thoughts, the mate did not at first see a shadowy figure slipping through the cargo hold. He caught a glimpse of a trailing robe—or blanket—as someone entered the room housing the wing and paddle machinery.

"You there!" Gaston called. There was no response, and the angry mate sped after the silent figure. He burst through the door and immediately staggered back from a fierce blow to his face. Gaston hit the deck hard and bounded to his feet, spitting out bits of broken teeth. The room was dark, but he could make out a tall elven figure swathed in flowing robes. Gaston's vision slipped into the night vision spectrum. To his horror, the elf-shaped assailant registered in a pattern of cool blue and green light, not the healthy red one expected of a warm-blooded elf.

Gaston drew his short sword and lunged. He connected—hard!—to the creature's midsection. The sword should have gone up and under the rib cage, but the only result was the sharp clunk of blade meeting tough plate armor. Before the first mate could recover from the failed lunge, he received a backhanded blow that shattered his nose and sent him reeling. The stranger advanced, raining blows so fast and vicious that Gaston could do no more than bring his arms up in a futile attempt to shield his face. The elf fell to his knees, and the room closed in on him with a rush of blood and darkness.

* * * * *

Sleep would not come to Teldin. He returned to the hammock in Hectate's cabin. Despite his exhaustion, he could not dispel from his mind the image of gray monsters with swords for hands and insatiable appetites for elven flesh. Vallus had called them Witchlight Marauders, and he'd also muttered something about them destroying entire worlds. From what Teldin had seen, he didn't doubt for a minute that such a thing was possible.

Also disturbing to Teldin was the choice that lay before him. He wanted to join forces with Pearl, and not only for what she could offer him. In many ways, the dragon was a kindred spirit. Her curiosity and love of adventure reminded Teldin of both his grandfather and Aelfred. She was an irreverent character, always poking sardonic fun at conventions and authority figures. Solitary by nature, the dragon prized her independence, yet, like Teldin, she enjoyed being with others from time to time. That, he realized, was one of the main attractions of the alliance. He'd been alone for too long. So many of his friends and companions had fallen victim to his quest that he'd isolated himself, fearing to bring danger to those he loved. A dragon would be not only a good companion, but a durable one. And he had a responsibility to make his comrades' deaths mean something.

On the other hand, Teldin felt torn by a growing sense of duty. The Witchlight Marauders had to be stopped. He wasn't sure what he could do about the monsters, but neither did he feel that he could just walk away. Like Hectate, he hadn't wanted to get involved in the spreading conflict between the elves and goblinkin, but it was starting to look as if he wouldn't have a choice. Until he'd seen the gray monsters on the man-o-war, Teldin wasn't sure he could have chosen one side over the other. Granted, the scro were vicious, brutal characters, but the elves' methods were not exactly beyond reproach either.

Teldin thought back to his first war, the War of the Lance, back on his native Krynn. He'd entered it believing in black and white, heroes and villains; he'd left it believing in very little and deeply suspicious of those in positions of power. Cynicism came easily; at least, it did until he himself had been faced with the necessity of making a decision. He was beginning to understand some of the problems of leadership, some of the pitfalls that came with power. There were no right answers, only the struggle to find the greater good—or the lesser evil. And power! He'd survived the attempts of a dozen races who were willing to kill him and others to possess the magic cloak. What would he himself become in the process of wielding the cloak? And what would he become as captain of the *Spelljammer*? Even now, there were days when he looked in the mirror to shave and felt as if he were confronting a stranger.

After half of a watch slipped by, Teldin was no closer to either sleep or answers. With a sigh of surrender, he swung himself out of the hammock and went in search of the dracons. They both were on duty this watch, and maybe one of them would be free to drill with him. Perhaps the activity would clear his mind. At the very least, it would help sharpen his skills for the next battle. If there was one thing Teldin *was* sure about, it was that there would be more battles.

* * * * *

Teldin was fending off Chirp's battle axe when Vallus came to the upper deck. "We must talk about Hecate Kir," the elf said without preamble.

Breathing heavily, Teldin wiped the sweat from his forehead and nodded to the dracon. Taking the hint, Chirp tucked the ornate weapon into its holster and ambled off, whistling as he went. "What is it?" Teldin asked anxiously, sheathing his own sword. "Did Hecate finally wake up?"

"So it would appear," Vallus said solemnly. "I am sorry to have to tell you this, but you must know. The first mate was found in the hold, beaten almost beyond recognition and left for dead. Under Deelia's care, he revived enough to describe his attacker."

Teldin's blue eyes narrowed. "I don't like where this is leading."

"Gaston claims that the being who attacked him was covered with plate armor, like an insect. There is only one person aboard who could fit that description."

"And that person is unconscious in my cabin," Teldin returned heatedly.

Vallus shook his head. "According to Deelia, the bionoid's injuries are not sufficient to explain his condition. Isn't it possible that he is feigning sleep to keep us off guard?"

"Let's say you're right. How did Hecate leave the cabin undetected?" the captain asked. "Someone has been with him at all times. If not Deelia or me, then Rozloom."

In response, Vallus merely turned and led the way to Teldin's cabin. When the elf eased open the door, they were greeted by a sonorous snore. Puzzled, Teldin peered in. Hecate still was unconscious. His breathing still was weak and shallow, and his unruly red hair was a shock of color above his pallid face.

Rozloom also slept. He lay on the floor, his booted feet propped up on Teldin's writing table and his vast belly rising and falling with each raucous blast of sound. An empty bottle from Teldin's sagecoarse hoard lay on the floor beside the snoring gypsy.

"Rozloom could have been asleep for hours," Vallus said as he shut the door.

"Days," Teldin corrected without humor. Experience had taught him that sagecoarse was potent stuff, and despite Rozloom's immense capacity for spirits, Teldin was surprised that anyone could put away an entire bottle and live to snore.

But even if Hectate could and did leave the cabin, Teldin did not believe that the bionoid was responsible for the first mate's injuries. As much as he hated to admit it, Pearl was a more likely suspect. The attack on Gaston was too much like her violent response to Rozloom's overeager courting. With her shape-shifting talent, she certainly could have taken on the armored form that Vallus had described. It had to be Pearl, unless . . .

"Paladine's blood," Teldin swore, raking both hands through his sandy hair. He turned back to the elven wizard. "You've searched the ship?" he asked sharply.

Vallus blinked. "For what?"

"An insectare," Teldin said. "I have no idea how it got on the ship, but I think we've got an insectare aboard."

"You want us to search the ship for an *insectare?*" Vallus echoed in disbelief.

Before Teldin could explain, the sound of fighting drifted up from the cargo deck.

"Don't bother," Teldin shouted as he sprinted down the stairs to the lower deck. "I think someone already found it."

Chapter Nineteen

• • •

Teldin and Vallus raced down the steps to the cargo hold, their swords drawn. They found several other members of the crew clustered at the base of the stairs, gaping at the peculiar battle.

Chirp and Trivit stood a dozen yards apart, using their enormous tails to bat a flailing, brown-robed creature back and forth between them. Despite the playful appearance of the scene, both dracons' faces were grim and tears ran in rivulets down Trivit's green cheeks.

Still in her moon elf form, Pearl came running down the stairs and pushed her way through the group. "I've got him, Captain," she announced. Drawing herself up, she inhaled slowly and deeply. Fearing the dragon intended to breathe a magic missile, Teldin clapped a hand over her mouth. Her gold and silver eyes widened in shock.

"Don't," Teldin said simply. He released her, then he drew her broadsword from her scabbard and handed her the ancient weapon. "If you have to fight, use this. Not as effective, but it won't blast another hole in the hull."

"Damned nuisance, being an elf," she muttered, looking with distaste at the sword in her hands.

Teldin turned away and cupped his hands to his mouth. "Trivit! Chirp! That's enough. Stop the insectare, now."

Chirp obediently stopped the tumbling creature with one foot, then quickly planted that foot on its prone body, moves

that appeared to have been learned on a kickball field. Teldin
hurried to the dracon's side. Although the insectare looked
battered and dazed, it glared up at him with malevolent black
eyes.

Teldin reached down and jerked back the creature's cowl.
Knowing what he would find did not make the sight any less
strange. The face was elven in form, but the peculiar color
of green apples. Long black antennae rose from a thick
thatch of wavy, flaxen hair to curl above its pointed ears like
fiddlehead ferns. Remembering that Vallus had said those
antennae could be used as lethal whips, Teldin seized the tip
of one and thrust it into Chirp's hand.

"Hold this. Trivit, you come grab the other. Keep them taut."
He prodded the insectare with his foot. "You, on your feet."

The dracons quickly got the idea and soon they had the
furious insectare standing immobilized between them. Teldin
was not insensitive to the humiliation he'd inflicted on the
creature, but he didn't want it using its antennae on the crew.

"Search it," Vallus directed, and two of the elves moved to
obey. In the pockets of the insectare's robe they found a
small lump of dried clay and an oddly shaped key. Vallus
examined these items closely, and his jaw tightened.

The elven wizard walked up to the insectare. "Who are
you, and what use have you for the ship's log?"

"You may know my name," the creature said in a dry,
brittle voice. "I am called K'tide. My purposes, however, are
my own."

"Sir," Trivit addressed Vallus in a tremulous voice, "if you
would be amenable to such, Chirp and I would be most
happy to encourage the creature to talk."

The insectare's eyes darted between his dracon tormen-
tors and the elven wizard. Obviously determined to get in the
first strike, the insectare began to chant a spell in a strange,
clicking language. His long green fingers gestured, and his
eyes glittered with hatred.

"Pearl!" Teldin shouted. "Silence it!"

The elf-shaped dragon responded with a quick smile and a countering spell of her own. A sphere of silence enshrouded the insectare, neatly cutting off his spellcasting.

"Now there's a philosophical question for you, wizard," Pearl casually said to Vallus, an edge of contempt in her voice. "If a spell is spoken but not heard, was a spell cast? Fits right in with the if-a-tree-falls-in-a-forest-and-no-one-hears-it nonsense your sort likes to ponder."

The insectare threw back his head and howled a soundless oath. Frustration and rage twisted his green visage as he drew a long, gleaming sword from the folds of his robe. All the crew members in the hold took a reflexive step back, in their surprise forgetting that the dracons had the creature immobilized.

No one expected K'tide to free himself by slashing off his own antennae. In two lightning-fast moves the insectare cut himself free and pushed Vallus Leafbower aside. Ichor flowed down the insectare's face and dripped off his chin as he rushed at Teldin. The creature's ghastly snarl was as rigid as a skull's as he charged forward, sword held overhead with both hands.

The startled captain groped for his sword. Time slowed down as the cloak's magic took over, and Teldin managed to raise his short sword overhead in time to meet the descending blow. The swords met with a bone-jarring clash, uncannily silent. The dragon's sphere of silence encompassed them both, absorbing all sounds of battle.

The insectare fought with a desperate, despairing madness, flailing wildly with its sword. Try as he might, Teldin could not get inside the creature's reach to land a blow. Even with his altered perception, it was all he could do hold off the frenzied insectare. From the corner of his eye Teldin saw several elves circle the battle, swords drawn. Elven blades struck silently and ineffectually against the insectare's armor, and more than one of Teldin's would-be rescuers reeled back under the force of the insectare's wild swings. Then a backhand slice caught Teldin's sword arm and opened a gash from wrist to elbow. An explosion of pain penetrated Teldin's cushion of slow, dreamlike magic. Time shattered and began to career dizzily around Teldin as the short sword dropped from his bloodied hand.

Acting on instinct, Teldin raised his other hand and pointed it at the insectare. Magic missiles shot from the Cloakmaster's fingers, one after another. The insectare stiffened, his body jerking in spasms as it was jolted again and again by the magic weapons. During the magic assault, Pearl's spell dissipated and a horrible searing hiss replaced the silence. The green face blackened, and fetid smoke rose from under the creature's exoskeleton. Finally the insectare tottered and fell to the floor with a dull clatter.

The stunned crew stared at the smoking remains. What moments before had been an insectare now was a pile of blackened plating and charred robe, nothing more. The creature's body had simply disintegrated from the force of Teldin's missiles. Awed and speechless, the elves and dracons raised their gaze to the human. Teldin, clasping his bleeding arm, stood over the dead insectare. His expression was dazed, and he looked disoriented and none too steady on his feet. Even so, power clung to him like a mantle.

"That was for Hectate Kir," Teldin said faintly, addressing the smoking pile.

Deelia Snowsong was the first to collect herself. She darted forward and helped Teldin sit down on a storage crate. After a quick examination of the man's injury, she ripped away his torn sleeve and doused the arm with a foul-swelling herbal wash from a small vial. She'd already begun to stitch the wound before Teldin's startled oaths died away. The dracons suddenly realized they still held the insectare's severed antennae. Both shuddered and threw the things aside. Chirp produced a kerchief from a pocket of his leather armor and fastidiously wiped off his clawed fingers, and Trivit dashed tears from his green cheeks with the back of his hand. No one noticed the troubled, speculative expression on Pearl's face as she fingered her long raven braid, and no one saw her slip away from the cargo hold.

A subdued Vallus quietly came over to the makeshift infirmary. He watched silently as Deelia put the last of many stitches in Teldin's arm. The tiny healer poured another quick dose of her liquid fire over her handiwork, then she quickly wrapped Teldin's forearm in bandages.

Only once before had Teldin seen Vallus at a loss for words, and the elf's silence unnerved him. Looking about for something to say, he noticed that Vallus still held the items taken from the insectare. Teldin rose to his feet, ignoring the new waves of pain that radiated from his arm.

"How do you think the insectare got those keys?" Teldin asked through gritted teeth.

"I believe I can answer that," Trivit broke in tearfully. The dracon turned and led the way toward the stern. The crew silently followed him past the machinery that drove the wing and paddle mechanisms. On the floor, in a scattered circle of tiny tools, lay Om's body. It was sprawled facedown, its head bent at an impossible angle. Around the neck was an angry red circle where the insectare's whiplike antennae had struck and killed. Teldin swallowed hard, and Trivit's tears began anew.

"Why would Om work with an insectare?" Vallus wondered, looking down at the gnome's body.

"More likely she bumped into it, like Gaston did," Teldin suggested. The elf shook his head and handed Teldin the key taken from the insectare. A glance at the outlandish handle betrayed its gnomish origin.

"If I were to choose the least likely person on board to play the traitor, it would have been she," Vallus mused. "To all appearances, Om cared for nothing but her machines. What could convince her to do something like this?"

Teldin's eyes widened as an answer occurred to him, and he groaned softly in self-recrimination. Once again, the truth had been just too damned obvious. "*Who* convinced her, not what," he corrected in a dull voice. "Om didn't make those keys for the *insectare*. I doubt she even knew an insectare was in the picture until she met up with it."

Without offering an explanation, Teldin turned and strode back to the cargo hold. He picked up his sword and hurried up the stairs to his own cabin, worry dulling his pain and speeding his steps. If his theory was right, Hectate could be in grave danger.

Teldin kicked open the cabin door. As he suspected, the aperusa was no longer sleeping off the pilfered sagecoarse. Rozloom was standing, bent over the writing table. The gypsy whirled to face Teldin, and his black eyes widened at the sight of the blade leveled at his heart.

"She is yours," the aperusa stated baldly, holding up his huge bronze hands in surrender. "From this moment, Raven is the captain's woman and Rozloom will kill any man who says otherwise."

"Just for the record, her name is Pearl, and you know damn well this isn't about her," Teldin said evenly. The sword felt awkward in his left hand, and he hoped he didn't appear as unsteady as he felt. The aperusa seemed suitably cowed, however, and he raised one hand to flick beads of sweat from his gleaming pate. Teldin's eyes narrowed. "What's that green stuff on your hand?" he demanded.

"Green?" Rozloom spread his hands before him and studied his fingers as if he'd just acquired them. Understanding lit his broad face, and gold teeth flashed in relief. "Ahh. Is nothing. Merely the healing herbs I grind to feed the captain's friend." The gypsy gestured to the small mortar and pestle on the writing table.

"Let me have them," Teldin said, holding out his free hand. Panic flared in the aperusa's black eyes, but his smile never dimmed. "I think not, Captain," he said. "Herbs, they can be dangerous if one knows little of them."

"You might as well know that K'tide is dead," Teldin said bluntly. Rozloom's jovial expression vanished, and he sank heavily into the chair. "So is Om," Teldin added quietly, but the second piece of information did not seem to register with the aperusa.

"I see." The gypsy's usually booming bass voice sounded strangely subdued, and his face sagged in the resignation of defeat. "And of course there are many questions. What would you have me to tell, Captain?"

The thunder of approaching dracons drowned out Teldin's response. Two green heads poked in through the door, their puzzled faces framing Vallus. "Get Deelia," Teldin told the elf.

"I'm here." The healer pushed her way into the room. Teldin pointed to the dish of crushed herbs and asked her what they were. Puzzled, Deelia went over to the writing table and touched the tip of one finger to the mixture. She sniffed it, tasted it, and spat.

"Nightsorrel," she breathed, glancing at the gypsy with dawning understanding. "No wonder the half-elf never woke up."

Rozloom sighed and removed a small green flagon from the folds of his sash. "This will help," he said, handing it to the healer. Again she tested it. Satisfied, she quickly poured the liquid into Hectate's slack mouth. She produced a vial of her own, a healing potion of some sort, and administered that to Hectate as well. Almost immediately the half-elf's color looked a bit better, and he sighed in his sleep.

"He should start coming around soon now," Deelia murmured. Teldin nodded his thanks and sheathed his sword. Feeling a little light-headed, he pulled the room's only chair over to Hectate's bedside and dropped into it. Leaving Rozloom to the furious elven wizard, Teldin renewed his vigil over his half-elven friend.

"How long have you been working for the insectare?" Vallus demanded, coming forward to stand over the aperusa.

"Work?" The gypsy shrugged off that concept like an ill-fitting garment. "My people salvage old ships. K'tide's money was good. The insectare, he wished also to buy information. The money for that was even better."

"What information?"

"Harmless things: Where the captain goes. What he does. What he wears. Very much K'tide liked stories of the cloak that changes color, so I tell what I see. Is business," he concluded with another shrug. Teldin, who had looked up when Rozloom mentioned the insectare's interest in the cloak, got the distinct impression that Rozloom had little notion what the fuss was about.

"Who else was with the insectare?"

A bushy brow arched. "The insect-elves, but this you know already, yes?"

Vallus winced visibly. "So it was K'tide and the bionoids who supplied spelljamming vessels to the Armistice goblinborn. Why?"

"That, I did not ask."

"All right, then, are the scro involved?"

"Scro!" Rozloom snorted. "Who is to say? What scro do is hidden even from those who read the cards. The aperusa trade but little with such creatures."

"Is anyone else working with you?"

"From time to time," the aperusa allowed. "For a good price, a beholder helped me to make the captain's acquaintance."

"In the tavern on Garden," Teldin said slowly, remembering the beholder who had fired over his head and sent him, the dracons, and Rozloom into flight. Rozloom's revelations also explained the insectare's appearance in the tavern that night, just before the aperusa troop's arrival. Still, Teldin was puzzled. The insectare wanted the cloak, yet its bionoid allies easily could have acquired the cloak and had failed to do so. There was something else going on, probably something that went far beyond Rozloom's involvement. Teldin didn't need his medallion's power to discern that: no reasoning being would trust an aperusa with all the details of a plot. There *was*, however, one mystery the gypsy could clear up.

Teldin turned to the aperusa. "Why did you keep Hectate from waking up? What possible purpose could there be in that?"

For the first time, the aperusa seemed at a loss for an answer. He cleared his throat and opened his mouth as if to speak, then his face went blank and he shut his mouth with a click. The aperusa's befuddlement surprised Teldin: Rozloom had never before stumbled over the creation of an entertaining explanation.

"Sir?"

The faint whisper brought Teldin's attention back to the half-elf. Hectate stirred, his eyelids struggling to open.

"I'm here, Hectate," he replied in a soothing tone. "You're back aboard the *Trumpeter*. You've been asleep for a long time, but you'll be fine."

Hectate went very still, and despair flooded his thin face. "Then I've failed," he whispered. Teldin's brow creased in surprise.

Vallus came to stand at Teldin's shoulder. "I'm afraid I'll have to ask him some questions."

"Later," Teldin declared, not bothering to look up.

"They cannot wait," Vallus insisted gently.

With a long sigh, Hectate opened his eyes and gave Teldin a sad, reassuring smile. "It's all right, sir. There is much you both should know."

With Teldin's help, the half-elven bionoid struggled to sit up, then began his story.

"After the insectare raid that destroyed my own family, Clan Kir took me in as one of their own. I still carry their name, but I left the clan years ago. You may know that bionoids are usually solitary folk, living alone or in small family units. On a few occasions, larger groups known as battle clans have been formed. Clan Kir is a battle clan, its formation fueled by hatred of elves. It was they who attacked the *Trumpeter*. One of them overpowered me and brought me aboard the insectare ship."

"I saw it happen," Teldin broke in softly. "The woman bionoid went right for your crystal eye, your vulnerable spot. I thought for sure you were dead."

Hectate shrugged, obviously uncomfortable with the direction the discussion was taking. "She pulled her punch," he muttered.

"Nice girl," Teldin said in a sardonic tone. He regretted the quip immediately, for Hectate looked as though he'd been struck through the heart. It took the half-elf a moment to collect himself. When he was able to speak, he went on to explain the bionoids' plan and their alliance with the insectare and scro, including the insectare's treacherous plan to release the primary Witchlight Marauder against the goblin races of Armistice.

Vallus questioned Hectate closely about the intended attack on Lionheart, but Teldin was almost equally disturbed by the proposed destruction of the ice world. He'd seen for himself the tertiary Witchlight Marauders' feeding frenzy, and Hectate asserted that the primary marauder was many times more fearsome, a giant land slug that could reduce the planet to a lifeless hull within a year or two. Teldin could well imagine the destruction a rampaging monster of that size might accomplish. He resolutely put the disturbing images out of mind, but he suspected that Witchlight Marauders would edge the spiderlike neogi out of his nightmares for many nights to come.

"I regret to have to ask you this, Hectate Kir," Vallus said in a soft voice when Hectate had finished his story, "but we must know where you stand in all of this."

Hectate held up a hand to stop Teldin's protest. "No, sir, it's a reasonable question. My clan fights for the scro, and I've been flying with an elven ship. That alone marks me a traitor. From either point of view, come to think of it."

The bionoid met Vallus's eyes squarely. "Those who choose not to fight in time of war are often named traitor. I had hoped to live in peace, but that was not among the choices offered me. The insectare K'tide put the lives of every member of my clan against the death of Armistice and the destruction of Lionheart." Hectate stopped and cleared his throat.

"I chose a third option," he continued in a barely audible voice. "I could not sanction the taking of so many lives. Yet, if I had defied the insectare, he would have found a way to carry out his plans without my help, perhaps even without Clan Kir. The small band of bionoids who traveled with K'tide eagerly supported his methods. Seeing no other way to stop them, I sabotaged the insectare's craft so that it would crash on Armistice and kill all those aboard. It was . . . I could think of no other way."

A subdued silence filled the room.

"That was a noble choice," Vallus said in an awed voice, but Hectate smiled sadly and shook his head.

"I'm not sure there's much nobility to be had in war," he replied. He turned to Teldin. "There were four other bionoids aboard the klicklikak. They all died in the crash?"

"Yes."

Hectate nodded, quiet resignation on his face.

Pearl spun into the room, her long black hair flying wild and unbound around her borrowed elven face. "Sorry to break up this tea party, but we've got company. *Lots* of company."

Teldin was on his feet immediately. His cloak flowed around him in sweep of dark maroon. The last time it had been that color was on Ironpiece, in the battle with . . .

"Scro?" he asked Pearl.

"First guess," the dragon dryly congratulated him. "There's a scro battlewagon out there, and they brought along a bunch of those weird patchwork ships for company. It's going to be a big one."

With a sigh of frustration Teldin turned to the aperusa. "We're not finished here, Rozloom. I can't spare anyone to guard you. Can we at least trust you to keep out of the way?"

The aperusa answered with an absent nod, his black eyes fixed on Pearl. Her beautiful face shone with excitement, and, as she dashed from the captain's cabin, her unbound hair swirled around her like a silken banner.

Rozloom walked slowly from the cabin, unnoticed by those who hurried to do battle. When he reached the relative safety of the galley, the gypsy pulled a leather thong from the pocket of his voluminous silk trousers. For a long moment he stared at the homely object, which to his eyes was lovelier than gilded ribbon. The strip of hide had bound the hair of Raven Stormwalker, the elven woman who now called herself Pearl. She had given it to him in the pledge he had so long sought, asking only that he deepen Hectate Kir's slumber. Of course, Hectate would have died from such a dose as Rozloom had prepared, but what was one half-elf to him? *After the battle*, Raven had promised him, after the battle.

An unfamiliar emotion stirred in the complacent heart of the aperusa. Concern for a life not his own rose in his breast like a swelling tide, and for the first time Rozloom suspected that there might be worse things to fear than death, and greater gains than riches.

Chapter Twenty

$\bullet\bullet\bullet$

As Teldin sent the crew members to their battle stations, he read on every face the belief that the battle ahead was to be their last.

The sheer numbers that had been brought against the swan ship were staggering. There were at least thirty orc ships, ranging from tiny, buglike flitters to crude versions of scorpion ships. The vessels flew in dizzy, drunken, seemingly random paths around the *Trumpeter*. Despite the lack of navigating skills shown by the orc spelljammers, it was apparent that they were acting under a seasoned commander. None of the ships ventured within ballista range and within an amazingly short time they had the swan ship surrounded.

The source of command was apparent; lurking in the distance was the ogre dinotherium, a long, massive oval plated with gray metal. It looked a bit like a void-traveling whale, except for the two long, curving rams that protruded from its bow like the tusks of an elephant. Lashed to the underside of the dinotherium's hull were several blunt, wedge-shaped vessels.

"Kobold arrows," a worried Vallus told his wizards, pointing to those small ships. "Their use is exactly what the name implies. The scro pack them with smokepower so that they will explode on impact. If one is launched at us, hit it with every spell you can summon before it gets close."

Yet there was no attack. The ships came to a halt as soon as they'd surrounded the swan ship. The *Trumpeter*'s crew stood by and waited, but the goblinkin showed unusual patience. After a time most of the elven crew drifted to the upper deck, their worried eyes flitting from one orc ship to another.

"Why don't they *do* something?" an unnerved Trivit wondered, nibbling at his claws. He and Chirp again flanked Teldin, ordered to his side by a vigilant Celestial Nightpearl. Teldin was becoming accustomed to having large green bodyguards.

"Maybe they plan to drop some of those creatures on us and watch the fun," Teldin said in a voice intended only for Vallus's ears.

The elf's face turned gray at the very thought, but he shook his head firmly. "They know you are on the ship, Teldin Moore. They would not be likely to risk the destruction of your cloak."

"Captain?"

The unexpected bass voice behind him made Teldin jump, and he turned to face Rozloom. With the threat of battle before him, he had forgotten about the traitorous aperusa.

"I wish to help," the gypsy declared.

Teldin hesitated. They certainly could use every fighter they could get, but—

"It might be safer to keep him out of the way," Vallus commented, echoing Teldin's thoughts.

"Oh, let him stay," Chirp said. "The aperusa could be of great assistance if we are boarded. The moment an enemy turns his back, Rozloom could stick a knife in it," he suggested with bitter sarcasm. The dracon glanced at the goblin ships. "*Will* we be boarded, do you think?" he asked Teldin.

"They probably expect us to surrender," Teldin observed.

With such a massive show of force, it seemed a reasonable assumption.

Rozloom nodded in avid agreement. "That would be the sensible thing, Captain," he said, earning himself scathing glares from both dracons.

"To surrender is to die," Vallus said simply. "When the scro conquered the world called Bondel, they systematically tortured and murdered the elven population. Their goal is the destruction of the elven people."

In that moment Teldin made his decision, and he turned and headed for the bridge. "Then let's make them work for it," he called over his shoulder in ringing tones. Surprised and strengthened by his answer, the elven crew responded with a cheer and hurried back to their stations. The dracons unceremoniously hoisted Rozloom between them and tossed him down the steps to the deck below, loudly suggesting that he occupy himself in the galley, baking cream puffs.

Teldin relieved the elven helmsman and seated himself in the chair. As he did, the captain told Quon to shoot at anything he thought the swan ship might hit. The weapon master flashed Teldin the peculiar, distinctively elven salute, and his eyes were fever-bright in his tattooed face. Teldin's cloak quickly became a mantle of brilliant pink light, and, as his will became motive force, the *Trumpeter* shot forward with incredible speed.

The swan ship hurtled toward one of the larger orc ships, a patchwork scorpion equipped with pincers that looked a couple of sizes too large for its hull. The moment the swan ship was within range, Quon fired the fore ballista. The giant bolt shot forward, tearing through the insect ship's left shoulder and into the claw machinery. The left claw drooped, useless, to the ship's gravity plane, and the weight of it tipped the ship dangerously to one side. Orcs on the upper deck tumbled overboard.

Before the surviving orcs could react, Teldin abruptly

pivoted the ship in a tight, fast circle, bringing its tail catapult to bear on another scorpion. Chirp and Trivit immediately sent a load of Om's spiked bolas hurtling toward the ship. The scorpion took only minor damage, but the dracons had no time for a second shot. The swan ship already was hurtling out of weapon range.

A familiar, whistling whine began approaching the swan ship, and in response the door to the captain's cabin flew open. Pale and far too thin from his long, drug-induced sleep, Hectate made his way unsteadily to the rail where the battle wizards gathered.

"The bionoid ships have a weakness," he said, speaking quickly in a race against the invisible, approaching shrike ship. "They've replaced the forecastle ballista with a magical crystal eye—can't explain that right now. A direct hit should make a magical backlash big enough to destroy the ship."

"How can we aim at something we can't see?" one of the wizards demanded.

"They'll hover over the deck so the bionoids can drop—"

"And the cloaking device might shut down when a ship comes to a halt," Vallus broke in. He eyed the half-elf with new respect, and his expression did not falter when Hectate abruptly transformed into his monstrous insect form.

The shrike ships whistled by, then began their circling approach, slowing as they prepared to drop the deadly warriors. Vallus looked inquiringly up into the bionoid's large frontal eyes, and Hectate nodded his insect head. The dorsal plates on the bionoid's armored chest folded back, and the membrane beneath began to glow with magical red light. At the same time, the wizards began the complicated gestures that summoned fireball spells.

When the first shrike ship came into view, a bolt of energy burst from Hectate's chest. The ball of red light scorched along the shrike ship's long, pointed beak and hit squarely between its domed forecastle windows. The red glow spread over the entire shrike ship, enveloping it in a crackling field of energy and holding it quivering in its grip. The elves braced for the explosion, but the shrike ship burned far too rapidly for that. To their astonishment, the ship blackened and collapsed into a cloud of fine ash. The destruction of the shrike ship took place so quickly that the other bionoid ships had no time to react. When the second and third shrike ships came into view, the elven wizards released a barrage of fireball spells. Some flew harmlessly off to fizzle in the blackness of wildspace, but one managed to hit its mark. A second ship disappeared into smoke and ash, which drifted with the ship's momentum to cover the deck of the swan ship and the unconscious form of a reluctant, half-elven hero.

"Return Hectate Kir to the captain's cabin," Vallus ordered. "He'll need a day's rest." Two of the wizards immediately stooped to do his bidding against a whirling backdrop of stars. The swan ship was making another rapid retreat. This time, however, the third and final shrike ship darted after it in furious pursuit.

The bionoid ship did not risk coming to a hover. Barely slowing its flight, it dipped low over the swan ship. Enormous weapons dropped from it and clattered to the deck, and several bionoid warriors leaped out after them. Five of the monstrous insects managed to land, tucking at the last moment and rolling to their feet with fluid, athletic grace. The sixth was less fortunate: it missed the ship entirely. Flailing its spiked arms, it floated outward toward wildspace and death. The surviving bionoids snatched up their halberds and formed a battle circle.

"Trial by champion."

Hectate Kir's hoarse whisper echoed in the unearthly silence. He gently pulled away from the elven wizards who supported him and made his way slowly over to the invaders.

"You know our battle codes?" one of them asked Hectate

in feminine, incredulous tones.

"Name your champion," the half-elf replied, his voice a little stronger this time.

"I am Ronia, captain and ranking officer of Clan Kir," the female replied. Her huge black head dipped slowly as her multifaceted eyes looked Hectate over. "But I cannot accept an honor challenge from such as you. You're a half-elf."

"As are you," Hectate said softly.

There was a hiss of anger from the bionoid warrior. She spun her halberd in a quick circle, signifying her readiness for battle, and the wicked blades at each end of the staff caught and tossed back the starlight in a gleaming arc.

"Weapons?" she snapped.

"Halberds," Hectate replied, holding out a hand to another bionoid. The creature slapped the enormous weapon into Hectate's palm, and the half-elf staggered a bit under its weight. He quickly rested the tip of one blade on the ground and balanced the thick staff with both hands.

"Terms?" Ronia's voice was inexorable.

"Victory by survival."

She let out a bark of laughter. "Of course. Conditions?"

"If I am slain, you avenge the deaths of Soona, Wynlar, Tekura, Enester, and Zeddop. If you die, the rest of the battle clan will withdraw with honor, leaving the swan ship and its crew unharmed."

"Agreed. You know much of our customs," she said with suspicion.

"I should. My name is Hectate, formerly of Clan Kir."

The bionoid woman recoiled with another hiss of rage, and she leveled her halberd's blade at Hectate's throat. "Change quickly, then, or I'll spit you like a skinned hare," Ronia gritted out. She charged forward, blade leading.

Hectate leaped aside and spun. As he did, the Change came over him and in a blink he was a ten-foot-tall insect, the mirror image of his attacker. As he whirled, he hooked one of his curved forearm blades over Ronia's halberd staff. He quickly bent forward at the waist, using the momentum of the female's attack to throw her up and over him. She flipped and landed on her back with a dull clatter.

Instantly Hectate leaped at the fallen bionoid, his halberd held before him. Ronia brought her knees to her chest and kicked out high and hard. Her foot spikes raked down Hectate's plate-armored chest with a sound like fingernails on a windowpane. Hectate staggered back, ichor dripping from the large dorsal plates on his chest; the plates had not yet sealed after opening for his ball of force spell.

Leaping nimbly to her feet, Ronia pressed her advantage. In a lightning-quick combination, she raised her left knee high and snapped a kick at Hectate's crystal eye, hit it again with a side kick from her right foot, and whirled to strike a third time with her left. She danced back, both hands holding the halberd before her in a horizontal line. An enraged oath escaped the bionoid warrior when she saw that Hectate still stood. The glow from his central eye had dimmed, but the crystal was not shattered.

Hectate mirrored her stance and the guard position of the halberd staff. A quick spring brought him toe-to-toe with Ronia. Thick oaken staffs clashed again and again as the two bionoids sparred viciously, each trying to work an opening for a halberd's blades. For many moments the battle went on. The monsters were so evenly matched that it seemed that only exhaustion could claim one of them.

Then Ronia spun, taking a sharp blow to her back but kicking backward hard. Her spiked foot smashed into Hectate's knee, and he went down with a sharp cry of pain and the crunch of cracked plate and bone. With a triumphant yell, Ronia raised her halberd high overhead and chopped down. Hectate rolled aside, and the blade bit deeply into the wood of the deck where his head had just been. Before Ronia could tug her weapon free, Hectate hoisted himself up on one elbow and smashed the back of her knee with a mailed fist. The joint buckled, and she went down.

Plate armor clattered against the wooden deck as the bionoids rolled and grappled, each trying to get the advantage. Finally one of the warriors lifted its head high, smashing its forehead into the other's face. The creatures' crystal eyes struck each other like flint and steel, and there was a bright spark and a sudden flare of red light. Then there was darkness, and both bionoids lay still.

In the aftermath of battle, elves and surviving bionoids eyed each other uncertainly, not sure what the strange outcome meant.

After a long, silent moment, one of the creatures stirred and rose unsteadily to its feet. There was an empty oval indentation on the other bionoid's forehead. Its crystal eye had shattered; the creature was dead. Everyone on deck held his breath as the onlookers waited to learn who had survived the challenge.

The dead bionoid quickly compressed back to elven form. A tall, rangy female elf lay on deck, her sweat-drenched black hair clinging to her head and her amber eyes open. Even in death those eyes held the wild, fierce expression of a hawk. Still in his monstrous form, Hectate stooped and closed Ronia's eyes with a gentle, taloned finger. He rose and faced the other four bionoids.

"Challenge was made and met. You will withdraw, as agreed."

The four bionoids inclined their heads in agreement, and one of them signaled the shrike ship by waving its arms at the shrike ship in an elaborate pattern. The bionoid ship circled, came to a hover, and threw down boarding ropes. One of the creatures gathered up the elven body of Ronia, and, without a word, the survivors of the once fearsome battle clan returned to their last ship. The shrike ship flew off, disappearing into the black vastness of wildspace.

* * * * *

Grimnosh pounded the railing with a white-hided fist. "The bionoids have failed again! Thrice-damned elf-spawned garden pests, fit only as food for giant Zenuvian flytraps!"

The scro ranted for some time, while the hideous ice orc general looked on impassively and waited for the storm to pass.

"What plan now?" Ubiznik asked at length.

"We must have that cloak!"

"Cloak, scro want. Elf blood, orcs."

"Indeed." Grimnosh's colorless eyes narrowed. "Perhaps it's time for both of us to take what we want. Choose four of your best soldiers and report to the landing dock immediately. We're going to board the swan ship."

* * * * *

Pearl came up onto the main deck just as Chirp and Trivit were dragging Hectate's limp bionoid form into the captain's cabin. "About time," she murmured with satisfaction. Turning to Vallus, she demanded to know what had just occurred.

"The bionoids have retreated," he said tersely.

"Good. An assortment of goblins is trouble enough. By the way, I'm supposed to tell someone that we're out of ballista bolts down in the cargo hold."

"Take some from the main deck," Vallus replied absently.

"Thanks, but I don't run errands." Pearl raised her voice and summoned Trivit, sending the dracon to resupply the lower level.

Elven crossbows twanged as the swan ship charged yet another orc scorpion ship, and the thud of the catapult sounded twice more from the stern.

"How long can he keep this up?" wondered Pearl, glancing up at the bridge with deep concern. "Sooner or later those scro out there are going to get mad, squash this sorry excuse for a ship like a ripe melon, and make off with the captain."

Vallus Leafbower turned to face the mysterious moon elf. "That would be convenient for you, wouldn't it. With Teldin Moore gone, you would have a clear path to the *Spelljammer*."

"Convenient? Ha!" Pearl said scornfully. "Teldin can have the captain's job, and welcome to it." She shot an arch glance at the elven wizard. "I'm sure *you* can understand that."

Vallus recoiled as if she'd struck him. "But how much does he know about the *Spelljammer*?" the wizard persisted. "Has he any idea of the dangers aboard the ship? Or that few who seek the ship are ever heard from again?"

Pearl's eyes mocked the elven wizard. "Not unless *you've* told him."

"You see what the elves are up against," Vallus said, a trifle defensively, pointing toward the ongoing battle with the orc fleet. "The Imperial Fleet faces destruction. We need the cloak."

"What do I care about that?" Pearl retorted. Her hand curved around her sapphire pendant in a gesture of deliberate menace. "I want Teldin Moore, end of story. If the Imperial Fleet interferes, I'll destroy it myself. That goes for anyone else who gets in my way. It's as good a hobby as any. Think about *that*, little wizard." She whirled and darted up the stairs to the bridge.

Teldin looked up briefly when Pearl burst into the room. "They're tightening the noose," he murmured in a distant, distracted voice. "They're starting to close on us, and we can't get them all."

"Can you break through? Outrun them?" she suggested.

"I doubt it. The swan ship's held together with string and spit," Teldin said ruefully. "Pieces of it fall off every time I make a run."

"Then it's time for us to leave," Pearl declared. "Turn the ship and its problems back to the elves, and come with me."

Her suggestion startled Teldin. "Leave? But how? On what?"

"Under your own power!" she said, and her voice sang with the exultant freedom of wildspace. "Think of it: Your cloak allows you to shapechange. What better form to assume than that of a radiant dragon? Ahh!" she broke off, her face glowing. "It would be good to fly again. Let's go!"

Teldin was too staggered by her suggestion to speak, and he just stared at Pearl's outstretched, entreating hands. Was such a thing *possible*? He had taken on other human faces and forms, had endured a brief interlude as a gnome, had fought in the body of an orc general, and had assumed the appearance of an Armistice bugbear, but a *dragon*?

Something hit the swan ship with an extended, rattling thump. The ship lurched, sending Pearl falling backward to land squarely on her backside. She leaped to her feet, eyes blazing. While she swore and rubbed at the offended portion of her inconvenient elven anatomy, Teldin swept his magically extended vision over the ship. One of the orc ships had loosed a catapult load of stones. Teldin could feel a crack along the lower part of the hull, slightly above the paddle line. They could fly and probably land, but they'd slowly sink once they *did* land. Still, it could be worse.

As if on cue, the attack began. A scorpion's jettison shot another load. Stones thudded against the swan ship like a summer hailstorm, and the cries of injured elves drifted into the bridge.

Still using his strange double vision, Teldin hovered over the ship. To his horror, he saw a small, triangular ship—one of the things Vallus had called "kobold arrows"—coming straight toward them. He brought the swan ship around, but then he noticed that the arrow had changed its course. The tiny vessel flew straight at the scorpion that had just attacked them. The two orc ships met in a ball of flame, and wave after wave of explosions rocked the burning remnants.

"Now there's an object lesson for you," Pearl said. "Someone on that battleship doesn't want this swan ship to be attacked, and they're letting the other orcs know it's not healthy to get carried away. They want something on this ship, Captain—probably that cloak of yours, though I never saw a scro who looked good in pink." Her facetious expression faded, and her face and voice became grim. "If you don't come with me now, the scro will get you. The elves can't stop them, and you know it. You've got to pick friends who'll be of some use, Captain, and that means me."

Teldin's eyes pleaded for understanding. "I can't just leave them here to die."

The dragon-in-elf's-clothing glared at him, and her elven eyes changed into compelling golden orbs slashed by vertical black pupils: *dragon* eyes.

One of Aelfred's stories flashed into Teldin's mind, a tale of dragons that could weave charm spells with their eyes. Indeed, Teldin could feel the warmth and power of the dragon's mind sweeping over his own, and the glow of his cloak dimmed a little as his hold on himself—and its magic—waned. Dimly he remembered landing on Armistice, when Pearl used her pendant helm to take over the spelljamming ship. He'd slept deeply and recalled few of the details of landfall. Had she charmed him then? And if so, would she *always* attempt to force his will?

No, Teldin vowed silently. He would not be owned, not by the elves and not by a dragon. Teldin gritted his teeth and struggled to throw off the dragon charm, to pull his gaze away from her compelling golden eyes.

An image forced its way into Teldin's mind, a memory of a childhood summer. He saw a much younger version of himself lying in the grass, looking up and marveling at the flight of the birds. The boy's timeless yearning for wings filled him, and he rose from his grassy bed, stretched his arms wide and prepared to soar up into the golden light.

Try as he might, Teldin could not break free of the vision. He summoned all the strength of his will and leaned *into* the waking dream. He recalled other boyhood pleasures—a fresh-picked apple, a swim in the creek, the scent of spring— and he visualized roots slipping from his small bare feet and tethering him to the land. The dream of flight faded.

Pearl tried again and again, projecting images into his mind of moments he'd treasured, people he had loved, all bathed in the warmth of golden light. One by one Teldin overcame them.

Gradually he came to realize that, under the power of a dragon charm, he could see into *her* mind as well. An overwhelming pride and immense vanity formed most of the mental landscape, but the dragon's image of *him* startled Teldin: Pearl saw him as more powerful than he dreamed possible. A mixture of awe and fear swept over him as he read Pearl's reluctant belief that he, Teldin Moore, potentially was the equal of a radiant dragon.

Equal. Partner. Suddenly Teldin knew how to break free from the dragon charm. Teldin concentrated on the pact Pearl had offered him, a pact that offered him a free choice. Next, he form a vivid mental picture of a forsworn dragon being driven from its lair in disgrace.

As abruptly as it began, the golden light vanished, and there was nothing stronger than exasperation in Pearl's gold and silver eyes. "Humans!" she grumbled. "I promise you a choice, and you have to start out with a bad one. Well, go figure."

"Thanks, partner," he said softly.

"Don't rub it in," Pearl groused. "If you're not going to get yourself out of this mess, I suppose *I'll* have to." She spun on her heel and stalked out of the bridge.

Teldin's magical vision followed her as she raced across

the deck. She made her way to the railing, hauled herself over it, and leaped far out.

His breath caught in his throat as he watched her float out along the swan ship's gravity plane, and he willed himself to soar high above the ship so that he could follow her. When she had put a safe distance between herself and the ship, a familiar gray mist enveloped her elven body, then shot out in either direction, firming immediately into shimmering black scales. Teldin had seen the radiant dragon through the eyes of the medallion's magic, but the full glory of the being called Celestial Nightpearl was overwhelming, frightening in its majesty.

The dragon was enormous; long and serpentine, her body alone was at least five times the length of the swan ship, and her tapering tail added perhaps four hundred feet more. She spread her glittering, translucent wings in flight, and Teldin guessed that a pair of elven armadas easily could sail beneath their shadow. The dragon's flight was not hampered by limbs, and she moved through wildspace with a fluid, sinuous grace. Her head was long, triangular, and studded with the compelling gold eyes Teldin had glimpsed moments earlier. Around her neck was the golden pendant, now bearing a sapphire the size of a small spelljamming craft. More wondrous still were her pearly scales; although darker than wildspace, they caught and reflected the light of a thousand stars.

Celestial Nightpearl threw back her head and roared, then, like a coiled spring, she lunged at and under the nearest ship. It flew upward like a bobbing cork, buffeted by the creature's powerful gravity force. As she sped past, she flicked her tail and two orc flitters crumbled into wildspace flotsam.

The orcs resumed their attack, throwing everything they had at the new threat. Almost playfully, Pearl dodged their pitifully small weapons and continued smashing ships with her tail or upending them with her gravity field. It seemed to be little more than sport for the radiant dragon, and the orc fleet crumbled before her might.

So intent on the battle was he that Teldin did not notice the elven man-o-war approaching from beneath them. Firing on orc vessels as it came, the patrol ship drew a tired cheer from the swan ship's crew.

The dragon spat out the claw she'd just bitten off a scorpion ship, and she hurtled toward the man-o-war. As she blazed past, a casual flick of her tail shattered one of the ship's enormous crystalline wings. The elven ship began to spiral out of control. Not content with that, Pearl wheeled around and came in for a second pass. Her enormous jaws opened, and blue light shot toward the careening vessel. A fireball of enormous power struck the hull, and the ship exploded into bright orange flame.

Pearl swooped down low, circling the swan ship so that the massive bubble air surrounding her melded with the swan ship's atmosphere. Her golden eyes sought out Vallus Leafbower, who stood transfixed with horror at the ship's rail. The dragon's head reared back, and a tremendous roar rolled over the swan ship. In the fearsome sound was the faint music of an elven woman's mocking laughter.

Throughout the one-sided battle, the scro command ship hung back. Teldin kept a close watch on it, however, and, with a sense of foreboding, he saw a sleek scorpion rise from the dinotherium's massive deck and begin a wide circle toward the swan ship. At the same time he noted a movement at the base of the ship's hull, and one of the small, wedge-shaped ships lashed there hurtled toward the radiant dragon like a giant arrowhead. It stuck her and exploded in a spray of metal shards and flying scales.

Pearl threw back her head and roared, and Teldin could feel both her agony and her rage. Bent on revenge, the dragon sped toward the dinotherium, leaving a trail of blood droplets floating behind her. With a sinuous, winding

motion she wrapped herself around the ship. She strained
and compressed as she squeezed the ship, crushing it in her
coils as if she were a giant anaconda.

The dinotherium's metal hull protested, shrieked, and
finally gave way. A huge crack ran up the dinotherium from
keel to upper deck. Still Pearl squeezed, and plates of metal
began to pop off. Finally even the ship's metal frame
buckled, and the ship began to break up into pieces. The
stunned elves stood gaping at the unusual attack.

With his expanded vision, Teldin was the first to see the
strange gray creature emerge from the crack in the cargo
hold and climb up the ruined ship as nimbly as a spider.
Perhaps twenty feet tall, the creature was dwarfed by the
powerful radiant dragon, but it was no less fearsome. It
appeared to be an overgrown version of the tertiary Witchlight
Marauders. Suddenly Teldin feared for Pearl.

Fast and agile, the monster ran along the dragon's coils
until it reached her neck. The enormous talons on its hands
found a purchase amid her scales, and the creature's enormous maw worked busily. Pearl's blood flowed freely over
the monster, increasing its feeding frenzy.

The dragon roared and twisted, but she could not dislodge
the creature from her throat. She released the shattered
dinotherium and took flight, weaving and pitching in an
attempt to rid herself of the clinging horror. Finally the
creature, in its frenzy, bit the gold chain that hung around
Pearl's neck.

Teldin sucked in a quick breath, knowing what was
coming. Anyone who'd tried to remove his cloak had
received a sharp, painful jolt. Sure enough, a brilliant spark
flared from the dragon's ultimate helm and the gray creature
was thrown off. It flailed wildly, and one of its hands
managed to thrust deeply into the base of Pearl's wing.

Six metallic talons tore through the membrane as the
monster fell, reducing the dragon's magnificent wing to

bloody shreds. The creature hung on briefly to the tip of the wing before it lost its grip and tumbled back down toward the icy prison that was its homeworld.

Pearl, too, was in trouble. Unable to use her ruined wing for flight, she began to spiral downward.

Change, Teldin urged her silently, but the dragon seemed to be too dazed to summon her shapechanging magic. He was forced to watch as the fire faded from her golden eyes. Teldin strained his magical ties to the ship, but he could follow the dragon's descent only so far. He stayed with her as long as he could, until his vision grew dizzy and faint, until he felt himself begin to fall into the darkness of wildspace.

Chapter Twenty-One

• • •

With a great effort of will, Teldin dragged himself back to the swan ship. As if in a dream, as if from a great height, he saw himself lying on the floor of the bridge. The pink light had faded from his cloak.

"Teldin Moore." Vallus's gentle voice pulled him more fully into the ship. Teldin took a deep breath and suddenly he was back in his own body. He remembered his duty, and in a sudden panic he twisted to look toward the helm.

"Kermjin is on the helm. Do not worry. He took over quite smoothly while you were . . . elsewhere."

Teldin slowly got to his feet. "I think Pearl is dead," he said, and the words seemed to echo in the empty place her absence had left inside him. His knees buckled underneath him, and wildspace threatened to claim him again.

Three sharp metallic thunks, in rapid procession, brought Teldin back to his surroundings.

"Grappling hooks," Vallus announced, his green eyes wide with foreboding. "The scro are trying to board."

*   *   *   *   *

The crew of the scro scorpion ship swarmed onto the *Trumpeter*'s deck, and the sounds of hand-to-hand combat rang out as the elves struggled to hold back the much larger scro.

One of the invaders, a seven-foot albino in magnificent battle gear, disdained combat and prowled about the ship as if seeking a worthy opponent. He looked merely annoyed when an aperusa stepped out of the shadows of the galley to confront him.

"The insectare is dead," Rozloom said by way of introduction.

The scro's pale eyes scorched up and down the gypsy, and his tusks flashed in a burst of derisive laughter. "*You're* K'tide's informant? That certainly would explain the confusion. Ah, well, I was rather hoping it had been an elf." Grimnosh shrugged negligently and drew a dagger—a lesser weapon and a scro insult. "Since I have no further need of information . . ."

With a flash of steel and gems, an aperusa dagger met and held the scro's weapon. The two huge combatants stood toe-to-toe, their weapons locked at the hilts and their strength equally matched. It would have been a deadlock, but for the second gypsy weapon that pricked the scro's side.

"We make new deal?" Rozloom asked, his black eyes boring into the scro's.

"Your negotiating style is impressive," the scro said with a note of irony, "but what could you possibly offer me now?"

"Your life." The aperusa's knife pierced the general's leather armor and pressed deeper until it touched a rib.

Grimnosh didn't flinch. "Well?"

"All is yours: ship, elves, the cloak that changes color. One elven woman I must have. Tell your men to spare the woman with raven hair and eyes of gold and silver."

"How poetic," said the scro with a sneer. "Very well, if she's still alive, you may have her."

"Swear it!" Rozloom insisted. "On the Tomb of Dukagsh, swear safety for Rozloom and the black-haired elven woman."

The scro grunted a response. Satisfied, the aperusa eased his knife out of the scro's hide and took a cautious step back, keeping the jeweled dagger before him.

Grimnosh spun in a swirl of midnight cape and stalked away. He sped up the stairs to the main deck, and his scowl turned to a delighted sneer when he at last saw the object he desired. The Cloak of the First Pilot billowed in a sweep of majestic crimson as its human wielder fended off Ubiznik Redeye's battle axe. Teldin Moore was rather good, Grimnosh noted with a touch of surprise as he watched the battle. Despite a rather nasty gash to the thigh and armed only with a short sword, the human managed to hold his own against the much stronger ice orc.

Caught up in the time-altering magic of the cloak, Teldin fought for his life against the squat, hideous creature. A strength he didn't know he possessed filled him, keeping him on his feet despite his exhaustion, the loss of blood, and the painful ringing in his head where the orc's axe handle had caught him. Dimly Teldin blessed Chirp for the hours the dracon had spent sparring with him. That practice against a battle axe would make the difference now, Teldin vowed silently.

From the corner of his eye Teldin could see Chirp circling the battle, his ornate axe held at the ready as he waited for an opening to chop down his *kaba*'s attacker. Teldin saw a huge white scro burst up from the lower level. With a fearsome sneer, the scro drew an enormous sword and, holding it like a lance, charged toward the preoccupied dracon and buried the sword to the hilt in Chirp's hindquarters. The dracon's mouth dropped open in surprise, then he tottered and fell like a downed tree.

Chirp's eyes sought Teldin, and he murmured, "*Kaba.*" With a final, great effort, he gave one sweep of his powerful tail. The tip whipped around the gray orc's ankles and knocked it off balance.

Immediately Teldin was upon the fallen orc, determined to use the opportunity Chirp had bought him. He leaned heavily on his short sword, pushing it through the orc's tough gray hide and up into its heart. Teldin yanked his weapon free of the dead orc and whirled to face the uniformed scro. Before either could strike a blow, Trivit gave an agonized shriek and thundered toward them. The dracon dropped his broadsword as he ran and drew a small throwing knife. He hurled it at the white scro, and the knife buried itself in the monster's shoulder.

With a contemptuous smile, the scro pulled out the knife and tossed it aside. Almost immediately, however, his sneer faltered and a violent shudder shook his large frame. The scro fell to the deck, writhing and twisting as spasm after spasm racked his body.

"Poison," Trivit said with dark satisfaction. "Chirp made it from the kelp of Armistice." The dracon cradled his fallen brother's head in his massive arms as he watched the scro's death agony. Finally Teldin could take no more, and he drew his blade firmly across the huge warrior's throat. There was a spark of surprise in the scro's colorless eyes, then nothing at all. With the death of the last of the invaders, the cloak's battle magic faded and Teldin's perception of time returned to normal.

Teldin drew a deep, calming breath and laid a hand on Trivit's shoulder, knowing he could say nothing that would ease the dracon's grief. The sorrowful scene was mirrored across the swan ship as the elves did want they could for their wounded and began to mourn their dead. The battle was over, but it had been costly. Only a handful of elves had survived, and it appeared that none had escaped injury. The swan ship was badly damaged. Teldin wasn't sure it would hold together during landfall, *if* they made it as far as Radole.

A shower of stones hit the *Trumpeter* and shattered Teldin's thoughts. One of the ill-built Armistice scorpion ships was attacking. It was quickly joined by three more, and then by a pair of wasps. Deprived of leadership, the remnants of the orc fleet gave in to generations of pent-up hatred for elves. A ballista bolt, a crude but effective weapon carved from the bone of some enormous creature, bit deeply into the swan ship's wooden hull. More weapons followed, and half a dozen orc ships closed in for the kill.

Vallus Leafbower staggered to Teldin's side. "We cannot repel another attack. Is there something you can do?"

There was little hope in the wizard's voice, but as Teldin surveyed the grim situation, he wondered if there was indeed something he might do. With a calm he did not expect to feel, Teldin silently acknowledged that he probably would die in the attempt. Better to die trying, he concluded. He made his way to the ship's railing, wildly dodged another spray of small stones, and vaulted over the side.

Teldin's stomach churned as he free-fell through the ship's atmosphere. The gravity plane caught him as if it were an invisible, elastic sheet, and Teldin slowly began to drift toward the edge of the air envelope. When he could wait no longer, he took a deep breath and closed his eyes.

Teldin summoned a mental image of his own face and body, then he replaced them with the golden eyes and glittering scales of Celestial Nightpearl. He concentrated as he never had before, struggling against both his belief that the effort could not succeed and his fear that it might.

Power surged through him, then he felt a cool satin rush of air. Teldin opened his eyes. Wildspace surrounded him, and he soared effortlessly though it with a sense of freedom such as he had never imagined. He twisted his head to look back at his new form. Disappointment mixed with amazement in his mind. He was only a fraction of Pearl's size, but one hundred feet of iridescent black scales flowed behind him, and around his massive neck was the silver chain of the cloak, its twin lion-head clasps now nearly life-size. Teldin threw back his head and let out a burst of incredulous, exultant laughter. He was not particularly surprised to hear his own voice thrumming with the power of a miniature dragon's roar.

In the distance was the swan ship, looking like a battered toy and besieged by the orcs. With effort Teldin drew his attention back to the battle. As he sped toward the first orc ship, he formed a mental picture of a fireball. Lacking hands, he wasn't quite sure how to cast the magic until he remembered what Pearl had done. Taking a deep breath, Teldin closed on the largest scorpion and expelled the air as hard as he could. Bright blue light shot from his mouth and seared across the blackness, and the orc ship exploded into flame. Again Teldin breathed a glowing pulse of force, and twice more, leaving four orc ships burning like candles against the backdrop of wildspace. He might not have had Pearl's girth, but speed and the essential powers seemed at hand. The two remaining enemy ships made a hasty retreat. He closed on them, only to find that his magical arsenal had been exhausted.

A solution seemed easy to a being as powerful as a dragon. Teldin closed on the small ships, his jaws open. There was a crunch of wood and steel, and he spat out the shattered remnants as easily as a boy might expel a mouthful of watermelon seeds.

Wheeling about, he came toward the swan ship. It was battered almost beyond recognition and lay silently in space amid the flotsam that once had been the orc and scro force. The battle was over.

Teldin's wings beat the air as he backpedaled, wondering what he should do next. He could not land on the ship as he was, but he dared not change back *where* he was for fear of missing the ship and falling into wildspace. As he surveyed the swan ship, he wondered whether he *should* land even if he could figure out how to do so; the last orc attack had left the ship beyond repair. Few elves remained standing on deck, probably too few to fly the ship. To return to his human form, to return to the elves, probably would mean death. Even if he lived, survival meant facing the elves' determined attempts to control the cloak. And, at the moment, exhilarated by the independence and power that came with the form of a radiant dragon, Teldin was ready to do almost anything to ensure his newly won freedom. He edged a little closer to the ship.

Vallus Leafbower clutched the rail with white-knuckled hands and gazed up into the unnerving cornflower-blue eyes of the wildspace dragon. The elf's face showed no fear, only deep weariness and resignation. The medallion's true-sight broke into Teldin's power-drunk mind, and the Cloakmaster recoiled from the knowledge that Vallus fully expected him to destroy the elven ship and make his escape. The idea tempted Teldin, and he saw no condemnation in the elf's eyes.

Almost without thinking, Teldin spread his wings and sped forward, this time dipping under the wounded swan ship. Recalling an image of Hectate's carefully marked star chart, Teldin set a course for Radole, carrying the battered elven vessel on his back.

The power of his miniature radiant dragon form and the magic of his cloak made the journey pass incredibly fast, yet even in his altered and enhanced state Teldin knew he eventually would pay for flying many days without food or rest. When the reddish gray sphere finally came into sight, Teldin headed carefully for the narrow ribbon that was Radole's only habitable land.

As the world hurtled toward him, it occurred to the numb Cloakmaster that he had no idea how a radiant dragon was supposed to land. He headed for a river and beat his wings furiously, trying to slow his descent.

Teldin did not feel the impact. The last thing he remembered was the roar of water as it closed over his head.

* * * * *

Voices swam in and out, their words as elusive as the colors cast through a dewdrop prism. Teldin tried to find meaning in the sounds, but he could not force his mind to focus.

Somehow, he knew it was important that he do so. He gathered the strength of his will behind the effort, and slowly the swirling haze of sound settled into conversation.

"It is my right," proclaimed a resonant bass voice just outside Teldin's door. "The aperusa, we avenge the death of those we love. If the woman Raven Stormwalker is dead, I claim the right of blood."

"Rozloom, try to understand this." Teldin easily identified the mellifluous, overly patient tones of Vallus Leafbower. "The woman you knew on the swan ship was not Raven Stormwalker. I don't know who she was, but Raven Stormwalker died many centuries ago."

The aperusa responded with a disbelieving snort. "Then vengeance is long overdue, is it not?" he retorted.

Vallus sighed. "What sort of vengeance did you have in mind?"

"Goblin blood." There was a new note, a grim and dangerous one, in Rozloom's rumbling voice. "I wish to take over where the green bug-creature left off. Give me a fast ship, a crew, and casters of magic, and I will return to Armistice. The Witchlight Marauder will lap goblin blood from the ice and the rocks."

Vallus was silent, and the aperusa continued with a description of the orc settlement, the location of the primary marauder, and a cogent, well-conceived plan for killing the orc priests and witch doctors who controlled the monster.

Teldin waited for Vallus's response, confident that the elf would refuse. "I will see that you get all you need," Vallus said in a strangled tone.

"Good. Is a deal," the gypsy concluded.

Frantically Teldin struggled to speak against the plan. Try as he might, he could neither move nor talk. There were limits to his strength, and he already had far exceeded them. Darkness and silence surrounded him, drawing him back into a vast and troubled dreamscape.

*   *   *   *   *

The aperusa slogged through the deep snow to the base of the tusk-shaped mountain. He found the entrance that the elven search party had used, then he counted off paces to the second hidden tunnel he had discovered when standing guard. Rozloom squeezed his vast, fur-clad bulk into the opening and made his way silently down to a ledge overlooking the cavern.

In the center of the stone chamber slept a hideous creature. Larger than a swan ship, the unhealthy gray thing resembled an enormous slug. Its flesh rippled and undulated as if its slumber were a tenuous thing. Surrounding the monster was a ring of orc priests, chant-singing endlessly in a coarse, guttural language.

Rozloom spread a collection of knives out before him. He waited until a second group of goblinkin, these hobgoblin witch doctors, entered the cavern to change shifts. To the aperusa's way of thinking, the more food the marauder had upon awakening, the longer he himself would have to make his escape back to the waiting ship. The moment had come.

With rare skill, the aperusa began to throw. One after another, the blades spun into the cavern and found homes in the hearts or spines of orc and hobgoblin priests. The chant faltered, and the marauder stirred. With barely a twitch, the creature sucked three of the fallen orcs into its cavernous central maw.

Rozloom noted this with dark glee as he continued to hurl

his weapons. Soon all the goblins on this frozen hell would meet the same fate. As the chant faded, the monster awoke and oozed forward, sucking in the goblin-creatures with frightening ease.

Rozloom backed out toward the tunnel, intending to make his escape. Then the monster belched, and foul gas roiled up toward Rozloom in a greenish cloud.

"Poison," murmured the aperusa, who knew enough of that dark art to recognize it in the hands of a master. The green gas worked quickly, and the last knife fell from his paralyzed fingers. The aperusa knew he was dead, but suddenly that knowledge was not disturbing. Rozloom had done what he'd come to do, and he was ready to die.

* * * * *

Teldin awoke two days later in a small tavern room somewhere on Radole. Vallus explained to him that he'd been unconscious for many days, gravely wounded in the crash and utterly drained, both by the use of magic and the marathon trip that had brought the swan ship to Radole. The captain listened to the explanation with little interest.

"Is Rozloom back yet?" he asked bluntly.

Vallus's eyes widened. "You heard our conversation?"

"Enough."

The elf lowered his eyes as if he were ashamed. "No. Rozloom has not returned."

That was almost too much for Teldin to take in. The instinct for self-preservation ran so strong and deep in the aperusa that Teldin could not imagine it failing to govern Rozloom's actions. "Was his mission successful?" he asked quietly.

"We do not yet know. It may well be that it was."

A wave of nausea washed over Teldin. If the enormous land marauder had been set free, an entire planet would be laid waste before the creature and its hideous descendants turned on each other. The magnitude of the carnage sickened Teldin, and he looked at the elven wizard with horror in his eyes.

Vallus did not shrink from the man's unspoken accusation. "I did what I felt I had to do, Teldin Moore. If you were in my position, you might have done the same thing." He rose quietly and left Teldin alone.

Several hours and much soul-searching later, a troubled Teldin concluded that Vallus may well have been right.

*   *   *   *   *

The Cloakmaster made his way unsteadily down to the main taproom, where he found Vallus deep in conversation with Hectate Kir and Trivit.

"I've come to say good-bye," Teldin said quietly.

The elf rose from his chair and extended his hand. "I shall miss you, Teldin Moore."

"That's it? No argument?"

A faint smile curved the wizard's lips. "There's an old saying that he who would argue with a dragon is either a fool or a corpse."

Teldin shifted uncomfortably. "I doubt I'll ever try to take that form again. It was, well, too . . . "

"I understand," Vallus said when the human faltered. "Yet the ability lies within you. The elves have problems enough without taking on a radiant dragon," he said with a touch of humor. "Therefore I will recommend that the Imperial Fleet break off its attempt to control you and the cloak. Once the grand admiral hears my report, I am sure she will concede. In her name, I offer you a separate peace . . . an armistice, if you will."

The elf extended his hand. Teldin accepted the pact, then on impulse he drew Vallus into a comrade's brief, hearty embrace.

"For a while, I thought I could fight with the elves," he said when they broke apart, feeling that he owed Vallus some explanation. "If Armistice turns out to be destroyed, well, I know you did what you had to do, but I can't be a part of it."

"Believe me, I understand," the elven wizard said quietly. "I wish I had that choice." A sad smile lit his angular face. "The gods go with you, Teldin Moore."

The elf turned and walked away. Trivit watched him go and turned to Teldin. "With your consent, *Kaba*, I would like to remain on Radole," he said hesitantly. "There is a dracon settlement here, and I, well—"

"Of course," Teldin broke in. The young dracon had been disconsolate since the loss of his brother, and a fictional clan comprising one lone human was no replacement for real family. "Give your new clan my regards, Trivit," he said warmly.

Wiping a tear away with one green hand, the dracon nodded and ambled out of the tavern. Teldin took the seat Vallus had vacated. "What's it like, being something you don't want to be?" Teldin abruptly asked Hectate.

The question took the bionoid by surprise. "You find ways to cope, sir, ways to compensate."

Teldin acknowledged the comment with a nod, but he wasn't satisfied. He'd seen what power had done to others, and he feared for what he might become as he wielded it. Would the duties of leadership crowd aside all other considerations until he was fully governed by that nebulous and demanding master Expediency? Or would power be like a drug that would take over his mind and overshadow dearly held values? Who *was* he? Teldin Moore or Cloakmaster?

"What if one part takes over?" he murmured, more to himself than to the half-elf.

"That's something we'll always have to live with, sir," Hectate said quietly.

Teldin looked up, and in the half-elf's brown eyes he saw

sympathy and understanding. He nodded his thanks, then he untied the small bag that held the medallion and held it out. "Are you ready to try again?"

A surprised smile lit Hectate's narrow face, lending the half-elf a decidedly elven appearance. The transformation no longer bothered Teldin, and he returned his navigator's smile with a conspiratorial grin. Together the two friends sought the privacy of Teldin's chamber. With the oaken door shielding the cloak's bright magic from curious eyes, Teldin Moore removed the medallion from its pouch and studied it for a long moment.

He took the artifact in both hands and began again the journey out of himself and into the *Spelljammer*'s eyes, not knowing where the new vision would take him.

BOOKS

The Cloakmaster Cycle
The adventure that began in
Beyond the Moons continued with *Into the Void*
and *The Maelstrom's Eye*.
Follow Teldin Moore as he persists in his search
for the ever elusive *Spelljammer*.

The Broken Sphere   Nigel Findley
After Teldin discovers that his magical amulet allows him to "see"
through the eyes of the great ship *Spelljammer*, he leaves the
Unhuman War behind to hunt for the great ship and its broken sphere.
At last he finds his quarry, but will he live long enough to claim the
ship itself? **Available Spring 1993.**

The Ultimate Helm   Roger E. Moore
Teldin battles for control of the great ship Spelljammer amid myriad
plots and conspiracies. Political intrigue mixes with fantastic elements
for an explosive ending to the series. Teldin must grapple with the
choice of taking the ship's helm, and his decision could change
fantasy space forever. **Available Fall 1993.**